Come Home
to DEEP RIVER

JACKIE
ASHENDEN

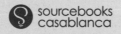
sourcebooks
casablanca

Published by Sourcebooks Casablanca, an imprint of Sourcebooks
P.O. Box 4410, Naperville, Illinois 60567-4410
(630) 961-3900
sourcebooks.com

Printed and bound in Canada.
MBP 10 9 8 7 6 5 4 3 2 1

To Maisey Yates and Megan Crane. For starting a conversation about small towns…

Chapter 1

FLYING INTO DEEP RIVER, ALASKA, TOOK A SPECIAL kind of grit. The airstrip was a narrow bit of gravel to the side of soaring mountains, with a river running along one edge, and there was always some kind of crosswind happening that would challenge even the most experienced pilot.

It wasn't a forgiving landing, and there was no room for error.

Luckily, Silas Quinn hadn't made an error in all the time he'd spent flying around the wilds of the Alaskan backcountry, and he wasn't about to make one now.

Particularly not when he was flying into the hometown he'd left thirteen years earlier and hadn't been back to since.

Especially not when he was coming back to what would probably turn out to be the most hostile reception since Mike Flint had once said at a town meeting that he thought the idea of a luxury motel on the side of the Deep River would be good and why didn't they build one.

Considering the reason Si was here was fifty million times worse than the idea of a luxury motel, the response he was likely to get once he'd broken the news would probably be more than the one month of cold-shouldering that Mike had gotten.

Si would be lucky if the town didn't kill him.

That was if this damn airstrip didn't kill him first.

The clouds were lowering, and the rain was coming down hard, and the wind was a problem, but with his friend Caleb's death still fresh, Si was in no mood to let the elements have their way with him.

He'd survived three tours in Afghanistan.

He'd survive this, even if it killed him.

He kept his nerve and brought the tiny plane down, the wheels bouncing on the gravel as he rolled up just shy of the lone hangar that housed Deep River's entire aviation industry.

As the spin of the Cessna's propellers began to wind down, Si sat in the cockpit trying to handle the rush of emotions that he had known would grip him the second he touched down. The usual mixture of grief, anger, and longing that Deep River always instilled whenever he thought of his hometown.

There was a special poignancy to it today though. Because Caleb was only a few weeks dead and the shock of the will was still ringing through Si's entire being like a hammer strike.

Deep River was an anomaly. The entire town was privately owned and had been since the gold rush days, when town founder Jacob West had bought up all the land around the Deep River and declared it a haven for the misfits and rogues who didn't fit in anywhere in normal society. He'd leased out the land to anyone who wanted to join him, getting them to pay him whatever they could afford in terms of a nominal rent, and in return, they could have a plot of land to call their own and do whatever they wanted with it.

The People's Republic of Deep River, some called it.

Most just called it home.

Even over a hundred years later, the town was still owned by the Wests.

And that was the difficulty. Caleb was the oldest West and had inherited the town after his father, Jared West, had died five years earlier. And he'd ran the place since then—or at least he had until his unexpected death in a plane crash while running supplies up to a remote settlement in the north.

But that hadn't been the end to the shocks that Si and his two other friends, Damon and Zeke, had had to endure in the past few weeks.

First, there had been finding out that Caleb had left the entire town to them in his will. And second, oil had been discovered within Deep River's city limits—oil that the town had no idea was underneath their land.

Oil that, once they knew about it, was going to turn the entire place upside down.

Heavy stuff for three ex-military guys who had nothing to their names but a small company doing adventure tours for tourists, transport runs for hunters, and supply runs for everyone else in the Alaskan bush.

Si stared out at the rain beyond the windshield of the plane.

It hid everything from view, which was probably just as well. He hadn't wanted to come back here, not considering what he'd been trying to leave behind, but it hadn't made any sense for either Damon or Zeke to be the advance party.

This was his hometown. He was the one who knew Deep River and the people in it. And he was the one who'd been closest to Caleb.

Therefore, it made sense for him to be the one to break the happy news that firstly, the fact that he, Damon, and Zeke were the new owners. And secondly, there was oil in them thar hills.

Some men might have kept the oil a secret and kept all the riches for themselves too, but Si wasn't that kind of man, and neither were his friends.

He'd been brought up in Deep River, an extreme environment where everyone learned to rely on each other since that could be all that stood between you and a very uncomfortable death. There was no time for petty grievances—though to be fair, there were a lot of those as well. But when push came to shove, the town pulled together. Because fundamentally, they were all the same. They'd all come here because they didn't fit anywhere else, because they were escaping something, because they liked the quiet and the isolation and the return to nature.

Because they just plain old liked it.

Si let out a breath.

And now he was going to give them news that was going to blow it all apart.

Since the rain didn't look like it was going to let up anytime soon and since sitting brooding in his plane wasn't exactly a power move, Si forced himself to undo his belt before reaching behind his seat to grab his duffel bag. Then, hauling it over his shoulder, he pushed open the cockpit door and stepped out into the rain.

Familiar, this feeling. The mountains like walls on either side, hemming in the narrow river valley, and the rain coming down cold and unpleasant, soaking him to the skin almost straightaway.

Yeah, he was home, and he wasn't sure how he felt about that.

As a kid, he'd loved this place with every fiber of his being. Hadn't ever wanted to leave. Those mountains had felt comforting, cradling a place of safety, where there was bush to run wild in and rivers to swim in, and the sea to fish in. He'd found it magical. There were dragons in the mountains, and castles, and armies to fight, new lands to conquer, princesses to rescue.

Then his mother had died, and his father had fallen headfirst into a vodka bottle, and all the magic had disappeared.

Now he was back and…

He looked around, scowling. Yeah, the magic was still gone.

There was only one way to get into the township of Deep River itself, since the highway ran alongside the opposite bank of the river rather than through the town, and that was by ferry. Old Jacob West had wanted to make it as difficult for the outside world to find the town as he could, so he'd positioned it very purposefully.

The few tourists that managed to make their way there loved that about it.

Right now, dripping wet and having to get a ferry across the river, Si didn't find it so amusing.

Gripping the strap of his bag, he made his way through the rain and down the gravel road that led from the airstrip to the docks.

It was early evening, and the weather was awful, and there was no one around. Which was probably a good thing.

Everyone in the town would already know about Caleb's death, and they would likely also know that the new owner wasn't Morgan West, Caleb's little sister and the town's only police officer. They might even have done some digging and learned about the will and how the town had gone to some "outsiders."

But they wouldn't know about the oil.

Hell, even he hadn't known about the oil, and he was Caleb's closest friend. The guy had kept that secret close to his vest, and understandably. Money brought out the worst in people, especially the kind of money that was tied up in oil.

In fact, now he was here, Si had to admit that there was a small part of him reluctant to tell *anyone* about that oil. But not because he wanted to keep it for himself—he had everything he needed in Wild Alaska Aviation, the small company that he and his buddies had started up. No, his reluctance was all about how the rest of the town was going to deal with the oil news. Especially when it was going to mean big things. It could change people's lives, that oil.

It could also mean the destruction of the town itself.

Still, the town had to know what was on their doorstep, and people had to make their own decisions accordingly, no matter his feelings on the subject. Even if he wasn't in any hurry to spread the news around.

Just like he wasn't in any hurry to get to his first port of call that night.

Seeing Hope Dawson, the third in his and Cal's friendship triad.

Hope. Who'd stayed.

A muscle leapt in the side of Si's jaw, but he forced aside thoughts of her, squinting through the rain as he stepped onto the dock, trying to see whether Kevin's boat was there—at least, he assumed Kevin's boat was still the ferry between the highway and the town. It had, after all, been a long time, and perhaps someone else had taken over the job.

But no, there it was, right down at the end, Kevin Anderson's faded red fishing boat.

Si steeled himself.

No one knew he was coming because he'd made sure no one knew. Which meant he was going to have to deal with people's shock.

He strode down the dock, wiping the rain from his face as he approached Kevin's boat. Hopefully the guy would be in there, because if he wasn't, Si would have to start making some calls, and he really didn't want to do that.

He wanted to speak to Hope before he spoke to anyone else.

But his footsteps on the dock must not have gone unheard, because the cabin door on the boat was jerked open and a large man in his late fifties, dressed in a scruffy-looking parka, stepped out onto the deck.

It was indeed Kevin Anderson. The Andersons had been doing the ferry service, as well as various fishing runs, for decades, so it was hardly surprising that he was still around.

"Who are you?" Kevin demanded in deeply unfriendly tones. "Saw you come in overhead. If you're expecting a run into town you're s—"

"Hey, Kevin," Si interrupted before he could get the whole outsider schtick. "It's me. It's Silas."

Kevin's craggy face froze. He squinted. "Silas? Silas Quinn?"

"Yeah." Si met the other man's surprised stare but didn't offer anything more. Not because he didn't have anything to say. It was just there was a time and a place for explanations, and that time was not now, and this was not the place.

"My God," Kevin said. "It *is* you. Geez, where you been, man? It's been years. Heard you and Cal went off to the army and…" He stopped suddenly and hunched his shoulders. "I heard about Cal. I'm sorry."

Si ignored the grief that tightened in his chest. There was plenty where that came from, but he wasn't about to indulge it now. He had too much stuff to handle first.

"Yeah, thanks. Look, I need a run into town." He didn't bother to phrase it as a request, not when he was all out of patience and damns to give.

But Kevin didn't seem to take offense. "Sure. Hop in."

The run over the river didn't take long—fifteen minutes on a bad day—and mercifully Kevin wasn't the chatty type. A couple of questions about what he'd been doing that Si answered as briefly as possible—army, then flying up in the bush. Yes, tourists. Yes, hunters. Yes, the business was doing okay—and the guy didn't ask anything more.

As Kevin dropped Si off on the dock on the town side, he gave him a brief wave before turning his boat around and heading back toward the airstrip side.

Si, by now thoroughly soaked and in a foul temper, didn't bother to watch as Kevin's boat disappeared into the rain.

He was too busy contemplating the reality of the town he thought he'd left behind years ago.

Deep River itself hugged the river it was named for, the buildings, on stilts and projecting out into the water, all linked by a covered wooden boardwalk.

It was a bit like Ketchikan, the nearest larger town to the south, except without the tourist vibe.

There was nothing touristy about Deep River.

It was…quirky. And that was being kind. The old wooden buildings were patched and worn looking, the paint faded from years of exposure to the harsh Alaskan elements, the signs on the stores barely legible. Apart from the general store, that was. Malcom Cooper, who owned the place, must have found some paint from somewhere because the words "Mal's Market" were painted in bright pink across the store frontage. Last time Si had been here, "Mal's Market" had been painted in fading orange.

It was not an improvement.

Si let out a breath and took a long look at the rest of the township.

There was April's, the diner that made the strongest coffee in Deep River, plus the meanest hash browns. Then the Gold Pan, the town's only hotel. Next to that was the tiny Deep River Tourist Information Center with the red marker pole standing outside it. The pole had "The Middle of Nowhere" painted down the side—one of Sandy's many "marketing" ideas—though the paint was wearing thin there too.

And then, directly opposite him, was the place he was headed for.

The Happy Moose. Deep River's one and only bar.

He didn't want to go inside. In fact, that was the very last thing on earth he wanted to do. But he had a duty, and if there was one thing he'd learned in his time away from Deep River, it was that a man couldn't shirk his duty, no matter how much he wanted to.

Si gripped the strap of his bag and strode toward the bar.

Hope Dawson leaned her elbows on the bar top and watched the argument between Lloyd and Joe escalate.

It was coming on seven, the point of the evening where their argument normally always escalated, so they were right on target. In another five minutes or so, they'd launch themselves off their barstools and start throwing punches, and then she'd get Axel to throw them out.

Same deal every Friday night, regular as clockwork.

They were a couple of old trappers who spent the summer months fixed to their barstools in the Happy Moose, and they had the same argument they'd been having ever since Hope's grandfather had owned the bar. Joe swore Lloyd had stolen a lynx from one of his traps, and Lloyd swore he'd found the animal dead under a tree. The actual truth had been lost in the mists of time and probably even Lloyd and Joe themselves had forgotten it, but that didn't seem to matter. Their argument had gotten to be habitual, a comforting ritual they'd indulged in ever since Hope could remember.

Really, it wouldn't be a Friday if Lloyd and Joe didn't get drunk and end up throwing punches at each other.

Hope flicked a glance at Axel, lounging beside the bar's exit. The tall ex-boxer glanced down at his watch, then nodded to her. He knew the drill well.

Another three…two…one and…

Lloyd shouted an obscenity, and Joe pushed off his barstool, his fists coming up. Axel moved toward the offending pair, grabbing both of them by the scruff and marching them, still shouting, toward the doors.

The rest of the bar didn't bat an eyelid, going on with their drinking and talking, the familiar click of the balls on the ramshackle pool table down on one end not missing a beat.

Hope gave a small, soundless sigh, the noises of the bar comforting.

She'd been managing the Happy Moose ever since her grandfather, who used to own it, had died, and she'd virtually grown up in the place. It was her home, its low heavy-beamed ceiling and rough-hewn wooden bar opposite the door and the few rickety tables as familiar to her as her own bedroom upstairs. The drunken singing and noisy conversation of the bar patrons had been her lullabies, the walls covered with the taxidermied heads of animals watching over her as she played. They were mostly old trophies from back in the seventies, when hunting and trapping still paid big bucks and Bill, her grandfather, had given out free beer to anyone who brought in a head.

No one brought in heads anymore, but some of the older hunters still paid for their beer in skins and furs, or whatever they'd managed to hunt that day. Old Bill had been okay with that, since bartering for goods and services in lieu of cash was an old Deep River tradition, and now that Bill was gone, Hope saw no reason to change it.

She might once have dreamed of leaving town, of heading on to college and a bigger, larger life somewhere else, but after her grandfather had drowned in the Deep River trying to save Joshua Quinn, her dreams had suddenly seemed not so very important.

Her mother, always emotionally fragile, had been even more fragile after her father's death, and Hope couldn't bear leaving her. Couldn't bear leaving the Moose to someone else to manage either.

So she'd stayed and taken on the bar. And now she ran it just like her grandfather had, with a combination of toughness, acceptance, and a little bit of mean to keep 'em in line.

It wasn't a decision she'd ever regretted, no matter that her two best friends in all the world had up and left without her.

A stab of grief hit at the thought, a reminder that at least one of those friends was no more.

Caleb. The news of his death had hit the town hard. If Deep River had been a country, Caleb West would have been its king, and no one knew quite where his death had left them, since the Wests owned the land that the town sat on. Most people had ninety-year leases for which they paid the Wests nominal rent, but with Caleb gone, uncertainty had gripped the town.

Not that Hope was thinking about rents quite yet. She was simply mourning the loss of a man she'd grown up with. A man she'd once thought she might have had a future with —or at least hoped for it.

Until he'd left, taking Silas, her other partner in crime, with him.

She turned away from the ruckus still going on near the exit, reflexively checking on the contents of the small fridge behind the bar that contained a few bottles of white wine and sodas that nobody but tourists drank.

Grief sat like a sharp stone in the center of her chest,

but she swallowed it down. Get on with it—that's what you did in Deep River. Life went on. You couldn't sit around feeling sorry for yourself and wishing things were different because they weren't.

She'd had to do that after her grandfather had died too. Had to after the night of the bonfire, when Caleb had told her that he and Silas were going to leave, that they couldn't stay. And that she should come with them.

Leaving had always been what she'd wanted, but after Bill had died, things had changed. The bar needed someone to manage it, but more than that, her mom had needed someone to look after her, and the only person who could do that was Hope.

How ironic in the end that it was Caleb who'd gone, taking Silas, who'd always been the one who'd wanted to stay, with him.

Something twisted in Hope's chest, something that wasn't grief, but she ignored it. Shoved it back down with all the rest of the icky emotions she didn't have time to deal with, not with a bar to run.

"I don't care." Axel's voice was hard, cutting through Joe's protests. "Go and cool off somewhere else."

Lloyd was still arguing, but then Lloyd never knew when to shut up.

Hope ignored them, focusing on the contents of the fridge and not on the ache in her chest. It had been a couple of weeks since the news of Caleb's death had filtered through the community. The funeral itself had been in Juneau, but Hope hadn't gone. The financial implications of closing the Moose for the necessary couple of days it would take to get up there and back had been too dire, so she'd attended the memorial service that Pastor Dan had given.

Morgan had been the only person who'd gone to Juneau. People had differing opinions on Caleb and the way he'd left town, and even though he'd visited a couple of times in the intervening years, some of them had viewed his leaving as abandonment. There had been a rowdy town meeting only a couple of days earlier about what was going to happen now, where Astrid, the town's reluctant mayor, had called for calm. That nothing was certain until Caleb's will was read. If Caleb even had a will...

It wasn't only the town he abandoned. It was you as well.

The feeling in Hope's chest coiled tighter, but she ignored that too, settling for rearranging the bottles aggressively, the glass making rattling noises.

Being emotional didn't help, and displays of grief weren't really done. It was very much a pick-yourself-up-and-carry-on kind of place here, which was how she'd gotten through her childhood and the pain of Caleb's leaving.

No doubt it was how she'd get through his death as well.

She straightened up and as she did so, became conscious that the bar had fallen silent.

Weird. It could only mean one of two things. Either Joe or Lloyd had managed to get a punch in on Axel, or a stranger had walked in.

Dear Lord, it had better be someone punching Axel. That was a whole lot easier to deal with than having a stranger turn up to disturb the already-disturbed populace.

Slowly, Hope turned around.

But Axel was standing there uninjured, and it wasn't a stranger.

It was much, *much* worse than that.

There was a man standing in the doorway. Massively tall, with wide shoulders, coal-black hair still long enough to curl at his collar…and those incredible eyes, the color caught between gold and green, like the glint of sunlight in the depths of the Deep River.

Her heartbeat caught, like an engine misfiring, her brain flailing around in shock.

Because it was Silas Quinn standing there. Silas, the inventive, imaginative kid who'd turned into a silent, brooding teenager after his mother had died. Who was the darkness to Caleb's light and who had half the female population of their high school swooning over his quiet intensity.

Silas, whom she hadn't seen since that night beside the bonfire, when she'd begged them not to go.

Silas, who'd offered to stay.

And whom you refused, because you wanted Caleb to be the one to offer. And he didn't.

The burst of instinctive joy that caught her in the chest faded at the memory, a wash of an old, half-forgotten shame following hard on its heels.

Yeah, she'd refused and hadn't been kind about it

because she'd been grieving and lost, and it had been Caleb she'd wanted. Caleb, who'd left anyway.

The bar was silent, everyone staring at the man in the doorway, and after a second the atmosphere changed, recognition setting in.

"Silas?" someone said. "Silas Quinn?"

And the man shifted, and suddenly, like a blurry picture coming into focus, it became clear to her that the Silas standing there wasn't the Silas that she remembered after all. And in fact, he *had* changed. He'd changed a lot.

His soaking wet clothing clung to shoulders wider than she'd remembered and a chest that was far more muscular and defined than it had been at eighteen. His features—almost pretty as a teen—seemed harder, more masculine somehow, his tanned skin drawn tight to the strong bone structure beneath it. She could see the white lines of scars here and there, and there were lines around his eyes and mouth, a darkness in his green-gold eyes.

The Silas she'd known had always been a serious type of guy. But she'd always known how to get a smile out of him. And those smiles…

She'd lived for those smiles.

This man looked like he'd never smiled once in his entire life. Like he didn't even know what a smile was.

He ignored the people staring at him, ignored the sounds of his name echoing around the bar. Instead, he looked straight at her. "Hello, Hope," he said at last, his voice as deep and gritty as the bed of the river that flowed outside the bar, and just as full of undercurrents.

A part of her, the wild and joyful teenager she'd once been before age and responsibility had gotten the better of her, wanted to launch herself over the top of the bar and into his arms. Because above all else, Silas had been one of the closest friends she'd ever had.

But she didn't.

She didn't let herself get carried away by wild extremes of emotion anymore and certainly not with a bar to run and an emotionally fragile mother to look after.

And she certainly wasn't going to hug the man who hadn't visited her once in thirteen years.

Hope forced all the old emotions down and locked them securely away. Then she folded her arms. "Hello, Silas," she said. "Long time no see."

Chapter 2

Okay, so that was clear—Hope was officially unhappy to see him.

Did you really expect anything different?

Si adjusted the bag on his shoulder, trying to ignore the stares from everyone else in the bar, not to mention the sudden, hollow feeling in his gut.

Yeah, he had expected different. Or at least, a part of him had hoped for it, especially after thirteen years.

Thirteen years and not one visit. Come on, man.

The hollow feeling yawned wider, but he didn't have a chance to examine it too closely, because questions were being shouted at him, and although nobody had moved, it was clear that everyone in the bar was demanding some kind of acknowledgment.

Deep River had never been an effusive place, but apparently people were pleased to see him, which was a little weird considering anyone who left the town was usually viewed with some suspicion.

But then being friends with a West usually had the effect of making people feel more charitable, and since he had a bombshell of his own to deliver at some point, he decided to be charitable back, even if he didn't particularly feel like it.

He nodded to a few people, endured a handshake here, a backslap there, took the condolences offered on

Caleb's death, and answered a couple of questions in as brief a way as possible, all the while making his way slowly, but surely, toward the bar.

Hope was standing there with her arms crossed, watching him approach, her dark eyes revealing nothing at all.

Yeah, she was *not* happy to see him, and he supposed he couldn't blame her. He hadn't been back here, not once, not even to visit, and he'd given himself a lot of reasons over the years for why that was. But it wasn't until now, until she was right in front of him, that he realized the real reason.

It was her. He hadn't been back because if he'd set even one foot in this town, he'd have stayed. For her. And anything more than friends would never work with Hope; he had too much of his old man in him.

Also, she didn't want you. She wanted Caleb.

Yeah, there was that.

Still, as he looked at her now, he was conscious that his heartbeat had gotten faster, a tightness coiling in his chest, a familiar, dark pulse in his blood.

She wasn't the eighteen-year-old girl he'd last seen beside the bonfire that night, the auburn glints in her long dark hair gleaming in the firelight. That girl had always worn her heart on her sleeve, her pretty face open, and that night there had been nothing but hurt written all over it. And anger. The firelight had picked up the tears in her black-coffee eyes too, and he'd known he'd said the wrong thing. Offering to stay had been a mistake. Caleb was who she wanted, not him.

He'd always been able to read her, but that night he'd gotten it wrong. And even now, as he stared at her, he couldn't tell what was going on in her head. Those eyes were still coffee-black, but there were walls behind them, and while that pretty, open face was still pretty, it wasn't open anymore. She was guarded. Giving him the face most people in Deep River gave strangers—the impassive "I don't know you from a bar of soap and I'm not interested in getting to know you either" face.

Her hair, though, that was the same. It wasn't wild around her head the way it had been when she'd been a kid, but worn in a long, practical plait. Yet the same auburn lights gleamed in it, like fire in the dark heart of a stone.

She had on a red plaid flannel shirt—which on some level made him want to smile, since old Bill had always worn red plaid flannel—and practical jeans, and on the surface she didn't look much like the old Hope Dawson from years ago.

But he'd seen the leap of anger in her eyes as she'd first met his gaze—and grief and something else he didn't recognize. And it made him think that the old Hope was still there somewhere inside her.

You better pray she's not. You don't want to go there again, buddy.

No fear of that. He'd learned his lesson. But what he did need was someone he trusted to talk with about the news he was bringing. Someone who wouldn't blab it instantly to the town at large and who could give him an unbiased opinion about where the town was at now and whether what he was going to tell them would cause trouble—and if so, what kind.

He'd learned a lot of things in the military and in the years afterward, getting Wild Alaska off the ground, not the least being that reconnaissance, preparation, and planning were key to the success of any mission, and he had a feeling he was going to need all of those now.

All of those things and Hope.

"Hey, Hope," he said, since there was no point beating about the bush. "I need to talk to you."

"No kidding." She crossed her arms, drawing his gaze to the soft curves beneath the flannel of her shirt. Which wasn't what he should have been thinking about, dammit. "Thirteen years, Silas. Thirteen years without any contact whatsoever and now you appear unannounced, in my bar, demanding to talk to me?" Her gaze roved over him in a long, leisurely, and very pointed survey, ending back at his face again. "Sorry, but that's a big no from me."

"I get it." He held that stare because he'd always been a man who owned his mistakes. "And you have every right to be angry with me about it. But I need to talk to you right now, and it's important. It's about Caleb."

Hope's guarded stare didn't so much as flicker, and from the way his back was prickling, everyone else in the bar was treating him to the same kind of attention.

He cursed silently. Arriving unannounced was always going to cause a commotion, but he hadn't wanted too big a fuss made about it. People would talk, and before you knew it, all kinds of rumors would be circulating, from the government coming to grab all the land and make people homeless, to aliens landing and the world ending.

Sadly, in this case, all those rumors might end up being true. Though it wouldn't be the government coming, it would be big oil. And the aliens could be seen to be his buddies—at least Damon was *very* alien to Alaska, that was for sure. And definitely the world as the people of Deep River knew it was going to end.

No one could stop it. All they could do was take the information and decide for themselves how they were going to deal with it.

Some of that must have communicated itself to Hope because she glanced over his shoulder at the suspiciously quiet bar, then let out a breath. "Okay, fine." Her arms dropped, and she turned toward the door that led to the little office out back. "You have five minutes."

He wouldn't need five minutes. Two would be enough.

But he didn't tell her that, rounding the bar and following her into the Moose's office area.

It was small, full of cluttered shelves and one broken-down old filing cabinet. There was a desk shoved underneath the sole window that looked out over the main street, though the window was a stark black square now, night pressing in against the glass.

He had memories of this office back from when he, Caleb, and Hope had used the bar like their own personal playhouse and Bill had let them. Si had been fascinated by the animal heads stuck on the walls, in particular one of a stag that everyone called Steve for reasons that were never explained to him. Caleb had thought the heads creepy and had been afraid of them, but Si hadn't. He was sure the spirit of the wild still lived in those glassy eyes, and he'd spent hours looking into them, imagining the lives of the animals they'd once been.

Seriously, he'd been an idiot kid.

Steve, he noted, was still in the office and still attached to the wall near the desk. But there was no spirit of the wild in his glassy eyes. Not now.

The magic was gone.

Hope pulled out the lone chair sitting under the desk and sat down, swiveling it till she was facing him. She'd kept her arms folded and there was an "impress me" look on her face. "Minutes are ticking, Silas. You've now got four and a half."

Si dropped his duffel bag with a thud and stared back at her. "I get it. You're angry. But trust me, this is too important to indulge in personal grievances right now, okay? You can talk about how mad you are at me later. This is about Caleb, and it affects the entire town."

The look on her face flickered, and she shifted in her chair. "Okay, fine," she said grudgingly. "What's this all about, then?"

He saw no need for preliminaries. Might as well tell her straight out. "Cal's will was read a couple of days ago. A couple of personal things he left to Morgan, but everything else he left to me, Damon, and Zeke. And I do mean everything, Hope. And that includes Deep River."

There was a moment's echoing silence, broken only by the sound of the ancient jukebox that someone must have put a quarter into, playing "Sweet Home Alabama" for what was probably the millionth time.

Hope's expressionless mask rippled again, shock flickering through her dark eyes, letting him catch a glimpse of that wild, passionate eighteen-year-old. The one who used to make his heart beat faster, make him smile, who'd been his ray of sunshine after his mother had died.

But then, like a light switching off, the shock was gone, the wary, guarded look replacing it once more. She wore a lot of armor, this particular version of Hope, and he wasn't sure he liked it.

"What do you mean 'that includes Deep River'?" she asked carefully.

"I mean, all the land that encompasses the town is now ours, and that includes the private funds and investments the Wests use to pay for the running of it."

Hope shook her head, as if she had difficulty processing it, which was fair enough, because he was still having difficulty himself even days later. "But…he can't have left it to you and…whoever those other people are. What about Morgan?"

"He changed his will after he came out of the army. I didn't know and neither did the other guys, and I have even less idea why he did it."

"Why you?" Hope fired back. "Why those other two?

And who are those other two, anyway? Have you told Morgan? Does she know?"

Morgan did know. She'd been at the lawyer's office in Juneau, looking small and pale, her pretty strawberry-blond hair, so like her older brother's, hanging lankly over her shoulders. She hadn't said much as the lawyer explained Caleb's will and Si remembered thinking that the one thing she didn't look was surprised.

But she hadn't stuck around for conversation after it was all over, and he hadn't thought to ask her about it, not when he'd been so shell-shocked himself.

"Yes," he said. "She knows. But, Hope, that's not even why I'm here. There's something more. Something that's going to affect the entire town."

"Like you owning all of it won't? Si, I hate to be a downer on this but—"

"There's oil under the town," he interrupted flatly.

This time, her guarded expression didn't just ripple; it fractured, her dark eyes going wide, her mouth, which he'd always fantasized about, opening. "What?"

"There's oil under the town," Si repeated. "Cal had some surveys done, and no, I didn't know he was doing them. He didn't tell a soul. But the results were clear. There's a large reserve, and the whole damn town is sitting right on top of it."

Hope blinked. "Uh…"

The look on her face now was one of absolute bewilderment and he knew the feeling. He'd had it the moment the lawyer had told him, since he'd had no idea Cal had

had some surveys done. Hadn't realized there was even a remote possibility of oil in his hometown.

But the remote possibility was now a reality, and there would be implications.

"Oil," Hope said slowly. "Under the town."

"Yeah." Si lifted a hand and ran it through his wet hair. His clothes were wet too, but that didn't bother him; he'd long become inured to physical discomfort. Life in Deep River had been physical, and life in the army hadn't been much different—except for the rules. He'd always had a little difficulty with those.

She was shaking her head again. "So…what exactly does that mean?"

Si dropped his hand from his hair. "It could mean nothing. Or it could mean everything. It could change everyone's lives here."

"But how?"

"Mineral rights," he said. "The whole town is leasehold, and every leaseholder can sell those rights entirely to an oil company. Or just sell the right to drill and take some of the profits for themselves."

Hope's eyes got rounder and rounder. "Every leaseholder? Every single one?"

"Yes." The lawyer who'd explained it all to him, and which his subsequent research had backed up, had been very clear. "The Wests persuaded people to move into the town on the possibility of everyone keeping their own gold, so the mineral rights were written into the leases. But no one back then thought about oil."

Hope shifted in her chair, and despite the seriousness of the conversation, he found himself glancing down at her legs, encased in blue denim. The jeans were tight, outlining the shape of her thighs and long, toned calves.

She'd always been athletic and fit, running in the bush with him and Caleb, playing knights and princes and princesses. They'd take it in turns to be the prince/princess and then the knight, with sticks as swords, fighting each other and the dragons that lived in the mountains. As a kid, she'd been so vital and full of life, a bright spark he'd been irresistibly drawn to in the last few months of his mother's illness. And then she'd grown up into a willowy woman, with breasts and hips and thighs, and he hadn't been able to take his eyes off her.

Seemed like he still couldn't.

Dammit. He didn't want to be noticing this stuff. Not now. He'd thought it might be a possibility that he'd still be drawn to Hope, but he'd thought that his physical response to her wouldn't be so instant and visceral. At least not after so long.

Apparently, that wasn't the case.

"That's insane," she muttered, her gaze sweeping, unseeing, around the room. "I can't even imagine…" She stopped and looked at him all of a sudden. "Does anyone know? I mean, you said they didn't, but are you sure?"

Slowly, Si shook his head. "That's why I'm here, Hope. Because nobody knows. And I have to tell them."

_____

Hope couldn't think. Her brain felt as if someone had pulled it out of her head and pummeled it before putting it back in.

Silas just stood in front of her, a massive, silent presence.

She didn't know how he managed to seem even bigger in her tiny office than he had out in the bar, but somehow he did.

He seemed even broader, even taller, his damp T-shirt pulling tight across the muscled expanse of his chest. Perhaps it was because she was sitting and he was standing, though why she was noticing his chest, she had no idea. Not when his chest had absolutely nothing whatsoever to do with what he'd just told her.

The town had new owners. Oil.

Oh God. Oil.

She took a shaky breath, staring up at him, her mind struggling with the implications, because there were so many implications. The town was owned by the Wests, but they had leased most of it to anyone who wanted to pay the nominal rents and live there. These days everyone paid with money, but sometimes people paid in furs or whatever else they managed to farm, trap, or fish. It had always worked because of the town's founder, Jacob West, and his belief that everyone deserved a place to be. A place where they felt safe and where they belonged. A home. And it was for that reason that the Wests had always refused to sell the land. Because while the Wests owned it, no one could muscle in and do things that would change the essential nature of the town.

Deep River might be literally in the middle of nowhere, but it was a haven and a place of welcome to everyone who lived there. Everyone was equal, and everyone had a say in the running of the place.

Except that was possibly going to change.

"You have to tell them?" she echoed blankly, trying to come to terms with the fact that somehow Caleb had willed the town to Silas and two other people she didn't know. To strangers. Outsiders. When Morgan was there, his sister and a West…

What on earth had Cal been thinking?

And that's not even the worst part.

No, the worst part was the oil discovery.

A cold shiver went down her back. The people of Deep River worked hard for their living, and some people had more than others, but no one was hugely rich—or at least, if they were, no one knew about it. But oil coming to town? That would mean money, and money always changed things.

"We can't tell them," she said before she could stop herself. "Can we not tell them? Can't we just keep it a secret?"

Silas frowned. "No, of course we can't hide it. People have a right to know."

"But once they do…" She stopped, took a breath. "Things might get very difficult."

"You think I don't know that?" He lifted a hand, ran it through his damp hair once again, the black strands gleaming in the light. "Believe me, I've done nothing but go over the implications of this since I heard about it. But the town has always been about the people, Hope, and you know that. We can't keep something like this a secret."

He was right, and she knew keeping it a secret was wrong, but fear and uncertainty were twisting deep inside her.

Ruthlessly, she shoved them aside the way she did with all her uncomfortable emotions these days, eyeing him instead. "What would you know about the town? You haven't been back for thirteen years."

His green-gold eyes glittered with what looked like anger. He'd always been a man of deep emotions, she remembered. He kept them far beneath the surface, but they were there, burning like lava inside a volcano.

The thought of Silas's deeply buried emotions made a shiver move through her, the way it used to do when she'd been a teenager. Back then, she hadn't known what that shiver meant, only known that there was something about Silas's reserve that got under her skin, made her feel uncomfortable. She'd always preferred Caleb's ready smiles and approachability. He'd been so easy to be with. He'd never made her feel like she wanted to crawl out of her skin like Silas did.

Seemed like that hadn't changed either.

Perhaps baiting him is not a good idea.

Perhaps sitting down was also not a good idea, not with him looming over her like the mountains loomed above the town.

She pushed herself up and out of the chair, moving over to the desk and yanking open one of the drawers where she kept her malt whisky Harry had given her. The most recent addition to the town—and *recent* being five years ago—Harry was an escapee from Florida, of all places, who loved the outdoors and wanted to live a home-steading lifestyle along with his girlfriend, Gwen. He had a still and made a pretty decent drop. It wouldn't win any medals, but at least it didn't take the surface layer of your throat off as it went down, unlike Lloyd's moonshine.

Hope pulled out the bottle, found a teacup that didn't have the remains of old tea in it, and poured in a splash. Then, holding on to the bottle, she turned and held the teacup out to Silas.

He glanced at it, then at her, then took it without a word. The teacup was bone china and delicate, and it should have looked ridiculous in Silas's large hands, but it didn't. He held it carefully by the rim and took a sip of the whisky.

Hope, meanwhile, took a gulp direct from the bottle. "So, what's your plan?" she asked as the good stuff went down, warming her insides, banishing the cold grip of fear. "A town meeting where you say, 'hey everyone, me and two complete strangers are the new owners of the town, and by the way there's oil, so have at it'?"

Silas's expression didn't change, his intense gaze unre-lenting. "Damon and Zeke were in the army with me and Cal. They're good men. I'd risk my life for them and have, and so did Cal. But the will is clear; the town must con-tinue to run the way it always has. We can't sell any of the land, even if we wanted to. And let's be clear." Gold gleamed deep in his eyes. "We don't want to. What we want is to get back to our business and leave the town to get on with running itself."

She didn't doubt him, not even for a second. It might have been thirteen years since she'd seen him, but she knew Silas Quinn. He'd always been a man of his word, a man of honor, and she could understand why Cal had thought to leave Deep River to him.

His two buddies, on the other hand... Yeah, that was a completely different story.

Another pang of grief hit her at the thought of Cal. He hadn't said a word to her about being in business with his buddies the last time he'd visited. All he'd mentioned was that he was flying, and she hadn't asked further about where or why. Perhaps she should have, considering how he'd died.

"What business?" She pushed herself up to sit on the desktop, deciding to leave the question of what to do with the town for another couple of minutes.

"It's called Wild Alaska Aviation. We have a few planes, a couple of choppers too. Running supplies up in the bush, transporting hunters and tourists—that kind of thing. We're thinking of branching out into wilderness tours as well, since tourism is becoming a big earner."

She didn't want to be interested in what he'd been doing the time he'd been away, yet despite herself, Hope was intrigued. It was annoying.

She took another swig out of the whisky bottle. "So where are these so-called buddies? Are they here too?"

"No." Si sipped from his teacup, his expression unreadable. "We decided it was better for me to come alone, since this is my hometown and we weren't sure of what kind of reception we'd get. Damon's in Juneau, looking after the business, and Zeke is..." There was a pause, and he glanced down at his teacup. "Having a few...difficulties."

There was a note in his voice that made Hope want to ask more questions, but asking about the doings of a couple of strangers didn't seem all that important right now. Not given the news that Silas had brought with him.

Oil. Hell.

She lifted the bottle and took another long sip, conscious of the tension in the silence. It never used to be like that between them. Silas wasn't much of a talker, and it had never bothered her. She'd once found it restful.

At least, until she'd turned sixteen and then things had changed between the three of them, and she hadn't found it so restful anymore.

Silas drained the rest of the whisky in the teacup, and Hope found herself staring, her gaze somehow drawn to the strong column of his neck and the movement of his throat as he swallowed.

Something stretched inside her, like a lazy cat turning over in its sleep.

She looked away quickly, uncomfortable with the feeling.

Silas put the empty teacup gently down on the desk. "Thanks for the drink."

"You want some more?" She lifted the bottle. "It's Harry's finest."

"No, thank you." His gaze settled on her. "You got a room free? I'm going to need a place to stay for a few days."

She blinked at him. Of course he would. The lease on the property Silas's father had owned had been signed over to a couple from Anchorage after Joshua died. So naturally he'd have nowhere to go.

Yet the thought of Silas staying at the Moose made her feel…unsettled. Though she couldn't think why.

And even though she didn't really want him here, there was no good reason to refuse. She could say that all the rooms were full, but they both knew that was a lie. The Moose only got full in winter, when the hunters and trappers came.

She was still trying to think of excuses when the office door opened and Axel put his head around it. His gaze flicked over Silas and then settled on her. "Carrie wants a cosmo. I told her we didn't do cocktails, but she's saying you made her one last night."

Hope hadn't made her one last night, and Axel knew that. He just wanted an excuse to see what was happening, and no doubt everyone in the bar had egged him on to interrupt them.

Good reason to end this conversation and now, because her head was threatening to explode with all the stuff Silas had told her.

Hope glared at Axel. "I'll be out in a minute." She tugged open another drawer in her desk and groped around in it, finding one of the room keys and pulling it out. "Here." She tossed the key over to Silas, who caught it easily. "Room on the end. The honeymoon suite."

Silas nodded, then picked up his duffel bag. He turned and gave Axel one hard, direct look. Instantly, the other man filled the doorway, lounging as if he was perfectly comfortable and planned to keep lounging there all night.

Hope rolled her eyes. "I'd like to say I love the scent of testosterone in the mornings, but it's not morning, it's night, and I've had enough male bullshit to last a lifetime. Axel. Haven't you got something else to do?"

The bouncer was staring hard at Silas. "Nope."

Hope sighed. Her life was spent managing difficult people of both sexes, both behind the bar and in front of it, and after today, she was kind of done. She opened her mouth to call Axel off when he abruptly turned and walked away.

She stared at Silas in surprise, unsure what had just happened. But all he did was shoulder his bag and give her one last glance, the gold depths of his eyes glittering. "We'll talk in the morning."

Then he strode out, leaving her alone with her whisky bottle and the sense that things were going to change, and not for the better.

Chapter 3

SILAS WOKE AT THE CRACK OF DAWN AS USUAL, AND for a moment, he lay in the dark, staring at the ceiling of an unfamiliar room, struck by the fact that it was utterly silent. Juneau was a big town, and there was always something going on somewhere, the sounds of traffic and people, the barking of dogs. Sirens. Music playing. Construction noise.

But there was nothing at all happening now, and he wondered what kind of apocalypse had come to silence the town.

Then he remembered.

He was in Deep River, and it was always quiet in Deep River.

He lay there another couple of minutes, relishing the silence more than he'd thought he would, remembering how he used to sit on the porch out front of his father's house when he'd been a teenager. Just sitting and looking over the mountains, feeling the silence of the landscape settle him, ground him. It had helped get him through another day of picking up after one of Joshua's drinking binges, another day mired in the old man's sorrow, as his own isolation deepened.

The memories weren't happy ones, so he shoved them aside and hauled himself out of bed. He had stuff to do and, more important, coffee to find.

Hope hadn't been lying about the room being the honeymoon suite. It was large—though in Deep River size was relative—with a table to do work at if you felt so inclined and a couch to sit on. There was also a balcony that looked out over the river and an en suite bathroom that, given the rest of the rooms at the Moose had a shared bathroom, was the very height of luxury.

He'd spent most of last evening battling the crappy cell phone reception as he gave Damon an update on the situation, all the while listening to complaints about how little there was to do in Juneau. Complaints which he ignored. Damon was a city boy whose plans for returning to LA had been disrupted by Cal's will, and he wasn't happy about it. He didn't want anything to do with Deep River and had been more than okay with staying in Juneau to keep things ticking over with Wild Alaska, leaving Si to handle breaking the news to the town.

Maybe a week max, he'd told Damon. Because he wanted to do this right. He couldn't simply lob the oil news into the middle of a town meeting like a grenade, then walk away as it blew everything sky high. He wasn't that much of an asshole. He needed to check out the town first, break the news in a way that wouldn't cause too much disruption, and then stick around to make sure any issues were handled.

It doesn't matter how you handle it. This news is going to cause problems.

The thought echoed the doubt sitting in his gut, but he ignored it. He had to. He had a business to get back to, a life he'd managed to build, and that didn't include staying in his old hometown. He'd spent most of his childhood years looking after one old man and getting absolutely no thanks for it, and then more years in the army looking after a platoon. He was done with responsibility. All he wanted to manage now was the business and himself.

He didn't need a whole damn town to look after.

Eventually, Si hauled himself out of bed, and since he'd showered the night before, he didn't bother now, pulling on fresh jeans and a tee before making his way downstairs in search of coffee.

Daylight wasn't the Moose's most flattering angle. What was cozy and warm at night turned dark and poky in the daytime, the animal heads on the walls looking moth-eaten and shabby. The place smelled of spilled beer and wet oilskins and—*yes, thank you, God*—freshly brewed coffee.

Hope was up, moving around the bar area with a broom, shifting chairs to get under tables, sweeping up after the previous night's revelries.

He watched her silently, his heartbeat accelerating the way it had the night before the moment he'd seen her. She was in jeans and a tee too, her hair in that severe braid down her back, though now it slid over one shoulder as she shoved a table to the side so she could get her broom underneath it.

Her movements were competent, practical, as if she'd swept this floor a thousand times before. Which she probably had. He hadn't asked her about what she'd been doing with her life last night, not when the news he'd had to break had taken up most of the time they'd had together. And after...well, after, he'd had to get away. He'd told himself at the time it was to do with updating Damon, but it wasn't. The effect Hope had had on him once before was there still, and he didn't like it. Not one damn bit.

He was older now, wiser. And he didn't have the time, or room in his life, to get tangled up with an old friend. Because that's what she was and always had been: a friend. And a friend she needed to stay, no matter that his body was trying to tell him otherwise.

Hope was bent over, her back to him, and even though he shouldn't, he couldn't stop his gaze from following the delicious curve of her rear, because he was a man, not a statue, and she was a fine-looking woman.

"You better not be checking me out, Silas Quinn," Hope said without turning around. "Not if you don't want this broom handle planted somewhere painful."

Amusement flickered through him, and it had been so long since he'd felt it, he almost didn't recognize the feeling.

He shifted against the doorframe. "What can I say? You've got a cute butt."

She straightened and turned, giving him one enigmatic glance as she moved back toward the bar, grabbing a dustpan and brush that were sitting on the bar top. Without a word, she went back to the table she'd been sweeping under and crouched, sweeping up whatever was on the floor into the dustpan.

So, no small talk then? Fair enough. He didn't do small talk himself, especially not when there was so much other important stuff to say.

He could feel the weight of that important stuff between them, hanging heavy in the early morning air. Hope was angry at him, he knew that, and eventually he was going to have to address it—or not. He could simply deal with the town stuff and not say a word about anything else.

But that was a coward's way out, and he'd never been a coward.

Seriously? Wasn't running away from here the first time taking the coward's way out?

Si shoved that uncomfortable thought away and moved over to the bar. There was a coffee maker behind it, the glass carafe full of fresh coffee, and it made the bar smell like one of the fancy new coffee places in Juneau.

"There are mugs under the bar," Hope said from behind him. "Though you might want to get a cup from April's if it's really strong you're after."

"Nothing to say I can't have both." He found himself a mug and poured a coffee. Then, after a moment, he found a second mug and poured some more coffee into that one too.

He preferred his coffee black, but Hope had always had a sweet tooth, and after a brief look around, he found cream in the bar fridge and some sugar beside the mugs. Doctoring her coffee the way she liked it—if she still liked it that way—he then put it on the bar top and shoved it in her direction. Then he leaned back against the counter behind him, holding his mug in his hands.

She was standing there holding her dustpan and brush, staring at him. "Just make yourself right at home."

"Thanks. I did."

An expression he couldn't read flickered over her face and then it was gone. She let out a breath, shook her head for some reason, then came over to the bar, dumping the contents of the dustpan into a wastebasket under the bar before putting the implements away tidily.

"That for me?" She straightened up, looking at the steaming coffee mug.

"No. It's for Steve out back."

She snorted. "Find a sense of humor while you were away, did you? I'd get it replaced, because it looks like it's broken."

Si ignored that, watching as she picked up her mug and took a sip. And since she didn't make a face, it appeared that some things hadn't changed. Hope still liked three sugars and a lot of cream in her coffee.

"Why are you still here?" he asked, because if he was going to be in Deep River anyway, he might as well catch up on what she'd been doing. Except as soon as he'd said it, he could hear the demand in his voice. Not to mention the accusation.

Strange. He hadn't thought he'd feel anything at all about her choice to stay, not after all these years. Though it was only now that he realized that he did, in fact, feel something. He was vaguely pissed, even. Cal had told him that she was running the Moose now, even though Si hadn't asked him about her, and that she was happy.

But he knew what a happy Hope looked like, and it wasn't this guarded woman sipping her coffee and looking at him over the rim of her mug with wary, dark eyes.

"What kind of a question is that?" she asked.

Si lifted one shoulder. "It's not an accusation." *Liar.* "I was just curious."

"Why? Because I was always the one who wanted to leave?"

He didn't answer that. He didn't need to.

When he didn't say anything, Hope shifted on her feet in a way he recognized from years ago; she could never keep still when she was uncomfortable. "You know why I stayed, Silas." There was a touch of impatience in her voice. "Do we really have to go into this now?"

Of course he knew why she'd stayed. Her grandfather's death.

A thread of old shame wound through him, because her grandfather would never have died if Si's own father hadn't been drinking so heavily that night. And Joshua mightn't have been drinking so heavily if Si had been around to keep an eye on him. But Si hadn't been around. He'd been down at the river, drinking beer with Hope, because she'd asked him to. Because Caleb was away in Juneau with his father, and she wanted some company. And he'd never been able to say no to her.

"I'm not talking about that," Si said, both to her and to the memories in his head. "I meant, what kept you here?"

He shouldn't ask. He really shouldn't. And he couldn't think why he was.

Another flicker of impatience passed over Hope's strong, angular features. "Why would I leave? When I have this paradise to manage?" She glanced around said "paradise," shabby and worn in the early-morning light filtering through the windows. Then again, he didn't know a bar that didn't look shabby and worn in the morning.

"You could have sold," he pointed out, not really knowing why he was pushing this. "No one forced you to keep it."

"Yeah, and no one forced you to stay away."

He let out a breath. That had been crappy of him, not to even visit, and she had a right to be angry with him. But it had been years. He'd have thought that after so long, she would have forgotten about him.

Seriously?

Si let the thought dissipate, silence falling, tension settling in the space between them.

"You want to talk about that?" he asked after a moment, feeling the need to address it at least, because having her angry with him wasn't going to make this situation any easier.

She looked away, her cheeks pink, and he knew she hadn't meant to snap at him. That she'd given something away and was annoyed about it.

A beam of early morning sunlight fell over her features,

highlighting the curve of her cheek and the fine grain of her olive skin. She was looking at the floor, her lashes swept down, dark and silky, with auburn undertones.

His chest ached all of a sudden, the ghost of an old longing gripping tight. He'd felt it that night beside the river—the night his father had drowned—sitting on the rocks near the bank, listening to her talk. Her hair had been a blaze of auburn in the sunset, her dark eyes full of light, and he'd ached and ached and ached. Because that night, she'd told him that she liked Caleb West a hell of a lot, and what did he think about that? What should she do about it?

She hadn't known how he'd felt about her, and he hadn't told her. Couldn't. He had a strong loyalty to Caleb and to the friendship between the three of them—it was the only thing he had that was wholly for him—and he didn't want to do anything that would put that at risk. Especially not when Hope clearly didn't feel the same way about him as he did about her.

So he'd stayed silent and let her chatter on about Cal, his chest aching, disappointment heavy and cold in his gut.

Are you sure the past is truly gone?

Sure it was. A ghost of a feeling was just that—a ghost. It didn't affect him anymore. He had another life now. A life where he had everything he'd wanted for himself. A home. A challenging business. A couple of planes and the wide-open sky. Friends…

"No," Hope said definitively, taking one last sip of her

coffee before putting it down on the bar. "I don't want to talk about it."

He should let it go, really he should.

"Seems like you do," he said, apparently unable to help himself. "Seems like you have some very definite feelings about it."

"Well, my feelings aren't your business anymore." She shoved her hands into the back pockets of her jeans, the movement pulling her red T-shirt tight across her chest, highlighting the soft curves of her breasts.

Which he shouldn't be noticing. Just like he shouldn't have been noticing her ass.

You sure those old feelings are just ghosts?

Oh, he was sure. This was only detached male appreciation now.

She gave him a distinctly cool look. "You want breakfast or what?"

He did want breakfast. But he also didn't want to let the subject go, and he couldn't figure out why because she was right—her feelings weren't his business. Hell, *she* wasn't his business, no matter the realization that had hit him the night before.

Maybe once he'd wanted her so desperately he thought it would kill him, but that was when he'd been eighteen, and he hadn't been eighteen for a long time. And okay, he hadn't been back to Deep River because of her. But she wasn't the teenager she'd once been either, and it was clear she'd moved on. They both had. So what was the point stirring up the past?

Anyway, he wasn't here to build bridges and mend fences. He was here to break the news to the town, then hand over responsibility for all of it to someone else, so he could go back to the life he'd made for himself.

So he put his mug down on the bar top. "Sure, breakfast would be good. You going to make it for me?"

She snorted. "You have two choices. You can go get some breakfast at April's, or you can go to hell, because I'm not cooking for you."

Definitely, she'd moved on. Or maybe she'd forgotten that she used to cook breakfasts for him and his dad on occasion, when Joshua was hungover and in one of his usual foul tempers. Not that it was the time to remind her.

"Been to hell," he said shortly. "Didn't like it. Looks like it's April's instead."

Hope gave him a wary look, as if she didn't know quite how to take that, but he didn't elaborate. No point getting into the specifics of his military experiences.

"You coming?" he went on. "We still need to talk."

She leaned against the bar and folded her arms, a crease between her brows. "Believe it or not, I have a job and things to—"

"This needs to be handled, Hope. And the quicker it is, the quicker I can go back to Juneau and get out of your hair."

The crease between her brows deepened. "What?"

And that was another thing he needed to tell her. If she thought he was back for good, then she was wrong.

"I'll tell you over breakfast," he muttered as his stomach reminded him that it had been hours since he'd last eaten. "Come on. My treat."

April's was renowned in Deep River for the kind of coffee strong enough to strip an engine. It was also the only diner in town, and as usual, when Si and Hope pushed open the door, it was full, even at this hour of the morning.

Burly fishermen in parkas sat at the tiny Formica tables downing mugs of the infamous coffee and inhaling April's big breakfasts before they went out in their trawlers for a day on the water. A damp fug lingered in the atmosphere, a combination of early-morning chill meeting the heat of the warm bodies and hot food, the smell of oilskins and coffee in the air, along with the clatter of silverware on plates and the buzz of conversation.

A wave of nostalgia washed over Si as the door closed behind them. He used to come here in the early mornings to get himself and his father coffee, because nothing else but a cup of April's joe would wake Joshua up sometimes. And then there were the dates he'd had here on occasion. There wasn't anywhere else to take a date in town but April's, and she used to make a mean milkshake. The fries weren't bad either.

As they approached the counter, a group of guys got up and several shouted greetings at Hope as they shouldered past, their gazes narrowing suspiciously on Si, giving him the stranger stare.

Typical but not unsurprising. What was surprising was

his own reaction, which was irritation, because he wasn't exactly a stranger, was he? He stared back, the nostalgia fading as the men moved past him, leaving room for another realization to hit.

There was a time when he'd come into April's and know every person sitting there. But he didn't today. He didn't know the fishermen glaring at him or the group by the door. Or the three guys sitting at the counter on barstools.

He didn't know anyone except Hope. The whole diner was full of strangers.

It's not your town anymore.

He shouldn't have felt that so sharply, almost like pain, not when it hadn't been his town for years. He'd left and hadn't missed it and didn't regret it, not once. So why he should feel a sharp, hollow sensation in his gut, he had no idea.

Dismissing the feeling, he and Hope took the vacated table by the window with its view over the boardwalk outside and, beyond that, the river. There was a line of trawlers already motoring in the direction of the bay, the morning sunlight glinting off the water.

It was going to be a beautiful day. The kind of day he'd once lived for as a kid because it meant joining Caleb and Hope in the bush near Caleb's house, where they'd play for hours, building fortresses and defending each other from dragon attacks until it was dusk.

"Silas?"

Realizing he was staring out the window like an idiot,

Si dragged his gaze from the scenery back to where Hope was sitting across the table from him.

"You okay?" she asked, frowning slightly.

Get it together, asshole.

Si shoved away the past and focused all his attention on the future sitting opposite him. "How quickly can we organize a town meeting?"

———————————

There had been a strange, faraway look on Silas's face just before, but now his green-gold eyes had narrowed on her so intently she felt like an elk in the sights of a hunter.

Weirdly, it made her skin prickle, but she ignored the feeling, not wanting to examine it too closely. Just like she'd decided to ignore the conversation they'd had just before in the Moose. Not to mention the way her stupid heart had jolted in her chest when she'd realized he'd come downstairs and been watching her while she swept the floor.

As well as checking out your ass, apparently.

Okay, she did *not* need to be thinking about that either. Or how uncomfortable that thought made her. A discomfort that had nothing to do with the fact that she didn't like it, but because she had a horrible feeling that she did. It had been a long time since anyone had checked her out, after all. She'd long since become part of the furniture with the locals and had rebuffed any advances from tourists. She wasn't going to be like her mother, falling pregnant by some stranger who was passing through and ending up a single mom with bad postpartum depression and living with her parents. Yeah, that definitely wasn't happening.

She'd once had a fling with one of the seasonal workers who came to Deep River on occasion, looking for work on the trawlers. He'd lasted a month, and she'd given the whole sex thing a go, got rid of her pesky virginity. But sex hadn't impressed her. She hadn't been able to understand what the fuss was about, and when he'd left, she'd given him a wave and hadn't thought about it twice since.

You're thinking about it twice now.

No, she wasn't. Silas was a friend—that's all he'd ever been and that's all he'd stay. And the weird, prickly sensation was only her ancient libido giving a couple of last gasps before it died completely, like one of Jason Anderson's old trucks.

Hope forced away the feeling, though her brain kept registering odd things like how the soft, well-worn cotton of Silas's dark green T-shirt was pulling tight across his wide shoulders and muscular chest. Or how the black shadow of his morning beard outlined his strong, sharp jaw. He'd looked dark and disreputable back at the Moose and he still did in the early-morning sunlight coming through the window, turning his black hair glossy. And apparently other people thought so too, given the number of female patrons in the diner looking his way.

He had his elbows on the table, the way his palms lay flat on the old Formica drawing attention to his long fingers. They were big, capable hands. Strong too, and crisscrossed with scars.

You idiot. Stop looking at his damn hands.

Hope gritted her teeth and dragged her gaze to his face instead, which, with the gold glinting deep in his eyes, wasn't any better, to be honest. What the hell was wrong with her?

"How quickly to organize a town meeting?" she repeated, just to be sure she'd heard him correctly and not give away the fact that she'd been staring at him like a lovesick teenager.

"Yeah." He frowned slightly, and it made him look very stern and rather intimidating. Same as it had years ago. "The whole town needs to be there to hear the news."

"What news?" someone else asked.

They both looked up to find a small, very round elderly lady in a pink-and-white uniform straight out of the fifties standing next to the table, looking at them. Her sharp blue eyes widened with sudden interest. "Silas Quinn?" Her softly wrinkled face broke into one of the brightest smiles this side of the Deep River. "I knew it was you! The second you walked in. Where you been, honey?" April Jones still had traces of a New Jersey accent, even though she'd left the East Coast behind over fifty years ago to follow her husband to Alaska. Now that husband was long gone, but April was still here, dispensing the murder brew she called coffee, freshly baked goods, and breakfasts, along with a fair helping of cheerful and mostly unwanted advice.

"Hey, April." Silas's hard mouth curved in a rare smile as he shoved back his chair and got up to receive April's hug. "How you been?"

Hope realized suddenly that if they were going to have a private chat about Silas's news, April's was probably the wrong place to do it. She could see April's son, Jack, behind the counter, looking interestedly their way. And that was a problem. Because if April liked a bit of gossip, Jack liked it even more.

Dammit.

Hope stood up too. "We'll take some coffees to go, April. Oh yeah, and a couple of those pies Jack makes. If there are any left."

April released Silas and tipped her head back, looking up at him, giving no indication she'd heard Hope. "My," she breathed, her eyes wide and admiring. "Haven't you grown up big?"

"Military rations." Amusement played around Silas's mouth, and Hope found herself staring at that mouth and the way it curved for no damn reason that she could discern.

"Uh-huh," April murmured. "So what's bringing you back to our neck of the woods?"

"Two coffees and a couple of pies," Hope repeated before Silas could answer. "To go."

Silas glanced at her, his gaze unreadable. But he must have figured out her reason for leaving because when he spoke, it was only to say, "Long story, April. I'll tell you about it some other time."

Five minutes later, they were outside on the board-walk facing the river, sitting on one of the rough wooden benches that Filthy Phil, a retired hunter who'd taken up the mantle of town eccentric with pride, had carved for tourists to sit on in the summer months.

"Sorry." Hope handed Silas the steaming cardboard cup full of coffee. "Too busy in there. And too many people who might overhear."

"Yeah, I remember." He took the cup, his eyes gleaming, though with what she couldn't tell. "Maybe you'll have to cook me breakfast after all."

Another current of that uncomfortable emotion rippled through her. The sun was in his dark hair and she was weirdly conscious of how much room he took up on the bench. One powerful, denim-clad thigh was right next to hers, and she'd only have to move an inch in order to brush up against it.

Great. Now she was thinking about his thighs. Not good.

Maybe if you'd played the field a bit more, you wouldn't be having such a strong reaction.

Maybe. Then again, what field? There was no field, not in Deep River. Not for her at least. She was the tough-talking, take-no-shit, capable owner of the Happy Moose bar, and no one thought of her as anything else. Not even as a woman.

And that was fine, absolutely fine. If she needed a salutary lesson in the dangers of hooking up with the wrong guy, she only needed to look at her mother, who spent most of her time sitting on the couch in front of the TV, watching soaps.

Hope glared at Silas and shoved the paper bag with the pie in it at him. "Absolutely not. Eat that instead."

He took it, opening the paper bag and glancing inside. "What is it?"

"Beef pie. Jack went to Australia and New Zealand last year on some kind of backpacking trip. This is apparently a speciality."

"Huh."

Neither of them said anything as they both ate their pies, sipping their coffee as the last of the fishing trawlers left the docks and the silence of the mountains descended on the town. And for a moment, Hope felt like she was twelve again, fishing with Silas and Cal by the river like she had in the old days. It was the only time Cal had ever been quiet, the three of them sitting in companionable silence with their rods, the hot sun on the backs of their necks...

Silas shifted, balling up the paper bag and throwing it in a nearby trash can with unerring accuracy, and Hope was back in the present again. Cal was dead, Silas wasn't the friend she remembered, and the kids they'd once been were long gone.

"A town meeting," Silas said, breaking the silence as he settled back against the bench, holding his coffee loosely in one long-fingered hand. "I need to organize one in the next day or two. The sooner the better."

A weird sense of regret had settled in Hope's gut and

she didn't know where it had come from, but she was very clear she didn't like it. Ignoring it, she balled up her paper bag too and threw it in the direction of the trash can. It went in, much to her satisfaction.

"Why the sooner the better?" she asked, relishing the burn of the coffee as she took another swallow, the caffeine buzzing in her veins. "Got something more important to do?"

Silas gave her another of those enigmatic glances. "I've got a business to run back in Juneau. Summer's nearly here, and it's going to be busy, and Damon can't handle it by himself."

The regret sitting inside Hope twisted, turning into a disappointment that she didn't quite understand. He'd mentioned that he wanted to get back to Juneau quickly before, which was fine. She didn't have a feeling about that one way or the other, right?

"So…what? Your plan is to call a town meeting, dump this news on them, and then go back to Juneau?" she asked, unable to keep annoyance from her voice.

He didn't react, simply eyeing her, the look on his handsome face unreadable. "No. I was not planning on 'dumping' the news. I was planning on handing this over to someone who was more qualified than I am to handle it."

"Well, Morgan should be—"

"Morgan didn't want it," he interrupted before she could go on. "We offered it to her after the will was read, and she refused."

Hope blinked, not understanding. "She refused? She refused what?"

"All of it. We offered to sign over the whole damn town, and she said no."

That was surprising. Morgan was Deep River's sole police officer, and she took the job of protecting the town very seriously. Hope would have thought she'd jump at the chance to keep the town as part of her family's legacy.

"Oh," Hope said. "Did she say why?"

"No. And I didn't sit down and give her the third degree about it."

The cardboard sides of her coffee cup were hot against her fingertips, but Hope barely felt it. She stared at Silas. "So you're really just going to dump and run?"

He looked down at his own cup. "I haven't lived here for thirteen years. I don't know the town anymore, or the people in it." He glanced up, his intent gaze catching hers. "I shouldn't be the one responsible for the Wests' legacy, and neither should Damon and Zeke. Hell, Damon doesn't even want to stay in Alaska, let alone be part owner of a small town like this one." He let out a breath and glanced away, out over the water glittering in the sun. "And you know the rules about absentee landlords. You have to live here if you want a lease, and that goes for ownership of the land too."

She did know the rules. The Wests had always been here, and Cal's father and his father before him had been very clear about the importance of living in the town that they owned and being part of its day-to-day life. That belief extended to the people living in Deep River too. Cal had told her that his father had often been approached by people looking to buy the land that Deep River was built on. For holiday homes for rich city folk and people wanting to build hotels and other tourist nonsense. But the Wests had always refused to sell. And it was even a condition of the leases they granted that the leaseholder had to live in Deep River.

So if Silas wasn't intending to stay, it was only right that he give responsibility over to a local. But the sense of disappointment sitting in her gut didn't budge, and she wasn't sure why. Because she didn't care. It had been thirteen years, as he'd said, and although he'd once been one of her closest friends, he wasn't that now.

It shouldn't matter that he wasn't planning to stay. It shouldn't matter at all.

"So what are you going to do?" Her voice sounded a little weird, so she took a sip of her coffee to cover it. "I mean, if you can't sell the land, where does that leave you?"

Silas's thumbs were moving on his coffee cup, rubbing slowly up and down in an absent movement that for some reason Hope found vaguely mesmerizing. "I want to sign the whole lot over to someone who loves this place. Someone who can look after it better than I can. Who'll look after its interests the way the Wests always did. I talked to the lawyer before I got here, and he said that it was possible."

Hope frowned, trying to think of someone who might fit the bill. There were plenty of people here who loved this town, it was true. Plenty of people who never wanted to go anywhere else. But when it came to looking out for Deep River's interests? To putting the town first before their own needs?

Yeah, that was tricky.

She sat there for a second, watching Silas's thumbs moving on the cup. He had a scar on the knuckle of his right thumb, the white line of it standing out on his tanned skin. "Who are you thinking, then? Do you have someone in mind?"

"Yeah." He glanced at her again, the gold deep in his eyes gleaming. "I was thinking of you."

Chapter 4

HOPE STEPPED INTO HER OFFICE AT THE MOOSE, SHUT the door, then leaned back against it and closed her eyes.

After delivering his bombshell, Silas had gone off to talk to Astrid James, Deep River's current mayor, about organizing a town meeting, leaving Hope to deal with the effects of said bombshell by herself. Which was the way she preferred it since she'd been dealing with everything by herself since the day he and Cal had left.

He wanted to sign the town over to her. The *entire* town.

Pushing herself away from the door, Hope crossed over to her desk, jerked out the chair and sat down. Then she pulled open the desk drawer that contained Harry's whisky and took out the bottle. She tugged the cork out, pouring a healthy dram into the teacup she'd used last night. It was far too early for alcohol, but this was an emergency.

She leaned back in her chair and sipped, the whisky sliding easily down her throat to sit warmly in her stomach, her thoughts careening wildly all over the place.

Steve the stag's eyes gleamed glassily at her from the wall.

After her grandfather had died, she'd known she wouldn't be able to leave the town, that she'd have to put on hold her dreams of going to college and getting a literature degree, of a life beyond Deep River's mountains. The Happy Moose had been owned by her family for decades, her grandfather's legacy, and she couldn't walk away from it. Couldn't walk away from her mother either. Angela Dawson had given up her own life and opportunities in order to have Hope, and Hope hadn't been able to bear the thought of abandoning her. She'd had severe postpartum depression after Hope was born, and if Hope had left, she would have no one and nothing but the Moose, which Hope knew full well her mother couldn't manage on her own.

So Hope had stayed. Put her college dreams aside and stayed while her friends had left. And she'd come to terms with that a long time ago. She was generally happy with her lot—after all, she could read wherever she was; she didn't have to study literature to enjoy books—and hadn't regretted the choice. So Silas handing over the town to her shouldn't have made her think twice.

Sure, there were a lot of better, more qualified people who'd perhaps manage Deep River better than she could, but if push came to shove, she'd step up. She wasn't one to shirk her responsibilities. Apart from anything else, she loved this town and the people in it. They all had their issues and some more than most, but they were good people at heart.

Except she'd felt a terrible sinking sensation in the pit of her stomach as soon as he'd said he wanted to sign ownership of the town over to her. A weight settling on her shoulders, like hands pressing down on them.

She couldn't work out why she felt that way. Or why her instinctive response had been no.

Silas had stared at her, and she'd had the uncomfortable feeling he'd seen her exact feelings about the subject—which may not have been much of a giveaway since she hadn't given him a rousing *oh yes, please* immediately. He'd only nodded, told her to think about it, then muttered something about needing to see the mayor before getting up and leaving her sitting on the bench.

The second time he's dumped you in it and walked away.

Hope knocked back some more of her whisky and glared at Steve, the stag's glass eyes reflecting the sunlight coming through the window.

Okay, she was being unfair. Silas hadn't exactly "dumped her in it" that first time. She'd chosen to stay. And yes, she'd asked them both not to leave, and he'd been the one to offer. She'd just refused him.

Anyway, he had a successful-sounding life he clearly wanted to get back to in Juneau, so it wasn't any wonder he didn't want to come back here.

Yeah, he gets to cut and run, while you stay behind to pick up the pieces. Like you did after Granddad died. And like you're going to do after Cal's death now.

Hope shook her head to get rid of the thought, but it stuck like a thorn. It *did* feel that way, that once again she was the one having to deal with the fallout of someone's death, while Silas Quinn got to fly away in his plane and never come back.

Her hand tightened on the teacup, and she drained

the rest of the whisky, wanting to drown the anger that had seemingly come out of nowhere to coil like a dragon in her gut.

It was ridiculous. If he wanted to sign the town over to her, then she'd take it. It didn't matter. She wasn't going anywhere.

You're certainly not going anywhere now.

Hope put down the cup and shoved back her chair. She couldn't sit here all day, brooding. She had stuff to do. Such as going next door to Mal's, the general store, and asking him to put up a sign letting people know about a meeting.

Mal's sold everything and anything, from hunting supplies to fishing gear, from ladies' clothing to stationery, from basic pantry supplies to gourmet ingredients (season and Mal's contacts dependent), and from books to souvenirs. Basically if you wanted something, Mal's would probably have it. And if he didn't, he'd get it in for you. Such as the collection of Charles Dickens's classics that she'd wanted that the library didn't have, plus some Jane Austen and *Wuthering Heights*, since she had a passion for nineteenth-century literature.

His store also housed a DVD library, since the broadband in Deep River was patchy at best, nonexistent at worst, and required a special wired workstation for consistent internet connectivity even when the rest of the town had no service. No one knew quite how he managed to achieve it, but he did, and it had been a lifesaver—quite literally—on a number of occasions.

Hope left the Moose and went up the steps next door, striding into the store. The towering wooden shelves on either side were stuffed with all kinds of things, creating a kind of tunnel to the back where the counter was. She'd thought Mal's was magical back when she'd been a kid, like the stores in the Harry Potter books her grandfather had bought for her, as if she'd discover a wand behind the cans of beans or a broomstick behind the fishing rods.

It didn't feel very magical just now though. Only familiar.

How is this going to change when the oil comes?

The thought hit Hope like a punch to the gut, and she had to stop in the middle of the aisle to take a breath.

Mal wouldn't want to take the oil money, would he? If it came to that? Surely he'd want his store to stay the same? Then again, what could he do with money? He might sell up and move out, start a bigger store somewhere else…

Something icy crawled through her. No wonder Silas had been so grim-faced telling her the news. He'd had time to think about the implications, and now they were hitting home for her too.

"Hope," someone hissed from behind her.

She turned, coming face-to-face with her mother, who on occasion helped Mal stacking shelves in return for a bit of pocket money.

Angela was a small woman, dwarfed by the shelves around her, looking even smaller in jeans and one of Hope's grandfather's flannel shirts that she persisted in wearing since it was a family tradition. Her long dark hair—same as Hope's—was pulled back in a ponytail, and her dark eyes—also the same as Hope's—were suspiciously bright.

In fact, there was something suspiciously bright about her mother in general this morning, and that wasn't a usual occurrence. Angela mostly sat around watching the soaps on TV, completely absorbed in a world outside of the town she'd gotten stuck in. And when she wasn't watching TV, she was bitterly listing an endless round of complaints about everything and anything to whoever was around to listen.

Except today her mother's usual discontent wasn't apparent. She was…excited.

"Come here," Angela whispered. "I've got something to tell you." Then she grabbed Hope's hand and tugged her around one of the shelves into a more private corner of the store. It was where the knickknacks were shelved, dusty porcelain shepherdesses and glass statues of cats and other things, plus hand-carved items from various locals. No one ever bought them and no one ever looked at them, which was why Mal never dusted this area of the store. In fact, Hope was pretty sure Mal had forgotten it existed.

"What?" she asked her mother, frowning.

Angela dropped her hand then glanced around, as if she was afraid of eavesdroppers. Which was stupid since there was no one in their immediate vicinity.

"Okay," she said, her gaze still darting around. "I have some news."

"What news?"

The glitter of excitement in Angela's eyes became more pronounced. "I got a call yesterday from a guy who was interested in buying the Moose."

Hope blinked at her. "What?"

"He wanted to buy our lease." Her mother leaned in closer. "And the money he was offering… Well, let's just say that it was a lot."

The subject was so out of left field that it took Hope a couple of seconds to process what her mother was saying. Someone had offered to buy the Moose's lease? Seriously?

"I…" she started, not quite sure what to say.

"I know." Angela reached out and took Hope's hands in her own, her long fingers still elegant and smooth despite the years of disappointments and bitterness. "It means we could leave, Hope. It means that we could finally get out of here. You could go to college or whatever, and I could move south. Go to Florida. California. Somewhere warm." Her mother's smile was full of excitement and anticipation. "We could finally do whatever we wanted."

The ice that had been sitting in Hope's stomach solidified, becoming strangely weighty.

For years, all she'd wanted to do was leave. She hadn't wanted to turn into her mother, stuck in the family home with a kid and a life hemmed in by mountains and small-town gossip. Where there was nothing to do but watch soaps and complain, too poor to do any of the things she'd always dreamed of doing. And then her grandfather had died, and Cal and Silas had left, and she'd had to shoulder responsibilities she'd never dreamed she'd have. She'd had to put those dreams of another life aside. But those dreams had never gone. They'd never disappeared entirely. They were still there, and suddenly she felt the weight of them acutely.

It was not a good feeling. Not given what Silas had just told her.

A call to buy the lease? That's never happened. Strange timing, don't you think?

Hope narrowed her gaze at her mother. "Did this guy leave a name?"

"John something or other." Angela lifted a shoulder. "Does it matter? The most important thing is that he wanted to pay good money for that lease." Her fingers squeezed Hope's, her eyes bright in a way Hope hadn't seen in years, if ever. "Aren't you happy?"

Interesting question. Happy wasn't a state she readily identified with. Contentment, sure, but happiness?

You're already turning into your mother. But instead of a kid, you have the bar. And now Silas has dumped the town on you as well…

Hope forced away the feeling of being helplessly crushed by stones people kept piling on top of her. She didn't want to be the one to pour cold water on her mother's obvious excitement, but questions needed to be asked. There was also a strange, secret part of her, a part she didn't want to acknowledge, that found the idea of selling the Moose's lease to a stranger almost painful.

"No, I'm not happy," Hope said flatly. "I'm weirded

out. No one has ever offered to buy the Moose's lease before. Never."

The excitement in Angela's eyes dimmed, and carefully, she withdrew her hands from Hope's. "What does that matter? Someone wants to buy it now."

"Who, though? Someone from here?"

"No. He said he was based in Juneau."

"So, what? Some random guy calls up out of the blue and offers a lot of money for the Moose's lease?"

Angela's expression darkened, the years of bitterness sitting more heavily on her, highlighting the lines around her eyes and mouth. "Yes, that's exactly what happened. What's the matter with that?"

Hope's heart ached at the dimming of her mother's pleasure. She hated to be the one to do it, but that had always been her role. She'd been the hard reality check since she was born. "Mom, you don't know who this person is. Or why they're suddenly offering you a lot of money. Didn't you even ask?"

Offense flitted across Angela's sharp-boned face. "Of course I did. I'm not an idiot."

"Mom—"

"He said he was looking for an escape from city life and had always wanted to own a bar. And he'd been investigating places of interest. He said Deep River sounded like just the kind of place he wanted to move to."

"So has he cold-called anyone else?" She should stop asking questions, stop making things worse, but she couldn't help herself or her suspicions. "Or was it just us?"

"No." Angela's expression was now full of her usual resentment. "He said the Moose was his first port of call. He'd been here, he said. And he'd liked it and he was calling on the off chance that we might want to sell." She glared at Hope. "I don't understand why you're being so negative. This could be just the kind of escape that we've been looking for."

"We? Why do you keep saying 'we'?"

Angela blinked, then frowned. "You always wanted to leave, Hope. Don't tell me you didn't. You wanted to get a degree. Go to college. And then—"

"And then Grandad died," she heard herself say, her voice unaccustomedly hard. "And I had responsibilities to shoulder. I can't just leave them because some random guy called you and offered to buy the lease."

Her mother drew back as if she'd slapped her. "So that's a no?"

Of course, that's how most of their arguments went. Every time her mother talked about selling and moving away, Hope would present her with the facts of their situation, the sharp pin that punctured the balloon of Angela's fantasies. Hope hated being that person, hated how she was forced into that role, especially considering what her birth had meant for her mother. But reality wasn't something Angela often concerned herself with, and someone had to be the one to present it to her.

"No," Hope said tiredly. "It's not." She took a breath, trying to temper her own feelings and not be so hard on her mom. "Okay, so what did you say to him?"

Angela sniffed. "I told him I'd think about it. He's going to call again in a couple of days."

That was something at least. That might give her time to investigate whatever this call was really about and who'd made it. And who knew? Maybe the guy was genuinely on the level.

He's not and you know it.

Hope ignored the voice in her head and instead gave her mother what she hoped was a reassuring look. "Okay, well, let's think about it. I can investigate him and see if he's genuine and then maybe we can discuss it."

Angela's expression was, for once, difficult to interpret. "Fine. But don't forget, Hope: When Dad died, the lease passed to me. It's in my name. Which means I can do whatever the hell I want with it."

The ice in Hope's stomach became a little thicker, a little weightier. Her mother wasn't wrong. The lease *had* passed to her. She owned it and the Moose along with it. Of course, Angela never actually wanted to own it and had even made some noises about transferring it to Hope. But that's all it had ever been—just noises. Her mother's name had remained on the lease.

It hadn't been an issue before, but Hope had a feeling it was going to be an issue now.

Dammit. She was going to have to find Silas and tell him, because the timing of this was just too convenient. It was about the oil. It had to be.

Silas stood in the doorway of the small Deep River community center and stopped dead. The center was comprised of one big open room with wooden floors, stacked chairs, and noticeboards on the wall. A big stove stood down at one end to keep it warm in winter, but it had always been a faintly chilly space. He had memories of huddling on one of the wooden chairs, freezing his balls off the few times his father had dragged him to town meetings and trying not to fall asleep as the adults talked about boring stuff.

But it wasn't chilly now. In fact, the temperature reminded him of a particularly grueling mission down in South America, where he'd sweated through miles of jungle, soaking his fatigues while insects ate him alive.

Yeah, exactly like that except with less insects and more women dressed in shorts and tanks contorting themselves into pretzels. Correction, not all were women. There were a couple of guys at the back doing the same thing.

A poster on the wall opposite told him exactly what was going on. *Hot yoga! Eight sharp every morning in the community center! Bring yourself and a positive attitude!*

Heads turned as he came in, and the woman leading the class—tall and willowy with blond hair and a tie-dyed tank—shouted, "Shut the door!" as he stood there staring.

He frowned, but shut it, conscious of everyone staring.

Hot yoga. In Deep River. He couldn't quite get his head around it.

"You want something?" the yoga instructor demanded. "If not, there's a spare mat by the door."

No, he was not going to be doing that.

He gave the woman—whom he didn't recognize, because there appeared to be so many people he didn't recognize—what he hoped was a smile and said, "I'm not here for the class. I need to speak with Astrid James."

A murmur rippled through the assembled class, and a woman in the middle of the crowd unfolded herself. Her pale gilt hair was tied in a knot on the back of her head, her gray eyes sharp and not a little suspicious. "Yeah?" she asked, giving him the usual Deep River stare. "What do you want?"

Silas ignored the pang that stare gave him and stared levelly back. "You're the mayor here, right?"

Her eyes narrowed still further. "Who wants to know?"

Damn. He could already feel the avid gazes of the assembled class becoming even more avid, and that was going to generate more interest than he wanted right now. But there was little he could do about it. Any newcomer was going to generate interest, and most especially when they barged into a yoga class demanding to see the mayor.

Hell. He should have waited.

"Can I talk to you for a moment?" he asked instead. "It'll only be five minutes."

At that moment, an older woman said, "Silas Quinn? Is that you?"

Silas threw her a smile. It was Clare, who owned the bed-and-breakfast. "Hi, Clare. How are you?"

The mayor abruptly rose to her feet. "I'll be back in five," she said to the blond instructor.

Silas gave Clare another grin, then pulled open the door and followed the mayor into the foyer area outside the hall. She was a small woman, with precise, petite features, yet projected the air of someone much larger and much more formidable. A very capable woman, this one, and certainly better than the goat the townspeople had elected once in protest at the yearly batch of candidates.

Astrid folded her arms and stared at him. Her pale skin was flushed from the heat they'd just exited, but she didn't look one whit discomposed. "Silas Quinn, huh?" she said, clearly having paid attention. "What are you doing here, and what do you want?"

Silas didn't beat around the bush. "I'm an old friend of Caleb West's. And I got some news concerning the town and its future."

"What news?" Astrid's gray eyes became even sharper.

He flicked a glance at the door to the hall. "Not here. Already too much gossip is happening, and I don't need any more. It's serious, and it's going to need a town meeting, where everyone can be informed."

The mayor said nothing for a long moment, then asked, "Is it going to cause trouble?"

"Yeah," he said, because it would—no two ways about it.

"It's about Caleb's will, isn't it?" Concern flickered through her eyes, which Si took to be a good sign. A mayor who cared about the town and its people was always going to be a mayor he could respect, and that was necessary, especially when he was going to be leaving said town and its future in hers and Hope's hands.

"Yeah," he repeated, and decided not to say anything more.

She could read his expression. She'd know it was serious.

And indeed, Astrid silently studied him another couple of beats, then gave a brisk nod. "Okay. Give me a half hour to get changed. You know where the mayor's office is?"

He appreciated that he was a stranger to her, but the pang inside him deepened at her assumption he didn't know where the mayor's office was. Like he hadn't been there on numerous occasions when whichever mayor it was gave him either a hard word about his father's behavior or a sympathetic inquiry as to how he was doing. The mayors of Deep River were always overly intrusive in the lives of the people they represented, in his humble opinion.

"I do," he said gruffly, not letting any of his irritation show.

"Good." She turned back to the hall. "I'll see you there."

Five minutes later, he was walking back down Deep River's main street, his head full of all the things he had to tell Astrid, when Hope stepped up beside him.

He stopped. "Got an answer for me already?"

She hadn't been pleased when he'd told her his plans to sign the town over to her, and he'd known it the second the words had come out of his mouth. What he'd thought was distress had flickered through her dark eyes, and he didn't quite understand that. He hadn't known what to expect when he'd told her, but upsetting her hadn't been the goal, that was for sure.

No, you just wanted to palm off your responsibilities the way you did all those years ago.

That thought irritated him. No, he wasn't palming off his responsibilities.

If he wasn't living here, he couldn't claim ownership. Cal had managed to twist the rules a bit, because he was a West and Morgan still lived here. And there were caveats that allowed for military service. But Si wasn't a West and his military service was done.

Anyway, he firmly believed that Hope was the best person to help deal with this situation. Everything he'd seen of her since coming back to Deep River had only confirmed his belief. Managing Deep River's only bar took a special sort of grit, and Hope had that in spades. Not to mention how she'd shouldered the responsibility of taking it on after her grandfather had died.

Only because she'd had to. And now you're giving her another no-win situation.

Yeah, well, however she felt, she'd told him that she'd think about it. Though he hadn't expected her to come back with an answer so soon.

"It's not about that." Worry glittered in her dark eyes. "I've just been talking to Mom. She got a call yesterday from someone wanting to buy the Moose's lease."

A cold feeling threaded through him. A familiar feeling. The sense that something was wrong. He'd experienced it enough times in the army that he'd come to trust it without question.

He gave Hope a narrow look. "Buy the Moose's lease? Seriously?"

"Yeah." She shoved her hands into the pockets of her jeans and looked around warily, for eavesdroppers presumably. But it was still early, and there weren't many people around, the sidewalk empty. "Mom said it was some city guy looking for an escape and wanting a bar to run. He apparently told her he'd been here and liked the place and wanted to know if she wanted to sell."

The feeling of wrongness deepened. Yeah, he was betting that phone call had nothing to do with some city guy wanting to cash in. "I guess you've never had anyone call out of the blue and ask about the Moose's lease before?"

Hope's gaze came back to his, sharp and clear. "Nope. Not even once."

There was a note in her voice that he didn't quite understand, but now wasn't the time to think about what it could be or why he might be interested in finding out, so all he said was, "You think it's not genuine?"

"Hell no. I tried finding someone to take on the lease after Grandad died, and no one was interested. And I tried again a few years after that, but again, no one wanted it. So this guy suddenly offering now? After Cal? It's sketchy."

Again that note in her voice, a hint of bitterness. So she'd tried to sell up.

And no one wanted it and so she was stuck with it. Just like you're sticking her with the entire town. Way to go, asshole.

Something ached behind his breastbone, an old regret that suddenly felt not so old anymore. But he couldn't go on thinking about it, and he couldn't have regrets—not now. He couldn't take on the responsibility that Cal had unexpectedly shoved on him, and neither could the rest of the Wild Alaska team. They had other plans, and none of those plans included Deep River.

"Yeah, it's sketchy all right," he said, ignoring the ache. "If Cal had someone here prospecting, then somehow word might have gotten out. Oil companies are shady as hell."

Hope let out a breath, as if he'd given her confirmation of something. But it wasn't satisfaction on her face. It was something more painful.

He stared at her, and the urge to lift his hand and cup the angular shape of her cheek gripped him. So strong that he had to close his fingers in a fist to stop himself. "What's up?" he asked instead, even though he shouldn't. Even though getting interested in Hope again was not something he should be doing.

And for a second, he thought she might answer him. Then she looked away, over his shoulder, to the street at his back. "Nothing. Well, not nothing. I wonder how many other people this guy has been calling. Or how many other people have gotten similar calls."

That wasn't what she'd been upset about, Si was sure. But again, this wasn't the time to be talking about it. "Okay, so that's a worry. We need to get this news out in the open so everyone knows and there's none of this shady shit happening." He nodded toward the buildings that faced the river. "I'm just on my way to meet with the mayor. Why don't you come along and tell her about that too?"

"Okay."

Without another word, she fell in step beside him as they made their way to the Deep River tourist information center, since the mayor's office was situated above it.

The buildings all faced the river and the boardwalk, but there was an entrance from the street that ran behind the buildings. Hope didn't say anything as Si pulled open the door and let her in first. She gave him an enigmatic glance, one he couldn't interpret, as she went past him and up the creaky, dark stairs. But he suddenly found that he wanted to interpret it. He wanted to know what was going on with her and how she felt about his plans to sign the town over to her, but wanting to know those things was a mistake.

He was only going to be here a few more days, then he'd be going back to Juneau and the life he'd planned for himself there. A life that didn't include this town. A life that didn't include Hope either.

Somewhere inside him, that ache deepened even though he tried not to let it, and he had to stop and take a breath before following her up the stairs.

No. He wasn't going back to those old feelings again. The longing and the need. The loneliness that had settled inside him after his mother had died when he was ten. The loneliness that had only ever eased when Hope smiled at him.

Shit, he'd thought those feelings were gone, that he'd excised them completely from his heart, but maybe he hadn't removed them as cleanly as he'd thought.

Maybe it was time for a second operation.

Chapter 5

THE MAYOR'S OFFICE WAS A CHEERFUL ROOM, WITH BIG windows facing the river letting the morning sun in and highlighting the almost stark tidiness that was the hallmark of Astrid's tenure. The previous mayor, Sonny Clarke, who managed the gas station, had shown his displeasure at being elected by being extremely untidy, the desk always full of half-drunk coffee mugs, balled-up papers, and half-eaten donuts. Not that anyone had cared whether he was tidy or not. Electing people who didn't want to be mayor was one of Deep River's favorite games, especially since the people who ended up being mayor never really had to do anything. The position was only for a year anyway, which meant most people suffered through it.

Hope had—thank God—never been elected, mostly because people preferred her behind the bar, serving them alcohol. This year it had been the town's librarian, Astrid James, who'd drawn the short straw. She was a frighteningly intelligent, sharp as a tack, incisive woman, and the town's little joke on her had rebounded on them when she'd started taking her position completely seriously.

She said nothing as Silas gave her the rundown on what was happening with Caleb's will and the town and the oil, and she continued to say nothing as Hope told her about Angela's phone call and the Moose's lease.

A silence fell after that, weighty and portentous,

making the room feel stuffy, and Hope longed to open one of the windows and let some fresh air in.

"Well," Astrid said finally. "That's certainly going to shake things up here, isn't it?"

Silas stood in front of her desk, his arms folded across his chest, the morning sun falling over his handsome features. There was an implacable look to him, like the mountains that surrounded the town, hard and absolutely impenetrable. And Hope had the oddest feeling that it should be him sitting behind that desk, taking charge and making sure that everything would turn out okay for the town.

Stupid. He wasn't going to do that, and he'd said as much. He was going to get back in his plane and fly out of here like he had all those years ago.

Leaving you to clean up the mess. Again.

"We need to call a town meeting ASAP," he said in a voice that brooked no argument. "If we already have shady assholes calling people and offering them money for their leases, there will be talk. And we need to handle this out in the open and directly. Make sure everyone knows where they stand."

Astrid leaned back in her chair and gave Silas a cool look. She was a single mom with a teenager who was a handful by all accounts, and nothing much seemed to faze her. Including returning prodigal sons bringing news that could change the town beyond all recognition.

"Are you sure they need to know quite so soon?" she asked, her voice neutral.

Silas's gaze narrowed. "Are you saying we should hide it?"

"No. I just wonder what the hurry is."

Astrid was, of course, playing devil's advocate as she was wont to do, much to most people's irritation. Hope opened her mouth to let Silas know, but it seemed he'd already figured it out, because he said, without heat, "I might have been away from Deep River for years, but I know this town. Gossip started the moment I landed my plane, and it's not going to let up until people know the score. Which means the sooner we tell them the truth, the sooner we can start dealing with the fallout."

"We?" Hope said sharply. "You mean me, right?"

Silas's gaze met hers, and she thought she saw a regret flicker in his green eyes. And she couldn't tell herself that didn't satisfy her on some level. A sign that he at least had an idea of the responsibility he was laying on her. "If there's going to be trouble, I can stay to help out," he said. "I don't have to leave immediately."

"What do you mean 'if'?" She couldn't quite temper the sharp note in her voice. "Of course there'll be trouble. Oil means money, and money always causes trouble."

"So that was your plan?" Astrid eyed Silas with some disapproval. "You were going to announce that the town was now Hope's and then you were going to go back to wherever you came from?"

Astrid had a whiff of stern teacher about her, something that made a lot of people uncomfortable, but Silas didn't move, didn't even look away. "I left this town years ago," he said flatly. "I'm not part of it anymore, and one thing I know is that the people here won't want an outsider getting all up in their business. It makes sense for this to be handled by the people who actually live here."

Damn him. How did he make all of this sound so logical? Because he wasn't wrong. People wouldn't want someone who hadn't been back for thirteen years telling everyone what to do and assuming they knew what was best for the town. So why did it still feel as if he was abdicating his responsibility?

You sure as hell don't want it.

Hope shifted on her feet, her hands clenching in her pockets. She couldn't stop thinking about her mother's excitement, about how that had dimmed when Hope had confronted her with the reality of the situation. About the anticipation in her voice as she'd told Hope that finally, they could leave. As if Hope hadn't spent years as a kid wanting to do the same thing.

You could sign that lease over to someone else. Let them take it. And then you and Mom could take the money and go, leave all of this behind. You could get your degree at last...

"That's true," Astrid was saying, and then she glanced at Hope. "And how do you feel about this?"

Hope took a breath, forcing away the thoughts of simply up and leaving. She'd made the decision years ago to stay, and she couldn't regret it. Couldn't change it. Her future— and all the responsibilities along with it—lay here.

"It was a shock, obviously," she said, conscious of Silas's gaze resting on her. "And I'm concerned about what it's going to mean for the town. Most folks here won't be swayed by the potential for money, but you never know. People do strange things when there are dollars to be made."

"What about Angela?" Silas asked, as if he'd known exactly what Hope had been thinking. "Did she want to sell?"

Hope felt the tension gather in her jaw and along her shoulders, but she tried to make herself relax as she met Silas's gaze. "Mom was excited," she said, because what else could she say? She had to let them both know that there was at least one person who was tempted by the offer. "She wanted to consider it."

Silas said nothing and she couldn't read his expression, but a part of her felt defensive, even though he hadn't said anything. "Hey, she's had a tough life. And being here hasn't been easy for her."

He gave her a steady look. "I didn't say anything."

"No, but just in case you're thinking it's about greed—"

"I'm not." His voice was flat and she could hear the truth in it.

But it didn't make her feel any better. "The Moose is in her name. She could sign the lease over whenever she wants."

There was silence.

Silas's gaze narrowed. "You didn't get your name put on it?"

"No," Hope said, the tension gathering and knotting in her shoulders and neck. "Mom inherited everything from Granddad, and honestly, I didn't think about getting it transferred because who wants to buy the lease of a rundown bar in a backwater town?"

"Do you think she'll do it, then?" he asked, the look on his face impenetrable.

"Honestly? I don't know. If you'd asked me yesterday, I would have said no, she'd never sell. But now..." Hope stopped, not wanting to talk about it all of a sudden. "Anyway, Mom's not the only person who might be an issue."

"I agree," Astrid said in a clipped voice. "There are certainly a few people around here who'll take this opportunity and run with it."

Silas's expression turned hard. "They can't. Because you know what's going to happen if they sign their leases over, or even if they give these assholes mineral rights. This whole town will be one big mess, and that's not even talking about the mess it's going to make of the environment if they start drilling."

Astrid gave him a cool look. "What do you care? You just said you were leaving, so it won't impact you in the slightest."

Good question. He did seem awfully invested in a situation he had no intention of sticking around to help out with. "Yeah," Hope added, "I'd like to know the answer to that too."

Silas regarded Astrid, then flicked a glance at Hope. He didn't seem discomfited by the question, which annoyed Hope for reasons she couldn't explain. "I care because I was born here," he said, his voice hard. "Because I grew up here. Because Cal was my friend and I owe him. Because this town stood for a way of life that meant something, and I'd like to see it stay that way."

Hope stared at him, catching the note of something passionate in his deep voice. As if, despite the fact that he'd left all those years ago and hadn't been back since, he still cared about this place.

Maybe there's more to him not coming back till now. A reason he's not telling you.

Emerald and gold glinted in his gaze, reminding her of how deep he buried his passions, yet also that no matter how deep he'd buried them, she'd always been able to see them. Yes, something serious had kept him from returning and maybe that same something serious was stopping him from staying now.

It's almost like you want him to stay.

No, that was stupid. Why should she care whether he stayed or not? Sure, he'd once been her friend, but he wasn't anymore. Thirteen years of silence had put an end to that.

"Nice speech," Astrid said. "But since you're leaving in a couple of days, what happens here won't be your problem anymore."

A muscle flicked in Silas's hard jaw, his expression becoming even more like granite than it already was. As if he didn't like having that particular truth pointed out to him.

But he only said, "Fair enough. Except I'd call that meeting soon, before gossip makes this mess even bigger."

Astrid gave a nod. "In that case, we'll need a decision

as to who the ownership of the town will pass to." She looked at Hope. "You want to make a call on that?"

What could Hope say? She had to take this responsibility, even though she didn't want to. Even though the thought of it felt like too much. Because who else would?

Silas's expression remained enigmatic, and she suddenly felt compelled to say, "Astrid should take it. She's the mayor."

"But I don't know Astrid," Silas said. "Sorry, Astrid. I'm sure you're fine, but there's a reason I wanted to sign the town over to Hope."

"No problem," the mayor muttered. "I don't want to own this place anyway. I didn't even want to be mayor."

"Well?" Silas arched a brow, not taking his gaze from Hope's. "Is that a yes?"

Someone had to do it. Someone had to help manage this situation, and since Silas wasn't going to do it, that someone had to be her. Even if she didn't want to.

"Okay," Hope said, crushing the doubts inside of her flat. "You can sign it over to me."

"So she's going to do it, then?" Damon's voice down the line sounded impatient.

"Yeah. She will." Si leaned back on the chair he'd put out on the small balcony of his room at the Moose and kicked his booted feet up on the rail in front of him. He'd told Damon all about Hope and his plans for her to take on what he, Damon, and Zeke couldn't, and they'd all agreed that she was the best person for the job. His two friends didn't quite have the same stake in the issue as he did, but they'd still taken the responsibility that Cal had landed them with seriously. They'd all been in the army together, had fought beside each other, had been through hell, and they had each other's backs. Neither Damon nor Zeke—no matter that the pair of them had their quite considerable faults—took what Caleb had left them lightly.

"Good," Damon said. "You think it'll be a problem for her?"

Si thought about the stoic look on Hope's face as she'd accepted the responsibility for the town. The same kind of look she'd had when she'd told him and Cal that she had to stay here now that her grandfather was gone. That she couldn't leave her mother. Someone had to stay and that someone had to be her.

An uneasy feeling twisted in his gut, the sense that he'd made a misstep somehow. She hadn't wanted the responsibility, that was for sure, and that had surprised him. She seemed confident and more than capable of tackling the issue.

Are you really surprised? Come on.

Yeah, he knew she'd had dreams of going to college and getting a degree, of having a bigger life somewhere else, but still…she'd chosen to stay. No one had forced her.

"I don't think she's all that happy about it, but she accepted it," he said. "Think we might have bigger issues than we first thought, though."

"Oh?"

"Some guy called her mom out of the blue, offering her money for the lease on her bar."

There was a silence.

Then Damon said, "Well, that doesn't sound at all shady as shit."

"I know."

"So what do you think that's all about, then? Someone heard about the oil, maybe?"

"Given the timing, it's hard not to think that. The Moose isn't exactly hot property. Hell, nothing in this town is."

Damon muttered a curse. "Great. So anyone else been called, do you think?"

"Don't know. And we won't until we have this town meeting, which we're hoping to have tomorrow night." He paused. "I have a feeling it's not going to be straightforward."

"Yeah, well, nothing with money ever is." Damon sounded annoyed.

Hell, Si couldn't blame him. The situation wasn't ever going to be without its complications, but it was turning out to have a few extra that he hadn't been anticipating. Which was irritating, since he liked to anticipate issues and plan for them, rather than being taken by surprise. And the call Hope's mother had received definitely counted as a surprise. An unpleasant one.

"No, it's not," Si said. "And if this person wanting the lease isn't on the level, then I'm going to have to figure out how he found out about the oil and who he's associated with."

"You mean your friend will." Damon's voice was uninflected. Very uninflected. "Because you won't be there. You'll be back in Juneau, meeting some guys who might be interested in buying out my share of the business, leaving me to get back to LA."

The uneasy feeling in Si's gut twisted tighter. Damon wasn't wrong. Going to the meeting, then heading back to Juneau was exactly what he should be doing. And yet...why did he feel like that would be a mistake?

You really want to leave Hope to deal with all of this?

Well, sure he did, didn't he? Hope was more than capable of handling it. Especially with the help of that sharp and icy mayor. They didn't need him, little more than an outsider these days, getting involved in decisions for a town he didn't live in and wasn't going to return to.

The late-afternoon sun was shining directly on him, the warmth of it gentle on his skin, instilling a sense of well-being. And since he led a life where physical discomfort was usual, he'd learned to enjoy the small pleasures.

And it hit him hard all of a sudden that this was one of those pleasures—sitting in the sun, with the river in front of him and the familiarity of the mountains around him. He felt...almost at home in a way he didn't in Juneau.

Can't escape this place and you know it.

"Yeah, I hear you," he said to Damon and to the voice in his head. Because he couldn't get involved in Deep River's issues. You couldn't ever go back, right?

Besides, he'd barely had a chance to get settled in Juneau before Cal had died. And once all this crap from Cal's will had been dealt with, he could concentrate on getting Wild Alaska up and running properly. Grow the business. Be his own man in a way he couldn't be in Deep River, with the past dogging his heels and all the expectations that came along with it.

That had been one of the great things about the army. He'd been just a cog in the military machine and no one was looking at him. No one had expectations of him. He was only a soldier, not the son of a drunk whose death had also caused the death of someone beloved in the town.

"Good," Damon said, satisfied. "Can you give me an ETA on when you're coming back, then? I really have got some guys who are interested in buying me out. But they're not gonna hang around forever."

Si scowled at the river, for some reason irritated by the reminder. "I told you, it'll be another couple of days. I need to be at that town meeting, see what the fallout is. I can't just cut and run if there's going to be trouble."

"I thought you said your friend could handle it?" Damon sounded as grumpy as Si was.

"I didn't say that. I just said she wasn't happy at having to deal with it."

"There are other people around to help her though, right?"

Tension crawled through Si, making his jaw ache, and he didn't know where it had come from. Because Hope did have the rest of the town to help her. She wasn't alone.

Not like she was thirteen years ago, right?

"She's my friend," he growled into the phone. "I can't just dump her in it."

"Sure you can," Damon said, apparently oblivious to Si's tone. "She's a grown woman, she can handle it. Anyway, you told me she probably wouldn't be your friend anymore, not after so many years."

Yeah, he had said that, blithely expecting his feelings about her to be long dead and gone. Except they weren't and this reluctance, this deep sense of unease, wasn't all about the town and his own problematic relationship to it. It was about her as well.

Suddenly he didn't want to talk about this with Damon anymore. "I can't hear you," he muttered. "You're breaking up."

"Hey, don't start that—"

"I'll call you after the meeting," he said, then hit the disconnect button before Damon could say another word.

Then he sat there for a couple of moments, staring over the balcony rail at the rushing green water of the river in front of him, tense and annoyed with himself for letting all this crap get to him.

You should have expected all of this. Coming back here was always going to be difficult.

Yeah, and he hadn't anticipated he'd feel quite so strongly about it. And no matter what he told himself, he *was* starting to feel strongly about it. About protecting this town from the troubles that were going to come with the oil money. And about Hope too, no denying it.

Especially now that her livelihood was at stake, considering the call Angela had had and Angela's own feelings on the subject.

He needed to figure out what to do about that before the meeting, since no doubt there would be other people who felt the same way. And he really needed to get together a plan for how to deal with it. Or rather, he and Hope had to get a plan, since the issue was her mother.

That Angela had been excited about the call hadn't surprised Si. Even thirteen years ago, Angela hadn't exactly been full of the joys of life. All he remembered about her was that she was a thin, angular woman who seemed to be always sitting on the couch, watching TV. She'd had issues with depression over the years in the same way his father had had issues with alcohol, and he knew that Hope had always worried about her. Really, it hadn't been any surprise that Hope had stayed here in many ways, despite that she'd always wanted to leave. Angela had been fragile, and he'd always known that to a certain extent Hope blamed herself for her mother's issues. Certainly her birth had resulted in a severe postpartum depression that had left Angela emotionally brittle for years afterward, so he could see why Hope thought that. Didn't mean she had to take all responsibility for her mother though.

You're a fine one to talk.

Ignoring that thought, Si decisively pulled his feet from the railing, got up from his chair, and went downstairs to the bar.

Chapter 6

HOPE SHOVED THE BOOK SHE'D BEEN READING UNDER the bar, served beers to a group of fishermen who'd come in from a day on the water, before nodding at a couple of the Moose's regulars. Not that most of the people in here as the afternoon headed into evening weren't regulars.

There seemed to be a few more people than was normal for a weeknight and she hadn't missed the open stares that had followed her around.

She knew what that was all about. The gossip mill had no doubt churned into life the moment Silas had turned up in the Moose the night before, and now that the news of an upcoming town meeting was flying around, people would be drawing conclusions.

Her mother had come straight in from her shift at Mal's full of questions about why Hope hadn't mentioned that Silas was back and what this town meeting was about. Did it have something to do with the call she'd gotten about the lease? Or was it about something else?

Hope had decided that she wasn't going to tell Angela about the oil or about the fact that Silas planned on signing ownership of the town over to her. Her mother would hear about it at the same time as everyone else, which was maybe slightly unfair, but Hope couldn't risk her mother accidentally letting it slip to the wrong person before the meeting. She couldn't bear the thought of the argument that would no doubt ensue either, or at least not yet.

Having the town signed over to her would naturally mean that she couldn't leave, and Angela would be pissed. And that wasn't even going into the issues with the lease for the Moose. That lease remained in Angela's name, which meant that legally she could do whatever she wanted with it, regardless of Hope's wishes.

And what do you wish? Really and truly?

Really and truly, what she wished was that Silas hadn't asked her to take ownership of the town. That Silas had never come back here at all. That Cal hadn't died and that oil hadn't been found…

But hell, what was the point in wishing for that? The reality was all those things had happened, and now here she was, having taken on a responsibility she'd never wanted, a responsibility that was only going to present her with yet more difficulties.

"Hey," a deep voice said, prompting a small shiver to go through her. "You got a minute?"

Hope turned, her gaze clashing with the deep green and gold of Silas's.

After the meeting with the mayor, he'd tried to talk to her about it, but she hadn't been in the mood for a discussion, feeling crushed by the weight of what she'd agreed to and needing some space to kind of forget about it for a while.

So she'd told him she was busy and had shut herself in her office, trying to lose herself in some accounts stuff. And that had worked until she'd had to open up the bar and found herself the object of interested gazes from the various locals who'd poured through the door. A few pointed questions had been asked that she'd neatly avoided, all the while becoming more and more irritated by the fact that here she was getting all the questions while the person who'd started all of this was safely ensconced upstairs, away from prying eyes.

"Not really," she said shortly, pretending to be absorbed at the till. "It's busy today."

"Looks like it." He glanced around the bar, then back at her. "Rumor mill on high alert already, huh?"

That he'd guessed what the issue was didn't make her feel any less annoyed. "What did you expect?" She closed the till with slightly more force than necessary. "After you appeared last night and then the news of the meeting today... Well. Everyone wants to know what's going on."

If her tone bothered him, he didn't show it. "And did you tell them?"

"No, of course not." She folded her arms and stared at him. "What do you want?"

He stared back. "We need to decide how we're going to handle your mother."

His casual assumption that they'd deal with this together shouldn't have annoyed her the way it did. Yet here she was, annoyed by it. "We?" She arched a brow. "Why should that have anything to do with you?"

Something shifted in his gaze. "Let's discuss this in your office."

But Hope was in no mood to discuss anything. "Yeah, let's not. I have work to do, in case you hadn't noticed."

He didn't reply for a second, his gaze moving over her in a way that made her feel restless and vulnerable, as if he could see right down to the roots of her and knew exactly why she was mad. "Let me help while I can," he said at last, quietly. "You don't have to do all of this by yourself."

There was an ache somewhere in the vicinity of her heart, longing curling through her. It was familiar, that longing. She'd felt it often after he and Cal had left, leaving her alone to deal with the Moose and her mother. As if some vital piece of her was missing, making everything that much more difficult. She'd been off balance, listing like a building with crumbling foundations, her only option being to shore herself up, because there was no one to do it for her, not anymore. It had been a hard lesson in self-sufficiency, and she didn't want to go back to depending on anyone else for support. Didn't want to have to relearn that lesson either. But the soft note of understanding in Silas's voice made her realize that even though she might have arranged her life so she was her own support, that didn't mean the longing for someone else to lean on had gone away.

Silas and Caleb had once been the most important people in her life. And now that Cal was gone, there was only Silas left.

And he's still important to you, no matter what you tell yourself.

"Fine," she heard herself say with very bad grace. "But I can't be away from the bar for too long."

She led the way into the back office, hearing the firm *click* of the door as Silas shut it behind him.

Not bothering to sit, she turned and met his gaze head-on. "Okay, so what's your plan?"

But Silas ignored that, his gaze far too sharp for her liking. "What are you mad about, Hope?"

"I'm not mad."

"Bullshit. You're pissed about something. Is it taking over ownership of the town? Or the whole situation itself?" He paused, studying her in a way that made her uncomfortable. "Or is it me?"

Of course it was him. Him and the way he'd come in here, dropping bombshell after bombshell, then expecting her to pick up the pieces. At the same time as he offered a helping hand. A helping hand that a part of her desperately wanted to take. But she couldn't let herself. Him and Cal leaving had hurt, and no matter how many times she told herself that she was over it, that it had happened years ago and it didn't hurt anymore, she still carried the scars. And the wound still ached. It hadn't healed as much as she'd thought it had.

No point in pretending otherwise, is there? He's not stupid.

Yeah, more's the pity.

"What do you think?" She didn't bother to hide the anger in her voice. "You waltz in after thirteen years of silence, bringing with you all kinds of trouble, and then you dump it straight in my lap. So yeah, I guess you could say I'm a little mad. After all, this is the second time you've done this."

A muscle flicked in his hard jaw, but he didn't look away. "I offered to stay. You refused."

Aw, crap. She hadn't meant to open up this particular can of worms. But the fact that he instantly knew what she was talking about was indication enough that it had been preying on his mind too, and she wasn't sure how she felt about that.

It didn't help that he was right. He had offered to stay. And she'd refused him because it hadn't been him that she'd wanted. Or at least, she'd thought it hadn't been him.

Maybe it was him, but he was always too dangerous for you. Caleb was safe because he never wanted you the way you wanted him.

A hot feeling crept through her, making her skin feel sensitized and her breath catch. Because if Cal had felt safe because she'd known he wasn't into her, then there was a reason she'd instinctively shied away from Silas. A reason he'd always felt dangerous, making her antsy and uncomfortable. And perhaps that reason was something she'd known on a very basic level but had never wanted to examine or think about too closely, since it would mean things she wasn't ready to face.

That he'd wanted her.

"You didn't want to stay," she said, even though she knew she should change the subject, that talking about this might open a Pandora's box full of implications she wasn't ready for even now. "You only said it because Caleb didn't offer."

The silence in the office was full of something sharp and electric, something that whispered across her skin like a fine current, making all the hairs on her arms stand up on end.

Gold glittered from beneath Silas's thick, black lashes, his gaze holding hers, making it impossible for her to look away. "I would have stayed," he said, his voice deep and dark in the silence. "I would have stayed for you."

A wave of heat arrowed through her, the electricity in the room crackling, sparks falling all over her skin in bright, hot points. She could see the truth in his eyes all of a sudden, the truth that perhaps had always been there and she'd never seen it because she'd never looked. Because she'd never wanted to look.

She'd been too young, too afraid of the intensity of her emotions. On some level aware that if she allowed herself to become more than friends with Silas, she might fall and fall hard—and never ever stop falling.

Hope wrenched her gaze away, acutely conscious of the distance separating them. Of how close he was. A very physical awareness that had her mouth going dry.

She'd never been so conscious of a man before, of his height and strength, the width of his shoulders and the hard muscle of his chest. His arms were folded, and she wanted to study the way the cotton of his T-shirt pulled tight around his biceps, wanted to touch that chest to see if it was as firm as it looked.

Hell, what was wrong with her? She wasn't a virgin, for God's sake; she knew what sex was all about. It was only that she'd decided it was more trouble than it was worth, and she'd been completely fine with that decision. She hadn't missed it. So why did she feel this way now? Was it him? Was it the past catching up with her? Was it because he was familiar? What?

Does it matter what it is? You're not going there with him.

No, she wasn't.

"Well, great to know," she said inanely, her voice sounding tinny in the small confines of the room. "I'll be sure to remember that. But right now, I have to get back to the bar." She took a step forward, hoping the towering wall of male muscle in front of her would move.

But he didn't. He simply stayed where he was, as unmovable as the mountains surrounding her home and just as hard.

"No," Silas said.

Hope, who was clearly expecting him to move, came up short, her dark eyes widening. "What do you mean, no?" she demanded.

"I mean no you can't go back out to the bar. It'll take care of itself for five minutes."

"Silas—"

"We haven't finished our conversation."

He was being a dick and he knew it, but he couldn't

help himself. There had been something in Hope's eyes that had caught him like a blow to the chest, something electric in the air around them that hadn't been there before.

An electricity he recognized and thought would never happen—not with her. But it was there now: sexual tension. He could feel it vibrating in the space between them and even though he knew he should let it go, he couldn't.

Once or twice, back when they'd been teenagers, he'd thought he'd caught a glimpse in her eyes of a response to him. But he'd never been sure and it had only ever been a glimpse, definitely not enough for certainty. So he'd let it go, told himself he'd been seeing things because that was easier than pinning his hopes on something that wasn't real.

Except the tension in the air now was definitely real and so was the glow in her dark eyes.

Telling her he would have stayed for her was probably a stupid thing to do, but he hadn't been able to help himself. If he wanted the truth from her, he'd have to give her some of his own.

Hope's gaze flickered over him, full of hot little sparks. "You might not have finished, but I have."

"Have you? You still look mad to me."

"I'm not—"

"Did you want me to stay, Hope?" Suddenly nothing was more important than the answer to that question. "Is that why you're angry with me? Why you were so angry with me yesterday when I first arrived?"

"Why do you want to know?" she snapped. "What does it matter? Haven't we got other more important things to discuss?"

He heard it then, underneath the anger—a sharp note of pain. And before he could stop himself, he'd raised his hand and cupped her cheek, an instinct bone-deep and years old gripping him.

As soon as his fingers touched her skin, she went utterly still, and it felt like the entire universe had gone still along with her, as if all of creation had taken a sharp breath and was holding it.

There was silence around them, even the sounds of the bar outside the door disappearing. Her fine-grained skin was warm beneath his fingers and as soft as he'd always imagined, and he knew he shouldn't be touching her and yet he couldn't bring himself to stop.

"I want to know because you're my friend." He let his thumb brush slowly over her cheekbone, relishing the satiny warmth of her. "And it matters because I hurt you."

She said nothing, standing unmoving, staring at him like he was a stranger. There were currents in her dark eyes, deep and powerful as those in the river that ran through the town, but unlike those, Hope's ran hot rather than icy cold. "It was years ago," she said, her voice a little husky. "And I'm over it. Are we done now?"

But she wasn't over it, not when that note of pain was still there, edged and jagged as a shard of broken glass embedded in a thick, soft rug.

He spread his fingers out on her cheek, continuing to

brush his thumb back and forth, wanting to soothe her, ease that pain somehow. Except he couldn't, not if she wouldn't acknowledge it.

You really want to push this? Why? What difference will it make?

Perhaps no difference. She was right; it had happened years ago, and maybe he was being a bastard bringing all of this up again. But…he couldn't let it go. He just couldn't. She was mad and she was hurt, and that meant something. And maybe he was reading things into it that weren't there, but it had to be about more than just friendship. Certainly the sudden sexual tension between them hadn't come from nowhere.

God, how many years had he wanted her? Too many. And he'd never done a thing about it, never crossed that line. He wasn't going to now, either, not given the situation with the town and the uncertainty around it. Yet even though it might be selfish of him, he wanted to know once and for all if she felt even a glimmer of what he felt for her.

"No," he said. "We're not done."

"What do you want from me?" She didn't pull away from his hand, but she didn't lean into it either, and he could see the tension vibrating through her, as if she was holding herself back from doing one thing or the other.

Either way, it meant his touch affected her.

Heat spread through him, quickening his heartbeat, all the blood flooding down to a certain part of his anatomy. Which very definitely shouldn't be happening, but he didn't drop his hand or step away.

"What do I want?" he asked instead. "I want the truth."

"The truth about what?"

"The truth about why you're really so angry with me."
He studied her face, watching the ebb and flow of emotions in her eyes. "Because I get the feeling that it wasn't
Cal that you really wanted."

"You have no idea what I really wanted." The hot glow
in her eyes burned brighter. "And why the hell would I
tell you anyway? What makes you think you deserve it?"

"Oh, I don't deserve it." He brushed his thumb back
over her cheek, the feel of her skin a glory he hadn't imagined. "But I'm asking for it anyway."

Her pupils had dilated, her eyes even blacker than
they were already and full of an expression he didn't
understand. There were too many things in them—pain
and anger knotted with other emotions too complicated
to name. "You left me," she said suddenly, her voice thick.
"Both of you left me. Grandad had died, and I had Mom
to look after, and I was afraid. And I needed *both* of you.
But you'd both gone. And then you stayed away, Si. For
thirteen goddamn years."

His chest tightened painfully. After he and Cal had left
Deep River, he'd told himself a lot of lies to make leaving Hope okay. But that's all they were. Lies. There had
been nothing okay about leaving Hope, and he'd always
known, deep down, that they'd both hurt her. Caleb had
at least gone back, yet he hadn't.

Because you're a coward.

Yeah, maybe he was. But the night he and Cal had told

her they were going, all he'd felt was pain. Her grandfather had gone into the water to save his father; his
father was the reason the both of them were dead, and he
hadn't been able to handle his own guilt about that, let
alone handle her grief too.

And he hadn't gone back because he'd told himself
she was better off without him. That she'd forgotten him.
That Cal had visited and Cal was who she really wanted
after all.

More lies—certainly judging from the hurt in her
eyes now.

"I had to go," he said. "Dad was the reason Bill died.
And I couldn't..." He stopped, trying to find the right
words. "I felt guilty." *You are guilty.* "And I didn't want
to stay and deal with the fallout," he went on quickly,
drowning out that particular thought. "I'd been dealing
with the fallout from Dad's drinking for years already,
and him and Bill... It was too much."

"I get that." Pain glittered in Hope's eyes. "But would
it have killed you to come back at least once to say hi?
You didn't have to leave me with no word for so long, Si."

The ache in his chest deepened, widened. "I didn't
think it would matter to you that much. It was always Cal
you wanted."

Her throat moved as she swallowed, her dark gaze
on his unwavering. "How could you think it wouldn't
matter? You were my best friend."

Yeah, and some best friend he turned out to be.

You never wanted to be her friend anyway.

And that was the problem. He didn't. He'd always wanted to be so much more than that.

Let her go. You're not going to follow through on this so what's the point insisting?

But he couldn't bring himself to step away. That tension in the air was still there, electric, and she wasn't pulling away from him. She was standing very still and letting him touch her.

So he stepped closer, cradling her cheek in his palm, staring down into her dark eyes. "There was a reason I stayed away."

"Don't," she began as if she knew already what he was going to say.

And maybe he should have stopped. But it was too late now. If it wasn't going to matter anyway, then why not say it? Why not tell her?

He brushed his thumb over her cheekbone again, conscious of the fact that he was standing very close to her and that she smelled sweet, like a field of wildflowers, along with a delicate musky fragrance that made everything male in him sit up and take notice. "That reason was you," he went on. "And it didn't have anything to do with being your friend."

Red stained the clear olive skin of her cheeks, yet again, she didn't pull away. She only stared up at him, the pulse at the base of her throat fast and hard. "What do you mean?"

"Do I really need to explain?" He pressed his fingertips lightly against her cheek. "I think you know exactly what I mean."

The blush in her cheeks deepened, the hot glow in her eyes glittering. "You know, I think you're going to have to spell it out for me. Just so we're clear."

Fine, he would. Because now they'd headed down this path, there was no reason not to keep going. "I want you, Hope," he said. "I've always wanted you. Is that clear enough?"

Shock flared in her gaze, unmistakable and bright, and her mouth opened, then shut. She shook her head. "No. No, you can't have."

"I did. Don't tell me you didn't know." She'd never let on that she had, but some part of him had wondered if she'd somehow picked up on his feelings for her. Because as teenagers, he'd often gotten the impression that she was uncomfortable around him. He hadn't made any move toward her, had tried to make sure that his true feelings for her stayed locked away so she saw nothing but friendship. But maybe he hadn't hidden them as well as he'd thought.

Something shifted in her eyes. "You never said anything."

"Are you surprised? After you told me all about your crush on Cal?"

Her expression was unreadable. "It wouldn't have made a difference, Si."

He pressed his thumb against her cheekbone, watching the shifting emotional currents in her eyes, seeing the gleam of heat in the depths of her gaze, glowing like banked embers. "Wouldn't it?"

He shouldn't push. He should let this go, let her go. Yet he wasn't going to. He wanted the truth, wanted to know once and for all if she felt anything at all for him. No, he didn't deserve it, but he wanted it anyway.

And surely she did. Because if she truly felt nothing but friendship for him, she wouldn't be standing so close to him. She wouldn't have let him touch her, let him stroke her cheek. She wouldn't be blushing. And those hot embers in the depths of her eyes certainly wouldn't be glowing the way they were now.

She stared back at him, unwavering. "No. It wouldn't."

"Really? You didn't want me to stay instead of Cal?"

"And why would I have wanted you to stay instead of Cal?" Her voice was husky, the look in her eyes challenging almost.

"Because you wanted me, Hope." He moved his thumb down in an arc, over her cheek, brushing the corner of her lovely mouth. "You wanted me the way I wanted you."

Her lashes fell, veiling her gaze. And there was a very long silence. "Whether I did or I didn't won't change anything," she said at last. "We can't go back to what we had before."

"I know that. And I'm not expecting anything from you. I just…want to know."

Slowly, her lashes lifted again, her eyes as dark as the river at night and just as deep. "I really did think it was Cal I wanted. And I really did want him to stay. I was disappointed when he didn't and angry that you were the one who offered instead." She paused. "But…maybe I was wrong."

It wasn't a shock. It felt like he'd always known on some level that she wasn't entirely immune to him the way he'd always thought.

Satisfaction stretched out inside him, a hungry, possessive kind of feeling following along in its wake, and if he'd been back in Juneau and she'd been a woman he'd met in a bar, he might have pulled her to him and kissed her.

But he wasn't in Juneau and she was Hope, his best friend, and there was too much history behind them and too many different futures in front of them.

Knowing didn't change a thing.

He allowed himself one last stroke of her cheek with his thumb before he dropped his hand.

Then he turned and walked out of the office without another word.

Chapter 7

THE COMMUNITY CENTER WAS PACKED. HOPE HAD never seen it so full of people, not even on Christmas Eve when they held the town's annual Christmas dinner there for those who could get through the snow.

Then again, it wasn't any wonder. After Cal's death, people were uncertain about what would happen to the town, and they were clearly hoping that the meeting that had been called was going to give them some answers.

And it would. They just wouldn't be the answers everyone was expecting.

Up at the front, Silas stood with his arms crossed over his chest, looking tall and powerful as he surveyed the crowd like a general surveying his army. That they were all surveying him back with varying degrees of suspicion didn't seem to bother him, or at least if it did, he didn't show it.

Hope leaned back against the wall and folded her arms over her frantically beating heart, tearing her gaze away from him and looking out over the assembled townspeople instead.

She'd spent all day berating herself for what had happened between them in her office the day before, for letting herself get caught up in a discussion that she didn't want to have and only made things more difficult between them. She should have simply shoved him out of the way when he'd stood in front of her, but she hadn't. She'd stood there and gazed back at him, mesmerized by the fierce look in his eyes instead.

She hadn't meant to give herself away like that, but she hadn't been able to move. And most especially not when he'd lifted his hand and touched her face. She'd felt the touch of his fingers move through her, sweet and bright as summer lightning, and something deep inside of her had trembled.

Then he'd told her he'd wanted her, that he'd always wanted her, and she'd been unable to breathe. She would have preferred it if the breathlessness had been due to shock, but it wasn't. No, on some level she'd always known that Si's feelings toward her had never been purely platonic, and it had been habit that made her ignore it. Or more accurately, self-preservation.

Admitting to herself that he wanted her would have meant she'd have to examine her own feelings about him, and they were complicated. They'd always been complicated.

You know what your body wants, at least.

She shifted restlessly against the wall, her gaze drawn yet again to the man standing at the front of the hall, tall and silent, his expression enigmatic. He was in his usual outfit of jeans and a T-shirt—this time a soft-looking gray one that clung to his broad chest, drawing attention to the hard muscle of his pecs and abs. He was built so very fine and a part of her, a part she'd never wanted to admit to herself, had always noticed. Just as she had always noticed his straight, sharp jawline and high cheekbones, and appreciated the fascinating shape of his mouth.

"You wanted me, Hope. The way I always wanted you."

Her breath caught, and she looked away from him yet again. God, she should have denied it, told him that of course she didn't want him, what was he thinking?

But that would have been a lie. And standing there with that electric tension crackling between them, it was a lie he wouldn't have believed anyway.

He wasn't wrong. She did want him.

Restlessness coiled inside her. Admitting that to him or even to herself wasn't going to change anything though. The past was dead and gone, and nothing was going to happen in the present. Sure, they didn't have a friendship left to preserve these days, but he'd be leaving soon, which made doing anything about their attraction pointless.

She didn't want to do anything about it anyway. There had been something hungry in his eyes as he'd looked at her, something that had told her that sleeping with him would change her and change her completely. That it would make things deeper and far more complicated than they already were, and she wasn't ready for that kind of thing in her life right now. Maybe she wouldn't ever be ready for it.

The buzz of conversation in the room increased as more people came in, the door banging shut behind them, and looking over the crowd in an effort to distract herself from Silas, Hope caught her mother's dark eyes looking suspiciously back at her.

Damn. She and Silas hadn't ended up talking about the phone call Angela received or formulating a plan for how to deal with it. In fact, Hope hadn't seen him at all the whole day today, which she had to admit to herself was deliberate.

Since when did you get to be such a coward?

Since she'd found herself helplessly attracted to her best friend, not to mention the owner of an entire town, neither of which she wanted on her plate right now.

"Is everyone here?" Astrid's cool voice rang out over the crowd and everyone quieted. "Let's get this meeting started then." She nodded to where Silas stood. "For those of you who don't know him, this is Silas Quinn, Caleb's best friend. He has some news that's going to affect the entire town, so if you could be quiet until he's finished speaking, I'd appreciate it."

A murmur ran through the crowd before it gradually died away, everyone looking attentively at Silas.

Hope tensed. Once everyone knew, things would change and there was no going back. No putting this particular genie back in the bottle. God, she hoped it wouldn't end up ripping the entire town apart.

Silas nodded, then began to speak, his deep, dark voice filling the hall. He stuck to the facts, delivering them levelly and stripped bare of any emotion or judgment. Telling them about Caleb's will and how Cal had signed the town over to Silas and his two friends. And once he'd gotten that out of the way, he told them about the oil.

It didn't take long, and once he'd finished

speaking, complete and utter silence reigned, shock rippling through the entire hall.

Then the whispers started, becoming mutters, getting louder, and several people got to their feet, starting to ask questions. Soon more people were on their feet and more questions were asked, some of them starting to be shouted, and in less than five seconds, pandemonium erupted.

"Be quiet!" Astrid's cool voice cut through the noise like a sword slicing through silk and just as precise. "I realize you all have questions, but shouting them all at once won't help. One at a time, please."

There was a sullen muttering at that, but people quieted, some of them settling back on the hard wooden benches that had been set up for them to sit on, but more than a few continuing to stand.

Hope felt her heart beating hard against her breastbone as she surveyed the familiar faces of the townspeople, seeing worry and concern and uncertainty, not to mention excitement too.

"Okay, first up, a few facts." Silas's hard voice fell over the few remaining whispered conversations like an iron bar, crushing them flat. "Since I don't live in Deep River anymore nor am I intending to stay here, I'll be signing my ownership of the town over to someone else."

"Morgan?" someone asked. Morgan was still in Juneau doing some kind of police training. "She's the logical person."

"No," Silas said. "I offered it to Morgan, but she refused."

Voices rang out at this, but Silas raised his hand, silencing them. "No, I don't know why. You'll have to ask her."

"What about this oil?" This was from Malcom Cooper, the big, bluff man who owned the market. "Did anyone know Caleb was prospecting? Why the hell was he doing that, anyway?"

Several other people began to comment, but Silas said over the top of them, "Again, I don't know. There was nothing about his reasons in the will, and he didn't say anything to me about it either. I was as surprised as you all were to hear he'd been getting Deep River checked out."

"So what does it mean for leaseholders?" This was, unsurprisingly, from Mike Flint, who'd never given up his luxury motel dream, no matter that the rest of the town had panned it. "Money-wise?"

People were nodding at this, a small chorus of yeses erupting, and Hope felt the tension grip her harder, because this was getting down to the nitty-gritty. Anticipation rippled through the assembled crowd, people looking excited, avid. There would always be a few blinded by dollar signs.

"That's a good question." Silas swept his gaze over everyone, his expression hard. "When Jacob began this town a century or so ago, he had a vision for it. A vision he wanted to preserve, and that meant it was always going to stay a leasehold town. But he needed to attract people here, so retaining mineral rights for leaseholders had to be part of the deal." Silas paused. "It's still part of the deal. In Jacob's era, it was all about gold, but that's gone now. You folks retain the rights to the minerals on your property and that includes oil."

There was another stunning silence.

"So, let me get this straight," Mike said, narrowing his gaze at Silas. "We have the rights to whatever's under the ground?"

"Yes." Silas didn't hesitate, and Hope couldn't help wincing at his honesty at the same time she admired the hell out of it. Some people might have kept all of this quiet, but not Silas. He remained true to the spirit of this town and always had, even if it meant things would change and maybe not for the better. "You can sell those mineral rights to an oil company or you can keep them for yourself, pay a share to a company to drill."

Another murmur rippled through the crowd.

"No, we can't do that!" Gwen, Harry the survivalist's girlfriend and instigator of the popular hot yoga classes currently sweeping the town, surged to her feet in a cloud of patchouli and muslin, long blond braids falling down her back. "We can't sell rights to an oil company. Think of the environmental damage!"

"Aw, pipe down, California," someone muttered from the crowd.

"Who said that?" Harry growled, standing up beside his girlfriend and looking menacingly around. "Gwen's got a right to speak, just as much as the rest of you. She lives here."

"Sure," Mike said, crossing his arms. "But she doesn't have any dependents. My mom needs to go into a retirement home because I can't give her the care she needs. The damn environment's not going to pay for that, is it?"

"So you'd rather have drills and heavy machinery raping the land?" Gwen exclaimed passionately. "Cutting down the trees and destroying the ecosystems that animals depend on?"

Hope muttered a curse under her breath because soon this would head into territory that'd put people at extreme loggerheads. And not just between people who cared about the environment as opposed to people who had more pressing and personal concerns. It would also be between the townspeople who'd been here for a couple of generations as opposed to the people who'd only been here a couple of years.

Money, as she'd feared, was a huge issue. And the irony wasn't lost on her that it had been money and the gold rush that had first brought the town into being. Maybe it would also be the thing that heralded its end.

She pushed herself away from the wall, not knowing what she was going to say, only that she needed to say something to defuse the situation, when her mother got to her feet and said loudly, "I had a call from someone wanting to buy the Moose's lease. He offered me a lot of money. Could this have something to do with the oil?"

Everyone quieted, starting at her.

It didn't surprise Hope that her mother had put two and two together. She might be mentally fragile, but she wasn't stupid.

"I had a call too," Nate Wilson, owner of the Gold Pan, put in unexpectedly. "He wanted to buy the hotel."

Hope watched as Silas narrowed his gaze at Nate. "Did he give you a name?"

"No," Nate said. "Only said he'd stayed in the hotel a year or so ago and really liked it. Really liked the town."

"He told me the same thing," Angela added. "Said he wanted to get out of the city, go somewhere small."

Silas's expression became even harder, the green in his eyes sharp as a knife. "Right, so conceivably this guy is the same person." He gave everyone a fierce look. "Anyone else get a call?"

"I had a couple of messages from some guy on my phone," Mal said gruffly. "Didn't call him back because he didn't leave a number."

Silas's gaze suddenly met Hope's, and she blinked, the air escaping her lungs for a couple of seconds, the impact of it almost physical. She couldn't read what was in his eyes, but there was a ferocity in them that felt familiar somehow. And she knew why.

He'd given her the same look the night he'd left.

Si wasn't sure exactly what had made him look at Hope, but suddenly he needed to know what she thought about all of this. Because given that three people had now been called by what was starting to look like the same shady guy, he wanted to see how she was taking it.

Not well, judging by the tension in her posture. Her expression remained mostly unreadable, but he recognized the uncertainty glittering in her eyes.

You can't leave her to deal with this alone. Not the way you did last time.

Something hardened inside him. A decision.

As he'd told the assembled crowd what was happening and watched the expressions on their faces change, he'd realized what his conscience had been telling him since the day Cal's will had been read—he couldn't simply drop this on his hometown and leave them to deal with the consequences. Couldn't leave this all on Hope either. And not because he didn't think she could handle it, but because it wasn't fair.

Thirteen years ago, he'd walked away from a situation he should have helped out with, and he just couldn't do it a second time. He wasn't twenty anymore. He wasn't that boy who'd been ground down by caring for an alcoholic father who only noticed him when he was drunk, by being in love with a girl who didn't want him. Whose fledgling hopes for his own future as a pilot seemed as though they would never happen.

No, he'd left that boy behind. He had his own life now, with the piloting business he'd always wanted, and a group of buddies who had his back. Things were different and so was he. And he wasn't going to run away like he had before.

Sure, Damon wanted him in Juneau, and he hadn't intended to stay in Deep River more than a couple of days, a week at the most. But maybe Damon could wait. And maybe he could stay to help Hope and the town figure out their direction. He was still the owner, after all, and no matter that he didn't live here, he had an obligation to make sure this transition ran smoothly.

Damon would be pissed, but he would live.

Nothing at all to do with the fact that Hope's not so immune to you after all, right?

No, of course it wasn't. He'd already decided he wasn't going to complicate matters by crossing the line with her, and he wouldn't. He'd stay to act as a support for her, nothing more.

He kept his gaze on Hope's a second longer, then looked back over the crowd. "I think we want to be careful of this guy," he said. "If he hasn't given you any details about who he is, then given the timing of his offers and the number of people he's called, I think it's sketchy as hell."

"You think it's a guy from an oil company maybe?" Mal asked.

Silas nodded. "I do. I'm pretty sure Caleb would have kept the fact that he was prospecting on the down low, and since no one else knew he was doing it, that was pretty successful. But maybe word's gotten around somehow that there's oil here, and there are some people who want to take advantage."

There was a rumbling of voices at this, people muttering things to their neighbors, some of them nodding their heads while others shook theirs.

More questions would no doubt be asked, and if this

wasn't managed carefully, it could devolve into a massive town argument. It was probably better to dismiss the meeting now, give people a chance to let the news settle in and figure out how they wanted to deal with it. They could arrange another meeting in a week or so, once everyone had had time to process what was happening, and then they could field more questions, get a sense for what most people wanted to do, and try to come to some consensus about how they were going to handle it.

A couple had already begun to throw questions around about money and what would it mean to sign away mineral rights, not to mention how drilling would work, but he shook his head. "Let's not get into discussing that right now," he said, raising his voice to silence a few of the conversations happening in the back of the hall. "I suggest you go away and think about it for a few days, decide what you think is the best course of action for you, and then we'll meet again to talk about it." He paused, staring out over the assembled crowd, conscious of all the people he didn't know and of all the people who didn't know him. Conscious too that this town wasn't what it had been thirteen years ago, that it had changed just as he had, and that he didn't know anything about those changes. He didn't know anything about this town as it now was.

But still, he went on, "Remember the spirit of Deep River. Remember why Jacob West created it all those years ago. He wanted to make this place a haven for people who didn't belong, a place of safety and shelter. And it's been that way for over a hundred years. Let's not ruin it now."

"Wait," Mal said as everyone prepared to rise. "You said you were going to sign ownership over to someone else. Who is it?"

Silas could feel the pressure of everyone's interested gazes as they all turned to look at him, and suddenly he didn't want to tell them about Hope, not yet. And not because of any open hostility or resentment or even suspicion. He just didn't want to leave her open to everyone's reaction, especially when she hadn't been all that happy about having to take on the responsibility.

So all he said was, "That's still under discussion. I will let everyone know when it's finalized."

Five minutes later, everyone had filed out of the community center, the buzz of conversation following them out the doors.

"Liked what you said about not ruining the spirit of the town," Astrid said, pausing beside him as she made her way out. "That was a good note to end on. Good plan to end the meeting and let the news settle in too."

"Thanks. Thought it was the best way to defuse any potential arguments."

Astrid glanced toward the open doors. "You might have a few of those waiting for you outside."

She wasn't wrong. He could hear a few people talking and not quietly, obviously lingering outside, perhaps to ask him some questions. Well, he was more than happy to answer them. He had nothing to hide.

"I can deal with it," he said shortly.

"I'm sure you can." Astrid gave him an unreadable

look. "You going to be around for the next meeting, then? Or was that for my benefit?"

Silas met her gaze straight on. "I thought I'd stick around. If it's all the same to you."

"Why?" Hope's voice at his elbow sounded sharp, and he turned to find her standing beside them, a suspicious look in her eyes. "I thought you said you had to head back to Juneau."

"And I think that's my cue to leave," Astrid muttered, obviously picking up on the tension. "Let me know when you need me to call another meeting."

Silas waited until Astrid had gone, then he said, "I do. But it can wait a week or so."

"You don't need to stay on my account." Hope folded her arms, giving him a challenging look. "I can handle it."

Even in the harsh light of the hall's fluorescents, her hair looked glossy, the deep auburn tones glowing like the embers in her eyes, all signs of the fire she kept smoldering under that tough, practical exterior.

He had a sudden, intense urge to pull at the tie that bound her ponytail and let her hair fall over her shoulders, bury his hands in the silken mass of it, release that fire he knew was inside her. Release the woman he remembered from years ago, passionate and wild, full of dreams and a relentless optimism that had saved him on more than one occasion.

He'd often felt that she hadn't been called Hope for nothing.

His fingers itched, but he folded his arms to stop

himself from reaching for her, because even though he'd decided to stay a little longer, that didn't mean he wanted anything more from her than friendship. Hell, he barely even had that. Perhaps instead that's what he could start rebuilding. He owed her that, at least.

"I know you can handle it," he said. "Hell, if you can deal with Joe and Lloyd every Friday night for thirteen years, you can deal with this damn town arguing about oil."

"Then why stay? You're not needed, Silas."

That stung, even though it shouldn't have. "Perhaps not. But I left when crap went down and I don't want to do it again."

Her jaw hardened, as if she found that offensive. "So, what? Is this some kind of redemption move? Making up for the past and all that bullshit? Because if it is, I'd rather you didn't use me to do it."

Mad. She was always so mad at him. Prickly and defensive and snappy. Yeah, he got where she was coming from, that she still hadn't forgiven him for the way he'd left years ago or for not contacting her. So maybe it was time he started working toward that. Maybe he could start rebuilding the friendship they'd once had.

"I know I screwed up, Hope," he said, addressing the anger still burning in her eyes. "I know I hurt you, that both Caleb and I hurt you. And I've already told you that I'm sorry about it. And I meant it. And I'm staying because I want to do better. No, you don't need me, and I know that. But I'm going to stick around anyway, just in case."

Hope stared at him, still radiating annoyance and something else he couldn't quite figure out. "You think an apology is going to fix thirteen years of absence?"

"No." He wasn't fool enough to think that. "But I think it's a start."

Her jaw was tense and so were her shoulders, and he knew she was fighting not to give him a single damn inch. God, she was stubborn. But then her stubbornness was the thing that had kept her going all this time, wasn't it?

"And what? You want to fix things between us? Is that what you're saying?"

"What do you think? Of course I want to fix things between us."

"Why? So you can get me into bed?"

An arrow of heat shot through him, no matter that it shouldn't have, which pissed him off. "No." He scowled. "Why the hell would you think that?"

Hope lifted her chin. "You told me you wanted me. And then after making a big song and dance about how you have to leave, you change your mind. What else am I supposed to think?"

Anger licked up inside him. "I'm your friend, Hope. Yes, I said that, but I already told you I don't expect anything from you. That's not why I'm staying."

"Well, I don't want you to stay." Her arms dropped to her sides, an intense, kinetic energy radiating from her, like she was a horse about to bolt. "I didn't ask you to." Then, weirdly, she stepped right up close to him, her head tilting back so she could meet his gaze. "I didn't want you to stay then and I don't want you to stay now." Her hand shot out, her fingers curling into the fabric of his T-shirt and holding on. "You should leave, Silas," she added fiercely.

Then, in a move he hadn't seen coming and would never have expected, not in a million years, she held on to his T-shirt as she came up on her toes and pressed her mouth to his.

He froze, his brain blanking, Hope's soft, warm lips against his own. The briefest brush and then she'd gone back down on her feet again, the banked embers in the depths of her eyes glowing bright.

He wasn't often taken by surprise, but he was now. And he had no idea what to do about it. "What the hell was that for?" he demanded, his voice little more than a growl, her kiss reverberating through him, striking white-hot sparks of heat through his entire central nervous system.

She didn't look away, her expression challenging. Daring him. "I just wanted you to know that if you think we could ever be friends again, then you can think again."

His hands were in fists at his sides and he could feel something in him begin to pull at the chains he'd put on it. Something hungry. "Really?" His voice had gone even deeper, even rougher. "That's a damn stupid way to prove it."

"Oh yeah?" Hope lifted her chin again. "Why?"

He shouldn't have done it, but it seemed like there were a lot of things he shouldn't do that he did anyway. And besides, he couldn't stop himself.

His hands lifted, his fingers in the softness of her hair

before he knew what he was doing, and he'd pulled her close, cradling her head in his hands, and his mouth was on hers again, taking what she'd offered him just before and more than that.

She didn't resist. Instead, she gave a little gasp and her mouth opened under his, her hands lifting to his chest and pressing against him.

The kiss was everything he'd imagined all those lonely nights when he'd been a teenager, fantasies of Hope playing in his head. Everything he'd imagined and more. Hot and sweet. He could taste the fire at the heart of her and it ignited something in him, setting him burning.

What the hell are you doing? You weren't going to go there with her, remember?

His heart was racing, the urge to pull her closer, kiss her deeper so strong he could barely think. Holding her was all he'd ever wanted to do and this was so much better than any of those fantasies...

But he couldn't take this further. He couldn't. He was going to leave in the end, and he didn't want to make things difficult for her. Didn't want to complicate this for either of them.

It was one of the hardest things he'd ever done, but he forced himself to do it, lifting his mouth from hers, then opening his hands, letting her go, and stepping away. He was breathing very fast and so was she, her eyes wide and so dark they looked fathomless.

Shock was written all over her flushed face, and she looked at him as if he were a complete stranger to her.

A part of him liked that look very much indeed, but it wasn't a part of him he was going to continue to indulge, so he forced the feeling away.

"That's why," he said.

Then, without waiting for a response, he turned and walked away from her for the second time in as many days.

Chapter 8

HOPE WAITED UNTIL MAL HAD FINISHED TALKING TO Debbie Long before she leaned her hip against the store counter and said, "Got a minute, Mal?"

Mal was a big man, tall and broad, in his midfifties, with a salt-and-pepper beard and tattoos up his heavily muscled arms. He'd owned Mal's Market for a couple of decades, and the place tended to be where people congregated to gossip during the day. At least once they'd had breakfast at April's and were waiting for the Moose to open.

His gray gaze was very direct. "Why? You got something to say about this oil business?"

"No. I was more interested in the phone calls you were getting."

After the meeting had ended the night before, Hope had decided to follow up on the calls that Nate and Mal had received, because they were suspiciously similar to the one Angela had gotten. Silas had said that it sounded like they were from the same person, but she'd wanted to be sure. Because if it was from the same person, then it was likely that the oil companies were aware of the reserves underneath Deep River and at least one of them wanted to get their hands on it.

Which was going to complicate an already complicated situation.

Even now, her mother had suspicions that Hope had

known about the oil before the town meeting and was annoyed that Hope hadn't told her, and she'd refused to talk about the phone call when Hope had asked her about it this morning. She'd told Hope she hadn't made any decision about the lease just yet so quit asking her.

That had irritated Hope, but pushing her mother wasn't going to help, so she'd decided she might as well follow up on those calls now.

It was certainly better than skulking in her back office and going over the accounts in an effort to avoid Silas and stop thinking about what had gone on between them the night before.

Oh God, that kiss.

She didn't know what had possessed her to grab him by the T-shirt and pull him close. To go up on her toes and press her mouth to his. She'd been angry, yes. Because he'd decided he was going to stay and she didn't want him to. She *really* didn't want him to. She'd accepted his presence here only because it wasn't going to be for too long, yet now he'd changed his mind; now he was going to stay on for a bit longer, and that made her...angry. And uncertain. And vulnerable in a way she hated. Then he'd started apologizing for how he'd left and mentioning that by staying and helping it would be a "start." And she had a horrible feeling that what he meant by that was rebuilding the friendship they'd once had. She didn't want any part of it, so she'd pulled him close and kissed him, thinking that it would distance him.

Did you really think that? Or did you just want a taste of him?

Hope shoved that thought away, as she did the memory of his hands in her hair, of how he'd tugged her close and kissed her back. A real kiss that time, not the light brush of her mouth that she'd given him.

And her brain had been wiped clean, a fire burning bright inside her, leaping high, heating her blood, making her heart race and her breath catch. Making her want to get closer to him, touch him. Reach the passion that she knew was buried deep inside him but was there and burning for her. Only for her...

"Phone calls from that guy, you mean?"

Mal's voice seemed to come from a long way away, and Hope almost shook her head to clear her brain of the memory of Silas's kiss.

"Yeah," she said, hoping her voice sounded normal and not as thick and breathy as she feared. "I'm pretty sure it was the same guy calling Mom."

Mal rubbed at his bearded chin thoughtfully. "Not sure what to tell you. He left a couple of messages, but not a number. Said he'd call back in a day or so."

"Right." Hope shifted against the counter. "I wonder if you should tell him that you're interested, get him to leave a number. We might be able to figure out where he's from if we have one."

Mal nodded slowly. "Yeah, was already considering doing that. I'm going to be asking him a whole lot of questions, believe me."

"Okay, sounds good." She hesitated because part of her didn't want to ask the question, let alone hear the answer.

But Mal was an influential person in the community. People relied on him and his store, and they respected him as a person too. His opinion might very well sway a few people, and if she was going to own all of this, she needed to know his feelings on the subject.

Except it seemed like he could tell that's what she was going to ask because he folded his arms and looked at her. "You want to know what I think about this oil stuff, right? Well, I think it's bullshit. I don't know what Caleb was thinking getting some prospecting done, but that boy was all about caring for this town, no matter that he ran off and left it. So it seems to me he was probably thinking about using that oil and whatever came with it to our advantage."

Hope let out a breath she hadn't even realized she was holding. "I think you're probably right. Cal would never have done anything to hurt this place, that's for sure. But…I'm not sure everyone's going to agree on the oil."

The burly storeowner dropped his arms, put his hands on the counter, and leaned on them, giving her another of those measuring looks. "You're taking a very dark view, Hope. The people of this town will put what's good for Deep River first, mark my words. Money is only ever a short-term fix, and I reckon everyone will soon realize that. They'll remember why they came to live here in the first place, what drew them, and they'll understand what's more important."

She didn't know if they would, but she liked his optimism.

You used to have that once.

Yeah, she had. Until her grandfather died and she was left all alone to deal with it.

Oh come on, when are you going to stop using that as an excuse to stay mad?

The thought shot through her brain like a shaft of bright sunlight, illuminating the darker corners of her psyche. Corners she didn't really want to examine, so she ignored it for the moment.

"I hope you're right," she said.

"Of course I'm right," Mal replied with a certainty that Hope found comforting. "You know I'm going to be talking to people about this and pointing out a few things to them. People might ridicule Gwen, but she's not wrong about the environment. If there's one thing we do well here and better than anywhere else, it's the quality of nature. We don't want to lose that to a bunch of rich assholes who only care about what's underneath the ground and not about what's on top of it."

But that was the problem—for most people, the environment was only a backdrop to their lives. It didn't actually impact them, not when they had more pressing concerns such as feeding their families and paying their bills, earning enough to get them through the harsh winter.

You need a plan. You need to figure out how to give those people something that the oil money can't.

"True," she muttered, an idea turning over and over in her brain.

"Hmmm," Mal rumbled. "Looks to me like you're thinking on something."

"Huh? Oh, maybe." Not really, but it might turn into a viable idea all the same. Still, she wasn't going to tell anyone about it just yet; she wanted to talk to Silas about it before—

Shit. Silas was her first go-to? Really? Talk about falling back into old patterns.

Or is it only depending on old friendships that never quite went away?

Hope swallowed, then shoved herself away from the counter, because that was yet another thing she didn't want to think about. "Thanks, Mal," she said. "Keep me posted on those calls."

"Sure." He gave her a speculative look. "So, I know the Quinn boy said he wasn't going to stay, but it sure sounded like he was…"

"No," Hope said as firmly as she could. "He definitely isn't."

Virtually the next second after sending the email, Si's phone began to vibrate on the desk. He glanced at the screen, knowing already who it would be calling him, and sure enough, it was Damon.

Si leaned back in his chair and stared at the angrily vibrating phone, irritated and vaguely guilty yet not guilty enough to change his mind. His buddy wouldn't like that Si had decided to stay another week, just until the next town meeting, but that was too bad. The guy would have to suck it up. He hadn't told Si what his hurry was for getting back to LA, and since he hadn't, Si had assumed it wasn't life or death. Knowing Damon, it probably had something to do with him not liking being stuck in what he termed a "dull backwater," but since dull backwaters wouldn't kill him, Si had no sympathy.

Still, that didn't mean he wanted to have that conversation with the guy, especially when Si hadn't fully sorted through his own strategy for staying here. And he needed to have one, especially after last night and that kiss.

He'd gotten exactly zero sleep afterward, tossing and turning, his body hard and his mind full of hot, sweaty scenarios involving Hope naked and in his bed. But since he'd already decided that wasn't going to happen, he'd had to get up and go stand under the shower with the water on cold for a good ten minutes.

Even that hadn't fully cleared his brain though, which was a problem. Because it meant another week in her vicinity, if not her company, and it wasn't as if he could avoid her, not given where he was staying.

Anyway, avoiding her would mean admitting that he was letting the attraction between them get to him, and there was no way he was going to do that. He'd spent thirteen years dealing with that particular problem, and he had it under control. One kiss wouldn't kill it. He wasn't like his old man, unable to resist the lure of his addiction.

Hell, he could even consider this a test. If he was able

to spend a week with Hope without touching her, with that kiss burning between them, he could do anything.

The phone stopped vibrating. Then after a couple of seconds of silence, it started up again. Clearly, Damon was royally pissed.

Si reached for the phone and picked it up, since he knew his friend wasn't going to let this go. "Yeah, I'm staying," he said before Damon could get a word in. "The situation is more volatile than I expected and I need to be here for Hope."

There was a silence.

"And what about me?" Damon demanded in aggrieved tones. "What about these guys I've got lined up for my share of the business?"

"You'll have to tell them I'll be another week."

"But—"

"It's just a week, Damon. You'll live, for chrissake. It's Juneau, not the pits of hell."

"Might as well be."

"You've been in worse places, come on."

"I know what's going on," Damon said, ignoring him. "It's this friend of yours, isn't it? Can't tear yourself away from a fine piece of ass, hmm?"

Silas scowled at the wall opposite him. "Call her that again and I'll punch you in the face next time I see you."

"Sure, sure. Just calling it like I see it."

"You see nothing."

"Yeah, I don't buy it," Damon said. "You were all impatient to get back here, and now you're making excuses to stay another week. That only happens when a woman's involved, and believe me, I know."

"You don't know a single goddamned thing since you never managed to stay with a woman beyond a single night."

"Lies. I've managed at least two."

"Whatever. This is about the town, nothing else. Now, got anything more you need to say to me?"

Damon didn't—or at least nothing but complaints, so Si cut short the conversation and disconnected the call before his friend could really get going.

He had better things to do than listen to Damon complain. He wanted to formulate some kind of strategy for dealing with Deep River's oil issue, especially for what to do with people who were thinking about signing over their leases or selling their mineral rights. And there would definitely be some people who wanted to do that—the town meeting had made that clear if nothing else.

The really thorny issue was that people were totally within their rights to do whatever the hell they wanted with their leases. Mineral wealth and its possibilities were what the town had been founded on after all, and this was really no different.

Except it was totally different. Oil drilling wasn't grabbing a pickaxe and striking it against a rock wall. It would mean trucks and machinery and strangers. Oil employees would flood into the town, and there would need to be places to put them. Sure, it would mean money for the people of Deep River, new business opportunities springing up, but it would also mean a lot of other things. Mainly out-of-towners coming in, and no matter if they were good people or not, they would change the fabric of the town.

Unease shifted inside him and he pushed back his chair, getting to his feet. He didn't like that thought, didn't like the idea of strangers suddenly living here, and not just oil employees either. There would be people who'd heard rumors of the oil reserves, all of them coming to see if they could grab a piece of it for themselves.

Shit. It would be the gold rush days all over again. And not all of that was good.

Thing was, the town was going to change whether everyone liked it or not, because the oil was a catalyst. They couldn't change what had been found under the ground, and they couldn't pretend it wasn't there, because news like that didn't stay buried. Hell, the phone calls people were getting already was a good indication of that.

Which meant that formulating a plan was imperative. Sitting back and doing nothing would only mean the change being dictated by other people, and if there was one thing he'd learned in the army, it was that he didn't like being dictated to by other people. He didn't want to be at the mercy of other people's decisions, and neither did the people of Deep River.

To stay in control of this, they needed to take charge, be proactive.

Luckily he knew exactly how to be proactive.

Time to go and talk to people, scout out the lay of the

land, see how many of them were considering taking this to the oil companies. But first he needed to know where he stood legally when it came to the ownership of Deep River.

Si reached for his phone and called his lawyer.

Chapter 9

HOPE SQUINTED AT HER COMPUTER SCREEN, LOOKING at the numbers that Sandy, who ran the Deep River Tourist Information Center, had given her. She'd swung by there after talking to Mal, the idea she'd had still turning over in her head, wanting to see what kind of info they had on tourist numbers. Sandy was an ex-marketing manager and had once worked for the Alaska Travel Industry Association. She was big into data and had run a few tourism campaigns for Deep River over the years. Her dating campaign—"Find love in the middle of nowhere!"—had been her most successful, and Hope had thought getting the numbers on that would be interesting.

Sandy, naturally enough, had wanted to talk about the oil and what it was going to mean and how it was going to impact the town, but Hope had managed to escape with a few vague promises of catching up for coffee at some point.

Sandy was lovely, but she did like to talk, and Hope had a few more important things to do right now.

Someone rapped hard on her office door. "Hope?" It was Axel. She'd roped him into bar duty tonight, since it was a madhouse out there and she really wanted to get started on her idea and didn't want to be disturbed. "Where's that cranberry shit you put in cocktails?"

Yet here she was, being disturbed.

Crap. If you wanted something done properly, you had to do it yourself.

She supposed she could have told Axel that the "cranberry shit" was on the bottom shelf, probably shoved behind the dusty bottles of liqueurs that no one drank, but since she was now distracted, she might as well get it.

She pushed herself out of her chair and stalked over to the door, pulling it open and stepping out into the main bar area. The noise hit her harder than it normally did, mainly because the place was packed, far more than usual.

People wanting to talk about Caleb and the oil, she guessed, and of course the Moose was one of the natural places in the evening where people could come together and talk about it.

She had to say, though, she'd thought the atmosphere would be a lot more antagonistic, yet there was almost a kind of…excitement in the air. Was that just the thought of money? Or was it something else?

Moving over to the bar, she ducked behind it to find the cranberry juice, grabbing the bottle and rising up to put it on the bar. And then she caught a glimpse of a tall, broad figure in among the crowd.

Silas.

He was leaning on one of the tables, talking to Mike Flint and a couple of Mike's fishing pals, and he was smiling, laughing with them as if Mike hadn't made a point of saying the money would be nice at the meeting the night before.

The mood of the table seemed jovial, and then Silas

pushed himself away, obviously excusing himself before moving on to another table and joining the conversation there.

What the hell was he doing?

Reconnaissance, a small part of her brain said. *He's doing reconnaissance.*

Because of course he was. He was ex-military and getting the lay of the land was probably the first thing a military person did when dealing with a situation.

Hope leaned her elbows on the bar, watching him as he moved over to yet another table, smiling at the group of women, Sandy included. They all melted visibly under the power of that smile, and Hope felt very bad-tempered all of a sudden.

Si's smiles had once been rare and precious, and every time he'd smiled at her, she'd felt like she been handed a diamond for safekeeping. Yet now, he was throwing that smile around to all and sundry, as if he had plenty to waste on people who didn't appreciate them like she did.

Surely you're not jealous?

No, she wasn't jealous. She didn't care that he was smiling and talking to those women. And she didn't care that those women were looking at him like he was the second coming, one of them even going so far as to put her hand on his arm as if she knew him. As if she had the right—

Hope pulled her thoughts to a screaming halt before they could get any more out of hand than they already were. Silas wasn't her boyfriend. Hell, he wasn't even her friend these days, so she didn't have any right getting jealous.

They'd shared one kiss, and yes, she was still trying not to think about that, but one kiss didn't make a marriage. Or even a long-standing relationship. It didn't even mean friends becoming lovers to share a few nights of casual sex.

Heat washed through her at that thought, and she shifted uncomfortably, trying to ignore the way her mouth had suddenly become sensitized, memories of the kiss they'd shared hitting her once more.

She'd had kisses before, from various men whom she'd found kind of interesting. But there had always been something wrong with them that had prevented her from taking it any further. They weren't tall enough. Had blond hair instead of dark. Their eyes were the wrong color, or their smiles didn't feel like precious gifts. They didn't look at her with enough longing, as if she was the most important thing in the world to them.

Yeah, you've told yourself a lot of lies over the years, haven't you?

She had. And the biggest lie of all was that she'd always preferred Caleb. That it was him she'd wanted. There had been a single moment between her and Cal, when she could have kissed him. It had been one night on the Wests' big porch, after Si had gone to deal with his father, and they'd been talking. And she'd had the impression that Cal wouldn't have minded if she'd kissed him. But for some reason she hadn't. She'd held back.

It wasn't Cal you wanted and you know it.

Of course it wasn't. It never had been. She'd even mentioned as much to Silas the night before. But she'd never really admitted it to herself. Not fully. Never let herself think about it either, and yet…

Yeah, she was thinking about it now. Thinking about that kiss he'd given her and how he'd taken charge of it, his hands in her hair, holding on, kissing her deeply, demanding a response. And she'd given it. In fact, she'd been desperate for more, which was when he'd pulled away. "*That's why,*" he'd said, letting her know in no uncertain terms that kissing him would do the opposite of distancing him.

Maybe you don't want distance after all.

The thought was searing, too bright to look at, and she had to wrench her gaze away from him, her lungs suddenly feeling like they couldn't get enough air.

"That the cranberry stuff?" Axel muttered from beside her, reaching for the bottle.

"Yes," she said, barely paying any attention to what she was saying, conscious still of that woman's hand on Silas's arm—Jenny Anderson, one of Kevin Anderson's daughters, who'd always had an eye for a good-looking man— and how she wanted to go over there and pull that hand away.

Crazy. Admitting to herself that she was attracted to the man who'd once been her best friend and that she might be a bit jealous was one thing, but going over there and laying some kind of claim on him was quite another.

Anyway, he'd been the one to end that kiss, not to mention walk away. He might be interested in her, but he was clearly not interested in taking it any further. Which was good. She didn't want to go there either, not with all this stuff happening in Deep River, not to mention him still planning on leaving.

Just at that moment, Silas lifted his head, his gaze clashing with hers. And she felt the jolt of electricity go through her like she'd wrapped her fingers around a live wire. Her mouth dried, her lungs trying and failing to find air.

Something gleamed deep in his eyes, and he kept on looking at her as if there were no one else in this bar. As if she were the only person in this whole damn town.

Walk away. You have to.

Hope wrenched her gaze away and turned, walking quickly back to her office, barely conscious of what she was doing, her heartbeat thundering in her ears. Axel said something to her, but she ignored it, retreating into the safety of the office and closing the door.

The noise from the bar was cut off, the silence of her familiar space watched over only by Steve the stag's calm glass eyes.

She put her hands on the wood of the door and took a couple of breaths, trying to get her heart rate under control again.

Well, this was going to be a fun couple of weeks if she had this reaction every time Silas happened to make eye contact with her. She was either going to have to avoid him completely or else...

Throw caution to the winds and see what happens if you kiss him again?

Uh, no. He'd already given her a taste of what would

happen, and she was pretty sure he wouldn't stop a second time—and that she wouldn't want him to.

That wouldn't be all bad, come on.

No. And if it had been a purely physical thing, it wouldn't have been an issue. But as she'd already noted, it would never be purely physical with Silas. They had a history, and it wasn't a comfortable one. A history that sex had the potential to exacerbate and not in a fun way.

Forcing those particular thoughts out of her head, Hope stepped away from the door and went back over to her desk, sitting down in the chair again. She glanced at the bottom drawer, where she kept Harry's firewater. Wouldn't hurt to have a shot or two, surely? God knew she needed it.

She had her hand on the handle, ready to pull out the drawer, when there was another knock on her door. Not Axel this time, she didn't think. The knock was firm but not quite the full-on hammering that Axel usually gave it.

And then she was certain it wasn't Axel, because the door opened before she could say anything and Silas walked in.

Her cheeks got hot, which was just plain stupid. "What the hell, Silas?" she demanded, instantly on the offensive. "I didn't say you could come in."

"I knocked," he said, as if that was explanation enough, before shutting the door firmly behind him.

"My complaint still stands." She knew she sounded graceless and grumpy, and wished she didn't. Because it gave away far too much. But it was too late to adjust her tone now. "What do you want, anyway?"

"To talk to you. What does it look like?" He came over to her desk as if he had every right to avail himself of her furniture whenever he liked, propping himself on the desktop and folding his powerful arms over his chest.

He was much too close, one hard, denim-clad thigh near to where she sat, making her very aware that because she was sitting down, he loomed over her. And it was very disturbing to realize that she kind of liked that he did, that it made a strange excitement pool in the pit of her stomach.

"About what?" She pushed her chair back to give her a chance to look at him properly, definitely not to put some distance between them.

God, if he wanted to talk about that moment just before in the bar, she'd get up and walk out. She didn't want to know whether or not he'd seen the jealousy she'd been feeling in that moment, and she definitely didn't want him to ask her about it.

His stare gleamed gold beneath his thick, black lashes, and she knew that, yes, he'd almost certainly seen her jealousy. And that he'd noted her moving her chair away just now too.

Damn, damn, damn.

So? Why are you letting him get to you? You've been dealing with aggravating men for years in the Moose. This is just one more, right?

That thought made something harden inside her, and she leaned back in her chair, lifting her chin, meeting him stare for stare. No, she wasn't going to let him get to her, not the way he had been. So he was hot. So he made her heart race. So what? She could handle it. She could deal.

"Come on," she said when he remained silent. "The suspense is killing me."

The gold in his eyes glowed brighter. "Just so you know, I'm not planning on kissing you again, if that's what you're thinking."

Another jolt of shock arrowed down her spine. "As difficult as it might be for you to believe, I wasn't actually thinking that," she said with as much cool as she could muster.

He raised one dark brow. "You weren't? Not even out there? While I was talking to Jenny?"

Oh, dammit. The asshole.

More heat was beginning to rise in her cheeks yet again, and her earlier urge to get up and walk out was starting to look real good. But that would be to admit she couldn't handle him, and there was no way she was doing that.

"So, is this what you want to talk about?" she shot back. "That kiss?"

He didn't even blink. "We need a plan on going forward, Hope. Because we need to work together to handle this oil situation, and that'll be difficult if we keep avoiding each other."

"I wasn't avoiding you," she lied. "I've just been busy all day. And anyway, we don't need to work together. You said you'd remain here as a support, which doesn't indicate 'working.'"

"If you're going to be the town's eventual owner, then

yeah, hate to break it to you, but that'll involve working with me, since I'll be the one signing it over to you."

"Hey, I didn't ask you to sign it over to me. You decided that all on your own."

Silas opened his mouth, shut it again. Then quite suddenly, he leaned forward and grabbed the arms of her chair, jerking it close. And Hope found herself sitting caged in the chair, his powerful arms on either side of her, his handsome face right in front of her, the gold in his eyes leaping high like a fire, eclipsing all the green. "Will you stop fighting me for just one damn minute?" he said in a low, intense voice. "This situation is too important to waste time bickering."

She barely heard what he was saying, her heartbeat racing yet again, and it was difficult to concentrate on the words because all she was conscious of was his nearness. The heat of his big body so close, the strength in his arms apparent in the flex of his biceps and the iron grip he had on her chair. The gleam in his eyes fascinated her, like sunlight on the river, or a seam of gold glowing at the bottom of the riverbed. He was angry, she could see that, and yet, just like her own anger, it wasn't really about her fighting him. About him staying when she didn't want him to or even how he'd left years ago.

It was about the fact that there was this attraction between them, an attraction that neither of them had expected and yet was there all the same, and they didn't know how to deal with it. And fundamentally, it was unimportant when faced with the larger issues the town was dealing with.

Silas was right, though. They had to find some way of handling it one way or another, so they could concentrate on figuring out what to do about the situation Deep River found itself in. And that only left them with two choices: they could either work this out by ignoring it, or…

Or they could work it out in bed.

Weren't you not *going to do that?*

Yeah, she was. But sitting here now, with him so close, the warm, familiar scent of him clouding her brain, she couldn't quite remember her reasons for not doing it or why they were so pressing.

"You're right." Her voice sounded thick and husky. "We need to deal with this." And before she'd fully thought through the consequences, her hands lifted almost of their own accord and came to rest on his where they gripped the arms of her chair.

Then, holding his gaze, she curved her fingers around his wrists and slid her palms up the undersides of his forearms, spreading her fingertips out and sweeping them across his smooth skin. "I guess it just depends on what you mean by dealing?"

———————————

There was no doubting the deliberation with which Hope touched him, her hands sliding up over his elbows, her fingers brushing his biceps as if caressing him.

Hell, there was no "as if" about it. That's exactly what she was doing.

In a dark, forgotten corner of his brain, a warning siren went off, but he couldn't concentrate on it. Not when every rational thought had been wiped out the second her palms had come to rest over his hands.

He shouldn't have lost patience, because that's what had happened. She'd done that challenging thing, lifting her chin, her dark eyes full of anger, and he'd abruptly had enough, leaning forward and jerking her chair toward him. Intending nothing more than to tell her to stop being such a damn nuisance, since he didn't have the time for it and neither did the town.

And then she'd touched him.

And everything he intended to say had gone right out of his head.

It felt like she was searing his skin with her touch, leaving scorch marks, making his body harden with every brush of her fingertips.

God, did she know what she was doing to him? Did she even understand? He'd thought that kissing her the way he had the night before had made clear that her pushing him by using their attraction was a very bad idea. But maybe he hadn't been clear enough.

Except, what she'd said about dealing with it…

He tried to keep himself very still, because if he moved, it would be to take her in his arms and he couldn't do that. He'd told himself he wouldn't.

"I think," he said, his voice gravely and rough, "you need to be very clear about what you mean. And when I say clear, Hope, I mean crystal goddamn clear."

Her gaze on him had darkened even further and she didn't snatch her hands away; she only swept her fingers over his skin again, obviously continuing to have no idea about how that touch affected him. "What do you think I mean? You're right, the situation with the town is too important to waste time in fighting over nothing. But we're not fighting over nothing, are we?"

They weren't. There was no denying the attraction between them, and it burned hot and deep, and if nothing else, that kiss had certainly proved how hot.

He stared down into her lovely, angular face, his body getting even harder as her fingers stroked his skin. "You want me. That's the problem, isn't it?"

The color in her cheeks was a deep and pretty red, making her eyes look blacker than the night sky. "And if I do? If that's the issue, how do you want us to handle it?"

Of course she wanted him, and that kiss they'd shared had only confirmed it. And it made the heat inside him burn hotter, brighter.

He tightened his grip on the chair, conscious of how close she was. Of how her red flannel shirt pulled tight across her full breasts and how the worn denim of her jeans accentuated the graceful flare of her waist and rounded thighs. Of how fast the pulse at the base of her throat was beating. Of how sweet she smelled.

Of how much he wanted her and always had, right from the very first moment he'd realized that he wasn't a child any longer and neither was she.

"Say it," he almost growled, because he was sick of her

pussyfooting around the subject. "I want to hear you say it. To my face."

Her throat moved as she swallowed, but again, she didn't look away. "Okay, fine." The fingers resting on his arms tightened. "I want you, Silas."

There was no stuttering. No hesitation. Her gaze absolutely level. And that satisfaction he'd felt before, when he'd kissed her, unfurled inside him again.

His breath caught. He'd dreamed for years of hearing her say those words, but he knew he never would. She'd never say them, not to his face. His fantasies would remain just that—fantasies. Dreams.

But he wasn't dreaming now and this wasn't a fantasy. This was goddamn reality. Hope Dawson, finally, after all these years, telling him that she wanted him.

"And what do *you* want to do about it?" he demanded, because he'd be damned if he was the one to say it first, not this time. Besides, as he'd already told her, she needed to be clear about what she wanted.

Why? Surely you're not going to take her up on it?

Oh, he'd told himself he wouldn't. Told himself very firmly that he wasn't going to cross the line with her. But that had been before she'd touched him. Before she'd told him out loud that she wanted him. And now that she had, the question wasn't whether or not he would take her up on it, but whether or not he could refuse. Because he wasn't sure he could, even considering how it would complicate just about everything.

Hope took a soft breath, her gaze dropping to his

mouth in a way that made a growl gather in his throat. "Well, avoiding you doesn't work, and as you've already pointed out, neither does fighting you. And since you're around for another week and we have some important things to concentrate on..." She lifted her gaze back to his again. "It only leaves one thing left, doesn't it?"

"And what's that, Hope?"

Her dark lashes fluttered. "Do I really have to spell it out?"

"Yes. I want to hear it from you, so there can be absolutely no argument." He held her gaze, the wood of the chair arms digging into his palms. And then he added, since if he wanted her to be clear, then he had to be clear in return. "Because once you're in my bed, I can't guarantee I'm going to want to let you out of it."

She searched his face—for what, he couldn't tell. "I'm not up for a relationship, Si. If that's what you mean."

Well, he didn't want one either, not with her. He wasn't staying here, and she plainly wouldn't be leaving. Plus, he wasn't relationship material. He was as selfish as his old man about a great many things, and he didn't want to inflict that on someone else, and most especially not her.

"No," he said. "That's not what I mean. I'll still be leaving, and that's not going to change. But if you're in my bed, Hope, I'm going to want to keep you there and for more than one night."

She nodded slowly. "Anything else I should know?"

"If you change your mind, I'm not going to take it well." He could be nothing but brutally blunt about this.

"Don't get me wrong, if you decide you don't want to take this step after all, I'll stop. But you can bet I'm not going to be happy about it. I've had thirteen years of thinking about you, Hope Dawson. And I can't honestly say I'm going to be able to hold myself back."

The pulse at the base of her throat had quickened, her eyes widening. "Well, okay. But don't go assuming that I'm going to want you to hold yourself back. Or that one night will be enough for me either." She paused, the flames in her eyes flickering higher. "You have no idea what I want, Silas."

"No, it's true, I don't," he murmured. "So, why don't you show me?"

She stayed still for a moment, staring at him. Then her hands on his arms moved higher, to his shoulders, and higher still, curling around the back of his neck and into his hair. And then she was pulling his head down at the same time as she lifted her chin, her mouth meeting his.

He held himself still as she began to kiss him, letting her take the lead for a moment, because there was something unbearably sweet about this, about her kissing him. Her mouth was so soft and so hot, and there was a little bit of hesitancy to the kiss. It was clear to him that she was inexperienced, and he was Neanderthal enough that he liked that she was. Not that it would have put him off in the slightest if she hadn't been, but there was a degree of possessiveness in him that made him want to be the only man for her. The only one she thought of. The only one she imagined at night, alone in her bed.

Tonight, he'd wipe her memory of every man she'd been with but him.

Yet still he held himself back, loving how she touched her tongue to his, seducing him, coaxing him the way he'd coaxed her. She tasted delicious, and he wanted to stay like this for a while longer, letting her find her way with him, but his own need was clawing his insides to shreds, and if he didn't take her now, he'd probably die. Literally.

So he moved, letting go of his death grip on the chair and leaning forward to grab her hips, pulling her up from the chair as he pushed himself away from the desk, holding her against him, her arms around his neck, her body arched into his.

Then he kissed her the way he'd wanted to the night before, deeper, hotter, exploring her mouth the way he'd dreamed of doing. He slid his fingers into her hair and curled them, gripping onto the silken mass as he took the kiss even deeper, becoming hungry, becoming desperate.

She shuddered in his arms, her mouth opening wider, her head angling back to give him greater access. And she kissed him back, just as hungry, just as hot. There was no hesitancy now, no uncertainty. She tasted of honey and fire, a sweet flame he couldn't get enough of, and he was so hard he ached.

Her fingers were curling in his hair, holding on so tightly it felt almost painful, but he didn't care about the pain. All that mattered was that Hope was in his arms, and she was kissing him every bit as desperately as he was kissing her.

He turned them both, backing her up against the desk, the kiss turning feverish. She felt so good against him, so soft and warm and feminine, her breasts pressed to his chest, the heat between her thighs against his aching groin making him even harder than he was already.

His hands dropped from her hair to her hips, and he gripped her, lifted her onto the desk before he'd even had a chance to think straight. Then he nudged her thighs apart with his hips so he could stand between them, pulling her to the edge of the desk and holding her there, fitting all her sweet heat against him.

The kiss sharpened his hunger, a knife-edge that could cut. It had been so many years thinking about being with her like this, dreaming about her like this, and now that it was going to happen, he almost couldn't handle it.

Her hands had dropped from his neck, and they were at the fastening of his jeans, her fingers fumbling with the button, brushing against the hard ridge of his erection, sending white-hot jolts of sensation through him and making him growl.

He had to brush her hands away; otherwise, this was going to get very real very soon, and he didn't want this to become some kind of hasty fumbling in her back office. He wanted her naked on a bed, where he could spread her out and take his time. Feast on her, savor her the way she should be savored.

Except…God, he didn't know if he could hold out. It had been too long, and her hunger for him was making everything that much more desperate. Her hands had now found their way underneath his T-shirt, stroking fire across his skin, and he couldn't stop himself from flipping open the button on her jeans, then tugging down the zipper.

She gave a soft moan as he spread open the denim, stroking over the front of her panties, the fabric damp beneath his fingertips. "Si…" She breathed his name, her voice thick, the sweetest sound he'd ever heard.

He wanted to hear it again, so he slipped his hand beneath the waistband of her underwear, his fingers sliding down and over slick, hot flesh.

Hope shuddered, gasping, and he nipped her bottom lip, making her tremble harder. "Si…" she whispered again. "Si…please…"

He stroked her, loving how she shook and trembled in his arms, kissing down her neck, nipping at the delicate tendons at the sides, licking the hollow of her throat, tasting salt and sweetness and heat.

Because that was Hope. She wasn't this tough, spiky, prickly woman who'd been arguing and pushing at him from the moment he'd returned to Deep River. No, she was more complex than that and always had been.

She was honey and fire, with a tart edge.

You're screwed. You know that, right? In every way.

The thought registered dimly in his brain, and he knew it for truth. Because now he'd had a taste of what he could have with her, nothing else would compare. But when had that ever mattered? Every other woman had always been like a candle flame next to the bonfire that was Hope, and he'd known that the second he'd walked away.

He didn't have to walk away now though. Now, he could make that bonfire leap high, burn bright. Now, he could burn along with her.

He stroked her, circling and teasing, making her pant and writhe on the desk, as if there wasn't a bar full of people right outside the door. As if the door wasn't unlocked and anyone could come in.

Her hands were on his shoulders, her fingers digging in, gripping him tight. And it became a matter of grim determination for him to keep going, to not just push her back onto the desk and sink inside her, because he wanted to give her this before he took anything for himself. Wanted her to feel what he could do to her, the pleasure he could give her, make her aware of what she'd been missing out on all these years.

There's no need to punish her.

And it was a punishment of sorts. Yet not one that she wouldn't enjoy. It was one that wasn't without pain for himself too, since it meant he had to wait. But he didn't stop, pressing his thumb down on the small, sensitive bundle of nerves between her thighs, finding the entrance to her body with his fingers and pushing gently inside.

Hope gave a small cry and turned her face into his neck, her whole body shuddering. He held her tighter, sliding his fingers in and out of her, pressing down lightly with his thumb, concentrating on the jerk of her hips and the soft, breathy sound of her panting against the side of his neck.

It didn't take long.

She gripped his shoulders and her body tightened, her sex clenching hard around his fingers. And then she was gasping out his name, shaking in his arms as the climax took her, and he turned his head, covering her mouth, silencing her cries of release.

He held her for long moments after that, kissing her slowly and leisurely as she quieted, easing her down. Ignoring the pain of his own desire because her going soft and pliant against him, knowing that he'd been the one to give her that, was one of the most satisfying experiences in his life.

But then he lifted his mouth from hers and stared down into her darkened eyes. "My turn, sweetheart," he said.

Chapter 10

SWEETHEART. HE'D CALLED HER "SWEETHEART." HAD anyone ever used an endearment with her before? Ever?

Hope's brain flailed about trying to remember and failed. But she didn't really care, because in that moment, nothing really mattered. Her body felt lax and heavy and supremely satisfied in a way she'd never felt before.

Except not entirely satisfied, it had to be said. There was room for more.

More of the way he looked at her, heat glowing in his gaze. Of the way he touched her, as if she was precious and rare. Of the intense pleasure he'd just given her, and yes, she definitely wanted more of that. A *lot* more.

"Your turn?" she echoed, staring up at him. She was leaning forward against his rock-solid torso, her head resting on his powerful shoulder, and she really didn't want to move.

The lines of his face were tense, and there was no green at all in his eyes now; they were a brilliant, burning gold. She could hear the beat of his heart beneath her ear and it was fast, getting faster.

He wanted her and badly—it was obvious. And it occurred to her that she really liked that. Because no one had looked at her with such open appreciation in years, and it made her feel good. Made her feel like a woman and not the tough, practical owner of the Happy Moose bar. Or the pessimistic daughter having to take care of her fragile, bitter mother.

It made her feel like she was eighteen again and there were still possibilities alive in the world. Possibilities that didn't begin and end in her small backwater town.

Silas's hands moved to her shirt, and he gripped the fabric, then pulled and she took a sharp breath as several buttons came loose, the material ripping. He pushed the shirt from her shoulders, leaving her sitting on the desk in her bra and jeans, still shaking from the orgasm he'd given her.

He didn't say anything, but his gaze dropped, following every inch of her body, and her heartbeat began to speed up, echoing in her head. A shiver went through her as his hands settled on her hips, before sliding up to caress her sides, making her shiver yet again, goose bumps rising everywhere he touched.

The hunger on his face intensified. "God, you're beautiful." His voice had deepened, full of gravel and sand, like it had been dragged from the bottom of the river. "You're the most beautiful thing I've ever seen."

And she trembled, because no one had ever told her that. Not once in her entire life.

She didn't know what to say, but then it became clear that she didn't need to say anything, because he'd slid one arm around her, his hand at the small of her back, and he was cradling her as he bent her back, his mouth at her throat, moving down. Then he was tugging down the cup of her bra, exposing her breast, and he bent his head further, his tongue teasing her nipple. She jerked in his arms, gasping, pleasure licking up inside her. And he kept doing it, kept lightly teasing the aching tip of her breast, before drawing it into his mouth.

Hope shut her eyes, all her awareness zeroing in on the heat of Si's mouth and the way he began to suck on her, every pull on her nipple arrowing intense sensation right down between her thighs.

"Si…" she murmured, her hands on his powerful shoulders. "Oh my God…"

His free hand roamed further south, pushing at the denim of her jeans, sliding around and beneath the waistband, curving over her ass, squeezing her gently in time with the suction of his mouth.

Light burst behind her closed lids. No one had ever touched her like this, not even that one guy she'd lost her virginity with. He'd been very matter-of-fact with her, and at the time, since she'd been nervous, she'd appreciated it. But she hadn't felt anything like this. That had involved some pain and then some mild physical pleasure, but she hadn't felt desperate the way she did now, like she would die if he didn't keep touching her. And she certainly hadn't ached to touch him back. Not the way she wanted to touch Silas.

She tried to move her hands from his shoulders, down to his T-shirt and under, to again feel the smooth, velvety skin of his stomach and the rock-hard muscles beneath it. To feel his heat, because he was so damn hot and she loved that; it was like coming inside after an icy winter's day and standing next to the furnace, a deep, sensual pleasure.

But then Silas was moving again, lifting his head from her breast and shifting his hold, gripping her jeans, then pulling them down, taking her panties with them, so she found herself sitting not just topless on her desk, but actually entirely naked.

There was a moment of exposure as the cool air hit her bare skin and she instinctively raised her hands to cover herself. But he took her wrists in his strong fingers and held them away from her body, the expression on his face suddenly ferocious. "No, don't. I want to look at you."

Heat swept through her. "Silas—"

"I've spent thirteen years fantasizing about having you naked," he interrupted. "And now that you are, I want to look."

She took a breath, as the reality of that began to filter through. Thirteen years he'd wanted her and she hadn't really grasped what that had meant for him until now. Until she could see the ferocity of his desire burning in his eyes. And there was a moment of strangeness, where it felt weird to be bare-ass naked in front of her best friend, and to have him look at her with such hunger. But then the moment passed, because this man in front of her wasn't her friend. Not anymore. He was something else entirely.

His gaze moved over her body, from her throat down to her breasts, to her stomach and hips, lingering between her thighs for so long that she felt she might burst into flame where she sat. Then he finally looked down over her legs to her feet, before raising his gaze again, his eyes full of heat.

Without looking away from her, he reached around to his back pocket and took out his wallet. Extracted a silver packet. Then he dropped the wallet to the floor and held out the packet to her. "Put this on me."

She didn't think about not obeying. It was clear he wanted her to protect them both and she wanted to. She so very much wanted to touch him.

Her hands shook as she took the packet, putting it down on the desk beside her, then reaching for the buttons of his fly. She fumbled a little with the button and the zipper, but he didn't make a move to help. Instead, he watched her as if she were the only thing worth looking at in the entire universe.

Her heartbeat accelerated, the pressure of his gaze doing things to her. Making her feel vulnerable and exposed, yet making the ache between her thighs more intense. And then the vulnerable feeling disappeared as she slid her hand inside his boxers, closing her fingers around him, finding him hot and smooth and hard. He took a short, sharp breath, and when she looked up at him, she could see the effect she had on him written all over his face.

He looked like a starving man seeing a feast laid out before him.

It thrilled her down to the bone.

She stroked him, loving the velvety feel of him and the way he tensed as she gripped him tighter.

"Hope." Her name came out as a growl, full of rough warning, and she loved the sound of it, another sign of the effect she had on him.

It made her want to tease him, push him more, but the moment felt too intense, too serious for that, so she let him go and picked up the condom packet instead. Her fingers felt clumsy as she got out the condom and rolled the latex down, especially since she'd only done this a couple of times before. Plus, she was starting to get as desperate as he was and part of her was a little afraid of how badly she wanted him. It had only been a few minutes since her last climax, and already she was breathless for the next.

Silas didn't move as she finished with the condom, then looked up at him, but the flames in his eyes almost burned her to the ground.

"Put me inside you," he ordered.

Another shiver worked its way through her, which was weird. She hadn't thought she'd find the rough way he told her what to do exciting, but she really did.

Breathless, her heartbeat like a drum in her head, she gripped him, easing herself to the edge of the desk and positioning him. He didn't wait, one hand coming to rest at the small of her back, holding her in place, then his hips flexed and he was pressing forward, sliding inside her, deep and slow and relentless.

A helpless gasp escaped her, the stretch and burn of

him delicious and too much, and yet at the same time not enough. And it took a few moments for her body to adjust, because he was big and it had been a long time for her, and she had to breathe through it.

He lifted a hand to cup her cheek, his fingers stroking her jaw. "Look at me," he said in a voice full of darkness and rough heat.

A small, vulnerable part of her didn't want to, but she did, lifting her gaze to his, feeling the same impact echo through her as she had in the bar just before, only this time it was sharper and there was an intimacy to it that stole all the air from her lungs.

He looked at her so intensely, focusing so completely on her that it felt as if he were reading the contents of her soul.

"Silas," she whispered, not quite sure whether she wanted to tell him not to look at her like that or to look away. But then the hand at the small of her back firmed, keeping her there as he pushed deeper, and everything she'd been wanting to say went straight out of her head.

He paused deep inside her, part of her, and just looked. And she had the impression that he was memorizing her, memorizing this moment, as if it was something he didn't want to ever forget.

You don't want to forget either.

Her throat closed for some mysterious reason, and beneath the intense physical pleasure, she could feel her chest get tight. Because it was true, she didn't. She had very carefully not thought about Silas like this, as her lover rather than her friend, and there had always been a reason for that.

But she didn't want to look too closely at that reason so she didn't. Yet as his other hand lifted, sliding into her hair and cradling the back of her head gently, her eyes prickled.

She wished they wouldn't. Wished he wouldn't see what this moment was doing to her, because it should have only been about physical pleasure, and it wasn't. Yet she couldn't look away. Because even though he was holding her so gently, it was his gaze that held her fast. Intense and brilliant, full of desire and heat, all those passions he kept buried finally there for her to see.

He stole her breath completely.

One of his hands dropped to the small of her back again, keeping her in place, while he continued to cradle the back of her head with the other, then he began to move, drawing himself out of her and then back in.

Hope shuddered, a deep, lazy pleasure stretching out inside her.

He didn't speak, his thrusts long and so achingly slow, as if he had all the time in the world and wanted to savor each and every second.

It drove her crazy.

The pleasure wound tighter, and she found herself holding on to his powerful shoulders, lifting her hips in time with the movements of his, trying to intensify the friction, urging him to go faster. But maddeningly, he kept up that same lazy pace, making her pant.

"Si, please," she heard herself say. "Faster. I need... more...please."

But he only caressed her jaw and the side of her neck, the hand at the small of her back sliding up her spine, pulling her in closer, yet not changing the movements of his hips one iota.

She moaned, shaking against him, and his head bent, his mouth brushing over hers.

"Hush, sweetheart," he murmured. "You got what you wanted. Now it's time for me to take what I want."

Then he kissed her, as leisurely as the way he moved inside her, and there was nothing she could do but give herself up to it.

Hope dug her fingers into the hard muscle of his shoulders, helpless against the pleasure that began to climb with a relentlessness that had her writhing on the desk and gasping his name, building and building and building, until the world began to turn to flame around her.

Only then did he lift his mouth from hers and look down into her eyes, and she could see the flames burning in his gaze too, leaping high. He slipped one hand down between her thighs, giving her one light stroke, and then she was burning too, crying out, a torch flaming in the night.

Dimly, she was aware that he was moving faster, harder, before his hands on her firmed and it was her name she heard, echoing around her, as he followed her into the flames.

Silas lay on his back in the bed and stared at the ceiling above him. There had been very few times in his life when he'd experienced utter contentment—sitting with Hope beside the river talking about nothing, holding his pilot's license in his hands for the first time, flying in the wide-open sky—but this was one of those times.

Hope was curled beside him, her head resting on his shoulder, her naked body pressed up against his, the warmth of her breath sighing over his skin, and he couldn't think of one single thing that he wanted to be different.

She was here, where he'd always wanted her to be, in his bed beside him, relaxed and warm and sated from the pleasure he'd given her.

The pleasure she'd given him too.

Making love to her had been everything he'd imagined and more.

He'd taken it slow down in her office because this had been the culmination of years of fantasies and yearning, and now that he had her in his arms, he hadn't wanted to rush. So he hadn't. He'd taken his time, savored all the firsts. The first time he kissed her throat, licked her skin, taken her hard nipple into his mouth. The first time he pushed inside her and felt that fire he'd always known lay at the heart of her wrap around him and hold him tight.

Yes, he wanted to remember that, keep it forever, because he'd be gone soon enough, and he had to have something to take with him. Not only that, though. He also wanted to leave her with something to remember him by. Something she maybe couldn't get from any other man.

A dark possessiveness moved through him at the thought of her being with someone else, making his jaw tense, and he had to shove the emotion away hard before he did something stupid like tell her he'd changed his mind and had decided to stay after all.

"How long?" Hope asked softly in the darkness, her fingers tracing patterns on his bare chest. "How long have you felt that way about me?"

After they'd recovered from the intense sex they'd had down in her office, he'd helped her get dressed, then had basically ordered her upstairs and into his room. She hadn't argued, not even once, and they'd both managed to get up there without anyone noticing, which was kind of a miracle.

Not that he cared if anyone had noticed. As far as he was concerned, Hope was his and would remain so for the duration of his visit; too bad what anyone else thought.

"A long time." He stroked his hand down the silky skin of her spine then back up again. "But if I was to pinpoint a moment, it was when you turned up at the swimming hole in that bikini." He grinned in the darkness, remembering. "I had to stand in the water for hours so I wouldn't embarrass myself."

She gave a soft laugh. "Oh really? I did wonder why

you kept on refusing to get out even though you were starting to go blue."

"The problems of being a guy." He spread his fingers out on her back, stroking his thumb across her skin. "Why do you want to know?"

"Just interested, I guess."

There was a silence, then she said quietly, "I'm sorry, Si. I told myself it was Cal I wanted, but I don't think it was, not really. He was the safe option, because he wasn't interested in me. And you were…" She stopped.

Not safe, presumably, though he didn't say it out loud. *And you weren't, not for her.*

No, he'd wanted her intensely and deeply, and that had always been his problem.

"Don't cry," his father had snapped at him during his mother's funeral, as he'd stood there with the tears running down his face. "I haven't got time for that bullshit."

But it wasn't time that his father didn't have—it was energy. His wife's death had left him grief-stricken and unable to cope with Silas's grief as well as his own, and so Silas had kept his feelings locked away so he didn't make things any worse. Had made sure his own sadness didn't impinge on his father's, that he didn't demand anything from him.

Not unless he was drunk, right?

That was the problem. His father was only mean when he was sober. Drunk, he was like the father Si remembered before his mother died. A loving, caring man.

Si had never known which dad he was going to get on

any given day, yet his own feelings remained, boiling away inside him, burning so intensely that it felt sometimes as if they were eating him alive. He'd needed some outlet for them, and that's when escaping into the sky had been a godsend. Where he could leave the deadweight behind and soar in the air with nothing weighing him down.

The upshot of that though was that he hadn't ever wanted to expose Hope to the need inside him, to the strength of what he felt for her. Because if his father hadn't been able to cope with him, how could she?

He'd wanted to keep her, make her his, make her stay with him forever, but Hope was fire, and you couldn't contain fire. It needed to burn. Keeping her would have smothered her, and he hadn't wanted to do that. Besides, she had so many plans, so much excitement for the future, and none of those futures involved staying in Deep River. And he hadn't been able to leave.

Things were different now; their positions were reversed—he was going to leave while she wanted to stay. Yet everything else was still the same.

"I'm still not the safe option," he said into the darkness, wanting her to understand. "If that's what you're wondering."

Her fingers moved in tiny circles on his chest, caressing him. "Why not? What makes you think you're dangerous?"

"Hey, you were the one who implied that I was."

"You were dangerous because I was eighteen and I wasn't ready for any kind of relationship." She let out a little breath. "You were also broody and silent and intense. And I didn't know what to do with intense."

He had been. That's why he and Caleb had worked so well as a team after they'd left, Caleb's easygoing personality lightening Silas's tendency toward darkness.

"It's okay," he said, savoring the feel of her against his palm. "You don't have anything to apologize for. It was a long time ago anyway." And he had her now. He had her just where he wanted her.

"I still wasn't very nice to you when you came back here." She drew another circle on his chest. "I missed you, that was the problem."

He shut his eyes a moment, his chest tightening at the wistful note in her voice, for a second too angry with himself and his decision to stay away to speak. "I should have come back," he said once he'd forced the anger away. "I was a damn coward not to."

"It was me, wasn't it?" Her voice sounded small.

He moved, unable to keep still, turning toward her and taking her into his arms, rolling them until she was beneath him, her soft curves pressed against his hard planes, making him feel hungry again, making him feel desperate.

But he framed her face with his hands, looking down into her eyes. "Yes, it was you, but not because I didn't want you, Hope. I stayed away because I thought if I came back and saw you again, I'd never want to leave."

She stared up at him, her expression difficult to read in the darkness. "But you don't feel that way now, do you?"

He searched her face, looking for what, he didn't

know. And maybe it didn't matter anyway because his answer was still the same. "No, I don't. I'm not staying, Hope. I can't."

"I know that." Her hands lifted, and she put them on his shoulders, stroking him, her touch light and yet searing at the same time. "I don't want you to stay, anyway. My life is here with Mom and the Moose."

He should have felt relieved about that, but he didn't. "Do you ever regret it?" he asked, not even sure why he was asking but needing to know all the same. "Do you ever regret that you stayed?"

Her gaze flickered and she glanced away, not answering for a moment, and he got the impression it was because she needed to think about it rather than because she wanted to hide something from him. "No," she said after a while. "I don't regret it. Mom needed me and I...I like managing the Moose. It's a challenge. And I like being able to provide a place for people to come and socialize." Her gaze came back to his. "What about you? Do you regret leaving?"

Two days ago, he would have said no, he'd never had one minute's regret about leaving Deep River. But now... now, with her in his arms and the taste of all those might-have-beens on his tongue, he wasn't so sure.

Except there was no point in telling her that. It wouldn't change anything and would only make things difficult between them.

"No," he said, swallowing down the lie. "I don't regret it."

She put up a hand, running her fingers along his jaw

as if she couldn't get enough of touching him. "You like being in Juneau?"

"Yeah. It's the best place for the business to be based. We get the tourists and the hikers. Not to mention all the hunters when hunting season comes along. Got a few businesses using us too, to get supplies to lodges and other places in the bush."

"Do you like it? Running your business, I mean. Is it what you wanted to do?"

"Yes." He brushed her cheekbones with his thumbs, caressing her. "I always loved flying, and this is one way I get to do what I love." He'd never talked to her about this before, and he hadn't realized how much he liked telling her about what he did until now. "It's not just about the hikers or hunters. Or running supplies. Or even tourists. Sometimes we get roped into helping search and rescue and flying injured or sick people back to civilization."

"Yeah, I get it. You like helping people." In the dimness, her mouth curved. "You always have."

He didn't, but he liked the way she said it. And he liked the look in her eyes as she did so. It made him feel good in a way he hadn't felt since...well, since he'd left Deep River, if he was honest with himself.

"I like the flying," he said, not willing to admit that it was the helping part that he liked too. "Cal liked that part as well. Though I think he preferred the business side of things."

A flicker of grief moved over her face, and he let her see a little of his own, sharing it for a second.

"Yes," she said quietly. "I know he did. That was his strength." Her fingers moved along his jaw once again. "So who have you got to replace him?"

"Truthfully? No one can replace him. But my buddy Damon's good with finance, and he's filling in for me while I'm here."

"And what? After all this oil stuff is sorted out, you'll go back to Juneau and keep on flying?"

He couldn't detect any undercurrents in the question, so he answered plainly. "That's the plan. What about you?"

"I've got the Moose to run. And then there's Mom..." A crease appeared between her brows. "I don't think she's going to want to keep the lease, Si. I think she wants to sell it, get the money and leave."

That would be an issue and one they still hadn't formulated a plan for. "What about her selling the lease to you?"

"I don't have the money. And it's the money she wants." The crease deepened. "She always wanted to leave Deep River. I mean, she was going to, and then she got pregnant with me, had some pretty severe postpartum depression. Which meant she ended up staying."

Si frowned, not liking the guilty note in her voice. "She could still have left, Hope. She could have left when Bill died."

"But she couldn't. She didn't have the money."

"You can't tell me she couldn't have gotten the money for a plane ticket to somewhere."

An expression he didn't understand crossed Hope's face. "You know she couldn't do that, not alone. She needs to have someone with her."

Si studied her for a second. "You mean your mother told you that you had to go with her, am I right?"

"But I would have to." Hope looked up at him. "Living alone would be very difficult for her. She needs someone to monitor her, see that she takes her meds. Stuff like that."

"That could be arranged with some mental health support. It doesn't have to be you. Because if all Angela wants is to leave Deep River, then hell, I'll see if I can help you get some cash together to buy the lease off of her."

Hope's expression hardened. "It's not that easy, Si. Mom's never lived anywhere else before. She's never actually had to look after herself either. Granddad had to support her when she got pregnant with me, and then after I was born, he had to take care of her because she could barely look after me, let alone herself. I can't let her go off alone. She wouldn't be able to function."

Si pressed his thumbs gently against Hope's cheekbones. "So, what? Are you going to let her sell the lease to someone else? Give up the Moose?"

Hope let out a breath. "I don't want her to. If she sells the Moose to someone else, I'm screwed."

"Or," he pointed out gently, because he could see even if she couldn't, "you'd be free."

Something crossed her face, and he wasn't sure what it was, but it vanished before he could name it. "I can't give up the Moose," she said, and this time there was nothing but determination in her dark eyes. "It's all I have left of Grandad."

She'd always been close to her grandfather. Bill had basically brought her up since Angela had spent the first couple of years of Hope's life in bed, in a fog of depression, unable to care properly for her daughter. So no wonder she wanted to keep the bar.

She wouldn't have had it though, not if her grandfather hadn't died and you know whose fault that was, remember?

His father's. Because his father had spent the night drinking at the Moose and then decided to go fishing. And her grandfather had gone after him...

Your fault.

"You wouldn't have had to deal with that if it hadn't been for Dad," he said roughly, unable to help himself.

Her expression softened. "Please don't tell me you're beating yourself up for that. It wasn't your fault your father decided to drink himself insensible that night."

"No, but he did. And Bill died rescuing him." There was no escaping that fact, no matter how badly he wanted to.

"Yes, I know," Hope said slowly. "What? Did you think you could stop him from drinking?"

You knew why he drank. And you never tried to stop him.

He gave a short, bitter laugh, ignoring the thoughts in his head. "Hell no, nothing could stop that bastard from drinking. I just should have been keeping an eye on him." But he hadn't. He'd wanted to sit with Hope down by the river, talking with her and drinking the illicit beers he'd stolen from his old man's beer fridge.

"You can't change what happened," she said. "No one can. And I don't blame you for it. I never did."

"But you would have had a different life." He had to name it, had to point it out. "You could have left if you'd wanted to."

"But I didn't." She touched his forehead gently, smoothing away the lines he knew were there. "I have the life I have, and I'm fine with it."

Except he couldn't shake his memories of the plans she'd made for college and the travel she wanted to do. See the world, be somewhere different. Learn new things, have new experiences.

Things she would never have now, and instead, he'd had them.

"Hope—"

But she put her finger over his mouth, silencing him. "No, I don't want to talk about this anymore." Her expression changed, becoming dark and smoky. "Show me something new, Si."

His body hardened almost immediately at the look in her eyes, and he became suddenly very conscious of the warmth and softness of her beneath him.

Yeah, perhaps now wasn't the time to talk about this, especially when they had better things they could be doing. He only had her for a limited time anyway, and it seemed a pity to waste it talking about things they couldn't change.

He took the tip of her finger in his mouth and bit it gently, making her breath catch. Then he gave it a teasing lick before gripping her wrist and pulling her hand away from his mouth, pushing it down onto the pillow beside her head. He did the same with the other hand, holding both of them down. Then he bent and kissed her deep and long.

But the conversation stayed in his head, and he couldn't shake the thought that she wasn't fine with it, no matter what she said.

She wasn't fine with it at all.

Chapter 11

HOPE CAME INTO THE KITCHEN THE NEXT MORNING and found her mother sitting at the small kitchen table with a cup of coffee in front of her and a frown on her face.

"Where were you last night?" she asked before Hope had a chance to open her mouth. "I looked for you and couldn't find you."

Well, that's because she'd been in Silas's bed all night.

Does your mother really need to know that?

No, she didn't. Especially when being with Silas was only going to be temporary anyway, and her mother tended to be judgmental about such things. With good reason admittedly, but still. Things were already thorny with the lease business, and she didn't need yet something else for her mother to use against her.

In fact, no one needed to know about her and Silas, and she'd make a note to tell him the next time she saw him. She'd woken up that morning alone, and she'd been quite happy about it, not wanting to go into a rundown of everything that had happened between them the night before.

And there had been a *lot* of things that had happened between them the night before. Interesting things. Very pleasurable and sexy things...

Heat coiled inside her, her breath catching at the memories.

"You're blushing," Angela said, frowning. "Please don't say that you and he—"

"No, of course not," Hope interrupted, irritated with herself. "I went to bed early."

She moved over to the kitchen counter and took a mug from the cupboard before going over to the stove. Her and her mother's one indulgence was the stovetop espresso maker and the beans she got Mal to special order.

Picking up the coffeepot, she poured herself some of the thick black liquid, conscious of her mother's gaze boring into her back.

"Anything in particular you want to talk to me about, Mom?" She put the pot back on the stove and then turned around. "I can see you're dying to."

"What do you think?" Angela's dark eyes gleamed. "I want to sell the Moose's lease."

All the pleasant heat and satisfaction that Hope had been feeling dissipated as if it had never been.

Slowly, she picked up her mug and wrapped her fingers around it, letting the hot pottery warm them. Normally she had cream in her coffee, but right now, she needed an intense hit of caffeine. "What? Just like that? You don't want to talk about it more?"

"You knew where I stood with this, Hope," her mother said flatly. "Surely you're not surprised."

"Yes, but I thought the meeting would have changed your mind."

"Why would it?" Angela stared at her. "Who cares if

the guy wanting to buy the lease is from an oil company? He offered me a lot of money."

Anger gathered in the pit of Hope's stomach. "Who cares? Mom, I care. You know what that'll mean, right? Strangers in the town. Machinery. Drilling. They might have to tear down half the town to get to the oil."

Angela lifted a shoulder. "So? It won't make any difference to me. I won't be here."

Hope stared at her, shocked in spite of herself. "So you don't care? About the town and what might happen? Is that what you're saying?"

For the first time, Angela's hard gaze flickered, and she glanced down at the tabletop. "Why should I care about the town? They never cared about me."

She should have known. And her mother wasn't wrong. Angela's unplanned pregnancy had apparently been the source of gossip for weeks and not a few people had had opinions about it. That they shared around and frequently.

At least until Bill had stepped in and told everyone to quit gossiping about his daughter; otherwise, they might find themselves unable to buy a drink in the Moose for the foreseeable future.

The gossiping had stopped then, or at least that's what Hope had thought. Because people had never treated her differently or made comments to her, not that she'd experienced.

Perhaps it was different with her mother though? Perhaps Bill hadn't protected her the way that she should have been?

An old and familiar guilt twisted in her gut at the thought. God, if she hadn't been born, none of this would have happened.

But it did. As you told Si last night, it happened and you can't change it.

Except she just couldn't quite stop wishing that she could.

You can't start thinking like that again. You can't.

No, she couldn't. If nothing else, having dreams and plans for a future that had never happened had taught her that sometimes it was better to take things as they came. To not think about what more she could have had.

"Mom," she began, not quite sure of what else she wanted to say.

"Well, they didn't," Angela snapped before Hope had a chance to go on. "No one cared that I was alone with a baby. That I had to bring that baby up by myself. Yet everyone had something to say about it."

"I thought Granddad told them to back off."

Angela turned her coffee mug around in a slow circle. "He did. But the damage was done. No one here gave a damn about how I felt."

Hope could hear the bitterness in her mother's tone, and it made the sting of guilt worse, though she tried to ignore it. She knew it wasn't her fault that her mother had ended up with severe depression. It wasn't her fault that her mother had ended up pregnant with her at all, yet that didn't stop her from feeling it.

Didn't stop her own defensive anger either.

"That's not strictly true," she pointed out. "Granddad gave a damn. And you weren't on your own. He helped you."

"Yes, well, regardless of that," her mother said, brushing that away, "I've finally gotten an opportunity to leave this godforsaken place and I'm going to do it."

The conversation she'd had with Silas the night before suddenly loomed large in Hope's brain, and she found herself asking before she could think better of it: "So why didn't you leave earlier?"

Angela looked up from her coffee mug, her dark eyes narrowing. "I never had the money, you know that."

"But you earn enough at Mal's for a plane ticket. So... why didn't you just go?"

Her mother shifted uncomfortably on her chair. "You kept telling me that I shouldn't go by myself. And that living somewhere else was expensive, so of course I had to stay here."

Perhaps a couple of days ago, Hope would have heard only the bitterness and resentment in her mother's voice and would have taken that to heart. Would have felt guilty for popping her mother's bubble with reality, and then felt angry for feeling guilty about it.

But today she heard more than anger and bitterness. She heard instead what sounded like justifications, and that was especially galling because her mother had said it in exactly the same tones as Hope had used last night when Silas had asked her exactly the same question.

"Are you sure about that?" she asked, recognizing that

it hadn't been true for her either. She did love the Moose, and she'd stayed because of her granddad. But there was more to it than that. "If you'd really wanted to leave, you would have. Except you didn't. Why not?"

Angela sniffed and looked away. "I couldn't leave you, could I?"

Which would have sounded better if there hadn't been so much annoyance in Angela's tone.

"When I was a kid, sure. But I'm nearly thirty, Mom. You could have left at any time in the past ten years."

Her mother turned her coffee mug slowly around once more. "Why does it matter? I'm deciding to leave now." She met Hope's gaze again. "You should come too, Hope. You had so many plans for the future. Why stay here in this old place?" She waved a hand at the kitchen area. "We could start again somewhere different. Somewhere out of this town. You could get the degree you always wanted, and I could get a job doing something more interesting that stocking shelves."

"Mom—"

"I know I'm the reason you're still here. That you stayed because of me. And I don't want you to do that anymore."

A small shock pulsed down Hope's spine because her mother had never said anything about this before. And Hope had thought she'd had no insight into how her mental health had impacted on her daughter either.

Clearly, though, she'd been underestimating her. Angela had not only thought about it, but she'd also felt unhappy about it.

"That's not why I stayed," Hope felt compelled to say. "It was the Moose and Granddad, and—"

"No, it wasn't. And don't try to placate me. I know when you're lying."

Hope bit off the rest of what she'd been going to say. Her mother wasn't wrong; she *was* placating her. "All right, fine," she said. "I did stay because of you. But I'm happy here, and I don't particularly want to leave."

"Are you happy?" Angela shot back. "Or am I just a convenient excuse?"

"No, of course you're not," Hope replied, irritated and not sure why.

Isn't she, though? Isn't she the reason you've been giving yourself not to leave?

But Hope didn't want to examine that thought too closely. It made her feel like she had the night before, in Silas's arms, his green-gold gaze looking down into hers, asking her questions she didn't want to think about the answers to. Seeing her clearly, too clearly. Disturbing all the little fictions she'd been telling herself about her life here in Deep River and how she felt about it.

She had to tell herself that she was content here, that she was happy, because what was the alternative? Thirteen years of doing all this for nothing, that was the alternative. And she couldn't face the thought of that. Wasting her life sitting here at the Moose when she could have been—

But no. She didn't want to think about what might have been.

Angela eyed her as if she could see every one of her

daughter's thought processes. "Fine, tell yourself what-ever you need to." She abruptly shoved back her chair and stood, picking up her coffee mug. "But just remember that I'll be doing this for us, not just for me."

And before Hope could say another word, her mother walked out.

Silas spent the day talking to people. He would have much rather spent the day in bed with Hope, but since they actually had stuff to do, he thought he'd better get on with it. Though if he was honest with himself, he needed some distance.

Every time he thought about the night before, her in his arms, his hands at last on her beautiful body, moving inside her, he got hard. He got breathless. He started to think about what it would be like to keep her in that bed for the foreseeable future, and since that wasn't happen-ing, distance it was.

At least enough to get his head back into the game with the town.

He'd left Hope asleep that morning, and because he hadn't wanted to wake her up for another round, he'd gone for a run instead, to try to burn off the lingering desire that still gripped him. Then he spent the rest of the morning visiting the various stores in the town and talking to people. April in the diner and then Nate at the Gold Pan. Sandy in the information center. Clare at Clare's Bed-and-Breakfast.

It had been all very useful, especially considering that none of the store owners were interested in selling their leases to any kind of oil company. None of them were happy about oil companies, period. Or the oil that Caleb's prospectors had found beneath Deep River. They weren't happy about a future containing oil company employees and drills and machinery. They weren't happy about the thought of the town changing.

They asked him a lot of questions about what would happen if the rest of the town wanted to sell and what was going to happen, and the prospect obviously worried them. He wanted to tell them it would be okay, but he didn't know whether it would or not, and he had no right telling them that anyway, not when he wasn't going to be here.

It would be one more thing Hope had to deal with after he was gone, and he didn't like that thought either. They were definitely going to have to think about a plan for dealing with the people who liked the idea of money and wanted to sell.

It was nearing noon by the time he stepped into Mal's Market, and he had to stop and take a breath at the sudden flood of nostalgia that filled him as soon as he walked over the threshold. The same scent of wood and spices and dust. The same feeling of magic at the towering shelves piled high with all kinds of things. There wasn't another place like Mal's, not anywhere. Not in all the towns and cities he'd been in, and he'd been in a fair few.

He had a sudden vision of Mal's not being here any- more, of a supermarket taking its place, and he didn't like that, not one bit. Mal's was part of the fabric that made up Deep River, and to not have it, or for it be a store reduced to selling cheap tourist knickknacks, would be to have a great gaping hole cut in that fabric.

Si walked through the aisle displaying candy, remembering how he and Cal had once dared each other to steal something when they'd both been kids, and how he'd nearly managed to smuggle a candy bar out under his sweatshirt before Mal had laid a heavy arm on his shoulder and demanded to know what he thought he was doing. There had been the rush of adrenaline and then the terror of being caught, and then the shame. Mal had made them dust the shelves for a whole month after that.

"Not thinking about stealing another candy bar, are we?" Mal asked, watching from behind the counter as Si approached.

"Nope." Si grinned. "Not after you made us dust those damn shelves. I sneezed for weeks afterward."

"Scared you straight, huh?" Mal grinned back. "Good to see you, Silas. Been a long time. Too long."

"Good to see you too." He shoved his hands into his pockets. "I expect you know what I've come to talk to you about."

"If it's what Hope came to talk to me about yesterday, then yeah, I do."

Si stared at him in surprise. "Hope came to see you?"

"Yeah, she wanted to know about this guy who's been calling everyone and offering to buy their leases."

He hadn't known Hope had spoken to Mal. Then

again, it hadn't been like he and Hope had actually talked. No, they'd been too busy doing other things.

"Right," he said. "Angela's been getting the same calls."

"That's what Hope said." Mal eyed him. "Said I'd let Hope know if I got another call from the guy. I'm going to try and get his number, so we can maybe find out where he's from."

"Good plan." He paused. "I guess you're not in favor of this oil business?"

Mal's expression turned grim. "What do you think?"

Of course Mal wouldn't be into it, and Si knew that would likely be the case. But he had to be sure. "Hey, I don't want to assume anything. You're a businessman after all, and this could mean good business for the town."

"It could, but it wouldn't be any kind of business that I'd want to be involved in." The other man glanced around the store, at the shelves piled high, at the barrels of dry goods, and the fishing rods, ski poles, shovels, and other objects stored in the rafters above their heads, at the doorway that led off into the small DVD library that people rented movies from since the internet up here wasn't great and most people couldn't get the streaming services available.

"This place is my livelihood," Mal said. "And it was Dad's before me and his father's before him. It's in the blood. I'm not giving it up, not for any amount of money."

Si watched Mal's expression as he said it and felt something shift inside him. Something that had been shifting ever since he'd landed here a few days ago. A knowledge that he hadn't at first wanted to be aware of, and yet with every minute that passed being here, with every person he talked to, it became clearer and clearer.

People loved this town and they were passionate about it. They believed in it. And he wasn't sure why he found that so very fascinating, but he did.

Maybe because it was something he'd once felt himself, before his father's drinking had sucked all the hope and joy right out of him. Before he'd realized that the town had become a prison for him and not the place of magic it had once been.

But for some people that magic had never gone away. It was still there, and they saw it every day.

You can see it too. If you look…

Si realized he was standing there holding his breath and that Mal was looking at him with a knowing expression in his deep-set gray eyes.

"You still planning on leaving?" Mal asked. "Because after the way you handled that meeting, I reckon the town could use a man like you."

"I think so," he said, that feeling shifting around inside him, becoming more demanding. "Got my own business in Juneau to deal with."

"Yeah, so I heard." Mal rubbed at his beard. "A bush pilot business, right?"

"Something like that."

"Well, you know you can be a bush pilot here. Doesn't have to be in a town."

Si found himself scowling. "I've got to be where the people and the tourists are, and there's none of that here."

"Uh-huh." Mal kept rubbing his beard. "Sure. Well, far be it from me to tell a man how to run his own business."

Si debated arguing with him and then decided to let it go. He wasn't here to talk about Wild Alaska; he was here to talk about Deep River. And besides, he had a few more people to see.

He said a few more words to Mal, then headed back out to the boardwalk that lined the river. The sun was out, but there was a bite in the air, the wind coming straight off the mountains.

As he'd hoped, Mike Flint was down on the docks with Kevin Anderson, the pair of them standing by Kevin's boat in deep conversation. Mike wasn't too pleased to see Si, and he had made no bones about it as Si came down the steps that led to the docks, frowning at him.

"You been buttering the town up?" Mike asked as Si approached them. "Lots of people have been in my face about this oil business and demanding to know if I was going to sell."

"You pretty much said you would," Kevin pointed out, scowling at Mike. "I mean you as good as—"

"No, I didn't," Mike snapped, clearly angry. "I just pointed out that I had responsibilities. Expensive responsibilities."

"And no one's saying you haven't." Si kept his voice neutral. "And no, I haven't been buttering the town up. I've been talking to people, that's all."

Mike's angry expression didn't lift. "Trying to convince everyone not to sell, right?"

"I just want to know what they think. To see what the consensus is."

"Yeah, and the consensus seems to be that they prefer animals and trees to people taking care of their own." Mike stuck his hands in his pockets, glowering. "The whole damn town didn't want my luxury motel idea, which was only going to benefit this place, and now they're getting up in arms because I'm considering taking advantage of what's mine anyway. Can't damn well win."

Si studied the other man for a second. The guy was well and truly pissed, and given what he'd said at the meeting the night before about his mother, Si could understand it. Retirement home care was expensive.

"So money's the issue?" he asked to be sure. "I mean, what would you have done if there hadn't been oil?"

"Of course money's the issue," Mike said angrily. "And if there hadn't been oil, I guess I'd be screwed."

"What if the money came from somewhere else?" Si persisted, following an idea suddenly looming large in his head. "You don't care too much about the oil?"

Mike's gaze narrowed. "Where else?"

"Yeah," Kevin put in, staring at Si, puzzled. "Where else are you talking about?"

"It doesn't really matter," Si said. "The point is, if you had enough money to ensure your mother got the care she needed, you wouldn't be too fixated on the oil."

Mike didn't say anything for a moment, obviously thinking. Then he said, "Look, don't get me wrong. Oil money could be good for this town. It could grow it, provide more opportunities for young people, shit like that. Because this place isn't growing, and last year we had more people leave than came in."

That was something Si hadn't known. But then, why would he know? He'd been away for so long.

Too long.

"There are leases vacant?" he asked.

"Yeah, a couple," Mike said. "I think Caleb was trying to find people to take them on. Maybe that's why he was prospecting for oil. Wanted to give people a reason to come here."

Hell, maybe Mike was right. That would be very Cal. He loved Deep River; it was his family's legacy, and if people were leaving and no one was coming in, he'd be worried about it. And he'd definitely want to try and fix it if he could.

"Could be." Si agreed. "But let's say there was another way to grow the town that would provide opportunities for young people, bring in money, you'd be supportive of that instead of, say, an oil company?"

Mike frowned. "What's the big deal about oil companies? They're businesses. Gotta make a buck like everyone else."

"They're big, though," Si said carefully, watching the other man as he spoke. "And when you have money, you can basically tell people what to do. Not sure you'd be happy with a bunch of suits swanning in here and laying down the law."

The other man's gaze narrowed; it was clear he didn't like that thought, not at all. "Huh," he said. "Maybe not."

Okay, so he'd given Mike something to think about it. That was good. That was a start. Maybe the guy would even take that to other people who thought the oil could be a good thing for the town.

Because if there was one thing the people of Deep River disliked more than anything else, it was being told what to do. Especially by a bunch of suits from the city.

"Food for thought," Si said. "Now, you guys need help with anything around here?"

"Was just talking to Mike about the boat engine." Kevin jerked his thumb at the boat docked behind him. "Using a bit too much oil."

"Want me to take a look?" Si offered, because he could do worse than to offer some help, perhaps get more of a feel for the mood of the town. After all, people were always much more talkative when you were helping them.

"Sure," Kevin said. "You know anything about boat engines?"

Si grinned. "Hey, I was born here. There's nothing I don't know about engines, period."

The two other men grinned back. Living in an isolated area meant needing to have a variety of skills, since it wasn't like a city where you could get someone in to fix it for you. If you couldn't fix it yourself, you were screwed.

It was a good reminder to them of who he was and where he'd come from, that he was one of them, and as he followed Kevin and Mike over to the boat, he very carefully didn't think about why that might be important to him.

He was going to leave. Nothing was going to change that.

Nothing at all.

Chapter 12

HOPE SPENT THE DAY IN HER OFFICE, LOOKING AT Sandy's numbers and thinking. And not about the idea she'd had, but about what her mother had said to her, about her being the excuse Hope used to stay in Deep River.

And instead of the research she should have been doing, she found herself looking at college websites and degrees.

It had been years since she'd let herself contemplate those dreams she'd once had. Of leaving and going somewhere else, living a different life. Going to college and learning, having new experiences, all the things she'd told herself she wouldn't be able to have staying here.

Her grandfather used to tell her stories of his life before he'd come to Deep River and bought the Moose's lease. Of his time spent in the navy, traveling to different countries. And then after that, of living in Florida and then moving north to New York, before deciding city life wasn't for him and going to Minnesota in search of a different lifestyle. He'd given that up too though, heading into the wild north and Alaska.

She'd loved those stories of his and she'd decided early on that she wanted to travel like he did, see all of those places. She definitely didn't want to stay in the Moose, didn't want to end up like her mother, whose life was spent sitting on the couch, watching TV, and going over all her bitterness. That seemed so small and limited, so unexciting.

You're going to end up like her anyway if you're not careful.

Hope nibbled on her bottom lip, staring at her computer screen.

Yeah, but she'd had to stay after her grandfather had died; there was no other choice. Her mother needed her and Hope couldn't leave her. She was, after all, the reason her mother's mental health was so fragile.

But…the years had gone on, and her mother had gotten better, and there had been plenty of opportunity for Hope to leave Deep River, to do the traveling and learning she'd always wanted to do. Yet she hadn't. She hadn't wanted to leave her grandfather's legacy to just anyone and…

Yeah. And?

Something that she really hoped wasn't regret twisted in her gut.

She'd told Silas the night before that she was fine with her choices, and she'd meant it. She *was* fine with them. She'd packed up her dreams, put them in a box, and shoved them to the back of her mind, never to be looked at again.

Because that was easier. Easier than wanting what you knew you couldn't have.

It had been, that was true. But what if she could have had them? What if she could have had those dreams all this time?

She didn't like that thought—which was probably why she'd never let herself think too deeply about the future, never let herself have too many plans—mainly because she didn't like what that said about herself.

You were afraid.

Hope leaned back in her chair, trying not to pay any attention to the nagging voice in her head. But the feeling didn't go away. Or the knowledge that maybe that voice was right. She had been afraid. Of failing maybe. Or of succeeding—she wasn't sure which.

One would have meant coming back to town with your tail between your legs. The other would have meant you didn't come back at all…

A knock sounded on her office door, mercifully interrupting her thoughts, and before she'd had a chance to reply, the door was opening and Silas was coming through, and all those thoughts disappeared entirely.

He didn't close the door this time, deliberately leaving it open, leaning one shoulder against the frame and folding his arms. His gaze found hers, the gold eclipsing the green, already burning.

For her.

Her mouth dried, her heartbeat picking up speed.

She'd always been very good at not thinking about things she didn't want to think about, but it had been tough not to think about him. Or about what had happened between them the night before. And she'd tried, because she didn't want that getting in the way of her day.

But at the sight of him now, tall and powerful, the dark

green of his Wild Alaska T-shirt highlighting the broad expanse of his chest and the gleam of desire in his eyes, the memories of the night before came flooding back.

He had touched her so deliberately, as if he'd relished every second, and he'd tasted her too, like she was something delicious he couldn't wait to eat. And after that initial hunger had been sated, after they'd talked, he'd shown her something new just like she'd asked. Then she'd taken what she'd learned and had given it back to him, touching him the way he'd touched her, as if he were a work of art.

And like a bottle of champagne that had just had its cork popped, all the need and desperate desire she'd been pushing down all day came rushing to the surface and she could hardly breathe through the intensity of it.

He'd told her that one night wouldn't be enough, but he'd been gone this morning, and she hadn't been sure whether he still felt that way or not.

Which is why you haven't been thinking about it. Because you wanted him too. And it's easier not to think about the things you want, right?

Of course it was easier. And she'd let a whole lot of things distract her today, since it meant she didn't have to think about Silas. Didn't have to wonder whether he would want a repeat of the night before. Didn't have to try and pretend that she didn't want it, that she hadn't been hoping for it with every breath she'd taken.

But it was clear he did still feel the same, since what flamed in his eyes almost burned her alive.

"Upstairs," he said roughly, and without giving her a chance to respond, he pushed himself away from the door and went back out into the hallway again.

She supposed she should feel offended at being ordered around so blatantly. Except she didn't feel offended. She felt turned on. That rough note in his voice told her that he was on edge and that likely the edge was all down to wanting her. Badly.

And she was not offended by that. Not offended in the slightest.

Hope pushed herself out of her chair and went quickly out of her office. The hallway outside was empty—thank God—and the stairs free of anyone hanging around. Not that she would have hesitated even so. She hadn't wanted anyone knowing she was sleeping with Silas, but right now, hiding where she was going wasn't the most important thing in her head.

He was.

She assumed he meant his room, so she went quickly up the stairs and down the corridor to the honeymoon suite. She didn't bother knocking, pushing the door open and stepping inside, and as soon as she did so, a pair of big, warm hands settled on her hips, and he was pushing her up against the closed door.

His mouth was on hers almost immediately, and she let her head fall back against the wood, threading her fingers through the thick black silk of his hair. She kissed him hungrily, opening her mouth and letting the kiss get deeper, hotter. His big body was pressing against her, all hard, muscled heat and the delicious scent of wood-smoke and cedar, and suddenly she was almost trembling with the need to get closer to him.

She arched up into him, sliding her hands from his hair and down his back, her fingers digging into the firm muscle, glorying in it.

A dim part of her was vaguely appalled at the intensity of her own feelings and how she was letting them run riot, but she ignored that part of her. Because Silas's grip on her was tightening, his kiss becoming demanding, making it very clear she wasn't the only one who was desperate.

She could allow herself this, couldn't she? She could let herself want him, want what he could give her, especially since right now there was no danger of her losing it. He would give her what she wanted because he wanted it too.

So Hope dug her fingers into his back, gripping him tighter, exploring his mouth with a little more confidence than she had before, letting the rich taste of him go straight to her head like a shot of Harry's finest home-distilled whiskey.

God, he felt so good. She couldn't believe they hadn't gone there together when they were younger, that she hadn't made a move on him. But then she'd had good reasons for not doing it. She couldn't have handled those raw sexual feelings at eighteen, but now she could. Oh yes, now she was more than ready.

His hands were at the buttons of her jeans, undoing

them, but this time she wanted to be the one to give him what he wanted first. He'd been so selfless the night before, holding himself back to give her pleasure, and now she wanted to return the favor.

Before he could do anything more than get her zipper down, she gave a little push to his chest, making him take a step back, then she dropped to her knees in front of him.

"Hope," he murmured, his deep voice rough. "What are you doing?"

Her heartbeat was getting louder, excitement crowding in her throat. She didn't look at him, not wanting to lose her nerve, because she hadn't done this before. "It's my turn," she said, as she reached for the button on his jeans. "So let me have it."

He gave a rough laugh. "Hell, if you think I'm going to stop you, you'd be wrong."

"Good." She got the button undone and then tugged his zipper down. He was already hard and ready, the outline of him clear beneath the black cotton of his boxers.

Her breath caught; he was big and she liked that. She liked it very much indeed. He'd filled her completely last night, and now she wanted to taste him, put her mouth on him. Drive him as insane as he'd driven her.

She reached out and stroked him, running her finger down the hard ridge, thrilling as she heard his breath catch as much as hers had.

"Are you teasing me, sweetheart?" His hands had dropped to her hair, lazily pulling her ponytail out.

"Maybe," she said breathlessly, tugging down his

boxers and reaching for him, curling her fingers around the long, hard length of his erection and drawing him out. "What are you going to do about it?"

"Nothing." He sounded even rougher now, his voice deepening. "Not a goddamn thing."

She wanted to stroke him, squeeze him, tease him the way he was accusing her of doing, but she didn't want to wait. So she didn't hesitate, leaning forward and touching her tongue to him, letting the salty flavor of him fill her senses.

He groaned, his hands tightening in her hair, the sound shivering across her skin like a caress. So she did it again and then again, licking him, tasting him. Then opening her mouth and taking him inside.

"Hope…" Her name sounded like a prayer. "God…"

She kept her fingers wrapped tight around him, taking him in as far as she could, then beginning to suck.

He muttered a low curse, his hips flexing, thrusting into her mouth slowly at first, as if he could sense her inexperience. She might have found that patronizing at another time, but right now she was glad. Because it meant she could make this good for him. And she wanted to make this good for him. She wanted this to be the best.

Why? You want to be special to him?

Of course she wanted to be special. She wanted him to have something good to take with him when he left, something to remember her by.

His thrusts sped up, getting faster, but by that stage, she knew what she was doing. She gripped one of his thighs with her free hand, changing up the rhythm, using her tongue, nipping at him a little, letting him feel the edge of her teeth, which he seemed to like because he growled low and deep in his throat when she did it.

She'd never thought she'd like doing this to a man, but Silas made everything different. He made everything exciting and new, and she loved that. She loved how she was able to drive him absolutely insane, making his fingers twist almost painfully tight in her hair, the rough sounds he made driving her own need higher.

And then things began to get faster, rougher, as he took control, and she loved that too. Especially when he groaned her name yet again, his body stiffening as he came. She swallowed him down, taking everything he had to give, and then afterward, she leaned against his denim-covered thighs, resting her head on his hard stomach.

She felt shaky and desperate all of a sudden, but also weirdly satisfied and pleased with herself.

His hands had loosened in her hair, stroking her, massaging her scalp gently, and it felt so good she wanted to purr like a cat.

"You're amazing, you know that?" he said in a deep, gravelly voice. "Absolutely fucking incredible."

She smiled and raised her head, looking up into the gleaming gold of his eyes. "I know there's beer goggles, but I feel like there's orgasm goggles happening here."

The expression on his face was as intense as it usually was, but then it relaxed and he smiled, and she found her heart clenching tight in her chest. There had always been a reason she'd hoarded the smiles he gave her. They were beautiful. And so was he.

"Orgasm goggles, huh?" His hands urged her to her feet. "Maybe you should try a pair on for size then."

"If you're the one giving them out, then definitely." She put her hands on his chest, looking up at him. "You should smile like that more often, you know."

As she'd hoped, the curve of his mouth deepened. "I'll keep that in mind. But note that it only happens when you're around."

"Lies. I've seen you smile at other people."

"Yeah, but I didn't mean it with them." He lifted one hand and hooked a lock of hair behind her ear, his fingertips brushing over her skin in a light caress, making her shiver. "I mean it when I smile at you."

The tightness in her chest increased, a bittersweet pain, and a wave of heat passed through her cheeks. "Si…"

His fingers cradled her head as he leaned down, kissing her. "No more of that," he murmured against her mouth. "I have a favor to return."

And thank God, because she didn't know what to say or how to deal with that pain inside her. A sweet ache that made her uncomfortable at the same time as it made her want more.

She hadn't had many people in her life tell her that she was valuable or even that her presence was welcome. Her grandfather hadn't been a demonstrative man, and her mother didn't have any emotional energy left for her. So the simple fact that she made Silas smile…

It meant a lot.

It shouldn't.

And she shouldn't let it. But tell that to the feeling inside her that only ached more as Silas lifted her into his arms and carried her over to the bed, laying her on it. Then he followed her down onto the mattress, his long, powerful body pinning her in a way that made the ache shift lower.

He settled himself between her thighs, kissing her long and slow, making her so aware of all the fabric that was still between them and how she wanted it gone. Right the hell now.

But he took it slow again, much to her annoyance. Taking off her clothes in a measured way, kissing every inch of exposed skin as he did so, stroking her and caressing her until she was naked and shivering, desperate for him.

Only then did he kiss his way down her body, his hands on her thighs, pressing them gently but insistently apart. Then he spread her with his fingers and bent his head, his tongue beginning to explore the hot, slick flesh between her legs.

Hope groaned, her hips lifting as soon as his mouth touched her, electricity crackling along every nerve ending, pleasure twisting and knotting inside her.

He explored her, taking his time, using his mouth and his tongue in the same way she had on him, driving her wild.

Oh, he was wicked. But then maybe she'd always known that as well, another reason eighteen-year-old

Hope had steered clear of him. Good thing the woman she was now absolutely loved it.

She sank her fingers into his hair, holding on as he pushed her higher, stoking her pleasure until she was shaking and writhing beneath him, and only then did he push her over the edge, making her gasp his name as she shook and shook and shook.

And it wasn't until she was lying there trying to recover that he pushed himself off the bed, slowly stripping off all his clothes until he stood by the bed naked and glorious.

She couldn't stop looking at him, at the broad width of his chest and shoulders, the sharp corrugations of his abs. Lean hips and powerful thighs. Oh lord, would she ever get tired of looking at him? Probably not.

"Now," he said as he came back down onto the bed, settling himself over her and between her thighs, his hot, bare skin on hers a delicious shock. "Let's try that again."

He was totally indulging himself, and he knew it. But he didn't care. Hope was naked and soft beneath him, and he was pretty much helpless to resist her. Not that he'd planned on resisting her, but when he'd come back to the Moose, he'd thought he might be able to hold out a couple of hours at least, take some time to think about what he'd found out from Mike about the leases, turning a few ideas of his own over in his head.

But the moment he'd walked into the Moose, he'd headed straight for Hope's office, his body already hard, unable to think about anything else but her. If his brain had been working properly, he might have asked her to bed a bit more nicely. But his brain hadn't been working properly. So he'd said the first thing that had come into his head, which was to order her upstairs.

Luckily she'd been into it, because if she hadn't been, he didn't know what he would have done. He certainly wouldn't have had her kneeling in front him, his cock in her mouth, giving him the most insane pleasure he'd ever had.

She lifted a hand and let her finger trail over his stomach as he dealt with the issue of protection, her dark eyes smoky with heat and pleasure. "You're pretty amazing too, you know that?"

He finished rolling down the condom, then positioned himself, looking down into her lovely face, unable to get enough of watching her as he pushed inside her, the moment when she became his and only his.

"What were you saying about orgasm goggles?" he murmured, flexing his hips and pressing in, seeing pleasure flare in her eyes as he slid inside her.

She inhaled sharply, her lashes fluttering. "I...can't remember."

He smiled, his heartbeat speeding up as her body clenched hard around him. "No. Neither can I."

Her hands slid up his arms to his shoulders, her body arching, her hips lifting to take him deeper, and they both groaned as he settled more fully inside her.

Oh God, she felt good, so incredibly sweet and hot. He could feel that fire burning inside her and it was all for him.

He bent and pressed a kiss to her throat, tasting the pulse that beat there, not moving for a couple of moments, wanting to savor this. Just the feeling of being inside her, of her welcoming him, having her fire burn all around him.

"Silas," she whispered, her nails digging into his skin. "Please."

He nuzzled against her neck, grinning, the husky, desperate note in her voice making him feel very self-satisfied. "Please what?"

She scratched at him. "Please move."

"Demanding." He bit the side of her neck gently, teasing her. "You know I don't like being told what to do."

"Don't be an ass." She arched beneath him, trying to urge him on, and the feel of her moving against him was so delicious that he thought he might let himself be urged. "Come on."

"Maybe I don't want to." He nipped at her bottom lip. "Maybe I want to lie here, driving you crazy."

"That would be mean, and you're not mean, are you?" Then she gasped as he shifted slightly on her. "Okay, scratch that. You *are* mean."

He laughed, sliding his hands beneath her butt, tilting her slightly, settling himself more completely and making her tremble. She was soft and she felt so good that he'd decided he'd had enough of teasing her. He began to move, gripping the curves of her ass as he slid out and then back in, watching the glow in her eyes become hotter, the flush in her cheeks intensifying.

Sexy Hope. Beautiful Hope.

You're such a goner for her.

Yeah, he was. He always had been. But even so, he wasn't going to make this into anything more than what it was: phenomenal sex with a woman he'd wanted nearly half his life.

You want more than that.

It wasn't anything new. He'd always wanted more with her. He'd wanted everything. But that wasn't something he'd ever allow himself. Because he'd always wanted more from people than what they could give. He'd wanted his father to go back to being the man he was before Si's mother had died, and because he'd been young, he'd thought handing the old man a vodka bottle would help. And it had.

His father had gone from never mentioning her name, never even looking in Si's direction, to reminiscing at length about her, giving Si drunken hugs and talking about airplanes and going fishing the way he used to do.

It was wrong to want his father to stay drunk. But that didn't stop him from feeling glad every time he came home to find the vodka bottle open and his father singing one of his mother's favorite songs in the kitchen.

And if he didn't exactly pour his father another drink, he didn't get rid of the vodka down the drain. Or tell Mal not to sell it to Joshua anymore. Or even tell his father that perhaps he might not want to open the bottle tonight.

He did none of those things. Because he'd wanted his

father back. He'd needed him so badly that he'd let him become a drunken wreck of a man.

He'd hated himself a little bit for that, and so he hadn't wanted to put that kind of need on Hope. Didn't want to be demanding stuff from her that she couldn't give. He'd keep this intensity in the bedroom and let himself have it here, where it could be mistaken for sexual hunger rather than anything else.

It was enough. It would have to be.

He moved deeper inside her, faster, and her head went back on the pillows as he increased the pace, her breathing coming in short, hard pants, her legs locking around his waist.

He bent his head, kissing her exposed neck, needing the taste of her in his mouth, because somehow it felt as if this wasn't enough. He had to have more.

You always have to have more. That's the problem.

Si shoved that thought away, gripping her hips as he thrust harder, her body so soft and hot he could barely handle it.

Her hands slid down his back, fingernails scratching him lightly before digging into the curve of his butt and holding on. She was making those husky, sexy little noises that meant she was close to the edge, and he wanted to keep her there, wanted to make her ride that edge for as long as he could.

But he was too desperate. All he could do was keep going, keep driving himself deep, the sweet musky scent of her and the tight clasp of her body making him slightly crazy. He slipped one hand between them, down between her thighs, stroking her, then giving her a little pinch.

Her body convulsed, his name a hoarse scream in his ear as she came, and then he let himself go, thrusting into her as the pleasure coiled tight as a spring before exploding outward, a bright burst of lightning sizzling up his spine and out through his head. He turned his head against her neck, biting down on the sensitive spot between her shoulder and neck as the climax took him, and for whole minutes—hell, maybe even hours, who could tell?—he was lost. Blinded by pleasure and by her.

It felt like a long time later that he opened his eyes to find her lying beneath him, looking up at him, her hands stroking slowly up and down his spine. Her skin was flushed and her eyes were glowing like dark stars, and he'd never seen anything as beautiful as she was in his entire life.

"You okay?" he asked, because he'd let himself go a little there and he wanted to make sure he hadn't hurt her. Though he had to admit she didn't look hurt, just well-tumbled.

"I am feeling...very good." Her mouth, reddened from his kisses and full and pouty, curved. "Very good indeed."

"I aim to please."

"And you sure do." She gave a sensual stretch, making parts of him that he'd thought well-sated start to be hungry for more. "You're good at that, by the way. Lots of practice, I take it?"

He couldn't tell if she was fishing for information, passing judgment, or something else, but he did catch the faintest edge in her voice. Which pleased the Neanderthal in him very much. "Why do you want to know? You jealous?"

She hit him lightly on the shoulder. "No. It was just a simple question."

It was more than that, he was betting; otherwise, why ask it in the first place? Then again, he didn't mind. He liked the idea of her being jealous extremely. "A bit. You know, here and there."

"What? A man who doesn't talk about his conquests?" Hope raised a dark eyebrow. "You're a unicorn, Si."

"No, I don't talk about them. And I prefer to think of myself as a gentleman."

"Yes, well, a gentleman doesn't order his lover upstairs without even a please, so I beg to differ."

He had to smile at that. "Depends on the gentleman and whether or not his lover likes being ordered upstairs." He brushed a lock of hair off her damp forehead. "You didn't seem to mind it."

She flushed. "Maybe."

"So what about you?" Because what was good for the goose, etcetera. "Have you got in much practice?"

Hope's gaze dropped to his mouth. "You know, I'd really like to kiss you right now."

He would really like her to kiss him too. But she'd just ignored him completely and he wasn't having that. "You can't ask me that question and not expect me to ask you the same thing."

She lifted her gaze back to his. "You didn't really answer me."

"No," he said bluntly, because he wanted her to know. "There's been no one else. I've had lovers, but no one serious."

"Oh." She blinked and glanced away. "Well…I haven't either. No one serious, I mean."

"Lovers?" She would have had some, surely? She was beautiful, and he couldn't imagine there wouldn't have been lots of men interested in her.

Hope sighed. "I don't really want to tell you."

"Why not?" He stroked her hair, loving the silky feel of it against his palm. "Have there been lots? Fifty? A hundred?" He wasn't quite sure why he wanted to know, because it didn't matter.

You don't want it to be fifty or a hundred.

Hell no. He already felt jealous of whoever it was she gave her virginity to, because she hadn't been a virgin. Some guy who didn't deserve it, that was for sure.

"Not fifty. Or a hundred." She let out a breath. "One. Lame, I know. But only one. A guy from the trawlers who was in town for a couple of weeks. He was interested and I thought 'why not?'"

He shouldn't have been happy with that, but he was. It pleased a very male, very possessive part of him. The hungry part he knew he needed to get a lock on. "That's not lame," he said, probably doing a very poor job of hiding just how much that pleased him. "You're choosy."

"Not really." She pulled a face. "I didn't have that much to choose from."

Surprise filled him, and he didn't bother hiding it.

"Seriously? You're gorgeous, Hope. You must have had guys lining up for a chance with you."

"Not really." She stroked her hands absently over his shoulders. "Bit difficult to find a decent partner when you own the bar and have a reputation for tossing people out when they cause trouble." She hesitated. "Plus it's a small town, and people always have something to say when you hook up with someone."

Oh yeah, he knew that. He remembered all too well the kinds of gossip that went around about his father. Most of it was benign, and there were more than a few people who checked in on Si just to make sure he was okay. The town had looked out for him in its own way.

But there would always be gossip. That was part of the deal.

"Did that bother you?" he asked. "I wouldn't have thought you cared about gossip."

An expression he couldn't quite read crossed her face. "It's all very well not to care if you don't live here. But when you're staying put and you manage a place that a lot of townspeople meet at, then yeah, it did bother me. Mom had to put up with all of that when she was pregnant with me, and I didn't want to have to deal with it myself."

Okay, so that made it clearer. Of course she wouldn't want to leave herself open to an experience like her mother's.

"Fair enough," he said. "Though that was a few years ago. People aren't quite as judgmental these days."

"Maybe not. But I still didn't want to have to deal with it. Even if the gossip isn't malicious, it's still annoying. And I didn't want the town looking over my shoulder, anyway."

There was a flat note in her voice that made him study her face intently, looking for what he didn't know. She'd had one partner in thirteen years... No one to touch her. No one to hold her. Had anyone told her she was beautiful? Had anyone ever let her know that she was sexy?

Ah, but he knew the answer to that already.

No one had.

Something ached in his chest. God, he hated the thought of her here on her own. Lonely. Because she must have been lonely. She'd always been so passionate, and that didn't just disappear. But she'd buried it, locked it away behind that prickly, tough exterior.

And she wasn't the only one who'd locked down a part of themselves. He'd done the same thing.

But right here, right now, they didn't need to keep those pieces of themselves hidden away, did they? Not with each other. With each other, they could be themselves completely.

"You don't need to worry about the town now," he said, staring down into her eyes. "What goes on between you and me isn't any of their business. And for the record, I don't care that you run the Moose, or that you throw people out who cause trouble." He ran his thumb across her lower lip. "As far as I'm concerned, you're the most beautiful woman in the entire universe, not to mention the sexiest, and I'm not letting you out of this bed until it's time for me to go back to Juneau."

She liked that, he could tell, because she blushed adorably. "Well, okay then."

He shifted his hands, cupping her face, letting her see how utterly serious he was. "I mean it, sweetheart. You're going to be sleeping with me here every night, got it? So if you don't want that, you'd better tell me now so we're both clear."

Hope stared at him for a second, not saying anything. And he found he'd tensed up because if she didn't want that, then he wasn't sure what he would do.

But then she said, "I want that, Si. I *really* want that." There was no mistaking the certainty in those words. No mistaking the longing he could hear in them either.

"Good," he said huskily, the ache in his chest intensifying for some reason. "Then that's what'll happen."

Then he leaned down and kissed her, making good on his promise.

Chapter 13

HOPE CAME OUT OF APRIL'S CARRYING A COUPLE OF paper bags along with two coffees, making her way along the boardwalk beside the river to the bench where she'd sat with Silas the first morning he'd arrived.

He was sitting there waiting for her, his long legs outstretched, his hands behind his head, his attention on the water in front of him, and for a second she paused, staring at him. He sat very still, a big, powerful presence. But a peaceful, restful one. She'd often compared him to one of the mountains that surrounded the town, silent and monumental yet protective too. Some people found mountains oppressive, but she never had. They were a defense, a barrier between the town and the rest of the world, and she liked that feeling. It was comforting.

He was comforting. She'd found that when they'd been teenagers, his silent presence was like a beam holding her up, supporting her, and she realized, almost with a shock, that she felt the same way now.

That could be a problem.

But no, it wouldn't be a problem. She wouldn't let it be a problem. Sure, she felt relaxed with him in a way she hadn't felt with anyone else in a long time, even going so far as to let her guard down, allowing herself to want and to be given what she wanted. Except only in bed. That's as far as she'd go. Out of it was a whole different ball game.

He'd told her the previous night, before she'd drifted off to sleep in his arms, that he needed to discuss with her what he'd found out from talking to people. So that morning they'd decided to meet for lunch on the boardwalk beside the river.

She supposed it might make people gossip to see them sitting together, but they were already gossiping. Besides, having lunch together wasn't unusual. They were old friends, after all.

Except her mother had given her a suspicious look as Hope had found her way into the kitchen that morning, though Angela didn't say anything. And it was a good thing that Angela didn't concern herself with the Moose because she might have had an observation to make about how Axel was behind the bar for the second night in a row.

Silas turned his head just then, and his green-gold eyes met hers and he smiled. And her heart fluttered in her chest like a wild bird, making her nearly spill the coffees she held.

Stupid. So he had a beautiful smile. So what?

She ignored the flutter, moving over to the bench and sitting down beside him. "Didn't think you'd mind if I bought lunch."

His smile deepened, lighting a flame in his eyes, making the fluttering even worse. "No. Especially not if it's one of those pies again."

"It is." She handed over a bag and one of the coffees, trying her best not to brush her fingers with his, because she was pretty sure she'd get coffee everywhere if she did that. God, was this reaction to him ever going to stop? They'd been burning up the sheets for two nights now and she'd thought the need for him would ease. But it wasn't easing. If anything, she thought it might be getting worse, which couldn't happen.

So stop, then.

She didn't think she could, though. And the only way to make herself feel comfortable with that decision was the knowledge that this was all temporary. He was going to leave again very soon, so really, what did it matter if she had him every night? What did it matter if the need got worse? By the time he was ready to leave Deep River, they'd have gotten it out of their systems and it would be all good.

Sure, tell yourself that.

Hope ignored that thought, taking a sip of her coffee instead, the scalding liquid burning its way down her throat, burning the doubt right out of her.

"So," she said, "tell me what's been going on."

"Well, most people aren't happy with the thought of big oil coming in here and taking over." Silas leaned back and made a start on his pie. "Which I'd pretty much expected, since this town isn't big on being told what to do by a bunch of rich suits."

"You said *most* people."

Silas finished chewing and swallowed. "Yeah, there're another few who want the money. And it's not completely selfish. Mike needs to care for his mom, and there's a couple of others who struggle with covering their bills, especially over the winter. They can see the good side of the oil money, which is opportunities for the town in terms of employment. There are a few vacant places around here, which I didn't know about."

Hope frowned, because she'd known that a couple of people had moved away and that no one had taken over the leases, but she hadn't thought about why that might be. "Has there been some difficulty finding people to take the leases over?"

Silas nodded. "Cal couldn't find anyone, or so Mike said, and I believe him. He didn't have any reason to lie about that."

"Cal never said anything to you?" Hope asked, taking another sip of her coffee, more than a little puzzled because he'd never said anything to her either.

"No, he didn't. Then again, I'd made it pretty clear I didn't want to talk about Deep River, so that probably had something to do with it." An expression of regret flickered over his handsome face, and Hope put her hand on his thigh, wanting to give him comfort of some kind.

He didn't seem to find it surprising, covering hers with his own in what seemed like an automatic gesture. "I shouldn't have shut him out like that. Especially if he was having problems. I just…" He stopped.

"You just what?"

Silas looked away, out over the water, but he didn't let go of her hand. "I didn't want to be reminded of this place. Or of everything I left behind."

Her mouth went dry; she knew what the implications of that were. He meant her, didn't he? He didn't want to be reminded of her.

A thread of guilt pulled tight inside her at what she'd said to him years ago, how she'd told him not to bother staying, and he must have sensed it because he said suddenly, "It's okay, sweetheart. Like you told me, we can't change what happened. You had your reasons for refusing me, just like I had mine for leaving. But yeah, I didn't want to be reminded. So I guess Cal just thought I didn't want to hear it."

She swallowed, the coffee in her cup burning against her fingertips. "Okay, so Cal didn't tell you about the vacancies. He didn't tell me about them either." She paused. "Do you think that's why he was prospecting for the oil? To see if he could attract people to the town again?"

Silas finally moved his hand from hers, grabbing his coffee from the bench beside him and taking a sip. "Yeah, I think that's exactly what happened. God knows what his eventual plans were, but I guess that's not his problem anymore. It's ours."

Hope let out a breath. "Mom's pretty fixed on selling the lease. She's bitter about the town in a way I hadn't realized she still held on to. And she as good as told me she doesn't care what happens to it, since she won't be here."

Silas's green gaze roved over her. "Is that really all there is to it?"

She didn't particularly want to tell him that no, it wasn't. Especially since the idea of college, now that her mother had mentioned Hope using her as an excuse to stay, had stuck in her brain like a particularly annoying splinter.

But she didn't want to reveal that just yet, not when she didn't know what she was going to do—if anything. Even if she did decide to leave, she still wasn't going to let her mother sign the Moose over to some oil guy, if it was an oil guy. No, she'd have to find someone who was prepared to pay her a fair price for the Moose's lease, who wouldn't then turn around and sell the mineral rights to someone else.

So all she said was, "Yeah, pretty much. I guess it means that for her it's the money, not the oil, that's important."

He was silent, studying her in that focused way he had that made her feel a little vulnerable at the same time it made her feel like the center of the world. "Mike said that too. He didn't care so much about the oil as the money and opportunities that came from it."

The idea she'd had the day before, that had gotten lost under thoughts of college and Silas, suddenly bobbed back to the surface again. "So, what?" She stared back at him. "We find something else that delivers the same thing to the town but that we have a say over. That doesn't involve signing rights over to a bunch of rich guys from the city."

The smile that turned Silas's mouth this time was like the sun coming out, warm and bright, making her want to bask in it like a cat. "Great minds think alike," he said. "That's exactly what I've been thinking too."

And she found herself smiling back, excitement fizzing through her. An excitement she hadn't felt for years— the thrill of a challenge, of a future full of possibilities, and not just an endless procession of responsibilities and things she had to do.

"Got any ideas?" she asked. "I mean, for this place, obviously tourism is the key. I got the numbers off Sandy yesterday to get an idea of how many people visit every year, and there were a few. There's potential there."

Silas finished up the pie and sat back, cradling his coffee, and she could see the same excitement she was feeling gleaming in his eyes. "I talked to Kevin and Mike yesterday, helped Kev fix his boat, and we got to talking about all those hiking trails in the mountains. There're a few beginner trails and some for experienced hikers, but Kev said they don't get many people walking 'em because not many people know they're there."

Excitement bubbled up inside her like soda from a shaken bottle. "We could run some kind of promotion, get people to see what there is here. I mean, that's what I was thinking yesterday. We've got people who could take tourists up the river, since there's some lovely scenery up there." Her brain ticked over, thinking about the places she and Cal and Silas used to enjoy going to. "Like the swimming hole and Bride Falls."

Silas was grinning. "Fishing charters. Taking people out to the coast. And then sightseeing around the islands."

"Oh yes!" She put her coffee down on the bench and turned to him. "And what about Phil's place?" Filthy Phil, the town eccentric, had a lease that encompassed a big area up in the back of the town, with lots of bush. He'd turned it into an animal sanctuary. "We could make his sanctuary official. He's got all kinds of wildlife up there, and tourists might like to see some genuine Alaskan animals."

The gleam in Silas's eyes got brighter. "It won't be enough revenue to match oil money, not initially. But there's potential there."

"And the best part about it is that Deep River is in control of it. We decide what happens and how to make it work for us." Anticipation coiled inside her, along with the excitement. "This could work, Si. This could be really good for the town." More things occurred to her. "Harry could teach some survivalist workshops, and there's also a few others who might like to teach climbing skills. We have so many people here who could offer their expertise to tourists and hunters and others. Oh, yes, and maybe when you get back to Juneau, you could look around for anyone with piloting skills who might want to come out here to offer scenic flights."

He didn't say anything for a long moment, watching her, the appreciation in his expression making something glow hot in the center of her chest. "Those are fantastic ideas, Hope. But then you've always been good at planning stuff." He reached out suddenly and cupped her cheek, the warmth of his hand against her skin sending a shockwave of heat through her. "I'm glad I'm signing this over to you, because the town could not be in better hands."

And just like that, her excitement came to a shuddering halt. Because she'd forgotten about how he was intending to sign over ownership to her. And she could feel that responsibility now like a millstone around her neck, pulling her down, suffocating her.

The feeling was familiar; she'd felt the same way the day her grandfather had died and she'd realized that not only did she have her mother to look after but the Moose as well. That she couldn't leave Deep River.

And all her dreams of a different life had crashed and burned.

She pulled away abruptly, looking down at her hands tightly clasped in her lap.

You'd better tell him you're having second thoughts.

Something inside her clenched tight at that, an instinctive reaction. Because she wasn't, was she?

You are. Come on. You know Mom was right. And not thinking about it isn't going to make those feelings go away.

Hope took a breath. And yes, those feelings were still there. Those plans for the future still burning as brightly as they had years ago. And all the excuses she was using not to do them were the same too.

Her mother had been right. She'd been using the Moose, using her mother's mental health as reasons not to leave, not to go out and take the future she wanted for herself with both hands. And she wasn't quite sure why.

A memory hit her then of a conversation she'd had once with her grandfather, when she'd told him she wanted to travel like he did, see the world like he had. And he'd smiled at her and shaken his head. "Why would you want to do that?" he'd asked. "I've seen the world, Hope. It's got nothing to offer you that you can't get right here."

She'd always thought her grandfather was wrong. That everything she needed *wasn't* here, because if it had been, she wouldn't be wanting to leave, would she? And then he'd died and she'd taken on the Moose, taken on looking after her mother, telling herself that maybe he was right. That maybe what she wanted *was* here after all. And it was something that she'd been telling herself for years.

But why? Why had she done that? Was it fear? Fear of having to come back in the end? Or was it fear that she'd leave and never return?

"What is it?" Silas asked, a note of concern in his voice.

She met his gaze, her heartbeat loud in her ears. He'd be disappointed and she didn't want to disappoint him, just like she hadn't wanted to disappoint her mother or the memory of her grandfather all those years ago. But she wasn't sure she liked the alternative either. She'd put everything she'd wanted on hold once before; she didn't want to do it again.

"I'm sorry, Si," she said, her voice sounding strange even to her own ears. "I don't think I can take on the town after all."

———————————

Si didn't know what he'd been expecting, but it hadn't been that. And he wasn't sure what to say. Yes, she hadn't exactly been thrilled with the idea of owning the entire town, but she'd agreed to take it on.

Then again, there had always been a part of him that hadn't liked what he'd asked of her. That still remembered the eighteen-year-old with tears on her cheeks, telling him and Cal that she had to stay. That she couldn't leave after all. He'd seen the death of her dreams in her eyes that night, and that vision had stuck with him all through the years.

Was he really going to insist on her staying true to her word now? Because clearly, given the glow in those same beautiful eyes now, she had plans again. And not just for the town, but for herself as well.

He couldn't kill those dreams—not again. Yet he felt an uncomfortable twist inside him all the same. "Why not?" He tried hard not to make it sound like an accusation. "You have something else you want to do?"

"Yes." She met his gaze squarely. "I know I said I'd do it, but…I can't stop thinking about what Mom said. You were right when you asked about her wanting to sell. There *was* something else going on there."

He'd thought as much, but he hadn't wanted to push it if she hadn't wanted to tell him. "What else?" he asked now, unable to keep the edge from his voice no matter how much he tried to mask it.

"I was trying to talk Mom out of leaving. But then she basically accused me of using her as an excuse not to leave myself. And…well, I can't help thinking that she was right. I have been using her as an excuse not to go."

Si found he'd curled his hands around his coffee cup again, holding on a little tighter than he should have. That thought had crossed his mind about Hope too, but he hadn't followed up on it since he had no right to accuse her of anything, still less of her using excuses.

"Why?" he asked instead, puzzled that he wasn't more disappointed, because he should be, shouldn't he? "Did you really need an excuse?"

"I didn't think I did, but you asked me once before why I stayed, and I think it's more than just being here for Mom or because of the Moose." She hesitated, glancing down at her hands a moment before looking back up at him again. "I think I stayed because when it came down to it, I was afraid to go. And I didn't want to admit it was fear holding me back. It was better to give myself other reasons to stay."

That made sense to him. At least using her mother and the bar as an excuse.

After all, not anything you haven't done yourself, right?

He'd told himself lies for a long time about why he'd stayed away from Deep River. Lies to mask the truth, which was he hadn't been back because of her. Because she was here and he was afraid of coming back in case he stayed with her. But that hadn't happened. He'd come back and they were sleeping together, which was better than he'd ever imagined, but he knew it was temporary. He'd be leaving and hadn't felt tempted to stay.

Bullshit you haven't. And now, if she's not going to take on the town...

The feeling that had been dogging him for a couple of days now tugged harder—the pull of a responsibility he hadn't asked for and didn't want yet was still there, nagging at him.

If she didn't want the town, then who else was there? Morgan had been unequivocal in her refusal, and he wasn't going to force her. There was Astrid, the cool and collected mayor. She looked more than capable, but he had a feeling she wouldn't want it either. Maybe Mal?

You don't want to give it to anyone else, though.

He shifted on the bench, uncomfortable with that thought, mainly because he had a horrible sense that it was true. He'd never thought he would want the responsibility, not initially, but after coming back here, after talking with everyone... Yeah, he was beginning to feel differently about staying away, and where that left him and Wild Alaska he didn't want to think about too closely just yet.

Or what it would mean for him and Hope.

"Okay," he said, trying to ignore that thought. "So what does that mean, then?"

There was a glitter in Hope's dark eyes—excitement, yes, and something else he couldn't decipher. "It means that I'm thinking of leaving, Si. Not that I'll sell the Moose's lease to whoever's been calling Mom, but maybe I'll find someone else to take it on. And then Mom and I can just...go." She gave him a small smile. "Maybe I can finally do the things I've been wanting to do for so long."

He should be happy for her. He should be pleased. But his stomach dropped as if he'd taken a dive off a rock and into a deep pool. A deep, freezing-cold pool. Which didn't make any sense, especially since this was what he'd always wanted for her. To follow those dreams she'd had when she'd been young.

"It was you that did it," she went on, apparently oblivious to his sudden silence. "You asking me why I stayed. In fact, I think it was just you coming back and offering me the town that got me thinking about things. And then Mom mentioning me using her as an excuse…" Her eyes were shining, and suddenly she was eighteen again, the object of all his fantasies, all his longings. Bright and beautiful and full of the thing she'd been named for: hope. "I put what I wanted on hold, Si. I locked it away for years, telling myself I couldn't have it. That I had too many responsibilities, too many other things that were more important. But those dreams never went away. And I…" She took a breath. "I don't want to put them on hold again. I want to do them. I want to get that degree. I don't want to get to the end of my life and realize there was a whole lot of stuff I didn't get to do because I was too afraid."

Shit, what could he say to that? Telling her to stay because he wanted to offload the responsibility for Deep River onto her was petty, not to mention selfish. And sure, he'd developed a bit of selfishness over the years, but not if it would cost Hope. She'd paid enough already.

"That's fantastic," he said, unable to say anything else.

And if he said it enough times, maybe that cold feeling inside him would go away. Not that it should be there, since what did it matter to him if she left?

The irony, though. You're considering the merits of staying while she's deciding to leave.

Oh yeah, he couldn't escape that. He was fully aware. And of course, if she was leaving, then didn't that solve the difficulties of him deciding to stay? Since there would have been difficulties. Their affair was based on the fact that it was temporary, and him staying would have been…problematic.

So her deciding to leave didn't change anything, did it?

Hope tilted her head, that small smile becoming uncertain. "You don't sound very sure."

"I am sure." He adjusted his tone, making an effort to sound as if he meant it this time. "It's really fantastic. I mean, you deserve this, sweetheart. And I'm happy for you, I really am."

She let out a breath, her smile relaxing, which meant he'd obviously been more convincing. "Good. It's kind of scary to finally accept that's what I want to do. But I think it is." Picking up her coffee again, she took a sip. "Of course, I can't do any of this without finances, so I'll need to think about who can buy the lease to the Moose. And that's not going to be easy."

"You don't have any savings? I remember you telling me about a college fund?" And she had once, years ago. She'd put in a lot of hours at Mal's stocking shelves as well as cleaning up the Moose in the afternoons, saving all that hard-earned money for a college fund that never went anywhere.

"Yeah, I did." She leaned back against the bench, the midday sun igniting the burn of auburn in her hair. She wore it in her usual braid, the red-brown coil hanging over her shoulder, and he wanted to take it in his hand and pull gently on it. "But it all got spent on various catastrophes over the years. The Moose isn't cheap to run, and we had a couple of winters that were pretty bad snow-wise, which meant everyone stayed at home rather than coming in for a beer."

Five minutes ago, he would have responded to that urge, grabbing her braid and tugging her in for a kiss. But he felt oddly hesitant about it now, though he wasn't sure why. Because again, nothing had changed.

"Well," he said, deciding on something then and there, "if you don't find anyone, come to me."

She blinked, her long, thick lashes as auburn as her hair, the perfect frame for her dark chocolate-brown eyes. "Come to you? What for?"

He couldn't bear it, he realized. He couldn't bear for her not to take this opportunity again. Which meant he was going to do what he could to make sure she realized all those dreams she'd had to give up.

"I'll buy the Moose's lease from you," he said. "What do you think?"

Shock moved over her face. "You will? But…you said you weren't staying, Si. And you can't buy it if you're not staying."

His jaw felt tight, but the certainty was settling down inside him, and he knew that of any decision he'd made recently, this was the right one. The only one. "Yeah, about that. I think I've changed my mind."

Her eyes went wide. "What? When did you decide that?"

"I've been thinking about it the past couple of days, and talking to people here has just made me realize that maybe I'm not as over this place as I thought. And Cal left it to me and the rest of the guys for a reason." He paused. "Now I think about it, I wonder if he was anticipating trouble with the oil and thought that we were the best people to handle it."

"But what about your business? What about you getting back to Juneau?"

"I'll have to figure out what to do with the business. And hell, Juneau was never my home." He glanced out at the river, the certainty inside him becoming fact, making a weight he'd never realized was there abruptly lift. "Not like this place is."

"Oh," Hope said. "Oh…"

He kept his focus on the river, still conscious of her shock. Conscious too of the pressure of her gaze, that she was looking at him like she'd never seen him before in all her life.

Tension pulled tight between them—a tension that hadn't been there for the last couple of days—and he was sorry for it.

"This doesn't change anything." He glanced at her,

meeting her dark eyes. "So if you're thinking this makes our little arrangement different, it doesn't."

Our little arrangement. Such a stupid thing to call what they did together in bed at night. A paltry thing to call something so raw and precious and real. Like a rough diamond mined straight from the rock. The pleasure she gave him and the pleasure he gave in return, the satisfaction he felt when she was in his arms, the possessiveness too. The hot, burning thing that lived in his heart, that blazed brightly whenever she was near. No words could describe that.

Hope blinked, and her gaze flicked away from his for a second. Then it returned, and this time there was nothing but her own ferocity meeting his. "Okay," she said, determined and sure. "Nothing changes."

And the weight in him lifted a little more, because thank God she wasn't ready for this to be over yet and he was glad. Ferociously, savagely glad.

It was still temporary, which meant this was all still possible.

"But," she went on, "just so we're clear, you're not staying for me, are you?"

"No." The word came out easily because it wasn't a lie—of course it wasn't. "I'm staying because Cal left this town to me. It's my responsibility. And I can't walk away from it. Not the way I did thirteen years ago."

The look on her face this time was indecipherable. "You don't have to, you know."

"I do know. But who else is going to do it? I could ask

around, see if someone else could take it on. Except…"
He stopped.

"You don't trust anyone else, do you?" she asked.

Yeah, that was the reason, wasn't it? It wasn't simply
because it was his responsibility. There was more to it
than that, and it could have been about his ego, about the
whole power trip of it. But he knew deep down that it
wasn't.

It was because this place was home to him and always
had been. He loved it. It was important to him, as was
carrying on the legacy that the Wests had founded the
town on. A haven for people who couldn't find a haven
anywhere else.

He wanted to make sure it stayed that way, make sure
the spirit of the town stayed alive.

"Maybe there are other people who could do a better
job," he said. "And maybe I'll hand it over to them if that's
what's required. But Cal gave it to me for a reason."

"Si—"

"It's not your responsibility anymore," he cut her off
as gently as he could, because he didn't want to talk about
this right now. "It's mine, okay?"

She gave him a long look, her dark eyes full of that
indecipherable expression. Then she said, "Okay."

"Good." He pushed himself up off the bench. "Let's go
see if Mal's had another call then, hmm?"

Chapter 14

"I WAS JUST THINKING ABOUT CALLING INTO THE Moose to tell you," Mal said. "The guy called me back this morning."

Hope stared up at Mal, who was currently up a ladder tugging down a fishing rod from where they'd been stuck over several ceiling rafters. "Did you get his number?"

Mal tugged again on the fishing rod and this time managed to pull it out without it getting tangled on the other rods or on the various other long-handled items that he kept stored in the rafters. "Yep," he said laconically.

Hope glanced at Silas, who was standing next to her, part of her dreading what Mal might say next. Silas gave her a minute nod that was somehow reassuring, then asked, "I take it you figured out where the guy is from, then?"

Mal tucked the rod under his arm and descended back down the ladder. "He was reluctant to leave it, but I got it out of him in the end," he said as he stepped onto the floor. "And sure, I checked on the number." He gave them both a meaningful look. "I think you know where he was from."

"Oil company?" Silas bit out.

"Yeah. Oh, he wasn't straightforward about it. The number was for some warehouse in Juneau, but guess who owned the warehouse?"

"Damn," Hope muttered, disappointment gathering in her gut. God, she'd really hoped it would turn out not to be an oil company sniffing around, since it would have made everything a lot simpler. But of course it wasn't going to be; of course there would be nothing but difficulty.

Mal lifted a shoulder. "It's nothing I didn't expect. When money's involved, word gets out fast, and I always knew those types were going to be looking into things around here."

"So what did you tell him?" Silas asked.

"That I was still considering it." Mal turned and went over to the counter, putting the rod down on top of it. "I expect Nate's had a call too, not to mention your mom." He looked at Hope. "She know this guy isn't on the level?"

"I told her." The disappointment shifted into a cold, sick feeling. "But she likes the sound of the money too much." And that was going to be an issue. An oil company with deep pockets would be able to offer Angela a lot of money, and who could compete with that? Could Silas?

She could feel him standing behind her, a tall, strong presence, and she still didn't know how to deal with everything he'd told her out there on the boardwalk. That he was staying. That if she couldn't find a taker for the Moose's lease, she could come to him.

Staying. He was staying.

What was she supposed to do with that? With the irony that, after thirteen years, he would be the one to return and she would be the one to leave? But then, did she have to do anything? He was right; it wouldn't change anything ultimately, so there was no reason for her to feel so…strange about it. As if she was losing something, which made no sense, since the thing she was losing had always been temporary anyway.

He still wanted to keep sleeping with her, and she was happy with that. More than happy. Especially since it meant she had some good memories to take with her when she left.

Don't you want more than good memories?

Hope swallowed, her mouth dry, the feeling of loss deepening inside her. It was inexplicable. She and Silas were never going to have any kind of relationship— never. Years ago they'd been too young and she hadn't seen him like that anyway—or at least never consciously. And now, sure, the sex was great, but to have anything more than that? Definitely not. She was too busy at the Moose for relationships and anyway she couldn't now. She was leaving and he was staying here.

Apart from anything else, he'd made it very clear he wasn't looking for anything more than sex. That was the whole reason they'd entered into this arrangement in the first place. Both of them knew it was temporary.

You do want more, though. You've been so lonely…

Hope pushed that thought firmly back into the box it had escaped from, bringing her attention back to what was going on, which was way more important than her stupid feelings.

"We'll deal with Angela," Silas said quietly from behind her. "I think it might be worth letting everyone know, though, that this guy has been calling around and offering people money. And most especially they need to know who he is. I'd say that if he's called you back already, Mal, he's feeling some urgency."

Mal nodded. "Oh yeah. I wonder if he heard about the town meeting and now knows that everyone in town is aware of the situation with the oil. He can't just pretend to be some random guy calling to offer shitty money on leases from people who don't know what's going on."

"Did he offer you more?" Hope asked. "Like, did he mention the oil?"

"Nope." Mal folded his arms. "But he upped the price a little." The store owner's eyes glinted all of a sudden. "I wonder what he'd do if I called him up and asked for a cool million?"

"I think," Silas said calmly, "that he would realize something was up and that his little secret is out, and do we want him to know that?"

"Good point." Mal stroked his beard. "Though I like the idea of having a little fun with him."

"Mal."

Hope glanced around and saw Nate coming, making his way down the aisle to where they were all standing.

"What's up?" Mal put his hands on the counter and leaned on them. "Seen Harry? Got the rod he wanted."

"No. Harry's not why I'm here." Nate glanced at Hope and Silas. "You might be interested to hear this too."

"Don't tell me," Hope said, having an idea already. "You got another call from the same man who offered to buy the lease on the Gold Pan?"

Nate frowned, his dark eyes narrowing. "Yeah, how did you know?"

"Because I got a call too," Mal said. "This guy is sure spreading the love around."

Damn. The sick feeling in Hope's gut churned. Her mother would be on that list no doubt. Maybe she'd even received a call already. Hell, maybe she'd even accepted the offer, because there was no telling with Angela.

"I've got to get back to the Moose," Hope muttered, already turning for the exit. She at least had to tell Angela that there was another potential buyer for the Moose's lease. That she couldn't sell it to some oil company who might potentially knock it down to get to the riches under the ground.

"Hope," Silas said.

But she ignored him, walking quickly out of Mal's and down the steps, stepping onto the boardwalk outside and heading toward the Moose.

Sandy was in the process of unlocking the tourist information center and gave Hope a wave, saying something to her. But Hope didn't have time for conversation. She gave Sandy a vague wave in return before hurrying on to the Moose and pushing the door open.

It was its usual dark and vaguely disreputable self, the way it always was in the afternoon, nothing unusual there. What was unusual was that her mother was standing behind the bar and appeared to be wiping it down with a cloth.

Hope let the door swing shut behind her, frowning. "Mom? What are you doing?"

Angela didn't stop her wiping. "What does it look like? I'm cleaning this place up." She gave a cursory look around, her gaze lingering on the taxidermied heads on the walls and the low-beamed ceiling, then sniffed. "It's a disgrace."

"Why are you cleaning?" Hope moved over to the bar, puzzled and not a little weirded out because her mother almost never set foot in the bar, let alone cleaned it. "I normally do that."

"I know. And I think you need to do a better job." Angela scrubbed at the bar top, not looking up.

Hope stood on the other side and stared at her. "What's going on?" She didn't really have to ask. She already had a suspicion, but she wanted to hear it from her mother first.

Angela scrubbed hard at a nonexistent spot. "We need to get this place looking good."

"Mom."

Finally her mother looked up. "Okay, so that guy called again with another offer. A better one. And you weren't here, so I thought, why not?"

Hope's heart sank. "Please don't tell me you agreed."

"Of course I agreed," Angela snapped. "It was a lot of money."

Anger turned over in Hope's stomach, a harsh, bitter feeling she could almost taste. "You know that guy's from an oil company, right? Mal got a call from him too and he managed to track down the guy's number."

Angela only shrugged. "So?"

"*So*?" Hope echoed, knowing the word was too sharp. Getting angry at her mother wouldn't help and it only upset her, but Hope couldn't keep it locked down the way she should. "Mom, do you have any idea what these people are like? What they'll do to the town?"

"No, I don't. And neither do you. And quite frankly, maybe it would be a good thing to have a whole bunch of strangers here. Shake this place up a bit, because God knows it could sure use it."

Hope stared at her mother, appalled. "So you have no problem with turning Granddad's bar over to someone who'll probably knock it down so they can start drilling? Who doesn't give a damn about the livelihoods of the people who live here?"

A bitter kind of fury etched itself into the lines of Angela's still-lovely face. "You think I care about this damn town? You think I care about this stupid bar?" She threw the cloth she was holding onto the bar top. "Well, I don't. I don't give two shits about it. It's a prison, this place. And you have no idea, but it was your goddamn grandfather who held the key."

A wave of shock went through Hope. Her mother never talked about her own father, and Hope had always thought it had something to do with grief. But there was no doubting the bitterness in Angela's voice. "What do you mean he held the key?"

Angela's jaw was set, her thin, angular face rigid. "I know you thought the sun shone out of your grandfather's ass, but he was no goddamn saint. Sure, he looked after me when you were born, helped me through the depression. But after I got better, I wanted to take you away. I wanted to get out of here, have a life somewhere else." Her mouth twisted. "Dad refused to let me go. Told me I didn't need to go anywhere else, that the town could give me what I needed. I was dependent on him, and he...made it difficult for me to go. I insisted and so he told me that if I was really set on leaving, then I could. But he would keep you here."

The shock inside Hope deepened. Really, it had been quite the day for surprises, and she was kind of over them. But her grandfather had really said that? Had threatened to keep her? Her grandfather hadn't been a demonstrative man. He'd been typical of the folk in these parts, tough, hard. No-nonsense in the extreme. But would he really have threatened to take his granddaughter away from his own daughter?

"But...why?" she asked. "Why would he do that?"

Angela lifted her chin. "He didn't like me being sick with that 'head stuff.' He was suspicious of it, didn't understand it. He thought you'd be at risk if I took you away on my own, told me that you would be safer here with him."

Hope's throat closed, guilt tugging at her. "So, what? You just stayed?"

"What else was I supposed to do?" The anger in her

mother's eyes glowed hot. "I couldn't leave you. And I didn't have any money of my own. So yes, I stayed."

The lump in Hope's throat grew bigger. "I was the key then, wasn't I? I was the key that locked the door."

"Yes," her mother said bluntly. "What kind of mom leaves her own kid? I'd already failed you by getting sick. I couldn't fail you by leaving."

Hope didn't know why she felt so raw about this, why it felt like this was scraping the edges of her heart. Her mother hadn't been demonstrative either, clearly taking cues from her own father, and there had been times when Hope had wondered whether her mother even wanted her at all. Whether she blamed Hope for how her own life had turned out. And part of Hope had already decided that no, her mother hadn't cared about her. Or at least she'd never seemed to.

But now, to hear that Angela had made the choice to stay because she hadn't wanted to leave Hope, well, it somehow made her guilt even worse.

"You didn't have to," Hope said before she could stop herself, her hands clenching. "You could have left years ago if you'd wanted to."

"Yes," Angela replied. "I could have. But I didn't."

"Why not? You could have at any time."

Her mother glanced away. "When someone tells you that you're not to be trusted on your own, that you're not to be trusted even to look after your own child…it gets stuck in your head, and sometimes it's difficult not to believe them."

Hope's own anger simmered inside her. A selfish anger. Because how could she direct that at her mother? If what Angela had said was true about her grandfather—and honestly, Hope thought it probably was—then what right did Hope have to feel angry about it? It was the guilt clawing at her, and she was so tired of it.

Don't make this about you.

No, she shouldn't. Her mother had obviously been treated badly by her father, but that didn't stop the feelings from flooding through Hope all the same. That her mother hadn't told her any of this. That she'd been used as a tool to manipulate Angela. That her mother had wanted to go, and yet, when the man who'd held that "key" to the doors of her prison had died, she'd stayed.

And Hope had stayed with her, thinking she had no other choice.

"Why did you stay?" she demanded, unable to keep quiet. "Why didn't you go after Granddad died?"

Angela's mouth was hard. "Why do you think? Because I was scared, Hope. Because I thought he was right."

"But I stayed." She shouldn't have said it, but she couldn't help herself. "I stayed here for you. You know that, right?"

Her mother was silent a long time, and Hope couldn't have said what was going on behind those dark eyes. Though for a moment she looked as hard and as blunt as Hope's grandfather had. "Yes, I know you did," Angela said at last. "And I was thankful that you did, don't get me wrong. But I also know it was me who kept you here."

"Mom—"

"For the longest time I was angry at you for staying, Hope. Because it felt like Dad all over again. It felt like you thinking I couldn't look after myself. And I was angry at myself too, for being too afraid to leave. For doing nothing here and letting all those years go by. But that phone call…" She stopped and took a breath. "It got me thinking about my life. It got me thinking about what I could do with that money. It made me see all the lies I've been telling myself, and I'm done with them."

Hope understood and she could see where her mother was coming from. But that didn't change the anger inside her, that didn't make it any less or make it go away. All she could think about was that she'd stayed here for nothing. She'd thrown all her dreams of a college degree away to look after a woman who hadn't needed it after all. A woman who'd simply been too afraid to leave.

Seriously? You've been using her as an excuse for years. And you're not angry at her. You're angry with yourself because now you're face-to-face with the reasons why you stayed.

But she knew that already, didn't she? That's why she'd made the decision to leave Deep River. So she could finally stop letting her fear of reaching for what she wanted stop her.

Fear is a nice excuse, but was it really fear? Or were you just happy to play the martyr? Because you wanted to prove yourself to her?

The thought whispered in the back of her head, insidious.

And then behind her, the door banged shut.

"Hope?" Silas's dark, gritty voice wound around her, and she had the terrible urge to turn and run straight into his arms, let him hold her.

But she resisted it.

"Silas," Angela said, giving him an unfriendly look. She'd never been approving of him, and Hope had always assumed it was because she wasn't approving of boys in general. Understandable given her own personal experiences. "Maybe you could come back at another time. Hope and I were just having a discussion."

"No, I don't think I will." Silas was suddenly right next to her, though she hadn't heard him move. The damn man was soundless as a cat. "What did you say to her, Angela?"

"This isn't any of your business," Angela snapped.

"Actually, considering I'm going to be buying the Moose, I'd say it's definitely my business."

Silas had no idea what was going on between Hope and her mother, but he knew the moment he'd walked into the Moose that something was going on. Hope had been standing there with her back to the door, but he hadn't needed to see her face to know that whatever was going down, it wasn't good. Hope's posture was rigid, her back poker-straight, her shoulders hunched. And her hands were in fists at her sides.

Angela was standing behind the bar, a hard expression on her face, though Silas had to say that was nothing new. Angela Dawson had always looked like she'd been sucking on a particularly sour lemon.

Except there was anger in the air, he could feel it, and it was sparking in Angela's dark eyes. And he knew that whatever it was, it had to do with the Moose. Nothing else would have gotten Hope so upset.

"What do you mean you're buying the Moose?" Angela demanded, her gaze narrowing on him.

"I offered to buy it from Hope." He put his hand on her rigid back to ease her, hoping the warmth of his touch would help. "She agreed."

Angela's dark gaze flicked to Hope, then back again, and he could see the suspicions growing, noting how close he was standing to her daughter and no doubt drawing her own conclusions. "I didn't agree. And my name is on the lease. And anyway, I already agreed to another offer, so you're too late."

An intense, protective urge washed through him, and he didn't fight it. Instead, he put one hand on Hope's hip and drew her in close to his side, making it very clear where his loyalties lay. "Whatever your offer, I can do better," he said, meeting her gaze squarely. "Name your price."

He couldn't really afford it, not when the business was just getting off the ground, but he couldn't let the Moose get into the hands of whatever oil person was making offers on all these leases. Even one property was one property too many.

Angela's gaze dropped to where his hand rested on Hope, then narrowed even further. "You can't afford it, I'm afraid," she said flatly.

Hope remained rigid for a moment, and then just like that, she relaxed against him. He was overstepping the mark by laying claim to her like this, but he'd wanted her to know that he was on her side.

Besides, it feels right to hold her like this, doesn't it?

It felt more than right. It felt like it was meant to be.

He let that thought sit a moment in his head, his fingers tightening on her, meeting her mother's disapproving gaze. "I think you'll find I can," he said just as flatly. "Name it, Angela. I won't let this property fall into the hands of people who are only going to exploit this town."

"Oh, the way you're exploiting my daughter?"

Hope's hand suddenly covered his. "Don't be stupid, Mom." Anger threaded through her voice. "He's not exploiting me. We're together for a little while, that's all."

"I see." Angela's tone made it clear that she did see and that she didn't much like it. "And so if she gets pregnant, you'll naturally stay here and bring up the child with her, right?"

"Mom, for God's sake!" Hope said angrily. "I'm not going to get pregnant."

"That's what I thought too and look what happened to me."

"Yes," Silas said, because he had to. "I would stay and help her bring it up."

There was a stunned silence.

Hope had stiffened, but Angela only gave him an intense, piercing look. "Really? Most men wouldn't."

"I'm not most men."

Angela snorted. "High opinion of yourself. Then you always did, didn't you?"

But Silas was getting impatient with this conversation, and he had no time for Angela getting annoyed with him for being with her daughter. "I've decided I'm going to stay anyway," he said. "So good luck with legally being able to accept the offer you received. It won't be binding unless this guy is actually planning on staying in town."

Hope's mother chewed on her lip for a second, obviously not pleased with having this pointed out to her. Then she glanced at Hope. "So I guess you're staying as well? Throwing everything away for someone else again?"

"No." Hope's voice was hard. "I've decided to leave."

Something passed over Angela's angular features that Silas couldn't interpret. "So you're okay with me selling—"

"No," Hope repeated. "I'm not okay with it. Yes, we'll need the money, but I don't want this place passing into the hands of a stranger. I want it to go to Silas."

Her mother said nothing, staring at the two of them. "I don't know why you have such a loyalty to this place, Hope," she said after a long moment. "It was never anything but a millstone for the both of us."

"Maybe it's not so much about the building," Hope said. "I know you were never happy here, Mom, but I was. And this town means something to me. Even if I leave it, I still want to know it's here and still the same.

That it won't suddenly be flattened by a whole bunch of rich assholes from the city."

Angela chewed again on her lip, giving nothing away. Then, finally, she said, "Okay, fine. If you have an offer, Silas, you'd better bring it to me and I'll think about it." She turned to the door that led to the stairs and strode out without another word.

Hope abruptly shoved his hand from her hip and stepped away from him, moving toward the bar before coming to a stop and turning. Anger glowed in her dark eyes, though Silas didn't know if it was all directed at her mother or whether some of that was for him. "You shouldn't have done that."

No, it was for him—and he probably deserved it.

"What?" He folded his arms, resisting the urge to go to her, pull her back into his arms again. "Show your mother the lay of the land?"

"I didn't want anyone to know. And you said it was just between you and me."

"I wanted your mother to know you weren't on your own. That I agreed with you."

"Which could have involved you simply standing beside me as a friend, not…" She gestured wordlessly.

"What? Not putting my hands on you and making it clear that we are an item?"

"But we're not an item, Si." She let out a breath and turned away. "That was the whole point of not telling anyone. And now you've just made this even more complicated."

He frowned. "How?"

"You know Mom's history." Hope went over to the bar, going behind it. "She had an affair with some guy and ended up with me and…" She stopped, picking up a cloth that sat balled up on the bar top. "Granddad kept her here. Mom just told me. She couldn't care less about the bar because she's still angry with Granddad. Because when she told him she wanted to leave, he told her that she could go but that I would have to stay here. He wouldn't let her leave with me."

Hell, had that been what he'd walked into just before? No wonder there had been so much tension in the air.

"And now I'm angry at her," Hope went on, looking up at him. "Which I shouldn't be. Because that's a terrible thing to do to someone, to use their own child against them like that. But…" Her hand closed around the cloth. "She stayed for me, she said. And because she was afraid that Granddad was right when he told her that she couldn't look after me. That's why she stayed here even after Granddad died."

Si studied her face. A kind of directionless rage that felt somehow familiar to him gleamed in her eyes. He'd felt the same way about his father, even though he knew he shouldn't. A helpless fury that the old man couldn't be happy without alcohol in him, even though his own son was right there to help.

"It's okay to be angry with her," he said. "She should have told you all of this."

"Yes. Yes, she should have. I just…what was the point

of me staying here, then? All those years ago? I did it for her, to look after her. And she didn't need it."

"But you did." He could see it now, the hurt gleaming in her eyes. And it made sense to him all of a sudden. "You needed her. You were trying to prove something to her, weren't you?"

Hope looked away. "She never told me she loved me, not once. Not in all the years since Granddad died."

The pain in her voice cut him like a knife, and it was all he could do to remain standing there, to not go over to where she stood and take her in his arms. Tell her the truth that had been in his heart so long that it had become part of him.

That he loved her. He'd always loved her. But telling her would accomplish nothing but adding more complications to an already complicated situation. She'd made a decision that had been hard for her, and he didn't want to do anything that might compromise it.

Besides, love was a burden, as he knew all too well, and she didn't need to carry that along with everything else.

So he didn't tell her. Instead, he said, "She does love you, Hope. If she didn't, she would have gone and left you with Bill."

"Maybe." Hope kept her gaze turned away. "Look, I've got a few things to do right now, so do you mind if we have this conversation later?"

"Hope—"

"Please."

The soft plea in the word caught at him and he was powerless against it, even though his instinct was to stay, to hold her, make her feel better any way he could.

If all you can think about is telling her you love her, maybe you could use some distance yourself.

Yeah, and wasn't that the truth?

"Okay," he said gruffly. "I'll be around if you need me." He turned to go.

"Si." Hope's voice was quiet.

He looked back, but there was a part of him that somehow already knew what she was going to say. "Yeah?"

The expression on her face was guarded, and the suspicion inside him became a certainty; she hadn't looked at him like that since they'd started sleeping together. But something had changed, and he wasn't sure what it was.

"I think I need a couple of nights on my own," she said, confirming it. "Just to get a few things straight in my head."

He wanted to ask her what it was that she needed to get straight, because he could help. She didn't need to do this by herself. And anyway, they didn't have much time together, so why waste it?

But that would have been selfish of him. So all he said was, "Fine. Just let me know if you need anything."

Then he turned on his heel and left.

Chapter 15

SI STOOD AT THE BOTTOM OF THE GRAVEL DRIVE THAT led up to Filthy Phil's place, having the kind of conversation with Damon that he should have had where the reception was better. But his friend had called him to update him on the situation with Wild Alaska, and he needed to tell Damon about his decision to stay in Deep River anyway, so he'd answered the call.

Damon had not taken any of it well.

"You're staying?" Damon sounded furious. "Why the fuck would you want to do that?"

Si gritted his teeth. It wasn't that he hadn't expected this kind of response, but after the past few days, he didn't have the patience for it. Not when he didn't have Hope in his bed at night.

She'd wanted distance, and so for the past few days, he'd given it to her, not imposing himself, waiting until she came to him. But she wasn't coming to him. She closed herself in her office during the day, and the past few times he'd knocked and gone in to see if she was okay, she'd barely looked at him.

He had no idea what was going on, but it was pissing him off, even though he knew he had no right to be pissed off. They weren't together in any real way. She wasn't his girlfriend. And if she didn't want to sleep with him, she wouldn't. But it still annoyed him.

"Because Cal left this town to us," he snapped down

the phone. "And because I was born here. It's my home-town. And I know you don't give a shit about that kind of thing, but I have a responsibility."

"What about your responsibility to me and this damn company?" Damon demanded. "What am I supposed to do now if you're staying in that little shithole?"

Si scowled. "You think I'm simply going to walk away and leave you and Zeke to deal with it? You know me, Damon. You know I wouldn't do that. Also, Deep River is not a shithole."

There was a silence on the other end of the phone.

"So what are you going to do, then?" Damon asked at last, still sounding angry, his voice crackling with static.

But Si wasn't in the mood to deal with his friend's anger, especially not when the reception was so crappy. "I'll call you when I know," he said and hit disconnect.

Then he stood there for a second, trying to get a handle on his temper, staring out at the mountains with their crisp caps of snow and the green tide of the bush lapping around their bases. The river flowed through all that green in a wide silver strip, and from where he was on the side of the hill, he could also see the town at the edge of the river below, all those familiar, slightly ram-shackle buildings clinging to its bank.

It was a beautiful day, with the air clear and the sky a brilliant blue backdrop, showcasing Deep River's true riches. It wasn't the black stuff underneath the ground, but those mountains and bush. The ribbon of the river and the small, quirky town that sat on the edge of it.

His anger dissipated, his heart abruptly full. And if he hadn't been sure before, he was suddenly sure now. *This* was what had brought people to Deep River—the environment that surrounded them—and this was what made them stay. This was what was going to make him stay too, because he couldn't let it all be given to people who cared only about what they could exploit from under the ground. Who cared only about the money.

It's the people who matter, too, don't forget that.

That was true. People like Mal, who'd made him dust shelves as a punishment, a punishment that Si had secretly enjoyed since it got him out of the house and away from his dad. And April, who used to sneak him donuts after school when he hung around the diner, not wanting to go home. And there had been others who were kind to him, who knew what had been going on with Joshua Quinn and his lonely son.

That was edging into territory he didn't want to think about, so he turned from the view and made his way up the narrow gravel drive to Phil's rundown old house.

He'd once spent a bit of time here. Phil had given Si odd jobs to do while telling him stories of his days on the traplines. He'd also let Si talk as much as he wanted about his mother, and that was something Si had never forgotten.

They called him Filthy Phil, but not because he was filthy, but because he'd once dropped a Bible on his foot in church and let forth such a stream of curse words that the whole town had been talking about it for days.

Now, the old ex-hunter was sitting on his porch in what was obviously a hand-carved chair and doing something with his hands. And it wasn't until Si got closer that he saw what it was.

Phil was knitting something small with bright red yarn. He didn't look up from his work as Si approached the rickety wooden stairs that led up to the porch.

"Good to see you, boy," was all he said. "Did you bring my books with you?"

Si had mentioned to Mal that he was going to visit Phil, and Mal had told him to stop by Deep River's little library before he went. Phil had a weekly delivery of library books, usually brought up to his house by Mal or Astrid, since the old man didn't come down into town often.

So Si had stopped by the library before he'd gotten a ride up to Phil's from Sonny Clarke, who owned the gas station, and had been amused at the selection. Apparently Phil's tastes in reading were wide ranging—there was a thriller, a mystery, one or two nonfiction books, plus a couple of romances.

"Yeah," Si said, coming up the wooden stairs. "I got them for you." He put them down on the small table that sat next to Phil's chair—another beautifully hand-carved piece. "You chose these yourself?"

"No. I let Astrid pick 'em." Phil finally glanced up from his knitting, surprisingly sharp blue eyes gleaming from underneath bushy white eyebrows. "And yeah, before you say anything, I like love stories." His grin turned wicked in his white beard. "Makes an old man feel young again."

Si grinned back. He hadn't seen Phil since he'd returned, but in many ways, the old guy hadn't changed.

He still looked like he'd been handcrafted out of old leather, his skin weather-beaten and lined by the years spent out in the elements, but his mind was still sharp as a tack and apparently his sense of humor was still fully operational too.

"Hey," he said, "doesn't everyone need to feel young again every so often?"

"True, true." Phil's hands worked rhythmically at his knitting, the metal needles clicking. "You want to talk to me about this oil nonsense?"

Si leaned back against the porch railing. "You know all about that?"

Phil snorted. "Of course I do. I may not go down into town much, but that doesn't make me ignorant about town goings-on."

"Fair enough." He stared at the old man. "What do you think about it?"

"It's bullshit. Not that it matters what I think. I'm not going to be here for too much longer anyway. It's a decision that you young folk will have to make."

Si raised a brow. "What? You planning on dying in the next few months?"

"Don't think that's up to me."

"Your opinion is still important."

"Didn't say it wasn't. Only that I don't have to deal with the consequences, which, come to think of it, might make me see things differently." The old man nodded to himself. "Could use a little money to make my old age easier."

"You don't want the money," Si said.

"Don't I?" Phil finished a row and then turned his work around to start the next. "My military pension doesn't stretch that far."

Yeah, sure. The old man was shit-stirring, and Si was well aware. Phil had been born in this town, had left to fight for his country a couple of times before returning to do what his father had done before him, which was to earn a living in the mountains he loved, hunting and trapping. In fact, quite a few of the heads on the walls of the Moose had come from Phil.

He was too old for it these days, and even before Si had left, Phil had started turning the property his family had leased into a wildlife sanctuary—giving back to the land what he'd taken, or at least that's what he'd told Si once.

Anyway, the upshot was that Phil loved this place, and Si knew it. The last thing he'd want would be to hand over his lease to some oil company that would ruin what he'd spent the last few years building.

"And yet your place is in pretty good repair," Si pointed out. "Though I see some of the shingles on the roof need replacing."

Phil gave a cackling laugh. "You notice things, boy. Always did."

"And you're a shit-stirrer. Always have been."

"True," Phil acknowledged, clearly enjoying himself.

"My grandson visits from Anchorage every so often. He fixes the place up for me."

"He does a good job." And the guy truly did, since although Phil's place was pretty ramshackle, it was all in good repair. "When is he coming back? Because if it's not for a while, I'll give you a hand with the roof."

Phil's bright blue eyes were suddenly very sharp. "Generous offer. I'll take you up on that. Especially since you're apparently going to be staying here."

"I see the jungle telegraph is still working. Who told you that?"

"I have my sources." The old man gave a satisfied nod. "I always knew you'd come back. And once you did, I knew you'd stay."

Si didn't quite know how to take that, whether to be offended that Phil could have anticipated him so easily or to be pleased that at least someone remembered that he wasn't a man to walk away from his responsibilities, even though he had at one time. "What makes you say that?" he asked, keeping his tone casual.

Phil's needles clicked. "Because the girl is still here."

Si went very still. "What girl?"

"You know who I'm talking about." The old man's gnarled hands moved steadily. "You're like your father, Silas. A man of deep emotions. And you can run from those emotions all you like, but they always bring you back."

Si gripped the rail he was leaning against very tightly. He wanted to deny it, say that he was nothing like his father, but in some ways, the old man was right. "Dad didn't run from his emotions." He tried to make his voice sound as neutral as possible. "He went looking for them in a bottle."

That you gave him.

Phil shrugged. "We all find ways of dealing with the shit life throws at us. Some ways are better than others."

"Yeah," Si said, unable to help himself. "And some just get you killed."

"Don't let anger get in the way, boy. Your father was angry at the world for taking June away."

June, his lovely mother. Who'd died very suddenly of a brain aneurysm.

"Yeah," he heard himself say. "Well, he wasn't the only one who was angry." Because in many ways, Si had lost two parents. His mother and then the father that he'd loved. The father who'd changed and only became that man when he'd had half a bottle of vodka inside him.

Phil's gaze was far too perceptive, and it felt like he was seeing past Si's anger and down beneath it to the hurt little boy that was still inside him. "It's not your fault, Silas. Don't take responsibility for your father's bad decisions."

But it was his fault. It always had been.

"I didn't, remember?" Si said shortly. "I ran away instead."

"Did you?" Phil stopped knitting for a second. "Or did you go away to prove a point?"

Something shifted inside him, something uncomfortable. "What makes you say that?" He couldn't quite keep the sharp note out of his voice. "You don't know me, Phil. You don't know why I left."

Phil stared at him for a long moment, then leaned back in his chair, resuming his knitting, his attention back on his hands again. "I was your age once. A bit of a rabble-rouser. A bit of a troublemaker. The town thought I was bad news, and so I decided why bother changing their minds? And I left. I thought I was escaping, but it wasn't until I came back that I realized it wasn't an escape I wanted. I left to prove myself, to show the town what kind of man I was and that they'd be sorry they made me leave. But you know, the funny thing was, they didn't really care what I'd been doing while I was away. The only thing that mattered to them was what I did when I returned."

Si shoved himself away from the railing, the uncomfortable sensation twisting around in his gut no matter how hard he tried to ignore it. "What's that got to do with anything?"

"The present is all that matters, boy. You might think that you're taking responsibility for the town, making up for past sins, yours and your damn father's, but ultimately, the whys don't matter. You don't need to prove yourself. It's the action you take in the present that's important, because the present is all any of us ever have."

Si didn't know what to say to that, because the old man was wrong. He hadn't left to prove himself; he'd left because there was nothing here to hold him. His final responsibility had gone and the last tie had been Hope. And she'd told him to leave.

"Yeah, well, thanks for the philosophy," he said, trying not to sound ungrateful. "But I got a few things to do."

"Sure you do," Phil said, unoffended. "You come up and see me again soon. And bring your hammer for the shingles. Oh, and some more yarn. Doesn't matter what color. It's for the birds."

Si frowned, distracted. "The yarn is for the birds?"

Phil grinned and held up his knitting. It looked like a tiny tank top with overly big armholes "Vests for birds. Keeps 'em from grooming if there's oil on their feathers." He winked. "Albert likes blue."

"Albert?"

"The albatross." Phil went back to knitting. "He's very picky."

Si decided that was his cue to leave.

"Oh, tell Astrid not to send me any of the love story books that stop at the bedroom door," Phil shouted after him as Si excused himself and went down the steps. "I want the hot stuff. I may be seventy-five, but I'm not dead yet!"

———————

Hope sat in front of the computer at Mal's—the one the whole town used when their personal internet connections weren't working, which was frequently. Mal had some kind of satellite link for the computer in his store, which was more reliable, and he'd made it publicly available. You had to pay for the privilege of course, since the link and the data weren't cheap, but Hope didn't mind paying. She was doing some more college research, plus a couple of other banking things, since the internet in her office in the Moose was down.

It had totally nothing to do with the fact that she was avoiding Silas.

Sure you're not.

She wasn't. Why would she need to avoid him? She only needed some distance from his distracting presence. Time away from the relentless pull of her attraction to him and the way he made her feel. The needy vulnerability that gripped her whenever he was around.

She hated that feeling. Just as she hadn't much liked him witnessing everything that had happened with her mother a few days earlier.

She shouldn't have gotten angry with Angela, and she definitely shouldn't have dumped it all on Silas after her mother had left. Shouldn't have said to him that stuff about how Angela had never told her that she loved her. It felt pathetic somehow to reveal that. Pathetic that she'd let it matter. And it shouldn't matter, because she knew on some level that Angela did love her. She didn't need to be told it a thousand times a day.

Don't you?

Whatever, she certainly didn't need Silas watching her with those sharp green-gold eyes, as if he saw all that neediness inside her, saw the depth of her loneliness.

"You needed her. You were trying to prove something to her."

Yeah, and that little observation he'd made hadn't helped. Especially when she had a horrible suspicion that he was right, that she'd stayed not because she was afraid to leave but because she'd wanted to show her mother that she was worthy somehow. That giving up all the things that mattered to her would somehow make her mother say those magic words in return.

But Angela never had, and so Hope had always wondered if there was something about her that prevented her mother from saying it. Perhaps the circumstances of her birth, that Hope was the reason Angela had been forced to stay in town, first because of her mental health after Hope's birth and then because of her father's manipulation.

Perhaps Silas was right. Perhaps it had been love that kept Angela here. Yet that love didn't feel like a good thing. It didn't feel warm or comforting. It only felt resentful and bitter.

God, if that was love, she didn't want any part of it.

That's why you pushed Silas away.

Hope shook her head as if she could shake away that particular thought. She didn't love Silas. As a friend maybe, but nothing more.

But if you don't feel anything for him, then why are you distancing yourself from him?

She growled under her breath and tapped angrily on the keyboard, trying to focus on the screen and not on the voice in her head.

"Hey," Mal said grumpily from behind the counter. "Don't hit the keys too hard. Those keyboards don't last that long."

"Sorry," Hope muttered. She gripped the mouse and

hit print for a few application forms, finished up her banking, then pushed the chair back, getting up to go and retrieve her forms from the printer.

"Town meeting tomorrow night," Mal commented. "Your boy going to be 'fessing up?"

Hope grabbed the forms, folding them up into small, precise squares. "Firstly, he's not my boy, and secondly, 'fessing up to what?"

Mal lifted one big shoulder. "The fact that he's decided to stick around. Which I'm sure means he's going to continue to be the town's new owner."

Hope felt oddly defensive. "Yes, he is. That a problem?"

Mal grinned. "Hey, I didn't say anything was wrong with that. In fact, I told him this town could use him, so I'm more than happy with the situation." He raised a brow. "You sure he's not your boy?"

She could feel her face get hot. "No. He's not staying for me. He felt some responsibility for the town."

"Okay, sure." There was so much obvious skepticism in Mal's voice that Hope couldn't help herself.

"It's *not* me. If it were, he'd be leaving with me, and he isn't."

Mal frowned. "Leaving with you? Where are you going?"

She drew herself up, feeling even more defensive. "I decided I want to go to college. I always wanted to get a literature degree but I never had the chance, and so I thought I'd take the chance now."

"Huh. You sure you need to leave for that? Plenty of colleges do degrees remotely." He grinned. "I got one myself."

It was just the kind of thing Mal would do, since he often came out with surprising things that no one knew about him. But Hope had her reasons for not wanting to study remotely.

"Yeah, well, I don't want to do that," she said. "I want to experience college life, go somewhere different."

"Different's good," Mal replied. "Nothing like going somewhere else to make you understand where you really need to be."

But that sounded too much like one of her granddad's old sayings for comfort, so Hope only made a few non-committal noises, then escaped outside.

She headed straight back to the Moose because she wanted to fill out the application forms ASAP and then get them in the mail. She could have sat there and completed them online, but filling out forms with a sketchy internet connection was a drama, and the mail tended to be more reliable. She was going to have to ask the high school for official transcripts of her academic records as well. Fun.

Pushing open the door to the bar, her head full of all the things she had to do, she didn't immediately see the two people standing behind the bar. Then she did, coming to a surprised stop.

Silas and her mother were looking at a document of some kind and talking. Her mother, for once, was almost smiling.

She hadn't seen Si for a couple of days, and the reality of his presence hit her like a punch to the stomach. He seemed taller somehow, broader, her mother seeming even more tiny and delicate next to him. One of his rare, precious smiles was playing around his beautifully carved mouth, the handsome lines of his face relaxed. He was so hot. He made everything inside her clench tight with longing.

Shoving down the need to go over there and touch him, she asked instead, "What's going on?"

The pair of them lifted their heads. Si's gaze was enigmatic, but she felt that gut punch again as she met it, because apparently that's the way she always felt whenever she looked into his eyes.

"Angela's just accepted my offer for the Moose," he said.

A small electric shock hit her, though she had no idea why, since that's what he'd offered to do a few days ago. "Oh," she said, not knowing what else to say.

"And you'll be pleased to know that I didn't make him go higher than what that other guy offered me." A satisfied look settled over her mother's face. "I'm not greedy. I just want enough to start again without having to struggle the way I did here."

Was that something to be glad about? Or did it just make Hope feel worse? She wasn't sure. She wasn't sure what she felt, period.

Oh, come on, you do. The Moose won't be yours anymore, and you don't like it.

She was conscious suddenly of the weight of the years pressing down on her, of the memories she had of this place. Not all of them good, but not all of them bad either. Her and Cal and Si playing in here in the early mornings, pretending to pull drinks. Making up stories about the animal heads on the walls. And when she was older, creeping downstairs to watch the adults talk and drink, watching Joe and Lloyd fight. And older still, wondering if her granddad would notice if she stole a beer from the fridge, since the problem with being the granddaughter of the bar owner was that you couldn't pretend to be of age, and all the fake IDs in the world weren't going to help.

Then as an adult, after her grandfather had passed away, managing this place and taking pride in how the bar was like a big dining room, with all the families clustered around, talking and drinking, arguing and laughing. A big community, making her feel connected.

A sharp pain started up behind her breastbone, and she had to catch her breath.

"Hope?" Silas's gaze was focused, and she knew that he'd read every thought that had just gone through her head.

So she shut it down, ignored the pain, pasted a smile on her face, since she was tough and she'd made a decision and she wasn't going back on it. "Great." She tried to sound like she meant it. "That's fantastic news."

"Isn't it?" Her mother gave one of Silas's broad shoulders a pat, which was weird considering a couple of days ago she'd looked at him like she wanted to kill him. "Well,

I'll leave you two to sort out the rest. I've got a few things to do."

"You having second thoughts?" Silas asked after Angela had gone.

"No, of course not." Hope forced a smile. "It's wonderful. Mom's obviously ecstatic."

But he clearly wasn't going to let it go. "You didn't seem to think it was so very wonderful just then."

"Of course I have a few regrets," she said, unable to keep the impatience out of her voice. "I've been looking after this place for thirteen years. But this is what I want, and this is what Mom wants, and it's great it's going to someone who'll look after it properly."

He said nothing for a second, only looking at her, and a sudden wave of anger washed through her.

"What?" she demanded. "Stop looking at me like that. It's great, it's wonderful. And I'm so pleased you and Mom are buddies again." She reached into the back pocket of her jeans, grabbing the application forms and brandishing them. "And look, I got all the forms I need for college." She began to head for the door to her office. "So, if you don't mind, I'll just go—"

Silas stepped out from behind the bar all of a sudden, blocking her way.

Brought up short, Hope glared at him. "What?"

He narrowed his gaze; he was a very big, very broad, and very solid brick wall. "What's going on with you, Hope? You've been avoiding me for days now, and I want to know why."

"What for?" she snapped. "Getting sick of your right hand?"

He'd always been slow to anger, those volcanic emotions of his buried so deep that sometimes it was impossible to reach them. But she'd clearly reached them now because an emerald glitter of anger leapt in his eyes.

"You think that's all that's bothering me?" he demanded. "That all I want from you is sex?"

"Well, isn't it?" She knew she was being unfair, knew that this wasn't just about the sex, but she couldn't seem to stop herself. "You haven't exactly been beating down my door to have an actual conversation."

"You told me you wanted distance. So that's what I was giving you."

Of course. So why she was getting annoyed with him she had no idea. And it had nothing to do with the unexpected feeling that kept shifting inside her, a kind of weightlessness, like she was a hot air balloon that had come untethered from its mooring and was floating away, nothing to keep it grounded anymore.

"Then why are you getting in my face again?" She couldn't shut herself up, couldn't stop all the words she didn't mean from coming out.

"Come on, Hope. You should know me better than that."

"Yeah, well, maybe I don't."

His gaze gleamed emerald. Then he reached out suddenly, his hand cupping her cheek in the way he'd done over the past few days, a gesture that never failed to make her heart ache in her chest. The look on his face softened, the anger vanishing to become something else, something more tender. "It's not about the sex though, is it?" His thumb brushed along her cheekbone. "Tell me what's wrong, sweetheart."

Her throat closed, and much to her horror her eyes prickled, and he must have seen it because then his arms were around her and he was gathering her close, and all the fight went right out of her.

She melted into him, completely unable to resist him, not understanding how starved for his warmth and strength she'd been until now. And it was so good to have his arms around her, so good to have him hold her.

Hope pressed her forehead to his chest, closing her eyes, her throat sore. "This was what I wanted," she said, her voice muffled against his T-shirt. "You buying the Moose's lease is perfect, so I don't know why I feel so crappy about it."

His hand was on the back of her head, stroking her hair. "Like you said, you have regrets. That's only natural."

She could hear the beat of his heart, steady and strong and certain, the sound of it soothing her. "I didn't think I would. I thought I could leave this damn place without feeling a thing."

Gently, his fingers came under her chin and he tilted her head back, the sympathy and understanding on his face making the ache in her chest even worse. "I know. I thought the same thing when I left years ago. It was . . . hard, and I didn't think it would be. And it's understandable,

Hope. This is your home. But you made the right choice, okay? You need to go and have the life you always wanted, otherwise you'll regret that more than you'll ever regret leaving."

He was right. She *had* made the right choice, and she knew it. Yet a tiny, almost forgotten part of her was uncomfortable with what he'd said. Almost as if that wasn't what she wanted to hear.

Almost as if she'd wanted him to say something else entirely.

But that was stupid. What else did she want him to say?

She put her hand on his chest, pressing it over that strongly beating heart. "I'm sorry I've been avoiding you." And right now, with his arms around her, she didn't understand why she had. Time with him was limited, and she was done wasting it. "I shouldn't. I don't know what's going on with me. I guess making all these decisions about my future has been tough."

He brushed a lock of hair behind her ear, his touch making her shiver helplessly. "Hey, I get it. Change isn't easy, especially when you've been doing the same thing for so long. But your mom is really excited about it, and I think you should be too."

Hope leaned against him, indulging herself totally in the hard warmth of his body. "You two seem to be friends now."

"Yeah, she forgave me for despoiling her daughter. Especially when I told her I'd match whatever that oil asshole promised her for the Moose." He smiled. "I think she thought I was going to insist you stay here with me and got a whole lot friendlier when I said that you weren't. That you were pretty set on this college idea."

Her stupid heart gave a little shudder at that, and she didn't understand why, so she ignored it. "I am." And she was. Very set.

"Of course you are." His thumb moved along her jaw, his gaze dropping to her mouth. "And now you'll have some money in that college fund."

"Are you sure about this, Si?" She couldn't help but ask. "It's a lot of money, and I know you've got your own business to think about."

"Yes, I'm sure. And you let me worry about my business, okay? Now…" The look in his eyes intensified, making her breath catch. "Are you still after that distance? Or would you mind me getting a little closer?"

There were doubts in her head, doubts she didn't understand, and she didn't want them there. So she put her hands on his chest and rose on her tiptoes, giving him her answer by pressing her mouth to his.

Because if she knew one thing it was that Silas Quinn was very good at getting rid of doubts. Maybe not forever, but for a little while at least.

Chapter 16

THE COMMUNITY CENTER WAS AS FULL AS SI HAD EVER seen it, with people packed in, sitting on the hard wooden benches that were set out in the middle of the hall and, when those had gotten full, standing along the sides and leaning against the walls.

The murmur of voices filled the space, people in deep discussion with each other. Some of the conversations looked heated, but he wasn't getting any angry vibes from anyone. Even from Mike Flint and his little contingent. Sure, Mike had given Si a skeptical look as he'd entered the hall, but it was more *convince me* than *nothing you say will change my mind*.

He hoped that was true. He also hoped it was true of the other people who considered that the oil might be a good thing for the town.

He and Hope had spent the night talking about their ideas for using tourism as an alternative moneymaking idea for Deep River—when they weren't totally indulging themselves in bed, of course—since he was going to be presenting the ideas to the town tonight. He'd wanted to have a strong, cohesive vision, so people knew exactly what they were making a decision about.

He hadn't wanted to tell everyone what they should decide, only present options to them. People had to make up their own minds, since if the whole town wasn't on board, this idea wouldn't work. And he wanted it to work.

Hope stood off to the side, leaning against the wall to his right. He'd asked her if she wanted to speak, but she told him that since she wasn't staying, she really didn't have a right to. He hadn't felt comfortable with that, since a lot of the ideas had come from her, but she'd been adamant.

There had been a moment in the Moose, after she'd found him and Angela making a few last adjustments to the agreement to buy the Moose's lease, where he'd thought he'd caught a glimpse of uncertainty in her eyes.

He hadn't expected her to arrive suddenly like that, especially given how she'd been avoiding him, and then she'd gotten angry. But he knew she was only angry because she was hurt, and the fact that she was having regrets was understandable. He hadn't wanted her to change her mind though. It was important she leave, get that degree she'd always planned on. That was the whole reason he'd taken on the buying of the Moose's lease, after all.

He'd been extremely glad he'd done that, even though it was going to cost him, not to mention cost Wild Alaska, but he'd worry about that later. Because then Hope had let him comfort her and the feel of her warm, soft body against his had driven nearly every other thought from his brain.

She'd forgotten about distance then—they both had—and just as well, since their time together was already limited and soon to get even more so.

Si let his gaze rest on her for a long moment, the lights

of the hall glossing her auburn hair. She was in her usual jeans and red-plaid button-down, nothing special yet she burned brighter than any other person in the hall. Her sharp, precise features were serious as she spoke to Mal, but there was an intensity burning in her lovely dark eyes, that fire that lived inside her.

It's going to hurt when she leaves.

It would probably hurt worse than he expected. But he'd dealt with the loss of her once before and he could again. And he wasn't going to do anything that would hold her back, that was for sure.

He had something special planned for after the meeting to celebrate the Moose and her decision to leave, plus his own decision to stay, and he hoped she would like it. He liked doing things for her since he had a suspicion that not many people did.

"Shall we get this show on the road?" Astrid walked up to him, her teenage son in tow. He'd spoken to her about his and Hope's plans a day or two earlier, and she'd been supportive. Though she'd wanted to know where the money for some of the promotion was going to come from, and that was still to be decided. Now he'd promised to buy the Moose money was going to be in limited supply, and he needed to get together a plan for raising more capital.

"Yeah, do it," he said.

Astrid nodded and called the townspeople to order, her cool voice cutting through all the conversations, and slowly everyone quieted.

"All right," she said, her hands on her hips. "So we all

know why we're here. We've had a week or so to think about this oil business, and we need to make a decision on how to approach it as a group. Because this oil guy who's been calling around is probably going to call around again, and we need to know how we're going to handle it." Astrid paused and gave everyone a stern look. "He won't be the only one, either. Things could get dicey around here in the near future, and the only way Deep River is going to survive it is if we all stand together."

Another murmur ran through the hall like the wind through the trees, a susurration of approval. Which was a good sign.

"Okay," Astrid said. "I'll hand you over to Silas since he's got a few things to tell you."

Si folded his arms and gazed out at the attentive faces turned toward him, and this time he knew every one. Because over the past week, he'd talked to them and he knew their stories. Knew their names. And that satisfied him on a deep level he hadn't been previously aware of.

"I've been talking to most of you over the last few days," he said, addressing them all. "And I think no one likes the idea of a bunch of strangers coming in and telling everyone what to do, people who don't understand us and the way we do things around here. But also, there's been some concerns raised about the vacant leases that have cropped up and the fact that we're not getting in any new blood. Some concerns, too, about finances and how to address them. Because let's face it, who doesn't like having some cash?"

Several people nodded in agreement at this, including Mike and not a few others who hadn't been into the idea of selling their leases. Everyone was worried about feeding their families, no matter where their allegiances lay.

"I have some things to say about that," Si went on. "But first you all need to know something. I've decided to stay in Deep River, which means I'm going to be holding on to the ownership of the Wests' property." He paused, scanning the hall. "Anyone got a problem with that?"

"As long as it doesn't affect the leaseholders, why would we?" someone piped up from the back.

"It won't," Si assured them. "Leaseholders have all the legal rights to their property, and the limitations on the ownership are very clear. Basically, I'm prohibited from selling any of Deep River, even if I wanted to. And let's be clear, I don't want to. Which is why I'm staying. I can't legally be an absentee owner, and since this place is important to me, I've got no choice but to return here to live."

"Great," someone off to Mike's left grunted. "But where does that leave us?"

"That leads me into the next thing I want to talk to you about," Si replied. "I think the town needs some future-proofing. We need to make sure people have a reason to stay here, not take their skills and their knowledge off somewhere else. Or if they do, they come back. And to do that, we need to create some opportunities."

"Sounds good," Mal said, stroking his beard. "But what opportunities are you talking about? It's not as if this place is a hotbed of industry."

"Hey," one of the fishermen said, only partly kidding, "I'm right here."

Mal waved a hand. "You know what I mean."

A ripple of laughter went through the hall.

Si nodded. "Good question. I'm not saying we don't have things to offer already, but what I'm getting from people is that we need more."

"If it's more ideas like Mike's luxury motel, then I'm out," one naysayer at the back shouted, prompting a few muttered comments, both in agreement and not.

"Yeah, that's something we need to discuss," Si said, raising his voice. "Because if we get one guy calling, we're going to get others. And they're all going to be after one thing. It's too late to pretend we can't change, that we don't want to change, because change is coming for us whether we like it or not." He paused, giving the hall another scan. "But what we can do is take charge of that change, be in control of it, make it ours."

"How?" Harry asked bluntly, sitting in the middle of the hall with Gwen, his hippie girlfriend.

"Well," Si said, meeting his gaze, "there's something Deep River has that the rest of the world doesn't. And it's not treasure under the ground. It's all around us. It's the environment we have here. There's magic in this place." His chest suddenly felt tight, but he needed to say it, so he forced the rest out. "I lost that magic as a kid, but coming back here helped me find it again, and I think that's what we could share with people. I think that's what we could use to get people to come here and stay. Deep River is a haven. A place of acceptance, and I think that's what we could offer."

People were nodding at this, approval rippling around the hall.

"That's all very well, but what about money?" Mike asked bluntly.

A few others muttered, but Silas waved them to be quiet, and they settled.

"Like I said, we can use what we already have, though if you're after immediate gains, you'll have to be patient. It's a long-term plan that's going to be more sustainable than oil drilling, and even more important it'll be something the town has control over." He looked away from Mike to include everyone. "I'm talking tourism here."

Several people immediately started to speak, but again he silenced them with a wave of his hand. "I know you don't want strangers, but like I said, leases are falling vacant and aren't being renewed. People are moving away, and hey, I was one of those people. Do we really want the town to disappear?"

There was a silence, but it wasn't one of disagreement, since the question was pretty much rhetorical. Of course no one wanted it to disappear.

"So we need to do something, and we need to use what we have, and tourism is the most logical thing. We can run sightseeing tours, wilderness skills workshops, fishing charters, climbing trips, hiking, animal sanctuaries, all kinds of stuff. And that's just the start. We have people here who have skills, who can share those skills with others too, and I think that's where our strengths are. In our environment and in ourselves."

More silence as people took this in, most nodding in agreement.

Silas went on, "Like I said, it won't mean instant money, but it's a start." He did another scan of the hall. "Now, if you have more ideas, then I want to hear them. Anything you can think of that we can use to promote Deep River and get people interested. This should be a town effort."

"What about the oil guys?" Harry asked. "What do we do about them?"

"We need a plan, but basically I need everyone to be in agreement about it first." He glanced at Astrid. "The mayor here decided that the best way to make a decision on this is to vote. And to make it a private ballot."

"Anyone got any issues with this?" Astrid asked.

No one did. It was the way they decided most things in Deep River, including voting on who got to be mayor. Mal would put a ballot box up on the counter at the market, and people could come in and vote.

"Okay," Mal said. "I'll get the box up tomorrow. How long have people got to decide?"

"Two days," Astrid said crisply. "We need to decide this ASAP."

No one protested, and soon the meeting was called to a close, people filing out of the hall talking furiously as they went.

Hope came up to him, her dark eyes shining with

approval, and a little jolt of pleasure hit him, because he liked her looking at him like that. Liked it far too much.

"That was good, Si," she said. "I think it went well. You gave them a lot to think about."

"I hope so." He quelled his instinctive urge to take her hand and hold it. "Hey, you got some time now?"

Her smile turned wicked. "Why? You have something in mind?"

"Yes, and save that thought for later. Right now, though, there's something else I want to talk to you about."

Her smile faded. "Oh?"

A couple of people were waiting near the door, and he knew they wanted to talk to him. "Can you meet me down by the river? I'll deal with this lot first."

A momentary ripple of puzzlement crossed her face. "The river?"

He met her gaze, hoping she would understand. "Where you, me, and Cal used to meet up. You remember, right?"

Her smile returned, warm and natural. "Yeah, I remember. Okay. Axel will be irritated to fill in behind the bar again, but he'll live."

Si couldn't help himself; he gave in to the urge and reached for her hand, squeezing it gently. "See you down there, then."

Chapter 17

HOPE HAD TO STOP BY THE MOOSE TO GET AXEL TO fill in behind the bar for her, especially since the place was packed with people wanting to gossip about the town meeting over a beer or five. Even Lloyd and Joe's usual evening fight was looking like it was going to be postponed; they were currently deep in discussion about taking potential tourists on a trapping run.

Refusing to let herself get sidetracked, she made her escape as quickly as she could.

It was a beautiful evening, the temperature mild, the stars like a scattering of diamonds across the black velvet of the sky, the mountains tall black shadows in the night. Her head was full of what Silas had talked about at the meeting, about how *this* was the real treasure of Deep River. The mountains. The river. The sky. The natural environment all around.

And the people. Because it was the people who made Deep River truly home.

A small pain tugged at her as she walked along the boardwalk to the end, taking the wooden stairs that led down to the riverbank and the little path that ran along it.

Truly home? It's almost as if you're regretting your decision to leave.

No, she wasn't regretting it. Not at all. College was what she wanted, and no matter how inspired she'd been by Si's speech and all the challenges and changes it was going to mean, she wasn't going back on her decision.

She walked down the path, smiling at the familiarity of it, the utter silence of the night broken only by the sound of the water rushing by and the occasional cry of nocturnal wildlife.

It had been years since she'd been down to the little clearing beside the river, the special place where she, Cal, and Si used to meet. At first she hadn't gone because it reminded her of too many things she hadn't wanted to be reminded of, and then because she'd gotten too busy with life.

A small part of her was afraid of the memories that coming here would prompt, especially after losing Cal, and yet as she walked along the path and saw light flicker and leap through the trees, it wasn't pain that filled her but an aching kind of happiness.

Si had lit a fire on the beach, and all she could think about was the times they'd sat around a fire just like this one, drinking stolen beer and toasting marshmallows. Talking about nothing. Talking about everything. Cal making them both laugh, because he could always make them laugh. Si making the odd dry comment. Herself teasing both of them.

Good times. Happy times.

She stepped off the path and walked slowly down to the sandy flat area beside the river, her eyes prickling with unexpected and very stupid tears at what awaited her.

Because not only had Si lit a fire but he'd also dug

little holes in the sand to put cans of beer in, the way they used to do, so they wouldn't fall over. And in lieu of the sweatshirts they would pull off to sit on, there were a couple of cushions. A giant bag of marshmallows lay between the cushions, along with some sharpened sticks—she and Cal had always agreed that Si made the best marshmallow-toasting sticks.

Best of all was Si himself standing there waiting for her, the flames flickering over his handsome face, highlighting his strong jaw and straight nose, the deep hollows of his eyes and his high forehead. A compelling face. Magnetic, powerful. And the way he was standing, certain and sure. Rooted to the earth like the mountains, a solid, comforting presence.

It struck her in that moment that although she was going to miss those mountains, the rushing river, and the big bowl of the sky, the clean freshness of the air and the ramshackle cluster of buildings that was the town, she was going to miss Silas Quinn even more.

It's not just the people that make it home. It's him.

This time, she couldn't pretend she hadn't thought it. Couldn't pretend that thought hadn't always been there, waiting in the back of her mind. That maybe, just maybe, Deep River hadn't felt like home all these years because he hadn't been there. And that the reason she was having these doubts about leaving now was because he was staying.

You're in love with him, fool. When are you going to admit it?

It felt like she'd ducked her head under the icy water of the river and now her hair was dripping, trickling under the collar of her shirt and sliding down her spine in cold rivulets, making her shiver.

She didn't want to admit it. She didn't even want to think it. But it seemed like the time for denial was done. Because the feeling in her heart was too big, too powerful to ignore. And more, it felt wrong to ignore it, deny it.

She did love him. Maybe she'd even loved him years ago when they were teenagers sitting beside the fire and talking. When they were children playing fairy tales in the bush.

As she'd told them both that terrible night that she had to stay, and then he'd offered to stay with her.

She hadn't been ready for everything it would have meant back then. Hell, she wasn't sure she was ready for it now.

His hands were thrust into the pockets of his jeans, and as she came to a stop on the opposite side of the fire, his mouth curved in a smile, his eyes gone a brilliant gold.

"Thought I'd recreate a little of the past." His voice was deep and dark over the crackling of the flames. "What do you think?"

She swallowed hard, forcing the words out. "It's fantastic, Si. I love it."

His smile deepened. "Good. Sit down, let's have a beer. I'll even toast you a marshmallow."

"Can't argue with that. You always did have the best toasting skills."

He inclined his head, obviously taking his due, and then they both sat. And a strange tension began to build inside her. Her heart felt too big for her chest, her skin sensitized like in the winter when she'd been wearing winter clothes so long she'd almost forgotten what it felt like to have the air on her bare flesh. And the thoughts in her head were going around and around.

Did he feel the same way about her? Was this why he'd asked her down here? He'd told her he'd wanted to talk to her about something... Was it a confession? That he felt the same way about her as she did about him? Maybe that he wanted her to stay? And if he did ask her to stay, would she? Would knowing he felt the same way change her decision to leave?

She remembered the day before when he'd pulled her into his arms after he'd signed the agreement with her mother, how he'd told her that she needed to go and have the life she'd always wanted. And she'd felt vaguely hurt by that. As if she'd been expecting him to say something else.

You wanted him to tell you to stay. Because the life you always wanted is right here.

Hope reached for the beer sitting in its little hole in the sand and pulled it out, the metal cold against her fingers. Her heartbeat was fast and her breathing had sped up along with it, and she knew she was thinking like a crazy woman.

He wasn't going to say any such thing, so why she was thinking that he might she had no idea.

She popped the tab and took a sip, watching as Silas took a couple of marshmallows out of the bag and put them on the end of the sticks.

"What are you doing over there?" Holding on to the sticks with one hand, he extended his arm, clearly indicating for her to sit right next to him.

"Hey, this is where the cushion is." Hope grinned, trying to quiet her raging heartbeat.

"Well, shift it over." His eyes gleamed in the firelight. "Come on, I'm cold."

She huffed a little to tease him but moved around the fire, coming to sit beside him, leaning in to the warmth of his body that somehow seemed even warmer than the fire itself.

His arm settled around her, holding her close as he extended the marshmallows toward the fire.

Silence fell, and the tension inside Hope gathered tighter for absolutely no reason.

"So," she said at last, when it didn't seem like he was going to say anything, "what's all this for?"

Silas inspected the marshmallows, then extended the stick toward the flames again, giving her a brief glance. "I thought a little celebration was in order."

"Celebration?" Her breath caught and she felt as if she was standing on the edge of a precipice. "What for?"

"You leaving. Me staying. And a pretty damn successful town meeting."

That shouldn't have made her stomach dip or cause a cold wash of disappointment to flood through her. Of course he wasn't going to tell her that he loved her or even that he had feelings for her. Why had she been expecting he would? Where on earth had that thought even come from? This affair they'd been having had always been temporary, and she knew that. Hell, she'd even insisted on it. There were no feelings, none.

So why are you feeling so very disappointed? So you love him. So what?

Hope swallowed and took a sip of her beer, conscious of the warmth of the hard, masculine body she was leaning against. And suddenly she couldn't bear to be near him.

She pulled away, sitting up instead, staring at the fire, fighting to keep her feelings from her expression, knowing she was probably failing.

"Hey," Si said, sounding puzzled. "What's up?"

"Nothing." A reflexive response that wasn't going to convince anyone, let alone him.

"Bullshit it's nothing."

She stared hard at the flames, holding on to her beer, not wanting to look at him. Afraid that if she did, everything would come spilling out. "Just tired."

"Hope."

There was tenderness in his voice that made her throat close, that made her want to cry. And she knew she couldn't lie to herself anymore. Couldn't pretend that she hadn't been secretly hoping he'd tell her that he wanted her to stay. That he loved her. That he'd always loved her.

She'd been running from that hope ever since he'd turned up at the Moose a week ago. Desperately telling herself that she didn't want anything more permanent, that she didn't want what her whole soul had felt starved of.

And it wasn't much to want, was it? Just to feel like she wasn't a burden to someone, the locked door of someone's prison. The sole caretaker of a legacy she'd never wanted in the first place. No, what she wanted was only to feel like she was important to someone. Precious to someone. That wasn't wrong—it wasn't.

A warm hand touched her back, searing her skin, and she'd shaken it off before she could stop herself.

"Hope," Silas said again, sharper this time. "What's wrong?"

"You want me to go, don't you?" She shouldn't be talking about this, shouldn't be revealing everything she was feeling, but she couldn't help it.

"Of course I want you to go. This is what you've been wanting to do ever since—"

"What if I changed my mind?" she interrupted and turned her head, meeting his gaze. "What if I decided I want to stay?"

An expression she couldn't read flickered over his face, then he frowned, the firelight reflected in his eyes, making them seem even more brilliantly gold than they already were. "You can't stay," he said, as if it were his decision, not hers. "You wanted to go to college, Hope. Get that literature degree. That's what you always wanted to do."

"I can get a degree remotely." She was holding her beer

way too tightly, but now that she was on this path, she had to keep going. "Mal told me he'd done one. I could stay here. I don't actually have to leave if I don't want to."

"But you do want to." Silas's expression hardened. "That's what you told me. That's what you wanted."

"Maybe I don't want that anymore." Her jaw was tight, her heart aching, and she knew she shouldn't tell him, but this was important. And she was tired of pretending, tired of denying. Tired of not thinking about things that made her feel uncomfortable.

It was time to confront them. Because if the past thirteen years had taught her one thing, it was that if you didn't at least try to reach for what you wanted, all you'd ever get was a handful of nothing.

And she was tired of having nothing as well.

She held his gaze. "Maybe I want something else."

His expression was absolutely unreadable. Abruptly, he dropped the marshmallow sticks and stood up in a sharp, jerky movement. Then he turned and walked toward the river a couple of steps and stopped, his back to her.

For a long moment, there was no sound but the rushing of the river and the crackle of the flames.

And the breaking of Hope's heart.

He didn't need to say anything. He'd obviously seen it in her eyes. And his reaction had told her everything she needed to know about his feelings on the subject.

He didn't want her to stay.

He didn't want her.

That's a lie, though. You know he wants you.

Only physically. And maybe he liked playing the supportive friend—he'd always liked to feel needed, Silas did—and he tended toward being a white knight. Obviously sweeping back into Deep River and dramatically rescuing the town and then rescuing her had been satisfying to him.

But it had never been about more than that. It was she who'd wanted it to be.

"Don't," Silas finally said in a low, fierce voice. "Don't stay because of me, Hope."

"Why not?" She had nothing left to lose now, so why not lay it all out there? "Why shouldn't I stay for you?"

He was a tall dark shadow beyond the firelight. "Because you wanted to go—"

"But what if what I really wanted, what I've wanted for years and years and never realized, was you?"

The words echoed around them, falling into a vast cavernous silence, and her heart ached and ached because he hadn't turned around. He wasn't coming over to where she sat and pulling her to her feet, kissing her, holding her as if he never wanted to let her go. No, he was only standing still, every line of him tense, as if he was bracing himself, waiting for a blow to fall.

"You don't want me, Hope." He stayed turned away. "It was just sex, that's all."

That hurt. That hurt a lot. "It was more than just sex, Si." She tried to keep her voice neutral, to not let the hurt show. "It was way more than that and you know it."

"But that's all it was supposed to be. That was all this whole thing was supposed to be."

Slowly, she put down her beer and then got to her feet. "I know it was. But then it changed. And you talking in the meeting tonight about the environment—about the people... I realized how much like home this place has felt recently. More than it has in years. And the reason for that is you, Si. You make Deep River feel like home to me, you always have."

He shook his head. "You can't—"

"Because I'm in love with you," she said, because she had to say it. She needed to. It was too big to keep inside anymore, no matter how exposed and vulnerable it made her feel. "I think I've loved you for years and never realized. Not until tonight. Not until now."

———————————

Every muscle in Si's body had gone tense, and he couldn't relax them. He stared into the darkness where the river flowed, his jaw aching, everything aching, the words he'd always fantasized hearing from her echoing around him.

She was in love with him. She'd loved him for years.

He'd imagined her saying those words, had imagined it many, many times. Yet now he had the reality, it felt nothing like he'd thought it would. He didn't feel happy or satisfied or relieved or overwhelmed.

What he felt was furious.

He was the one who was in love. *He* was the one with

all the helpless longing, not her. She was never supposed to reciprocate. She was never supposed to fall for *him*.

What she was supposed to do was leave, to go and have a goddamn life, while he was supposed to stay here. Alone.

Safe, don't you mean?

No, it had nothing to do with safety. Or certainly not about his. It was about hers. It was about protecting her. Protecting her from himself and what he wanted. Because he always wanted more than people could give, and hadn't he learned that from his father? His constant need for more had driven the old man to the bottle, and there was no knowing what it would drive Hope to do.

He couldn't expose her to that. He wouldn't.

Slowly, he turned around to face her.

She stood next to the fire, the light igniting the red in her hair, making her blaze, and her eyes were darker than the night sky above, looking at him… God, the way she looked at him hurt.

She was so beautiful. But she'd never been for him.

"You can't love me." He kept his voice flat, crushing the fragile hope in hers. "And I'm not worth sacrificing everything you wanted for."

Shock rippled over her features. "What? Why would you say that?"

"Because of Dad." He'd never told anyone this, not one person, and he didn't want to tell her now. But she had to know.

"What about him?" Hope frowned. "He was an alcoholic, sure—"

"But he didn't start out that way. Not at first. He was a good father, and then Mom died and he changed."

"He was grieving, Si."

"I only wanted him to feel better," he went on, ignoring her. "I only wanted him to see that though he might have lost Mom, I was still alive. That's all I wanted." His heart rate was through the roof, adrenaline pumping through him, but he forced himself to keep going. "But he wouldn't look at me, wouldn't even speak to me, and that went on for weeks. Then I remembered that the night of Mom's funeral he'd had a couple of beers and he'd seemed... better." He had to take a breath, force the rest out. "I found a bottle of vodka in the back of the pantry, and I thought that if beer could help, then vodka would be even better. So I gave it to him, and he nearly drank the entire thing. And that night he talked about her. He smiled and he laughed. Christ, he even gave me a hug." Si's heart twisted in his chest at the memories, a raw bitter anger coursing through him. "Then the next day he went out and bought another bottle. Then another and another. And I didn't stop him. I was ten, and I liked it when he was drunk." He bared his teeth in a feral smile. "Because when he was drunk, he was my dad again."

Shock rippled over Hope's face. "Oh, Si..."

"So you see, don't you?" he demanded, ignoring the soft note in her voice and how it hurt. "You see now. He wasn't an alcoholic. I turned him into one. Because I wanted my dad back. Because I wanted more than he could give."

Sympathy had replaced the shock in her expression,

a terrible sympathy that cut him to shreds. "You didn't tell me." Her voice was hoarse. "Why didn't you tell me?"

"What? That I caused my father to turn to drinking? That I was ultimately the one responsible for his death?" He couldn't keep the sharp edge from the words. "Why the hell would you think I'd tell *anyone* that?"

"I was your friend. I would have understood." She took a step toward him and stopped. "God, you can't blame yourself for that. You were ten, and you'd just lost your mom."

"But it wasn't just me being ten," he said bitterly. "How does that excuse me at fourteen? At sixteen? Letting him buy all that vodka. Letting him drink it. I could have stopped him, and I didn't."

"You were lonely, and you wanted him to be there for you."

"That's no goddamn excuse." His heart beat out of control now, and she looked like she wanted to close the distance between them, and he had no idea what he'd do if she got too close. *Hold her so tight. Never let her go.* "Dad told me once when he was sober that I wanted too much from him. That he didn't have anything more to give me. And he was right. I did want too much. I still do."

The firelight flickered over her lovely face, gleaming on the telltale signs of tear tracks on her cheeks. They felt like a knife in his chest.

"That's not wrong, Si," Hope said. "I'd give you everything you wanted and more, and I think you know that. So why can't you take it?"

But he knew. He'd always known, deep down inside. He stared at her, the distance between them not so very far and yet vast enough that he couldn't cross it. "I don't deserve it," he said, hard and cold. "I'll never deserve it."

She blinked. "What? Why on earth would you think that?"

"Why the hell would you think I would?" He flung up a hand. "After everything I've just told you?"

"But…" Her gaze searched his face, nothing but puzzlement on it. "That's not true. That's so not true I don't even know where to start."

"Start with a goddamn bottle of vodka."

"Si—"

"Dad died, Hope," Si ground out, trying to make her understand. "He died in the end because he was drunk. Because I didn't stop him from drinking. And because of him, Bill died too."

"But I've never blamed you for that and you know it," she shot back. "I would never judge you, either."

"No, but I do." He couldn't say it any plainer than that.

She stared at him for a long moment. "What? So that's it? I tell you that I love you and you throw it back in my face, giving me some crap about how you don't deserve it? And all because you gave your father a stupid bottle of vodka?"

Pain and fury knotted inside him, rough as old rope. She made it sound ridiculous, so simple, but it wasn't. "I'm sorry, Hope," he said roughly. "But that's all I've got to give you."

Her hands closed into fists, her own anger stark on her face, her eyes glittering with pain. She swallowed, and he wanted to go to her, pull her into his arms and tell her everything would be okay.

But it wasn't okay. Nothing would ever be okay again.

"Would you listen to yourself?" she said hoarsely. "It's not all you have to give. You have so much more, and I know because I can see it in your eyes every time you look at me." She took in a shaky breath. "It's not that you don't deserve it. It's that you're too much of a coward to take it."

"No, that's not true—"

"Yes, it is." Her voice was unsteady, tears glittering on her cheeks. "You told me that you'd wanted me for years, and here I am, giving you exactly what you want, and now suddenly you've changed your mind?"

She's right. You are a coward.

"You don't understand," he said.

"No, it's you who doesn't understand." Abruptly, she came toward him and every muscle in his body locked. Because if she touched him…

But she didn't. She stopped right in front of him, the look on her face brighter than the fire, ablaze with something that hurt to look at. "I've spent my life being afraid, being too scared to reach out and take what I wanted. Until you, Silas Quinn. Until you came back into my life and showed me everything I was missing out on." Her voice shook with passion. "You made me want things. You made me think I could have them. You gave me the courage to reach for them and I did, so don't you dare tell me that I don't understand. I put away my fear, Silas. What's your excuse?"

"I'm not afraid," he growled. "All I'm doing is trying to protect you."

"From what?" she demanded. "From you? Well, it's too late for that. Too goddamn late!"

His heart ached. Everything ached. He'd never wanted to hurt her. All he'd ever wanted was for her to be happy. But she'd never be happy with him. Because what she wanted he couldn't give. And love had already cost her so much with her mother. He couldn't be like Angela, holding on to her, taking from her. Taking and giving nothing back.

Forcing aside the anguish, he only stared back. "I've told you why it won't work between us. And I never promised you anything more."

"Oh, I know you didn't," she said bitterly. "You were always very clear." Her throat moved as she swallowed. "And if that's the way you want it, that's fine. I won't force you. But just remember that this time it was me who offered something more. And it was you who didn't have the guts to take it."

Somewhere inside of him a knife twisted, pain echoing through him.

But he didn't say anything. He had nothing left to say. He'd made his decision and he wasn't going to change it, and it had nothing to do with fear.

Nothing at all.

Hope turned without another word and walked away, leaving him standing by the leaping fire.

He didn't stop her.

He'd done the right thing—he had.

And maybe if he told himself that enough times, he'd believe it.

Chapter 18

Silas hammered in the last nail on the shingle he was attaching to repair Phil's roof, and clearly he was using a little more force than was strictly necessary because Phil yelled up at him, "Hey, you're supposed to be repairing the roof, not beating it down!"

Si grimaced, gave the shingle one last—lighter—blow before examining his work. Seemed good. Then his phone vibrated in his pocket, and he took it out, his heart beating for a second far too fast. But it was only yet another call from Damon.

Ignoring it, Si put the phone back in his pocket, hooked his hammer into his tool belt, then made his way back to the ladder propped against the side of the house.

Phil was standing beside the ladder, scowling as Si came down and stepped onto the ground.

"My house won't stand up to any more of your repairs if beating my roof in is what you call repairs," Phil said grumpily. "What's gotten into you, boy?"

"Sorry." Si knew he didn't sound sorry in the least, but he was beyond caring. "It's all done, though."

Phil eyed him. "It's that girl, isn't it?"

A hot shock pulsed down his spine. "No, it's not the damn girl," he snarled before he could stop himself.

But that was a lie. Of course it was the girl.

For the past few days, he'd been keeping busy, figuring

out where he was going to live now that he was staying and viewing a couple of the vacant lease properties as potential homes. And when he wasn't doing that, he was helping out around the town, responding to people's questions that had come up following the town meeting.

Which was great, because he needed to be busy. He needed to be doing something so he didn't have to think of Hope. Didn't have to keep replaying the sympathy and understanding on her face as he'd told her about his father, didn't have to see the tears on her cheeks as he'd told her he didn't want what she had to offer. Didn't have to see the pain in her eyes before she'd turned her back on him.

That she was avoiding him made things easier. She seemed to spend all her time in her back office, which was good, because it was bad enough hearing her voice at night, talking to the regulars behind the bar, the sound of her laugh drifting up the stairs. Making him want to go down there and haul her over that bar and into his arms.

But he'd made his decision. And it would be better for both of them in the end. Yes, much, much better.

Phil didn't seem bothered by his foul temper, only nodding sagely as if Si had just confirmed something for him. "Heard that she's planning on leaving," he said. "And that you're taking on the Moose."

Si ignored the way his chest ached at the thought of Hope leaving. Because it shouldn't ache. He knew she was going to go, and he was pleased that she was. "Yeah, that's right," Si muttered. "That's the plan."

Phil's bright blue gaze seemed to see far more than Si

was comfortable with. "You seem real happy about it," the old man observed.

"She needs someone to take on the lease," Si bit out, not really sure why he was explaining himself. "I offered."

Phil tilted his head, the movement making him look like one of his birds. "Seems to me that it's not the lease you want to take on."

Si stared back, belligerent. "Got something to say to me, Phil? Because if so, out with it. I haven't got time for games."

"Fair enough." The old man's gaze was steady. "Word is something's up with her, that she's walking around looking like a woman with a broken heart. And it seems like she's not the only one."

Another shock, a cold one this time, rippled down Si's spine, and for a second he couldn't speak. "I'm fine," he managed when he could find his voice again. "It just didn't work out."

"Huh." Phil rubbed at his chin. "You don't look fine to me."

His heart ached, throbbing and raw, the memory of Hope's face and the anguish in her dark eyes pulling at him, eating away at him.

Yeah, you broke her heart. And broke your own in the process.

"It's none of your business," he said roughly, not wanting to go into it.

"Maybe not," Phil conceded. "Or maybe I know more than you do about broken hearts and how to heal them."

Si stood there, suddenly very conscious of the crack that ran through that heart of his. Because yes, it was broken. It had broken when his mother died, and over the following months, as he'd realized that his father didn't want him when he was sober, only when he was drunk, it had broken again.

And again the night Hope had walked away.

It had broken so many times he was sure there was nothing left of it.

But apparently not, since nothing else could explain this pain.

"You can't heal it," he heard himself say in a raw voice. "Sometimes things just stay broken."

Phil shook his head. "That's bullshit, boy, and I think you know that. Everything can be fixed, otherwise why would you be up on my roof hammering at those shingles?"

Si almost laughed. "It's not the same thing."

"Sure it is. And I'll tell you this for free. The only way to heal a broken heart is not to give it less love, it's to give it more. Give it as much as you can handle."

He took a breath, unable to look at the old man. Because he thought if he did, he'd probably break in two. "And what if I don't have any of that to give?"

Phil gave a quiet laugh. "Everyone's got love to give, boy. No matter what they tell themselves."

"But not everyone deserves to have it," he said before he could stop himself.

The old man was silent for a long moment. Then he

said, "I think if someone is loved, then they deserve it. But love hurts. And not everyone can handle that kind of pain."

Si had no answer to that, because he sure as hell couldn't. And he didn't know why that stuck with him as he finished up Phil's repairs and began the walk back into town. A mistake to walk, because it left him with too much time to think—about the crack in his own heart. About the crack he'd put in Hope's. About love and worthiness.

About pain.

Love hurt, Phil had said, and he wasn't wrong. Love had never meant anything but pain for Si. Yet he couldn't stop thinking about what had blazed in Hope's face as she'd confronted him down by the river, telling him about how he'd shown her what she'd been missing and how she'd put aside her fear to take what she wanted.

You've loved her for years, and you never told her the truth. She loved you in a week and gave you her heart the first moment she had a chance.

Si came to a sudden halt at the side of the gravel road, looking sightlessly over the mountains.

She was brave. Braver than he'd ever been either before or since. She'd had the courage to open her heart to him, while he'd kept his locked.

She'd shown him her soul, her fears, and her hopes, while he'd kept his wrapped up tight and secret.

Safe. You kept it safe.

The thought was like a bucket of ice water dumped straight over his head.

Yes, he had. That's exactly what he'd been doing: keeping himself safe, protecting himself. Using his own sense of unworthiness as an excuse. And that's what it was, an excuse.

Because she was right, he *was* a goddamned coward. He was afraid. He'd had his heart broken so many times and it hurt, it just goddamn hurt. And if he gave it to her and she broke it...

Shit. He wouldn't survive it.

Si stood there staring out at those damn mountains, the pain in his chest nearly unbearable.

So where did that leave him? Phil had told him that more love was the key to healing a broken heart, but when that love could also destroy him, what should he do? What *could* he do?

You have to trust her.

The thought was an arrow straight from the sky, skewering him right through.

She was his friend. She'd always been his friend, no matter what. And she loved him. Even after he'd told her about his father, she'd looked at him as if that didn't matter to her in the slightest and told him that she'd give him everything he'd ever wanted.

And he did want it. He wanted her.

Hope. Her name was a promise, a prayer, a magic spell, holding the grief and the loneliness at bay. A light in the dark, the sun breaking through the clouds.

That's what she'd always been, his hope. And if he couldn't trust her, if he let her go, all that hope would be gone. And without that, he might as well be destroyed already.

Si took a shuddering breath, the knowledge sweeping through him like a wave.

She loved him, and he had to trust that love, trust her, even though he might not deserve it. Even though he was afraid. Because without her, he couldn't survive.

Si began the long walk back into town, moving faster and faster. And then he was running. Running back to her.

After all this time, hope was the one thing he couldn't bring himself to let go of.

Hope leaned on the bar as Joe and Lloyd began their usual argument. Tonight's was a little different, somehow morphing into which one of them had the best wilderness skills and which one could best teach those skills to the vast number of tourists that would soon be flooding into Deep River.

It would have amused her if she'd cared, but she didn't care. In fact, for the past couple of days, she'd cared about nothing. Even filling out her college application forms and sending them off hadn't made her feel anything.

Her heart had crumbled in on itself, leaving only an empty space where it should have been, a void that nothing seemed to fill. Which was maybe being unnecessarily dramatic, but even so, that's how it felt.

Everything had been made even harder by the fact that Silas was still ostensibly staying at the Moose. She'd managed to avoid him since that terrible evening beside the fire a few days ago, and with any luck, she could keep on avoiding him. At least until the moment when she left, which would be soon. Her mother was already drawing up an itinerary of potential cities they could live in, though that was going to be dependent on which college accepted her.

She wished she could feel more excited about it, but she didn't.

Perhaps that would change, though. Once she got away from here, away from Silas, she'd feel better. Perhaps she'd regain the excitement she'd once had for new possibilities and new challenges.

You won't. Not when all you want is him.

She did. But he didn't want her, and even though she knew that wasn't true, that he was only afraid, that didn't make the reality any easier to bear. She'd tried to make him see that he had nothing to be afraid of, nothing to feel unworthy about, but he'd refused. And she couldn't force him. All she'd been able to do was walk away.

God, if only it wasn't so hard…

Joe and Lloyd's argument was reaching its usual crescendo, and she began looking around for Axel to do his usual excellent job of kicking them out when suddenly the doors to the Moose were jerked open.

And the dusty remains of Hope's heart shivered.

Silas stood in the doorway, breathing fast, his chest

heaving as if he'd just run a hundred miles. A wild sort of energy was rolling off him, making everyone in the entire bar stop what they were doing and look.

Then his gaze—brilliant gold and green—came to hers, and all of a sudden she couldn't breathe. She wanted to turn and run, escape back into her office, but he was already coming toward her, determination in every line of him.

She reached for the anger she'd felt that night by the fire, lifting her chin, determined to challenge him the way she had when he'd come into her bar just like this only a week or so earlier.

Axel, obviously picking up on the tension, started toward Silas, maybe to stop him, but Silas only gave him a look that made the other man step back.

Well, the bastard might be able to intimidate Axel but he wasn't going to intimidate her. No freaking way.

She stood tall behind the bar, waiting, and Silas kept on coming, shoving between Lloyd and Joe as if they weren't there, much to their annoyance.

"Hope." His gaze was fierce and he ignored the muttered curses of the two old men on either side of him. "Can I talk to you?"

But she was angry. So angry she was shaking. Did he think that he could just waltz back in here after he'd basically thrown her heart back in her face? That she would agree to speak to him? Just like that?

"No," she said, equally fierce. "You can't talk to me. And if you don't get out of my bar—"

"Five minutes. That's all I want. Just five."

The shaking got worse, and she had to fold her arms over her chest to ease it. "Why? What's it going to change? I think you said everything you needed to, didn't you?"

"No." His voice was full of something intense and dark, a note she hadn't heard in it before. "Turns out I have a few more things to say. But not in front of anyone else." The intensity in his gaze burned. "If you need me to beg, I will."

Silence had begun to ripple outward, people turning to stare.

She was creating a scene and she hadn't meant to. Dammit.

Silas didn't seem to notice, still staring at her as if her answer was the most important thing in the entire universe.

"You got some nerve, Quinn," Lloyd muttered, because of course gossip about her and Silas and what was happening between them was already circulating. "You'd best apologize to the lady."

"That's exactly what I want to do," Silas said, still looking only at her.

She couldn't let this go on. The sooner she dealt with him, the sooner he'd be out of her life. So she lifted a shoulder, trying to hold on to her anger and not the pain, and said, "Fine. Five minutes."

He said nothing, paying no attention to all the stares thrown their way, following her silently as she led the way to her office.

"Why are you here, Silas?" she demanded, taking refuge against her desk as he closed the door behind them. "Because if it's to—"

"Stay, Hope." The look on his face was suddenly blazing, some powerful, fierce emotion vibrating in his voice. "Stay with me."

Shock rippled through her. "W-what?"

"I don't want you to go. I want you to stay here with me instead."

The shock deepened, widened. "But...you wanted me to go."

"I know I did. But I was wrong." He shoved a hand through his hair, the same wild, passionate energy as he'd had out in the bar pouring off him. "Turns out you were right that night beside the fire. You accused me of being a coward and... You're right. I am."

Her mouth was dry, the crumbled remains of her heart gritty as sand. "I don't understand. What are you talking about?"

He stared at her. "You were never supposed to love me back. You were always supposed to be unobtainable. Because that made you safe. That meant I could love you without fear, because if you never loved me back, I could never have my heart broken."

She swallowed, trying to follow what he was saying, her brain not working quite right. "But I—"

"And then you did," he went on, moving closer. "You gave me your heart, and I had no goddamn idea what to do with it. Love had been nothing but pain for me, and here you were, offering me yet more. I had to protect myself. Because I didn't want to face the reality of my feelings for you."

Hope blinked. "What feelings?"

Silas took another step and then stopped, the look in his eyes so focused and intent she could barely breathe. "I should have told you years ago and I didn't. Because I'm a goddamn coward. You always were braver than me, sweetheart." The gold burning in his gaze was as brilliant as the fire beside the river that night. "I love you, Hope Dawson. I've always loved you. I've loved you for years and years, but I was too afraid to say it. I was too afraid of the pain. Too afraid of what I felt for you, because my heart's been broken before, and if you broke it, I knew I wouldn't survive."

Her eyes prickled, her throat getting sore, all her anger draining away. "Si—"

"No," he said hoarsely, "let me finish. I told you I didn't deserve it, that I didn't deserve you, and maybe that's true and maybe I don't. But I'm not going to use that as an excuse anymore. Instead of you breaking my heart, I broke yours, and I'm sorry. I want to fix it. I want to heal it. I want to give you back all the love you should have had from me years ago, and not holding anything back this time. I want to—"

But Hope couldn't keep still any longer. She closed the distance between them, stepping up to him and raising a hand, laying a finger across his beautiful mouth to silence him. Her throat was so tight she could barely speak, yet she forced the words out because they were important. "If there's one thing you need to understand, Silas Quinn, it's this. You don't need to deserve me. And you don't need to become worthy. You already are."

His mouth moved against her finger, but she pressed it down, keeping him quiet, because she wasn't done.

"I know you had a crappy time of it with your dad. I know you blame yourself. And I get it. That's how I felt about my mom, too. But we can have this without needing to deserve it or be worthy of it. We can have it because we both want it, and that's enough, don't you think?"

He lifted his hand, his fingers circling her wrist and pulling her finger away, and he gave her his answer by bending his head and kissing her.

Then he put his arms around her. Holding her tight. Never letting her go.

"I love you, Silas Quinn," she murmured against his lips, giving him more of the truth that lived in her heart. "You're strong and honest and passionate. And you have the biggest heart. You're a good man—you always have been."

His arms around her tightened. "And I love you, Hope Dawson. You're the bravest woman I've ever met, not to mention caring and smart. Tough too, yet underneath, you're all flame."

Hope pulled away a little, reaching up to thread her fingers through the thick black silk of his hair, her heart so full it felt like it might burst. "Actually, underneath I'm all marshmallow, but please don't tell anyone."

He laughed, the sound natural and warm and like nothing she'd ever heard. "Don't worry, sweetheart. Your secret is safe with me."

She had to rise on her toes to kiss him again then, because she loved the sound of that laugh. But only a light brush, because there was something else she wanted to know. "What made you change your mind and come back?"

Silas's arms tightened around her. "Phil, oddly. He said the only cure for a broken heart was more love, and when I argued, he told me that love hurt and not everyone was built to handle that kind of pain." His mouth curved in that way she adored, one of his special, rare smiles. "It got me thinking about Mom and Dad. About pain. About you. About how brave you were telling me that you loved me and how it was fear that kept me from doing the same, despite having loved you for years." His smile faded, his expression turning serious. "I always thought love was a choice, but in the end, it wasn't. I could either have you or live without hope. And I couldn't live without that."

Her heart got tighter and tighter, but it was a good pain. A sweet pain. "I'd really like to tell you something meaningful about your name too, but Silas doesn't really mean anything else."

He laughed that gorgeous laugh again. "Actually, it means 'of the forest,' which is kind of apt."

"No, it doesn't." Hope put her hand on his chest, right over that big heart of his. "I think it means love."

His smile made the sweet pain in her chest worse, but she didn't mind.

She knew what that pain was now.

It was happiness.

Epilogue

SI LOOKED OVER THE FINAL CONTRACT, THEN GLANCED at Hope, who was standing at the bar next to him. "You good with that?"

She smiled, and the Moose seemed suddenly full of sunlight. "Abso-goddamned-lutely."

He lifted the pen. "For you, madame."

Hope grinned, took it, and signed her name with a flourish.

Finally, the ownership of the Happy Moose's lease was now Hope's, as it always should have been, and Si was glad. The town had voted to keep the oil companies out by a narrow margin, which meant he was going to have a lot on his plate, and though he liked the Moose, he'd rather not have to manage it.

Not that Hope was going to have a lot of time to deal with the Moose herself. Not since she'd decided that a double major in literature and business would be a good idea. It was going to mean she'd have very little time for anything else, but if anyone could handle it, it was her.

And she wouldn't have to do it alone this time.

This time, she had him, and together, they could do anything.

Si pulled her in close, kissing her, as always loving her passionate response to him.

"Ahem," someone said from the direction of the doors.

Silas didn't stop what he was doing. "We're closed," he growled.

"Are you?" a familiar voice said. "The doors aren't locked."

Si snapped his head up.

A tall man with golden brown hair stood in the doorway of the Moose, a duffel bag over one shoulder.

Dammit. It was Damon.

"What the hell are you doing here?" Si demanded.

"You weren't answering my calls," Damon said, his sky-blue gaze flicking from Si's arm around Hope's waist to take in Hope herself. "And I can see why." He grinned the grin that usually had anything female panting after him. "Hey there, pretty. The name's Damon."

"I'm no one's 'pretty' but Si's," Hope said calmly. "And the name's Miss Dawson, Damon."

Si grinned. God, he loved this woman.

Damon, who didn't get offended easily, laughed. "You're sharp. I like you." He moved from the doorway, strolling in and looking around as he came toward them. "So this is the bar you've been staying in, Si. And I'm using the term 'bar' in the loosest possible sense."

Si, who'd been hoping for some uninterrupted time in the honeymoon suite with Hope, gave him a glare. "Like I said, what the hell are you doing here?"

Damon came to a stop in front of the bar, his gaze utterly unreadable. "Thought I'd come and see what all the fuss was about. Also, since you wouldn't answer your damn phone, I thought I'd better check you were still alive, not to mention perhaps needing a reminder that you still have a business to run."

Oh yes. The business. That he hadn't thought once about in the past few days.

A flicker of guilt caught at him, but he refused to let himself feel too bad about it. Not when he'd had a few good reasons not to contact his friend.

Reasons such as the woman standing next to him and how he couldn't keep his hands off her and loved her to distraction.

"Yeah," he said shortly. "I've had a few things to do."

"Things such as this pretty little redhead and this weird yet oddly cozy pub?"

Hope cleared her throat. "First, *Damon,* I did tell you my name so feel free to use it. Second, the Moose isn't weird. Third, I'm right here."

Damon looked at her, then at Si, still grinning, the bastard. "Ah. I see how it is. I wondered since it was all 'Hope this' and 'Hope that.'"

"I didn't—" Si began.

But Damon rolled right over the top of him, glancing in the direction of the stairs. "And speaking of hope, I sure hope you've got a bed available in this apparently not weird pub, because the weather's closing in and it's looking like I can't fly out of here tonight like I planned."

And just like that, Si suddenly had a very wonderful idea.

"You know about finance, don't you?" he asked, knowing full well that Damon knew about finance. Quite a lot, in fact.

The other man's expression turned suspicious. "Yeah, why?"

This time, it was Si's turn to grin. "In that case, let me tell you a little bit about a town called Deep River."

Acknowledgments

I would like to acknowledge my agent, Helen Breitwieser, for her work on selling this series. My editor, Deb Werksman, for loving this book so much. And Sourcebooks, for my wonderful cover. You all rock!

Can't get enough small-town charm? Settle down in Blessings, Georgia, with bestselling author Sharon Sala!

count *your* blessings

a novella

Chapter 1

RUBY DYE SHOWED UP IN BLESSINGS, GEORGIA, twelve years earlier with nothing to her name but her divorce papers and a cosmetology license. She had just enough money from her divorce settlement to set up a beauty shop she called The Curl Up and Dye, with very little left over. It was a simple plan. If she didn't cut enough hair, she wouldn't eat. But as it turned out, she had arrived in Blessings to provide a service that had been missing. Before the first week was out, she was booked solid. Considering it was the first good thing that had happened to her in a long time, she was grateful.

She made it a practice to change her hair color and style on a biyearly basis as a means of advertising her own skill, and last night had been the night for another change. She'd gone home with shoulder-length brown hair and auburn highlights. This morning her hair was chin length and red. Audacious Red was the color on the box, and she considered it a good measure of her attitude.

She came in the back door, unloaded the box of dough-nuts fresh from the bakery, and started coffee.

Vesta and Vera Conklin, her fortysomething identical twin stylists would be here soon, and neither one of them was fit for conversation until they'd had something sweet and a cup of coffee in their bellies. Ruby loved the both of them, but they were the most opinionated women she'd ever met, and their confrontational attitude was probably why neither one of them was married.

At thirty-two, Mabel Jean Doolittle was the youngest employee. She did manicures and pedicures at The Curl Up and Dye and, when they were extra busy, helped out on shampoo duty, as well.

She was a feisty little blond with a scar on her fore-head from going headfirst into the windshield of her boyfriend's car when she was only sixteen. It was a daily reminder to never make stupid-ass choices in men again.

Ruby was proud of what she'd accomplished. The one thing she hadn't expected was for the shop to become the local confessional, which it had. Eventually, every secret in town came out at The Curl Up and Dye.

She was running the dust mop over the black and white tiles when the back door opened. Vesta and Vera entered, both wearing pink smocks and the same pissy scowl on their faces.

"Morning, girls. Coffee is hot. Doughnuts are fresh. Help yourselves," Ruby said.

"Morning, Sister," they echoed, then stopped. "Nice hair color," they added, and headed for the break room.

Ruby smiled as she headed for the register to count out the money for the till. Nearly everyone in town called her "Sister," and she liked it. It made her feel like she was part of a great big family. Once the money was in the drawer, she moved to the front door. She was just about to turn the Closed sign to Open when she saw Alma Button pull up in front of the shop.

The fact that it was August 15 and Alma was driving the family van made Ruby wince. It must be time for back-to-school haircuts for Alma's six boys. When she saw the side door open and boys spilling out like puppies turned loose in a barn full of chickens, she took a deep breath and yelled out, "Girls, grab your scissors! Here comes Alma and her boys."

The twins stepped out of the break room. On a scale of one to ten, their tolerance for children was a three, and judging from their expressions, that had just plummeted to a one.

Vera was muttering beneath her breath as she brushed powdered-sugar crumbs off her smock.

Vesta frantically stirred a second packet of sugar into her coffee.

Ruby turned the sign to Open and unlocked the door. "Morning, Alma. Y'all are here early."

She smiled at the boys trailing in behind their mother.

From the looks on their faces, they were no happier to be here than Ruby and her girls were to see them coming.

"Morning, Ruby," Alma echoed, and gave the boys a warning look. "You know Joe down at the barber shop is still in the hospital from his hip replacement, and I didn't want to have to drive all the way to Savannah with six boys just to get their haircuts. I figured if we came early we could avail ourselves of your 'walk-ins welcome' offer."

Ruby pointed to the three open stylist chairs. "Yes, I heard about Joe. They say he'll be out of the hospital in another couple of weeks but won't open back up for a while yet."

"That's what I heard, too," Alma said.

Ruby pointed at the chairs. "Okay, boys, who's first? Three of you grab yourselves a seat and we'll get this over. My goodness, you all have grown. Looks like no more booster seats for the Button boys, right?"

"I'm six now and tall for my age," Cooter announced.

Billy Joe punched his little brother on the arm.

"Big deal, Cooter. I'm almost eight."

"Shut up, the both of you," Larry muttered. At ten, he considered himself beyond that.

Ruby heard what sounded like a slight whistle, followed by the scent of an odorous fart. She turned on the ceiling fan and pretended not to notice, but was guessing it was either Jesse or James, the twelve-year-old twins, who were suddenly interested in the display of hair gel.

"*Madre*, someone farted!" Cooter yelled.

Alma glared at her son. "Hush your mouth," she hissed. "He's learning Spanish from *Sesame Street*," she added, hoping the use of a second language overrode her other child's social faux pas.

Vesta's nose wrinkled in disapproval, both for the smell and the task ahead.

Bobby Button, who had been nicknamed Belly before he started first grade, took a seat in Ruby's chair, refusing to acknowledge the boys he'd come in with. He would turn fifteen in a week and eyed his hair with regret. He'd been growing it all summer and was pissed at having to give it up. When he saw his mother watching him, he glared.

She glared back. Whether they liked it or not, part of getting her six boys ready for a new year of school meant buzz cuts, and they had Belly's entrance into second grade to blame. Before his first month in second grade was over, he had been infected with head lice and proceeded to share the infection with everyone else in the family before Alma knew that he had them.

By the time she had the scourge under control, she'd quit having sex with her husband, claiming it was partly his fault for giving her nothing but boys; burned every piece of bed linen she owned; and shaved the boys bald. Her skin had crawled for months afterward. Although it had never happened again and she finally went back to her wifely duties of submitting to her husband's sexual advances, she was thoroughly convinced the scourge remained under control because of her due diligence to cleanliness and the removal of most of her sons' hair.

The twins climbed up in the other two chairs, somewhat fascinated by the fact that the women who were about to cut their hair were also twins. They looked in the mirror, then at each other, and giggled. Then they looked at the expressions on the hairstylists' faces and frowned. Obviously, Vera and Vesta were not as amused.

"The usual?" Vera asked, as she put the cape around a twin.

"How short?" Vesta asked.

Alma folded her arms across her bosom. "The usual. Very short."

When the clippers began to buzz, Cooter covered his eyes. Billy Joe fell backward onto the floor, pretending he was dead, and Larry was picking his nose.

It was an auspicious beginning to what would turn out to be an eventful day.

◎◯◎

By noon, the foot traffic in the salon was slowing down. Mabel Jean didn't have another manicure until after 1:00 p.m. and had gone across the street to Granny's Country Kitchen for lunch. Vesta and Vera were in the back eating lunch they'd brought from home, leaving Ruby up front to finish Patty June Clymer's weekly hairdo.

Patty June's husband, Conrad, was the preacher at the Freewill Baptist Church. Up until the last few weeks, he always had his hair trimmed when he brought Patty for her appointment. But for the past six weeks, Preacher Clymer had been a no-show.

The first trip Patty June made alone seemed of no consequence to anyone, especially Patty June. The second one she was a little bit miffed but made all kinds of excuses. After that, she hadn't mentioned his name again.

But when she arrived alone today, Ruby could almost feel her anger. The little preacher's wife hadn't said a word to anyone from the time she walked in the front door. Ruby knew better than to ask what was wrong.

Then the bell jingled over the door.

"Hey, Patty, excuse me a sec," Ruby said, and headed for the front of the shop as a tall, leggy redhead walked in.

"Bobbette. Long time no see," Ruby said.

"Hi, Sister! I haven't been here in a while. I moved to Chesterville after Daddy died."

"Well, I'll say! I didn't know that," Ruby said. "How can I help you?"

Bobbette batted her fake eyelashes in double time and held out her right hand.

"Can you believe it? One of my nails has popped off. Makes my finger looked naked. I was wondering if Mabel Jean had time to put on a new one."

"That's acrylic, right?" Ruby asked.

"Yes. I tried silk wrap once but I didn't much like them. So can she fix it? I have a hot date and I don't like to keep my honey waiting, if you know what I mean."

"Ooh, so you've got yourself a fellow, do you? What's his name?"

Bobbette giggled. "I never kiss and tell. So can Mabel Jean work me in?"

"She's across the street eating lunch at Granny's. Why don't you run over there and ask her?"

"Thanks, Ruby. See you in a bit."

Bobbette Paulson made a quick exit as Ruby went back to Patty June.

"Sorry for the wait," Ruby said and picked up the hair dryer, then caught the pissed-off look on Patty June's face.

"Is everything all right?" Ruby asked.

Patty countered with a question of her own. "Sister, can I ask you a question?"

"Sure."

"How do you feel about fornication?"

Ruby blinked. "Excuse me?"

Patty lowered her voice. "How do you feel about people who fornicate with someone other than their spouse?"

"Oh. You mean cheat? Sleep around? You're asking me? Girl, that's why I'm not married. My old man cheated on me for a year and I didn't know it. Might never have known it if it hadn't been for our next-door neighbor's kid. He asked me who the blond lady was who came to my house every Tuesday and Thursday, which happened to be the days I went in to work early. Can you imagine?"

Patty's eyes narrowed. "Yes, I can imagine. What did you do?"

"I left him, that's what."

"But what did you do to *him*?"

Ruby frowned. "Nothing."

Patty's face turned a bright shade of pink.

Ruby blinked. "Is everything okay?"

Patty's mouth pursed tighter than a miser's fist. "Why, everything is just fine, and thank you for asking."

"Okay, sure," Ruby said. She grabbed the hair dryer and the vent brush and started styling Patty June's hair.

A few minutes later the door jingled again. Ruby looked over her shoulder, but it was just Mabel Jean coming back with Bobbette.

"So, Patty, is the economy affecting the collection plate on Sundays?" Ruby asked.

Patty didn't answer. She was staring into the mirror, her gaze locked on the two women sitting at the manicure table behind her. Every time Bobbette tossed her long red hair and laughed at something Mabel Jean said, a nerve twitched at the corner of Patty's eyes and her lips clenched a little tighter.

Ruby knew that look. It was pure, unadulterated hate, and that's when it hit her. What if the reason the preacher had been absent for so long was because he was cheating on Patty? And what if Bobbette Paulson was the hussy he was banging, and Patty June knew it?

All the hair stood up at the back of Ruby's neck. If this was so, the fact that they were, by accident, suddenly sitting in the same room was a recipe for disaster. The faster she got these two women separated, the better.

She turned the dryer up on high and finished off Patty's hair in record time, grabbing the hair spray and blasting the style into the little brown helmet Patty June preferred. Ruby whisked the cape from around Patty's shoulders and all but dragged her to the counter to pay.

"There you go, Patty June! Want me to put you down for the same time next week?"

Patty laid a twenty on the counter, set her purse down on the floor, and looked Ruby straight in the face.

"I'm not sure if I'll be out of jail by then."

Before Ruby could react, Patty made a run for the manicure table. Ruby gasped and tried to head her off, but Patty was faster.

Patty snatched the battery-powered clippers from Vesta's work station as she passed, then grabbed a hunk of Bobbette's long red hair and yanked down as hard as she could.

Bobbette screamed as her head popped back.

Mabel Jean jumped. The nail form on Bobbette's finger popped off, and the liquid acrylic Mabel Jean was using turned over and began running off the table onto Bobbette's shoe.

Vesta and Vera flew out of the break room, still holding their salad bowls and their forks, saw what was going on, looked at each other, and then took another bite, chewing faster as they watched what ensued.

Ruby was reaching for Patty's arm, but it was all too late.

The clippers were buzzing on high when Patty made the first swipe through Bobbette's long red hair, cutting a neat swath from the hairline all the way to the crown. Then she shoved Bobbette's head forward, smashing her nose against the manicure table, and finished the cut all the way to the nape of her neck, leaving a gap in her hair a good three inches wide.

Ruby moaned. There was no way that was ever going to pass for a part.

Bobbette's top lip was busted; her nose was leaning sideways on her face and bleeding profusely. She was screeching bloody murder when she flew out of the chair to face her attacker. Then she saw who it was and choked down the next screech as Mabel Jean shoved a towel under her nose to catch the blood. Bobbette's mind was racing, but her speech was seriously impaired by a swollen mouth and broken nose.

"Uh… well, by lord, Batty Jude, hab you lost your bind?" Bobbette cried.

"No. Just my husband, and for what it's worth, you can have the little bastard. He's not worth beans when it comes to sex, but I suspect you already know that by now. What you don't know is that the money in our family is mine, not his. So once the Baptist ministry has their weekly meeting and fires his ass for fornicating with a harlot, he's not only going to be out of a job, he's going to be broke and homeless… bless his heart."

Bobbette was blinking back tears of pain, but her mind was racing. This was definitely not good news.

"Do you have anything you want to say to me before you call the police?" Patty asked.

Bobbette tilted her head back and shoved the towel tighter against her nose to stanch the flow. The last thing she wanted was to get the police involved.

"I'b not calling the bolice," she mumbled.

"Really? I've just assaulted you and started a fight in

The Curl Up and Dye. I'm sure there's damage to the property and—"

"No, no damage here," Ruby said quickly.

Bobbette groaned as she traced the path of stubble that began at her widow's peak and went all the way down to the back of her neck.

"Lord hab mercy," she mumbled, then rolled her eyes. "I'm sure this was an accident and—"

"No, it wasn't an accident. However, it wasn't premeditated. That I can swear to, because I did not know you would be here." Patty handed the clippers to Ruby. "When you talk to the police, tell them I did not run from the scene of the crime and that I will be at home when they come to arrest me."

Bobbette rolled her eyes, then winced because even that hurt.

"I'b not pressing charges."

Patty frowned. "A harlot and a coward! You must be such a disappointment to your mama." Then she smiled at Ruby. "So, I guess you can put me down at my regular time next week after all. Y'all have a nice day."

The door jingled when she opened it, and then she was gone, leaving the women to stare at each other in disbelief.

Vesta handed Vera her bowl and fork and went to clean up her station. She had an appointment due in about fifteen minutes and needed to sweep up the red hair before she arrived.

Mabel Jean grabbed some rags and began sopping up the acrylic, then went to the back room to get some more cleaning supplies, leaving Ruby with the task of dealing with Bobbette.

"Uh, do you want me to call an ambulance?" Ruby asked.

Bobbette thought about the future and the fate of her hot date, and frowned.

"Dough, but I deed a ride to the Hoddywood botel to pick up by car."

There were several reasons Vesta and Vera Conklin had reached the age of forty-two without getting married, and they were looking at one of the reasons why. Men could not be trusted around easy women.

"Why don't you call your hot date?" Vesta asked.

Bobbette glared, pulled out her cell phone, and punched in the number to her mother's house.

Vera snickered and then ducked back into the break room.

"Baba, it's be, Bobbette. I'b at duh booty shob here in town. Cub get be. Hurry."

She dropped the cell phone in her purse, then yanked the cape off the back of Vesta's chair, threw it around her shoulders, and proceeded to shave herself bald.

"What in the world?" Vesta cried.

"I'b baking lembunade out of lembuns. Had accident. See... bwoken dose. Busted lib. I'll work dis look till by hair grows out."

Then she pulled a scarf out of her purse, tied it turban-style around her head, and handed Ruby two twenty-dollar bills.

"For duh mess and duh towel," she said, and sailed

out the door with her head up, the bloody towel pressed against her nose and her backside swaying.

Moments later, her ride pulled up in front of the shop. They saw her mother scream, although the car windows were up so they didn't actually hear it, and then watched as they drove away.

"Well, that just about takes the cake," Vera said, as she came out of the break room.

They were still giggling as they began putting the shop back together. A couple of minutes later, the bell jingled over the door yet again. They looked up.

Conrad Clymer was standing in the doorway with an uneasy look on his face.

"By any chance would… I mean, is—"

"Who are you looking for? Your wife or your whore?" Vera asked.

He gasped, as all the color faded from his face.

"I beg your pardon?"

"You're gonna be begging for more than a pardon before this day is over," Vesta said, as she continued to sweep up the red hair at her station.

He looked down. He'd had some damn good blow jobs with his fists wrapped in hair that color.

"Sweet Jesus," he muttered. "Is that… uh, what…"

"Bobbette Paulson's hair? Why yes, it is. Patty June shaved part of it off. Never would of guessed it, but she's got a real mean streak. And, you can tell Bobbette is a stickler for style. She shaved the rest off herself so it would match. Nothing worse than a messy hairstyle," Vesta added.

"I, uh…"

He pivoted on one heel and flew out the door.

The four women looked at each other and then burst out laughing.

Their day was about to level off, but Patty June's day had just shifted gears.

◎◎◎

Patty June had been thinking about this day for weeks. She knew in advance what she would do once it all came undone, and the first place she stopped after she left the salon was at the First National Bank of Blessings. She was operating on adrenaline as she walked up to the vice president and sat down without being asked.

"I need to move some of my money," she announced.

Lawrence Cornwall smiled and started to wave a teller over when Patty June stopped him.

"No. You do it, Larry. Please."

Lawrence blinked. It was the tremble in her lower lip that did him in.

"Why, certainly, Patty June. Tell me what you want and it's done."

"I need to open a new account in just my name. Then I want you to transfer all but fifteen-hundred dollars of the money in our personal checking account into the new one. Then I need all of my IRAs and the saving account moved into just my name."

Lawrence gasped. "Patty June… is there—"

"Conrad has been fornicating with Bobbette Paulson, and I'm tired of pretending I don't know about it. The money is mine. I'm leaving him his last month's salary, and it's more than he deserves. Move it all now, please. I will wait."

"Oh my stars, I am so sorry," Lawrence muttered.

"Yes, well, so am I, Larry, but it is what it is."

"Sit tight, Patty June. This won't take long," Lawrence said.

And it didn't. Once it was finished, Patty stood abruptly, shook Lawrence's hand in a forthright manner, and walked out of the bank with her head held high.

She didn't remember driving home. It wasn't until she started up the steps of her house that she realized what she'd done. By the time she got indoors, she was shaking. She made it down the hall, but when she walked into the bedroom, she dropped to her knees.

All the little lies she'd been telling herself to excuse Conrad's behavior were gone, and now everyone in town would know it, too. There was nothing left to face but the truth. Her husband was a cheat. Her marriage was over. She'd known it for months, but today it was final. She rolled up in a little ball on the floor and proceeded to cry until her head was throbbing and there was snot all over her face. She was thinking about getting up to get a tissue when she noticed dust bunnies underneath the bed. It appeared she could not keep a house *or* a husband.

Wearily, she pushed herself up off the floor and staggered into the bathroom to clean up. When she came back, she headed for the closet and began dragging his clothes out by the armfuls, making trip after trip to the front porch until his side of the closet was empty and his clothes were all over the porch and the yard.

Next, she went to the kitchen for a trash bag and began emptying the dresser drawers and all the drawers in his office. Then she dragged the bag out onto the porch and threw it into the yard.

Next stop was his office, and she cleared it as well, dumping computer equipment in the yard. When she began emptying two shelves of his reference books from the bookcase, she was more careful, taking special care of his big Bible with all of his favorite highlighted passages. She could have happily set fire to everything he owned, except the books. There was no need to destroy words from the Good Book just because he'd touched it. She hated Conrad, but she didn't hold a grudge against God.

Once the books were out, she went back into the house and began going from room to room, taking down the personal pictures of their wedding and the holidays they'd taken together. Every family memento that had his face on it was going in the garbage. She would not lay her head on a pillow tonight until she made sure every trace of his presence had been removed from this house. Her heart was so full of rage that there were no more tears. The only positive in this mess was that they'd never had children to suffer this disgrace with her.

She had just carried the last stack of pictures outside to the trash and was coming in the back door when she heard the front door slam and then the sound of running feet.

Her heart jumped, but then she took a deep breath and curled her hands into fists. She heard him running from room to room, and waited. Eventually, he'd get to the kitchen and then she would have her say.

Chapter 2

IF MARVIN SCHEFFLER HAD BEEN WATCHING WHERE he was driving instead of trying to get a fly out of his truck, he wouldn't have had a wreck on his way out of town or been transported to the hospital in Blessings, afraid he was going to die. And if Marvin hadn't been afraid he was going to hell for boycotting the church for ending bingo night, he wouldn't have insisted on seeing Preacher Clymer before he went into surgery, and the entire day would have evolved quite differently for a lot of people. But being what it was, life was full of surprises and Marvin's wreck was only one of them.

⊚⊚⊚

Conrad had just met up with Bobbette at the Hollywood Motel and wasted no time getting naked. He was, as his daddy used to say, primed and ready to go. They were about to get down to business when his cell phone vibrated all the way across the end table beside the bed.

Bobbette frowned. "Don't answer it, sugar bear. You're not a doctor. No one's gonna die if you don't show up."

He stifled a frown as he glanced at the text.

"It's Melba, and it's an emergency," he said.

"How do you know that?"

"The only message on her text is a 911." He quickly dialed the church. "Melba, what's wrong?"

She relayed the message and asked him what he wanted her to do.

"Tell them I'm on the way," he said and disconnected.

"Someone had a wreck. They're afraid he's dying. I have to go," Conrad said, and began grabbing his clothes.

Although she knew better than to argue, Bobbette began complaining as she proceeded to get dressed.

"This just messes everything up. What am I going to do? I don't want to sit and wait here all by myself."

"We can hardly go into Blessings together, and you know it," Conrad said.

Bobbette pouted even more as she began yanking on her clothes and, in the process, broke off one of her artificial nails, which brought on a fit of monumental proportions.

She cried, then she pouted again, and then she promised Conrad to add a special little trick to the next blow job if he'd take her with him. Before Conrad knew it, they were in the car together on their way back to town.

Even though he'd driven around to the back side of the hospital to park, he'd been a nervous wreck that they would be seen together. They'd parted company in the parking lot, with the agreement to meet back there in an hour. She was going to get her nail fixed, and he would go pray with Marvin Scheffler so he could go into surgery.

Conrad had known all the way into town that it was a risk, just like he'd known from the start of the affair that he was committing a sin. But this woman had been scratching an itch Patty June could never reach. The possibility of getting caught had always been in the back of his mind, but he had a just-in-case plan.

Years ago, televangelist Jimmy Swaggart had been caught chasing tail and begged for forgiveness in front of his congregation on a nationwide broadcast and got away with it. Conrad had gone along with his own cheating with something similar in mind.

Once inside the hospital, he prayed with Marvin and sent him on his way to surgery, then went out to the parking lot to wait for Bobbette.

But she never showed up, and it kept getting later and later. The only place he knew to look for her was at The Curl Up and Dye. He'd thought seriously about leaving her to her own resources, but he didn't want to make her mad. He'd thought to just walk in, pretend to be looking for his wife, and if Bobbette was still there, he'd soon know it.

So he headed to the beauty shop, careful to keep an eye on the streets for Bobbette as he drove. Once he arrived, he got out with his usual aplomb and poked his head inside to look around. But after Vesta's comment about whores and wives, and seeing all that red hair on the floor, it became apparent that the train his Jimmy Swaggart plan was on had already left the station.

Conrad drove home, shaking like a sinner at the altar praying for redemption and so damn scared he felt like puking.

When he came around the corner and saw his things out in the yard, he swerved, barely missing a parked car. He wheeled into the driveway, then stumbled to the house, his legs shaking so hard he could barely stand.

"Oh my God, oh my God, please, please, please," he kept muttering.

Unfortunately, he had not been specific enough with his prayer, and Patty June was obviously not a bit inclined toward forgiveness. He staggered past computers, office equipment, books, clothes, and what appeared to be everything he'd ever owned strung all over the porch and the yard.

But the bigger shock was the empty walls inside. It was if their marriage had never happened. He ran through the hall to their bedroom, then back through the house toward the kitchen, so damn scared now that he couldn't call out her name.

When he rounded the doorway into the kitchen, he stopped short. He'd found her, but from the look on her face, he was regretting the search.

"Patty June, I—"

"Shut your mouth, Conrad. There is nothing on this earth I want to hear from you. You have defiled me. You slept with me at the same time you slept with your whore. You have shamed me, your church, and your congregation. You are a lying, cheating bastard, and you should be grateful that my father has passed over, or he would have shot you dead where you stand. Get out of my house. Get your things off my property or I will set them on fire. When you get wherever you're going, send me a mailing address for the divorce decree. If you do not, I will hire a private investigator to find you and proceed to ruin your name everywhere you go for the rest of your life."

Conrad gulped. All of a sudden, he needed to pee.

"I am so sorry—"

"Yes, you are. As sorry a man as ever set foot on this earth. Get out of my sight."

"Please. I'll go to counseling. I'll—"

Patty June pulled a knife from the knife block. "I won't tell you again," she said and started toward him.

"Jesus Christ! Patty June, have you—"

She came at him, and Conrad turned tail and ran screaming out of the house.

She stood in the doorway with her eyes blazing, the knife held tightly in her grip, watching him carry away his things. Every time he came back to the porch to take another load, it was all she could do not to take the butcher knife to what was left of his hair, the same way she'd marked his damn whore.

◎◎◎

Conrad kept an anxious eye on Patty June as he gathered up his things, frantically stuffing them into the trunk, then on the car seats and in the floorboard, until the car was so packed he couldn't see anything through the rearview mirror. He knew the neighbors were watching. A couple of them had even come out to their front porches for a closer look. If it would have been possible to drop dead at will, he would have already passed on. Apparently God was not inclined to let guilty bastards out of their own messes that easily.

Finally, he had everything packed in the car. He stopped by the door and looked back at his wife, unable to believe fifteen years of marriage were ending like this.

"Patty June, I—"

She went back in the house, slamming the door to punctuate the fact that she had just shut him out of her life.

His heart hurt as he got in the car and started the engine, but the car was so full that he had to hang his head out the window to back up.

It didn't occur to him until he was driving away that he didn't know where he was going. He'd blown a career and a marriage for the pleasure of Bobbette Paulson's blow jobs. Looking back, he could honestly say it was not a good trade-off.

He was halfway down Main Street when it occurred to him that he would need money. He made a quick stop at the bank, then grabbed the checkbook from the console and ran inside, not realizing everyone in the bank already knew what he'd done.

He stopped at the nearest teller and began writing a check, then tore it off and scooted it toward the teller.

She looked at it and shoved it back.

"Sorry, Preacher, but that check will bounce."

"What? But that's imposs—" *Oh shit.* He cleared his throat. "What *is* the balance?"

She wrote it on a piece of paper and slid it toward him.

He swallowed past the knot in his throat and rewrote a check for the entire fifteen-hundred dollars, pocketed the money, and walked out with his steps dragging.

He thought about going to check on Bobbette before he made himself scarce, then decided against it. It wouldn't be the same getting a blow job if he didn't have all that hair to hold on to.

⊚⊚⊚

By the time the sun went down, nearly everyone in Blessings had heard about the preacher's fall from grace. The board of directors from the Freewill Baptist Church arrived just as Patty was about to sit down to a solitary supper. She saw them drive up and went to the kitchen to turn the fire off under her stew. If she did what she wanted, she wouldn't even go to the door, but eventually she would have to face them. Might as well get all the ugly stuff over in one day.

When the doorbell rang, she stood in the kitchen, waiting until they rang it the second time before she went to answer. They were rude in showing up without calling, so she didn't feel any immediate obligation to be prompt. Once she got to the foyer she took a deep breath, patted her hair to make sure it was still in place, then let them in and proceeded to play dumb. From the looks on their faces, they were less than pleased with the day's events, but she could have cared less. She wasn't all that happy about them herself.

"Titus? Willy? Carl Wayne? What on earth are y'all doing here? The board doesn't meet for another three weeks."

The three men had two things in common. Aside from being on the board together, they were all three big worrywarts, in Patty June's opinion. She could only imagine what was on their minds.

"We're not here for a board meeting," Titus said. "May we come in?"

"I suppose. I was about to sit down and have my supper. What can I do for you?"

The three men frowned. "As if you don't already know," Willy said.

Patty June stared, refusing to bite.

The men began to fidget. Finally it was Carl Wayne who broke the silence.

"When were you going to let us know about Conrad?"

"I'm sorry?"

"We have a duty to the congregation, you know."

"I suppose you do. I, however, do not."

Titus frowned. "Seriously, Patty June, the pastor's wife always—"

"Technically, you no longer have a pastor, and I no longer have a husband, so—"

Willy sighed. "Is he coming back?"

"Not if he knows what's good for him," she muttered.

"I don't understand," Carl Wayne said. "We thought you two were quite suited."

"Whatever we were, we aren't anymore. He's been fornicating with Bobbette Paulson. He is no longer a part of my life. What else do you want to know?"

The men turned three different shades of red.

Titus sighed. "Did it not occur to you to try counseling? I mean… this puts us in a terrible position. Sunday's coming and we are without a pastor."

Patty June's eyes narrowed. Had they been wise in the ways of women, they would have known that meant she was pissed. But two were divorced and the other one had never married, which made them seriously ignorant of the warning signs.

"Get out," she said softly.

They heard her but didn't really think she meant it.

"If the church paid for the counseling, would you consider taking him back?" Willy asked.

Patty doubled up her fists. "Get out of my house," she repeated.

"Titus is right. We are in a terrible position here, and your marriage vows *were* for better or worse," Carl Wayne added.

"I cannot believe two divorcés and an old bachelor are trying to give me marriage advice! My husband fucked a whore on a regular enough basis that I considered killing him. Were it not for my faith in God and my adherence to the *Thou shalt not kill* rule, he would be dead and I would be in jail. Whatever happens at that church, I will no longer be a part of it. I was raised a Methodist. I will be returning to that church to worship. You three have outstayed your welcome!" She strode to the door and yanked it wide. "It wasn't enough that my husband has betrayed me, but you three have just added insult to injury. Get out of my house!"

"Now see here, Patty June, you have no right to—"

She screamed.

Later, Titus would swear she hit a high C with the first breath, but it served the purpose. They ran into one another trying to be the first one out the door.

For the second time in one day, Patty June slammed her front door. It wasn't ladylike, and she knew it wasn't good for the etched-glass insets, but there were times when manners were highly overrated, and this was one of them.

"I swear to my time," she muttered and went back to the kitchen to reheat her stew.

Ordinarily, this would be when Conrad helped set the table and lay out the condiments. When she made stew, he was partial to having bread-and-butter sandwiches with it. She blinked away tears and, out of spite, made herself a bread-and-butter sandwich.

"Damn Conrad Clymer to hell and back, and I'm not a bit sorry for saying that," Patty June said, then sat down at the table, shove

helmet of hair, an

cold all over agai

For the next

people were

if Conrad's misdeeds were

the preacher. She heard the same two p

over and over. People make mistakes. People should

forgiven.

It was the revenge she'd taken that had caused the uproar. It made men nervous to realize there were women strong enough to exact that kind of retribution. It made them look at their own women in a different light. The last thing they wanted was to give them the notion that they had that kind of option.

And so they began a subtle mission, hoping to influence their females into thinking that cutting hair off a whore's head and kicking a cheating-ass husband out of the house were the two worst things a woman could do. They were turning Patty June into a raging feminist in a culture known for its sweet, southern charm.

For Patty June, it was as if she'd been cheated on all over again. When she needed support most, the people who should have been there for her were condemning her instead. She went through shock, disbelief, and despair.

When the day rolled around for another hair

rl Up and Dye, she almost didn't
self to even more ridicule? But if
ran, then she was admitting she was
was never going to happen. So what to
s when it hit her. All of her life she'd been
Maybe it was time to find out how the other
d. She had the money to travel and the time to do
th two full hours before her hair appointment, she
in her car and drove downtown to the Miller Travel
Agency. She'd always wanted to go to Italy, and there was
nothing stopping her now.

⊚⊚⊚

Willa Dean Miller owned the Miller Travel Agency and
liked to think that, of all the residents of Blessings, she
was the most widely traveled, even though her travels
had all been online.

She was pouring herself a fresh cup of coffee when
she happened to glance out the window. She had always
liked Patty June Clymer and was somewhat impressed
by what Patty June had done, but at the same time, it
didn't pay to be different in Blessings. After all, she had
her business to consider. If she went against the power of
public opinion and stood on Patty's side, that business
might suffer. The economy had already slowed it down
considerably. The last thing she needed was to tick off
her clients. So she turned on the sarcasm and waved at
her assistant, Precious Peters.

"Hey, Precious, look who just parked out front. It's Patty June Clymer, as I live and breathe."

Precious jumped up from her chair to run to the window, but when they both realized Patty June was coming into the shop, they made a fast scramble toward their desks instead.

When Patty walked in the door, she could tell by the flush on their faces that they'd been talking about her, but she was past caring. She strode to the front and plopped her purse near her elbow as Willa Dean came to the counter.

"Good morning, Patty June. I can't say as I've ever seen you in here before," Willa Dean said.

"Then that's proof your memory is just fine," Patty said. "I want to book a trip to Italy."

Willa Dean was torn between staying snarky or getting her act together and treating Patty June like a paying client. The money won out.

"That sounds exciting," she said. "Do you have any particular destination in mind? Maybe Rome or Venice? I hear Venice is stunning. Or maybe Milan! So many fabulous places to see in Milan. I have tours available at any of those cities. Just take your pick."

"I was thinking I'd hit them all," Patty June said. "I mean, now that my cheating, whoring husband is gone and I have divorce proceedings in progress, I see no reason to grieve myself silly here in Blessings while the people I thought were my friends proceed to judge me."

Willa Dean paled. "Why, I never—"

"Oh shut up," Patty muttered. "Everyone has. What I don't understand is why. If that had been Harold, would you have still crawled into bed with him at night and spread your legs knowing he'd been fucking someone like Bobbette Paulson?"

Willa Dean gasped. She didn't know what shocked her more: the idea of Harold committing adultery with anyone, or the fact that Patty had said the word *fuck*.

Patty frowned. "I see you have no opinion, which I find interesting. However, I'm not interested in who Harold might be doing on the side. I want to book a trip to Italy. Are you going to help me, or do I have to drive to Savannah?"

Willa Dean was still trying to get past the image of Harold doing it with anyone. She couldn't get him interested even once a month, and the moment that thought went through her mind, the next was that she'd never wondered why. What if Harold was already "doing" someone else? What if that was the reason Harold didn't want to have sex with her anymore?

It was all she could do to focus on booking this trip, which would be big income for the agency. Time enough to deal with Harold—the lying, cheating bastard—later.

Willa Dean waved Patty toward the chair at her desk.

"No, of course you don't need to drive into Savannah. Sit down, honey. Precious, get Patty June some coffee, or would you rather have tea? I have a nice lavender tea I think you would just love."

Patty June blinked. She wasn't sure how to take this

about-face, but it was nice to be treated normally, regardless of the reason.

"I believe I'd like to try that tea, thank you very much."

Willa Dean smiled. "Perfect. Now about that trip."

An hour and a half later, Patty June left the agency with a handful of pamphlets and an itinerary that would have made world travelers Brad Pitt and Angelina Jolie blink. Not only was she stopping in every big-name city in Italy, but she wasn't coming home for a month. She could hardly wait to go shopping, but first things first. Next stop, The Curl Up and Dye.

◎◎◎

Willa Dean watched Patty leaving with no small amount of envy. She'd always wanted to go to Italy, but Harold, the sorry bastard, didn't much like the idea of travel. She needed to talk to her friend Myra, who ran the flower shop. Myra had been a woman of the world before she settled down and married her husband, George.

Willa Dean made the call and then peeled the foil off a Hershey Kiss and popped it in her mouth while she waited for someone to answer.

"Pots and Posies, this is Myra. How can I help you?"

"Myra, it's me, Willa Dean. I think Harold might be cheating on me," and then she choked on the chocolate and broke down in tears.

◎◎◎

Unaware of the seeds of discontent she had just sown, Patty June drove down the street to the beauty shop and parked. The moment she got out of the car, she began to relax. This was probably the only place in Blessings where she would not be judged.

The bell jingled over the door as she walked inside.

Ruby looked up, waved, and smiled.

"Be right with you, honey! I'm just finishing up LilyAnn's hair. Vesta and Vera brought cake today. It's their birthday. Go on over to the table and cut yourself a piece, and don't tell me you can't eat cake before lunch 'cause I'll know that's a big, fat lie."

Patty smiled. She had tickets to Italy, a new outlook on life, and she was about to eat dessert in the middle of the morning. Talk about living in the fast lane.

She set her purse down on the table and cut herself a big square of bakery cake, making sure to cut a pink sugar rose with it, then sat down to eat while watching Ruby finish up LilyAnn Bronte's hair.

As she eyed LilyAnn's profile, Patty suddenly appreciated her own screwed-up life. At least she'd had fifteen years of being a wife. Poor LilyAnn's boyfriend had died right out of high school before the couple had gotten past a promise ring.

Patty June lifted the icing rose off the cake and popped it in her mouth, letting it melt slowly on her tongue as she thoughtfully eyed the tall blond. It was hard to imagine LilyAnn ever being the Peachy Keen Queen, although, as she remembered, LilyAnn had been a real looker in high school. Now the woman was overweight, never wore makeup, and her clothes were so oversized that they hung on her like sacks. She had such a pretty face. It was a shame she'd let the rest of herself go to pot.

Patty June took another bite of cake as guilt washed over her. Of all people, she should be the last one to judge. Patty June's man had not gone to war in Afghanistan straight out of high school and gotten himself killed. He just fucked a whore and got himself caught. Poor LilyAnn. Surely she had grieved herself into this condition. That was all.

A few minutes later, LilyAnn left the shop. As soon as she was gone, Ruby waved Patty over and gave her a hug.

"What was that for?" Patty asked.

Ruby smiled. "Are you trying to tell me you didn't need it?"

Patty June sighed. "No. It was nice. In fact it was the nicest thing anyone's done for me since I was here last. According to the people in town, I have gone from goody two-shoes to hell on wheels, just because I kicked my lying husband out of the house."

"Well, you did shave a path through his whore's red head wide enough to park a car on," Ruby added.

They stared at each other and then burst out laughing.

"Put your cake down and let's get you shampooed," Ruby said.

"Okay, but I want you to do something different today," Patty June said.

Ruby stopped.

Vesta and Vera came out of the break room, and Mabel Jean stopped folding towels.

"Really?" Ruby said.

Patty June nodded. "Sister, my hair has been the same mousy brown all my life. I want to do something different with it."

This set the women in the shop abuzz, offering one suggestion and then another. Finally, Ruby called a halt.

"Girls, that's all well and good, but Patty is the one who's gonna be wearing it. What do *you* want, honey?"

Patty June eyed the array of swatches in her lap and then looked up and grinned.

"I don't know. I don't care. Just give me a color with edge. You know what I mean. I want you to color me bad."

Chapter 3

Thanks to the inquisitive nature of small-town America, the news that Patty June Clymer was coloring her hair spread through Blessings faster than butter on a hot biscuit.

The postman was dropping off the mail at the front counter of The Curl Up and Dye when he saw Patty June sitting at Ruby Dye's station. He paused just long enough to see the color squirting out of the bottle onto Patty June's head and then he was gone. After that, he finished his route, delivering the morning's mail with a little dose of gossip.

The regular delivery boy for Pots and Posies was laid up at home with a broken arm, leaving Myra and George to take turns making their own floral deliveries. Myra was on a second trip to The Curl Up and Dye with orders for the Conklin twins' birthday. Even though there were no men in their lives, their clients were obviously loyal because floral gifts kept coming.

Myra came in with her arms full of vases and a smile on her face.

"I'm back. It's wonderful you girls have so many people who love you, but it's also great for business."

Vesta and Vera were beaming.

"This is so sweet," Vera said.

Vesta was touching up her client Rachel Goodhope's roots. Rachel ran the Blessings bed and breakfast and liked to keep herself sharp for her public persona. She was probably one of the few people in Blessings who empathized with Patty June. She was on her second piece of cake and third husband and understood all too well how shit like that happened.

"This cake is really good," Rachel said.

"Looks yummy," Myra said, as she set the vases down by the others she'd delivered.

Vesta pointed. "Get yourself a piece and take one back for George, too."

"Don't mind if I do," Myra said.

She cut two pieces of cake and slid them onto one plate and was about to leave when she noticed Patty June sitting in Ruby's chair. She started to speak and then saw what Ruby was doing and nearly dropped the cake. All of a sudden she was talking too fast and trying to get out of the shop to spread the news.

"So, thanks for the cake, y'all. George is at the shop by himself so I better hustle."

Ruby kept working.

Rachel kept eating cake.

Patty June was already beyond worrying about public opinion and thinking about how many words she knew in the Italian language, all of which had to do with food. She didn't think she was going to get far on marinara, linguine, and gelato. She needed to make a trip into Savannah and pick up an English-to-Italian dictionary.

Ruby kept working and time kept passing until she finally stepped back and eyed Patty June's hair.

"Okay... that takes care of the color. You still up for that cut we talked about?"

"Yes, and make it sassy."

Ruby laughed. "You're the best, you know that?"

Patty rolled her eyes. "I doubt Conrad would agree with that. Obviously Bobbette had something I don't."

Vesta snorted. "Yeah, big, fat collagen lips. Smack, smack."

The women's eyes widened from the image that brought to mind and then they snickered.

Ruby picked up the scissors and swung the stylist chair away from the mirror so Patty couldn't watch. She wanted her to get the full effect after she was done and not before.

Patty closed her eyes, imagining the snip, snip of the scissors cutting the last of her ties with her old life. When she walked out of there today, the preacher's wife would be gone.

A short while later, Ruby grabbed the hair dryer and began styling the cut. Patty could tell it was significantly shorter and was suddenly anxious to see what Ruby had done.

Finally, the dryer went off. Ruby squirted some

product onto her hands and then rubbed them together before combing her fingers through Patty's hair a few times.

"I think that's about it," Ruby said, and spun the chair around. "Patty June Clymer, meet P. J. I think you two are gonna get along just fine."

Patty's eyes widened as a big smile spread across her face. Her hair was as black as the funeral parlor's hearse and almost as short as the hair of the man who drove it. Ruby had spiked the very tips just enough to give her a windblown look.

"I love it," Patty said, feeling the tips with the palms of her hands and giggling because they were stiff. "I can't imagine what this is going to look like in the morning."

Ruby laughed. "That's the beauty of this style. A little product on your hands and your windblown look is good to go. It will make getting ready a breeze."

Patty jumped out of the chair and gave Ruby a hug.

"Thank you for giving me such a cool look."

"Honey, you wanted badass. You've got it."

Patty stood. "Put me down for the same time next week, and then after that, I'll be gone for a while."

Now she had the attention of everyone in the shop, including Rachel, who was getting ready to leave.

"Where are you going?" Rachel asked.

Patty couldn't even say it without grinning. "I'm going to Italy."

"Oh my word, I would love to go to Italy," Rachel said.

"How long are you going to be gone?" Vera asked.

Patty's smile widened. "A month."

They groaned, and then they squealed. The women were still talking about it when Patty June left.

She had purposefully parked a block away so that she could show off the new look, and it was working.

She saw people in the window at Granny's Country Kitchen pointing and staring. She waved and kept walking. Myra was putting a new display in the window of the flower shop when Patty June passed. Patty tapped on the glass and waved, stifling a giggle when Myra looked up and dropped the bowl she was holding. Water splattered up her pant legs all the way to her knees as Patty kept walking.

By the time she got to the car, there was actually a line of people standing on the curb across the street, staring in disbelief. She knew the look would be shocking, but she was a little irked that they were so blatant. Impulsively, she pulled out her cell phone and took a picture of them. When they saw what she was doing, they scattered.

She snorted beneath her breath as she got in her car and drove away. *Big bunch of cowards. They can dish it out, but they sure couldn't take it.* Fine with her. She had a lot of thinking to do while she was gone, like what she was going to do with the rest of her life when she got back.

⊚⊚⊚

Willa Dean Miller had not been home for lunch in ages. Partly because Harold's insurance office was in what used to be their garage, which limited parking if he had customers, and partly because Harold always ate nearly everything at supper, so there was never anything left over for the next day to eat at noon. But Patty June's off-hand comment had planted a seed and Willa Jean was going home—just to make sure Harold wasn't cheating on her, too.

When she turned the corner on their street, instead of driving all the way to the house, she parked in the middle of the block and began walking the rest of the way. A part of her felt silly for acting in such a suspicious manner. But she never would have believed Pastor Clymer would cheat on his wife and he had. This was something she had to do for herself, and Harold would never have to know.

The sun was warm on the top of her head. Her heels made little clip-clop sounds as she walked. A butterfly flitted across her line of vision on its way to the roses blooming on the other side of the street. Willa Dean had always admired those roses, but today their picture-perfect blooms were taking a backseat to the high-noon investigation.

Clip-clop, clip-clop went the heels of her shoes, marking off the distance to the front door of her house.

Mrs. Mason's black and white cat was lying on the top step of her porch licking its balls. It was a bit unseemly, although Willa Jean supposed that could be excused because it was a dumb, four-footed animal. But she was in no frame of mind to be generous with the dumb two-footed kind.

Clip-clop, clip-clop, only a few more yards to go.

In a way, this was all Harold's fault. If he hadn't turned into such a cold fish, it would never have crossed her mind that he might be cheating.

"Yoo-hoo! Willa Dean! How y'all doin'?"

Willa Dean cringed. Her next-door neighbor had just walked out onto her porch.

That Sue Beamon has probably been watching me ever since I got out of the car. Dang nosy woman.

"Hi, Sue. I'm just fine. Thank you for asking."

"Did your car quit on you?" Sue called out.

Willa Dean frowned. If Sue didn't shut the hell up, Harold would know his wife was coming and the sneak attack would be a bust.

"No. I'm walking for my health. See you later."

Sue smiled and waved and went back inside, but Willa Dean knew she was still watching from behind the curtains.

Clip-clop, clip-clop.

The closer she got to her house, the faster her heart began to beat. What was she going to do if she found out something she didn't like? She was honest enough to admit that it all came down to exactly what he was doing and how badly she still wanted to be a married woman.

There were no other cars in the driveway except Harold's six-year-old Jeep, which meant he was home and probably didn't have any clients in the office.

She dug the house key out of her purse as she went up the steps, and then opened the door and slipped inside.

The moment she closed the door behind her, she stepped out of her shoes and then listened, trying to figure out where Harold might be.

She was certain he wasn't in the kitchen eating lunch because she would have heard the clink of silverware against the dishes. It was a habit he had that drove her crazy—that and filling his bowl with dry cereal in the morning and then crushing it down with his hand so he could get more in the bowl before he poured in the milk. Absolutely disgraceful.

She took a few tentative steps toward his office, listening for the sound of computer keys clacking or the scratch of pen to paper, but it, too, was silent.

A door opened somewhere in the back of the house. When she heard the creak, she recognized it as the door in their bathroom. She'd been asking Harold to oil that thing for a week and he still hadn't done it; little did he know it would become a homing beacon, like belling a cat. At least now she knew where he was. He had simply gone to the bathroom, and she was making a big deal out of nothing.

She was about to say hello and suggest they go to lunch at Granny's Country Kitchen when she heard music. She frowned. "Moon River"? She hadn't heard that in a good four years. It was the song they used to play back when they still had regular sex.

Her heart thumped. All of a sudden she was scared. Did she really want to see what was happening in her bedroom, or should she play dumb and go on with her life regardless? Then she thought of Patty June kicking her cheating husband out of the house and lifted her chin. Whatever will be, will be, she told herself, and tip-toed down the hall.

The door was ajar.

She could hear the sound of footsteps sliding across the hardwood, like someone was dancing, which would be weird—unless Harold wasn't alone. She clenched her jaw and pushed the door open just enough to peek in.

Her heart stopped and then kicked against her rib cage so hard that she lost her breath. She slapped a hand over her mouth and backed up so fast she slipped and almost fell. By the time she got to the living room, she was shaking and breathless. She grabbed her shoes and purse, let herself out of the house, and ran all the way back to the car barefoot, well aware that Sue Beamon was probably watching.

It wasn't until she got in the car that she let herself feel the shock of what she'd seen. She needed to get away before she came undone, but when she tried to get the key in the ignition, she kept dropping it. On the fourth drop, she beat her hands against the steering wheel and screamed.

"Fuck, fuck, fuck!"

Hearing herself curse was so startling that she finally got the car started and drove away. She drove all the way out of town without a destination in mind. What she wanted to do was hide, but she couldn't. She had a decision to make and she needed to do it with a clear head.

When she was a teenager, Gray Goose Lake was the place where everyone used to go park and make out. She hadn't been there in years, so it would be the last place anyone would ever go to look for her. She wheeled off the highway and took the blacktop down to the landing, then parked beneath a grove of shade trees and killed the engine.

Her heart was pounding as she opened the car door and got out. Then she did an about-face and staggered toward the back bumper and threw up until there was nothing coming up but dry heaves. When she finally quit, there was as much snot on her face as there were tears on her cheeks. She pulled the tail of her blouse out of her pants to wipe her face and blow her nose. It was not her finest move, but need required invention. Still barefoot, she headed toward the lake.

The water was so still that it looked like glass. Not a leaf was stirring, or even a blade of grass. It felt like everything was holding its breath, waiting to see what Willa Dean was going to do. She spread her jacket on the weathered wood and sat down, dangling her legs off the edge of the pier. A pair of wood ducks paddled by, and a big snapping turtle took offense at her presence and shoved off shore into the water and swam away. She looked down at the ripples it left behind, then took a deep breath and closed her eyes.

A thousand thoughts ran through her head, everything from confronting Harold with the truth, to jumping in and swimming toward the middle of the lake.

She would be too tired to swim back and it wouldn't be exactly like suicide, but it was still a cowardly way to die. Or, she could pretend she never saw what she saw. Did she have the guts to do that? Did she want to be Mrs. Harold Miller bad enough to lie to herself?

She didn't know how long she'd been sitting there, but when her cell phone began ringing, she guessed it had been too long. It was most likely Precious, wondering where she'd gone. She thought about not answering, but that would create its own set of issues. Willa Dean was known as a punctual woman, and the last thing she wanted was for her secretary to alert the local police and have them put out a bulletin listing her as missing. Then she would have to explain why she was hiding out at the lake, so she cleared her throat and answered the phone instead.

"Hello."

"Uh, Willa Dean, it's me, Precious. I didn't remember you telling me you weren't coming back this afternoon, so I got worried. Are you okay?"

"I'm fine. I should have called. Something came up. Just take names and numbers, and I'll call them all back tomorrow."

"Sure thing," Precious said and disconnected.

Willa Dean had just told a lie and felt guilty. She wondered if that was how Harold felt when he turned his back on her in bed. Their relationship was a lie. The sorry bastard. Why had he bothered to get married if he didn't want the life that came with it?

Her truth was an ugly one, but it did finally explain why the elastic in her panties kept wearing out so fast. Harold had at least forty pounds on her and was obviously squeezing his fat ass into them on something of a regular basis. Lord. All that hair and manly bulge spilling out from under her dainties! She'd probably die with that image burned into her brain. And that red lacy bra he'd been wearing. It wasn't one of hers, which meant he'd actually gone to the trouble of buying his own, which offered yet another set of questions, like where the hell did he hide that stuff? Had to be in the office. That had always been off limits. Now she knew why.

Another thought shifted to the forefront. He'd been wearing makeup—her makeup. Damn it to hell, she spent good money on her makeup so her skin wouldn't break out and he was smearing it on his whiskery stubble. She could brain him gladly for that alone.

Her shoulders slumped. Her chin dropped toward her chest. What to do? What to do? She remembered Oprah having a show about people like this once. She couldn't remember the proper terminology, but it didn't mean he was seeing another woman or, for that matter, another man. So did she tell him she knew? Did she have it in her to keep silent? Was it a big enough deal for a divorce, which would lead her down another road altogether? She would lose the house. It wasn't paid off, and she didn't make enough money at the travel agency to live alone.

She thought of her Rose Garden Club and the Ladies Aide at church. She always read the Bible passages during the church play at Christmas and donated the best prizes for the silent auctions. How would that change? Did she care? Should she care?

She sat for a long time, staring at the water while the sun slipped toward the western horizon. It wasn't until the sky turned gray and the birds began coming in to roost that she got up and headed back to the car.

She drove back into town and stopped at the pharmacy. It was fifteen minutes until closing. The store was empty except for the pharmacist in the back and Mitchell Avery, the clerk. Mitchell was a little strange, but after everything that had been happening in Blessings lately, he seemed to be in the right place.

"Hey, Willa Dean."

She waved at Mitchell and kept walking, all the way to the back of the store, down the aisle where condoms were shelved, past the feminine hygiene products, to the bottom shelf below scented oils where the vibrators were sold. She chose one that ran on batteries, which were not included, and paused to gather some of those up as well before heading to the checkout counter.

Mitchell's face turned pink when he rang up the purchases, but he never said a word. He sacked them up, tossed the receipt into the bag, and looked her straight in the face.

"I'm saving up my money to book a trip to New York City."

She paused. "Just let me know when you're ready to go and I'll find the best deal. I promise."

He smiled. "Thanks. Have a nice evening."

"You, too, Mitchell."

She got in the car and drove home, hoping Harold had started supper. If he hadn't, they were going to Granny's Kitchen to eat. Tonight was not a night for her to be anywhere close to boiling water and knives, and tomorrow was a new day for a lot of things, one being the bullshit being dished out to Patty June. She'd just gotten a dose of how life could deal you a felling blow without warning, and it wasn't fun. What was happening to Patty June was about to stop.

◎◎◎

Conrad Clymer found a semipermanent address on his second day in Savannah, then began going through the help-wanted ads. There was no way a church would ever hire him again, and he wasn't so sure he wanted the burden of trying to maintain a spotless conscience anymore. He was obviously no good at it, or none of this mess would have happened.

He was sad on so many levels that it didn't bear thinking about. He missed Patty June's cooking. He missed the way her nose wrinkled up when she laughed. He even missed the nagging whine in her voice when he left wet towels on the bathroom floor.

Well, he didn't have to worry about the nagging anymore, and if the bathroom in this apartment got the cleaning it needed, he was going to have to be the one to do it.

It had taken him over an hour just to unload the car. Climbing the stairs to the third floor over and over had been exhausting, but there was an upside. It might help him take off some weight.

Once everything was inside, he began putting it up. The last thing he began to work on was setting up his computer. Having Internet access had been a deal breaker when he was searching for apartments, and he'd been lucky finding one cheap enough for him to take it. Once he got the computer up and going, he began searching online for available jobs in the area. The problem he had was lack of experience. He'd been a preacher all of his adult life. The only thing he was really good at beyond that was working with computers. He offered up a prayer and then began to search for listings in that field and hoped God wasn't holding a grudge as big as Patty June's.

◎◎◎

By the night of Patty June's makeover, everyone who mattered in Blessings knew about her new hairstyle and that she was about to travel abroad. The husbands were still on the "bash Patty" track, but some wives were secretly envious and gave their husbands a hard look that quickly ended the comments. The winds of change were in the air, but the men still didn't know it.

Two days later, Patty June was in the kitchen when she heard the mailman drop the mail in her box. She put her cookies in the oven and went to get it. It had been threatening to rain all day and the sky was gray and overcast, which was why she was in the kitchen. When a day was gloomy like this, baking always lifted her spirits.

She grabbed the handful of letters, went back to the kitchen to sort the mail so she could keep an eye on the cookies, and poured herself a cup of coffee before sitting down. She took a quick sip and then began putting bills in one pile, junk mail in another. When she saw the writing and the city stamped on a long, blue envelope, the skin crawled on the back of her neck. It appeared Conrad had settled himself in Savannah, which was fine with her. It was large enough that when she went there, she'd be unlikely to ever see him.

She opened the envelope. A single note card fell out with an address. Now she had a location for the lawyer to mail the divorce papers. She laid it aside and picked up a rather ornate envelope that smelled like roses.

Curious, she tore into it and then leaned back in her chair in disbelief. It was a personal invitation to attend a special tea hosted by the Rose Garden Club. She glanced at the date. That would be noon this coming Saturday.

She wasn't going anywhere else, so she might as well go see what the biddies had to say. She hoped it wasn't going to be a public flogging, and then she sighed. She'd lived here her entire life, as had her parents, and their parents before them. It would be sad if all this mess caused her so much distress that she had to move.

She noticed there was a number to RSVP. What the

hell, she thought, and grabbed her cell phone. She quickly punched in the numbers and waited for an answer.

"Miller Travel Agency. We can make your dreams come true."

She stifled a grin. They really needed to reword that. It could be misconstrued in a number of ways.

"Hi, Precious. This is Patty June. I'm calling to RSVP on the invitation from the Rose Garden Club."

"Oh, hi, Patty June. So is this a yes or a no?"

"It's a yes, and tell Willa Dean thank you for asking me."

"I sure will, and Patty June…"

"Yes?"

"I just love your new hairdo. It's amazing."

"Thank you, Precious. I like it, too."

She was still smiling when she disconnected. Now she had to figure out what she was going to wear. Did she go for shock value or understated class? Since they were the Rose Garden girls, she decided to go with understated class. The average age of that bunch was probably around seventy-five years old. She didn't want to be responsible for someone having a heart attack over lobster rolls and sweet tea.

◎◎◎

The women of Blessings were on a mission. All it had taken were a few phone calls to start the ball rolling in Patty June's favor. They'd let down one of their own, and why? Because their husbands had suggested she was a feminist? So what? Southern women had been feminists a long time before that tag had become a buzzword. They'd hidden the iron in their backbones with a smile and a "bless your heart," and not a man was the wiser.

Not only that, but they also were all taking stock of their own men, and a good many of them were falling short. The winds of discontent were rising. Women weren't giving out the details, but it was obvious which families were having their own little crises. Hair colors were changing, hems were coming up, and necklines were going lower. Houses were getting new paint jobs, and there were a few places in town with new cars in the driveway. The ration of shit the men had dished out on Patty June's behalf was coming back to haunt them.

◎◎◎

When Saturday rolled around and Patty June drove up to the community center, her eyes widened in disbelief. This wasn't just a meeting of the Rose Garden Club. There were at least fifty cars here, maybe more.

She tapped the brakes and circled the parking lot until she found an empty spot, then parked and got out, smoothing down the front of her little pink dress as she headed inside.

As she started down the hall, she caught a glimpse of her reflection and almost stumbled. This look was going to take some getting used to.

It occurred to her that the last time she'd been here had been for a family dinner before a funeral. Conrad had preached the sermon. If she remembered correctly, it had been for Bobbette Paulson's father. She wondered if Conrad had been screwing her then, or if it had all come later. Either way, the old man was dead, Conrad was gone, and last she'd heard, Bobbette was bald.

She followed the rumble of voices all the way to the dining area and then stopped in the doorway, stunned by the sight of so many women standing beneath a banner with her name on it.

"What on earth?" she muttered. Then Willa Dean saw her and she was swept up into the gala.

"What's going on?" Patty asked.

Willa Dean grabbed her hand and pulled her into the room.

"This is in your honor. We all owe you a huge apology, and rather than do it one at a time in mutual embarrassment, we decided to make an event of it. Besides, you know how we like events."

Patty June laughed. It was true. The women in Blessings *did* like their parties.

"Come with me. You're sitting between me and Rachel, and I hope you went light on your breakfast. I promise this is going to be the best lunch you've ever had."

Patty giggled. This was promising to be the best day she'd had in ages. Having the best lunch to go with it seemed only fair.

And Willa Dean was right. It was amazing, from the salad course through the entrée, all the way to the desserts, which held some of Patty June's favorites. When she saw the key lime pie, she groaned aloud.

"I love key lime pie."

"I made that," Myra Franklin said, her smile a little too wide to be humble.

"I made the Coca-Cola cake," Willa Dean added.

"I made the Mississippi mud cake," Sue Beamon said.

Patty was overwhelmed to the point of tears, but she wouldn't cry. This was a happy day.

"I'll have a little bit of all three," Patty said, and took her plate back to the table and dug in.

Coffee was being served when Willa Dean stood up and moved to the podium, tapping the microphone to make sure it was on.

"Can y'all hear me?" she asked, pointing to the back of the room. When they waved and nodded, she cleared her throat.

"All of you know why we're here. The only one who doesn't is Patty June. Patty, would you please come stand beside me?"

Patty resisted the urge to lick her fork as she laid it on the plate and got up and walked to the podium.

Willa Dean was still struggling with her own personal issues and was overly emotional, but such was life. She cleared her throat again and took Patty June's hand.

"We are begging your forgiveness, Patty June. You are our sister, and when you needed us most, we let you down. We admit it, and we're sorry and ashamed. Just so you know, your bravery prompted a lot of us to face our own personal issues. There are quite a few here who have had their own little revelations in the past few days, evidenced by new cars in the driveways and some new jewelry on our fingers."

A nervous round of laughter moved through the room as the women all looked at each other and then quickly looked away.

Patty June was shocked. She'd been so wrapped up in her drama that she'd been unaware of the subtle changes going on in her little town.

"However, we're not here to talk about us. We're here to honor you. You did something very brave. You faced your devils and dehorned the both of them in as fine a fashion as I've ever seen. And we wanted you to have this little gift as a memento of your finest hour. I'm sure you'll find a place for it in somewhere in your house."

She handed the gaily wrapped box to Patty June and then stepped back, giving Patty June the podium to unwrap it.

Patty was already so overwhelmed by the personal backup and the fine dining that she could hardly speak. Her fingers were shaking as she pulled off the gold ribbon, then the shiny white paper, then finally the lid.

The women watched as she dug through the tissue paper and then saw the shock on her face as she froze. The room went silent, the women waiting to see her reaction.

Patty June grinned. It was Vesta Conklin's clippers, spray-painted gold. She took them out and hit the Power button. When the sound system caught the buzz, the room erupted in laughter. And just like that, the last of Patty June's humiliation was gone.

She stepped up to the microphone, still clutching the clippers against her breast.

"Thank you so much! You girls are the best, and if any of you ever need to borrow them, you know where I live."

The room was filled with applause and laughter as Patty June went back to her table, but now the women were on their feet and heading to her table, wanting to talk to her personally.

Myra Franklin caught Willa Dean's eye. She knew her good friend had a problem at home, but didn't know what. What she did know was that Willa Dean was about to burst into tears. She wiggled her fingers, indicating she should slip out the back door now that it was over.

Willa Dean sighed and mouthed a quick thank-you as she began to gather up her things. She felt lighter, like a weight had come off her shoulders. A wrong had been righted with a public apology and good food. Unfortunately it was going to take a lot more than an apology from Harold to fix what was wrong under her roof.

He knew she was pissed, because she'd moved everything that was hers into the spare bedroom, but he wasn't sure why. And she knew the reason he hadn't confronted her was because he had secrets of his own to hide. Right now they were sharing a house and polite company, and she'd smiled just about all she could smile today without bursting into tears. Once she gathered up her things, she slipped out the back door.

Chapter 4

HOWARD FRANKLIN TYPED IN THE BIT OF INFO INTO his computer and hit Send, then leaned back in his chair and rubbed his belly. He was hungry and there wasn't a leftover in the house. It was almost time for Willa Dean to come home from her luncheon. Maybe she would bring leftovers, which she sometimes did.

He didn't know what was going on with her, but he guessed it had something to do with Patty June Clymer. Every man in town knew the women were up in arms on behalf of the preacher's wife, and the men were all treading easy, hoping the mass indignation soon passed.

He liked his life. He liked selling insurance, and he liked being married to Willa Dean. He had a few fantasies on the side that he indulged in now and then, but they were harmless. Certainly nothing like what Conrad Clymer had done. Still, he lived with a measure of both fear and guilt that Willa Dean might find out.

He got up to get himself a snack and, as he did, heard the front door slam. Willa Dean must be home. He walked out into the hall to meet her, but she sailed right past him, carrying her things into the kitchen. He followed, talking as he went.

"So how did the luncheon go? Did everyone make up and play nice?"

Willa Dean set her dirty dishes in the sink and then turned on him like a scalded cat.

"You're a fine one to talk about makeup and play acting."

The moment she said it, she wished she could take it back, but it was too late. She saw the shock on his face, and then fear.

"What do you mean?"

She sighed. His voice was shaking. Poor Harold. But then her instinct for survival kicked in. Poor Willa Dean, too.

"Do you really want to have this conversation?" she asked.

Harold felt sick. She knew! He didn't know how it had happened, but she knew, which suddenly explained the move into the spare bedroom.

"Are you going to divorce me, too?" he whispered.

"Obviously not, or I wouldn't have moved my things. You can rest assured your secret is safe. I don't want anyone knowing this any more than you do."

"I don't mean anything by it. It's just something I like to do now and then."

"Yes, well, I bought a vibrator. If you hear it buzzing in my bedroom, you will know I, too, am enjoying a thing

I like to do now and then. You will also leave my makeup and underwear the hell alone. It costs a fortune. If you want to play dress up, buy your own. Do you hear me, Harold Wayne?"

He nodded.

"I'm sorry, Willa Dean. It's nothing against you. I love you."

She sighed. "I suppose that you do. Unfortunately, I may never get over the sight of your fat butt in my panties."

"Oh lord," he muttered, and sat down with a thump. "I've ruined everything, haven't I?"

She wanted to stay angry, but she was beginning to feel sorry for him.

"Not everything," she said. "I'm still here. We'll just have to see how it goes. Oddly enough, there is a bit of good that has come out of all this."

"Like what?" he asked.

"I don't have to pretend I'm done having sex when you are anymore. That vibrator lasts as long as I do, which is a hell of a lot longer than your pitiful forty-five seconds."

He glared. "You never complained before."

"That's because you weigh two hundred and forty-five pounds and I couldn't breathe."

"Well seriously, Willa Dean. This is a hell of a time to be complaining. We've been married for twenty-three years and you never said a word."

"Look at it this way, Harold. You had twenty-three years of wedded bliss before I blew your cover, so the next twenty-three are mine. We're married. I'll keep your secret and you can keep mine."

His thoughts were racing. She hadn't blown her top and she was still here. It was way better than he would have imagined.

"I guess I can live with that," he mumbled.

"Good. I'm going to change clothes and then get back to the agency."

"Did you bring any leftovers?"

"No."

"I guess I could heat up a can of soup."

"Look at it this way, Harold. You can do anything you want to now, so knock yourself out. I'm going back to work."

He watched her stride out of the kitchen with her chin up and her shoulders back. He'd escaped public shame by less than a pubic hair and he knew it. The next time he went into Savannah he'd do a little shopping, something more in his size and style. In the meantime, he could certainly refrain from indulging himself in his little fantasies until the waters had calmed, so to speak.

⊙⊙⊙

The following Tuesday, Ruby came in extra early to open The Curl Up and Dye. The beginning of her workweek wasn't usually all that busy, but she had four haircuts this morning and a root touch-up and a permanent this afternoon. It made her back ache just thinking about how long she would be on her feet.

She was taking a load of towels out of the dryer when she caught movement out on the street. Alma Button was driving a new car. She knew the story behind the requests for new hairdos and new jewelry showing up on her customers' hands and wondered what Alma's husband had done that warranted buying Alma a new car. Whatever it was, Ruby just hoped none of the ramifications of their problems leaked into The Curl Up and Dye. She had enough on her hands without turning her shop into a version of *The Jerry Springer Show*.

THE END

**Keep reading for a sneak peek
at the next book in Sharon Sala's
Blessings, Georgia series**

ONCE *in*
a BLUE MOON

Available August 2020 from Sourcebooks Casablanca

Chapter 1

STREAKS OF MOONLIGHT SLIPPED BETWEEN THE blinds in Cathy Terry's bedroom, painting silver-white stripes across the dark hardwood floor. The lights of a passing patrol car swept across the wall where she lay sleeping, but all she saw was the man coming at her in her dream.

Blaine Wagner's face was twisted in rage—his fists doubled, ready to strike a blow.

"You're not going anywhere, dammit! Nobody walks out on me!"

Cathy was scared of him, but she'd had enough, and the luxury of their lifestyle was no longer the draw it had once been.

"I'm not nobody! I am your wife, not one of your whores, and I've had enough! You have cheated on me for the last time. I've already contacted a lawyer, and I'll be staying in the Luxor here in Vegas until I can find an apartment."

"Like hell!" Blaine roared, and swung at her.

Cathy ducked and ran, locking herself into their ensuite, and then called the police, crying and begging them to hurry as Blaine pounded on the door in continuing rage.

The sirens and the flashing lights pulling up to the house gave her the reprieve she needed. The moment she heard him leave the room to answer the door, she flew out of the bathroom, grabbed the bag she'd already packed from the closet, and followed him down the stairs.

He was already playing the part of the surprised spouse and telling the police it was all a misunderstanding when Cathy appeared. Her eyes were swollen from crying, and her fear was unmistakable.

"Help me! I've filed for divorce and he won't let me leave!" she said. She was trying to push past him when he grabbed her by the arm.

In the dream, she was struggling to get free, just like she had that night. The police had come into their house at that point, yelling at Blaine to let her go, and he was screaming in her ear, *"I'll make you sorry. You'll never have another moment's peace as long as you live!"*

Her heart was pounding when she heard a voice from her childhood.

Wake up! Wake up, Mary Cathleen! Wake up now!

She gasped, and then sat straight up in bed and turned on the lamp. The hundred-watt bulb put a whole new light on the moment, helping pull her out of the dream, but she couldn't deny what she'd heard. That was her mother's voice, and it had been two years since she'd heard it.

"Oh, Mama, you're still on my side, even from the grave." Cathy glanced at the clock.

It was twenty minutes to four, and going back to sleep after that dream wasn't happening, so she turned on the television, plumped up her pillows, and began scanning the available movies. She didn't much care what she watched. Anything to get her mind off her ex would suffice.

She was thinking about going to the kitchen for something to snack on when she saw actor Jeffrey Dean Morgan's face flash on the screen, and she stopped and upped the volume. He was one of her favorites, and being tall, dark, and handsome was the antithesis of Blaine Wagner's stocky build and blond hair.

"That actor is one pretty man. I don't care what this movie is about. I can mute the whole thing and just sit and look at him. That should get my ex-husband's face out of my head."

But she didn't mute it after all and wound up watching almost two hours of the movie. It wasn't a happy-ever-after movie, but she didn't live in a happy-ever-after world and was fine with that.

Cathy ran to the kitchen during a commercial and made herself a peanut butter and jelly sandwich, then brought it and a glass of milk back to bed.

By the time the movie was over, the memory of the dream had mostly passed and morning was imminent. She turned off the television and took her dirty dishes back to the kitchen, started a pot of coffee, then headed back to her room to get dressed.

A short while later she was in the kitchen, contemplating her day of doing little to nothing here in Blessings, and remembering her old life in Vegas.

The divorce had taken six months to finalize, ending with a lump-sum payment of thirty million dollars to her bank account. It wasn't like Blaine couldn't afford it. He was a billionaire…a fourth-generation Wagner, a name famous in Nevada. In early days, it was silver mines, and during the past seventy-something years, casinos had become the family business.

After the divorce was final, she thought that would be the end of it. But she'd been wrong, and it was what he did on the courthouse steps as they were leaving that scared her.

When both lawyers walked off, Blaine stayed behind. Cathy thought it was for a final parting of the ways, until he grabbed her arm and whispered in her ear.

"You do understand I now view you as a threat. You know things about me and my life that aren't healthy for you anymore."

Cathy tried to pull away. "Don't be ridiculous."

"This isn't a joke, Cathy. I'm just giving you fair warning. I don't trust you anymore, and I have no intention of spending the rest of my life looking over my shoulder and waiting for the feds to come knocking. Your days are numbered."

Cathy's heart skipped a beat. *Oh my God. He's serious!*

"I don't have the faintest idea what you're talking about. Our world consisted of your country club, our personal friends, and hosting dinner parties for your business associates now and then."

His eyes narrowed. "Exactly."

"I still don't get it," Cathy said, pretending total oblivion, although she was beginning to remember that some of those associates had dubious reputations, even though she knew nothing incriminating about any of them. "Go away, Blaine. Just leave me alone."

She twisted out of his grasp and walked away, resisting the urge to run. This was a shock. She'd never seen this coming, but she needed to disappear, and she was going to have to be smart about doing it.

By the time she got home, she had a plan. The first thing she did was fill out papers online to change back to her maiden name. After two tense months of waiting, it was done, and that's when she amped up the plan. She was setting up a new life with a renewed driver's license, a new phone plan, and a new credit card.

She knew Blaine was having her followed. She didn't know if that was just intimidation, but leaving town with his knowledge of where she was going wouldn't assure her safety. He'd just have her tailed to other places, and if he was still in the mind-set to get rid of her, it would be all too easy to make a death look like an accident.

But she already knew how to disappear. She'd spent the first twelve years of her life living off the grid in Alaska. The last thing Blaine Wagner would ever expect was for her to take to the back roads of America on foot.

Cathy ordered everything she needed online so her ex wouldn't know what she was buying, and thanks to him, every friend she'd ever had in Vegas had shut her out. No more lunch dates with girlfriends. No more girlfriends. So she holed up in her apartment and quit going anywhere, and when she got hungry, she ordered in.

The last thing she did was disperse the money from her divorce settlement into three different banks across the country.

And early one morning she walked out the back door of her apartment, caught the Uber she'd called to take her to the bus station, and took a bus to Colorado.

She got off in Colorado Springs and rented a motel room. She stayed long enough to buy a handgun and ammunition, and one morning just after sunrise, she shouldered her hiking gear and left the motel heading east.

She hiked along highways, sidestepping cities for the more rural areas, and the weeks went by until she finally reached Springer Mountain, Georgia—the beginning of the Appalachian Trail. It was a place she recognized true wilderness, and one in which she felt comfortable.

She knew how to forage, and how to fish from the rivers and streams teeming with fish. But the trail went north from there, and it was getting too close to winter to hike north, so she started hiking south. She made it all the way to a little, out-of-the-way place called Blessings, Georgia, before something about it spoke to her, and here is where she stopped. And now here she was, in something of a holding pattern. Not really participating in life. Just hiding from it.

Cathy set aside the memories, finished her morning coffee, and got ready to go for her morning run.

It was mid-November, but it promised to be a nice day in the high fifties. She was wearing her running shoes, sweatpants, and a long-sleeved T-shirt as she pocketed her phone and left the house, pausing beneath the porch light to scan the area for signs of things that didn't belong.

The streetlights were already fading with the growing light of a new day. The morning was still, the sky cloudless. She walked to the edge of the porch and waited for the car coming up the street to pass, and then waved when she recognized the boy who delivered the morning papers. He saw her and waved back. She still didn't know his name, but this town was friendly like that.

She came off the porch, pausing in the driveway to stretch a few times, and then took off down the sidewalk at a jog, relishing the impact of foot to surface. The rhythm of her stride soon caught up with the thump of her heartbeat, and by the time she was making her second pass by the city park, she'd been running for an hour.

The fat raccoon scurrying through the green space was heading for the trees and the creek that ran through the park.

On the other side of the street, a young woman came running out of her house toward the old car parked in the drive. Cathy recognized her as one of the waitresses from Granny's Country Kitchen. From the way she was moving, she was likely late for work.

The thought of Granny's led Cathy to wanting some

of the gravy and biscuits she'd had there before, but she couldn't go there all hot and sweaty and was wishing she'd pulled her hair up in a ponytail before leaving the house. Even though the morning was cool, the weight of the curls was hot against the back of her neck. She turned toward Main Street as she reached the end of the block, thinking to make one last sweep through Blessings and then head home.

Traffic was picking up on Main, and even though she'd been running every morning since her arrival, people still stared. No one jogged in Blessings, although she had seen some kids running at the high school track field, but she didn't care. She wasn't here to fit in.

She ran past the florist, and then the quirky little hair salon called the Curl Up and Dye, and was moving past Phillips Pharmacy as a huge black pickup pulled up to the curb.

It had been months since she'd been behind the wheel of any kind of vehicle, and she was toying with the idea of leasing one for the winter. She didn't know she'd caught the driver's notice, and it wouldn't have mattered anyway. She just kept running without noticing how far she'd gone until she saw the gas station at the far end of town and the city limits sign just down the road.

"Well, shoot," Cathy muttered. She made a quick turn on the sidewalk and was heading back into Blessings when she came down wrong on her foot, and before she knew it, her ankle rolled and she was falling.

The pain was instantaneous and excruciating, and as

she was reaching out to break her fall, she jammed her hand against the concrete and then landed on her side with a thud.

"Oh my lord," she moaned, then slowly turned over onto her back, only vaguely aware of screeching brakes and then the sound of running feet.

———————

It was just after 8:00 a.m. when Duke Talbot drove into Blessings and pulled up to the curb in front of Phillips Pharmacy. He was reaching for the list he'd put in the console when he caught movement from the corner of his eye and looked up just as a young woman in a long-sleeved T-shirt and sweatpants ran past the store. She was gone before he got a good look at her face, but all that curly red hair bouncing down her back was impossible to miss.

He couldn't remember seeing anyone jogging here before and was curious as to who might have taken it up. He didn't know any woman with hair that color, either, but considering the Curl Up and Dye was just down the street, Ruby or one of the girls could be responsible for that. He watched the jogger until she turned a corner and disappeared before he got out.

The bell over the door jingled as he entered the pharmacy.

LilyAnn Dalton looked up from behind the register and smiled.

"Good morning, Duke. You're out early," she said.

"Morning, LilyAnn. Just getting an early start on a long day." He picked up a basket from the end of the counter and started down the aisle where the shampoo and conditioners were shelved, then stopped and turned around. "Hey, LilyAnn, I just saw a redheaded woman with long, curly hair jogging past the store. I don't think I ever knew anyone to take up jogging here in Blessings. Who is she?"

"Oh, that's Cathy Terry. She's new here. She's living in one of Dan Amos's rental houses."

"What's she do?" he asked.

LilyAnn shrugged. "I don't know. She comes in here now and again. Really nice lady, but she sort of keeps to herself."

Having his curiosity satisfied, Duke began picking up the items he'd come for. It didn't take long for him to get everything on the list, and then he was back in his truck.

He stopped and used the ATM drive-through at the bank for cash, and then realized he was still a little early for his haircut appointment, so he headed to the gas station to get his oil checked.

He was thinking about the day ahead when he realized the redhead he'd seen earlier was on the sidewalk running toward him. He had a clear view of her face, and despite the pink flush on her cheeks, his first thought was how pretty she was.

Then all of a sudden she was falling, and he groaned aloud at how hard she hit. He stomped the brakes, slammed the truck into park, and got out on the run.

He was down on his knees beside her in seconds, and when he saw the blood on the palm of her hand, he knew that was going to burn later. Then he saw her ankle, and was shocked by how much it was already swelling.

"Your ankle! Don't move, it might be broken," he said.

And then she looked up at him, and Duke took a deep breath. He'd never seen eyes that blue, and they were swimming in tears. It took everything he had not to sweep her up in his arms, but he was afraid to move her.

"Did you hit your head?"

She wasn't sure. Maybe. She'd just watched a movie with Jeffrey Dean Morgan in it, and now either she was hallucinating, or his doppelgänger was leaning over her.

"Uh…I don't think so. Just the right side of my body. My ankle turned, and I think I need a little help getting up."

"My name is Duke Talbot. I saw you fall, and from the looks of your ankle, I think you need to go to the ER," Duke said. "Will you let me take you, or would you rather go in an ambulance?"

Cathy frowned. "I don't think I—"

"One or the other," Duke said.

She sighed. *Dictatorial male. Just what I don't need.* But both her hip and her ankle were throbbing now, and he did have a sweet, concerned expression on his face.

"If it's not too much trouble, maybe you could just drop me off at the ER, then."

"Yes, ma'am," Duke said, and then reached toward her hair, but when she flinched and then ducked, he frowned.

Those were instinctive reactions someone might make from fear of being struck. "I'm sorry. You have a piece of grass in a curl. I didn't mean to startle you."

Cathy sighed. "Then, thank you," she said, and closed her eyes as Duke pulled it out.

When she opened them again, he was on his feet and she was in his arms, and he was carrying her toward his truck.

At that moment, a police car pulled up, and Chief Pittman got out on the run.

"Hey, Duke! We just had a call come in that someone fell. I see you beat me to her," Lon said, as he ran toward Duke's truck and opened the door.

"I saw it happen," Duke said, as he eased Cathy down inside and then quickly reclined the seat back. "I'm taking her to the ER."

"I'll lead the way," Lon said. He glanced in the truck as Duke was buckling her in and recognized who it was. "Miss Terry, I don't know if you remember me, but we were standing in line together at Crown Grocers last week. I'm Lon Pittman, the police chief here in Blessings. My wife, Mercy, and Duke's sister-in-law, Hope, are sisters, which in the South means we're all kin. You sit tight and we'll get you to the ER in style."

Cathy nodded, then closed her eyes. But even after he'd shut her in, she could still hear them talking. A couple of minutes later Duke got back in the truck, and as he made a U-turn in the street, she grabbed onto the console to steady herself.

"Lon's just ahead of us, leading the way with his lights flashing. Just hang on for a few minutes more. Are you hurting very much?" he asked.

"Enough, and I really appreciate this," she added.

Duke glanced down at her briefly. Again, their gazes locked, but this time she was the first to look away. He could tell he made her uncomfortable, so he turned his attention to driving.

As soon as he pulled up at the ER, everything began happening at once. Two orderlies came running out so quickly that Duke guessed the chief must have radioed ahead that they were inbound. He jumped out as they were transferring Cathy from his truck to a gurney, and then walked beside her as they wheeled her inside.

"Is there anyone I can call?" Duke asked.

"No, but I'm fine, and thank you again for all your help," Cathy said.

Duke watched until they wheeled her out of sight and then shoved his hands in his pockets. He was still standing in the middle of the hall when Hope came around a corner. When she saw him, she came running.

"Duke? What are you doing here? Did something happen to Jack?"

"No, no, nothing like that," Duke said. "I came in to get a haircut this morning. I was going to have my oil checked when I saw a woman take a bad fall. I just brought her in."

"Oh no! Who was it?" Hope asked.

"Her name is Cathy Terry."

"Oh, Mercy mentioned her a time or two. She's renting from Dan Amos. Was she hurt bad?"

"I don't know. I felt bad leaving her here on her own, but when I offered to call someone for her, she shook me off. I think I make her nervous…not me personally, but me being a man."

Hope was a little surprised by Duke's insight and concern. Most of the time her brother-in-law was either critical or dismissive of just about everything and everybody.

"I'm working in the ER today. I'll check on her," Hope said.

"Okay. If she needs help, let me know," he said, then left the ER.

He got back in his truck and headed for the Curl Up and Dye for his appointment. The last barber had left Blessings some years back, so it was either a haircut at the ladies' hair salon, a drive all the way to Savannah, or do it yourself. Duke had only tried DIY once when he was twelve, and the results had been disastrous. But his thoughts were no longer on the day ahead of him. He was thinking of the little redhead he'd left all alone in the ER.

Cathy was disgusted with herself and, at the same time, a little anxious. Being self-reliant was fine when all your moving parts were working, but from the swelling on her ankle and the huge bruise already spreading on her hip, she wasn't going to be jogging for a while, and getting to the Crown for groceries wasn't going to be easy, either. She didn't have one person in town she knew well enough to ask for help, and she was wishing she'd already leased a car.

Cathy was watching Rhonda, the nurse who was cleaning the scrape on her hand, when another nurse walked in. She was tall, dark-haired, and looked vaguely familiar.

"Hi, Rhonda, how is she doing?" Hope asked.

"We're waiting for Doctor Quick," Rhonda said.

Hope moved to the other side of the bed.

"Hi, Cathy. I'm Hope Talbot. Mercy Pittman, the fabulous baker at Granny's, is my sister, and it was my brother-in-law, Duke, who brought you here. Has someone been in yet to get your personal information?"

"No, not yet," Cathy said, but now she knew why the woman looked familiar. She looked like the woman she'd seen at Granny's.

"Then they will do that shortly. Is there anyone I can call?" Hope asked.

"No, but I have a question. Does Blessings have a taxi service?" Cathy asked.

"We don't have an official taxi service, but we have a whole lot of good people who will gladly give you a ride home. Do you live alone?"

Cathy nodded.

Hope glanced down at Cathy's swollen ankle. "You won't be driving for a while."

"I don't have a car here," she said.

"Ah... Came in on the bus, did you?" Hope said.

"No, I had been backpacking for several months when I got to Blessings. I decided it was time to find a place to spend the winter."

Hope's eyes widened. "Wow! Go, you! As for getting home, that's no problem. We'll get you all sorted out. All it will take is one phone call. Have you met Ruby yet?" Hope asked.

"No, who's Ruby?" Cathy asked.

"Ruby Butterman. She owns the Curl Up and Dye. She's the go-to person in Blessings when someone is in need. Her husband, Peanut, is the local lawyer."

"Her husband's name is Peanut Butterman? For real?" Cathy asked.

Hope giggled. "Yes. He always says his parents were smoking weed when they named him."

Cathy grinned, and then winced when Rhonda poured some antiseptic on the palm of her hand.

"I'll go make a couple of phone calls," Hope said. "I'll be back later to check on you. Don't worry. We'll get you home."

Once again, Cathy was struck by how friendly people were here, and as Hope had predicted, a couple of minutes later, a man came in and got her personal information, and as he was leaving, the ER doctor arrived.

Rhonda looked up. "Good morning, Doctor Quick. This is Cathy Terry."

He smiled. "Morning, Rhonda," he said, and then he shifted focus to his patient. "Hello, Cathy, I'm Dr. Quick.

What have you done to yourself?" he asked, as he began eyeing the bruising and the swollen ankle.

"I turned my ankle and fell while I was jogging."

Dr. Quick was already feeling her ankle. "Can you move it?" he asked.

"Yes, it hurts, but I can move it," she said, and proceeded to show him. "Fell pretty hard on my right side. My shoulder and hip are beginning to hurt, too."

"Did you hit your head?" he asked, glancing at her thick, red curls.

"No."

Dr. Quick nodded. "Okay, I'm sending you down for X-rays. We'll know more after I see them. Just bear with us."

A couple of minutes later, an orderly arrived with a wheelchair, and all the way down the hall, Cathy kept thinking… *Nightmare or not, I wish I'd gone back to bed.*

About the Author

Jackie Ashenden has been writing fiction since she was eleven years old. Mild-mannered fantasy/SF/pseudo-literary writer by day, obsessive romance writer by night, she used to balance her writing with the more serious job of librarianship until a chance meeting with another romance writer prompted her to throw off the shackles of her day job and devote herself to the true love of her heart—writing romance. She particularly likes to write dark, emotional stories with alpha heroes who've just gotten the world to their liking only to have it blown wide apart by their kick-ass heroines.

She lives in Auckland, New Zealand, with her husband, the inimitable Dr. Jax, two kids, one dog, and one cat. When she's not torturing alpha males and their obstreperous heroines, she can be found drinking chocolate martinis, reading anything she can lay her hands on, posting random stuff on her blog, or being forced to go mountain biking with her husband.

You can find Jackie at jackieashenden.com or follow her on Twitter @JackieAshenden.

THE ONE FOR YOU

Secrets come to light and lovers learn to heal in this
steamy series by bestselling author Roni Loren

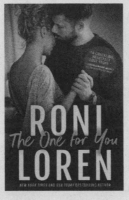

Kincaid Breslin is a survivor. She doesn't know why she got the
chance to live when so many of her friends died when prom
night turned into a nightmare, but now she takes life by the
horns and doesn't let anybody stand in her way.

Ashton Isaacs was Kincaid's best friend when disaster struck
all those years ago, but he chose to run as far away as he could.
Now fate has brought him back to town, and Ash will have to
decide what's more important: the secrets he's been hiding, or a
future with the only woman he's ever loved…

*"Absolutely unputdownable! Roni
Loren is a new favorite."*

**—COLLEEN HOOVER, #1 *New York Times* bestseller,
for *The One You Can't Forget***

For more info about Sourcebooks's
books and authors, visit:

sourcebooks.com